AF578275

THE FRATERNAL ORDER

If you purchased this book or came across it and enjoyed it, the author thanks you. Available in paperback, hardcover and e-editions.

Special thanks to the Albuquerque Police Museum and Albuquerque Police Records Department.

In honor of all the Officers around the world. And their families. A portion of all proceeds will be donated to C.O.P.S Concerns of Police Survivors- Chapter of New Mexico.

Photo dedications from: Officers Down Memorial Page, Retd. Mark Bralley, Kelly Casey and family.

Cover design: Kristen Bryant

Formatting by Daniel Morales

Library of Congress U.S. Copyright #TXu002492778

Nogales, Adrian, 1984-
The Fraternal Order
ISBN 979-8-9927515-0-5
ISBN 979-8-9927515-5-0

Pima Publishing Company
Taylor Ranch 87120
Printed and available in the United States and U.K.

THE FRATERNAL ORDER

INSPIRED BY REAL EVENTS

ADRIAN NOGALES

For Shawn McWethy

Scan this QR Code
To learn about more hero's
www.odmp.org

Contents

Part III

Part II

Part I

Introduction

Friday December 1st, 1989 - 3:37pm

Cowboys and Indians read the antique store's sign down the street, painted up high on the brick facade in three-foot-tall white letters with a black outline. The horses and banjos of the old Wild West have given way to rap music and lowriders by the end of the 1980's. Sitting in the heart of Native America along Route 66 is one of the United States largest cities. Nearly 380,000 citizens of Albuquerque go about their daily routines peacefully, but a group of Police Officers are investigating a violent gang fight in broad daylight that included the stabbing of two 14-year-olds walking home from their school bus stop. It seemed like a nice day to most, but the four Cops convened near a trail of blood that had splashed along the concrete sidewalk and onto the black asphalt of a normally quiet street.

This wasn't their first rodeo and each Officer could easily trace the trails of blood where the victims crawled from. The bloody scene juxtaposed by a beautiful day. A bright sun sweeping in across a vast blue sky that sits still above the wild desert surrounding the city. Light shined across the tree lined valleys of the Rio Grande River running through the middle of the city. The desert is full of extremes, despite a sunny sky with hardly any clouds, it was a chilly and windy winter afternoon. One Officer watched the trajectory of a tumbleweed blowing along the street and went to kick it to alter its path from coming into the scene and contaminating the blood stains.

Rising over 10,000 feet to the East, the Sandia Mountains are still dusted white from a winter storm the previous week and patches of un-melted snow can be found in shaded areas across the Metro. Cold weather changed the crime scene conditions for Police. Puddles of the young victim's blood coagulated along the cold sidewalk and some spots of blood were degrading from the sunlight. The Police did a good job securing the scene and collecting evidence.

The fight started on a sidewalk in front of a large chain link fence, topped by barbwire and leading to the lushly landscaped Fairview Memorial Park Cemetery on the other side. The gravestones in the backdrop give an eerie visual to what fate may have in store for the teenage stabbing victims, who were now being operated on at University Hospital.

With 10 years of experience, Officer Joseph Alvarez has just photographed the scene. He and other Police Officers on scene huddle together across the cemetery next to an un-kept yard of a brown flat roofed adobe house where one of the victims had tried to crawl to. The Police stand in a tight circle to minimize the punishing wind and discuss their findings. At 31 years old Officer Alvarez is a physically fit, handsome man. He is an imposing figure in his black uniform, standing 6 feet 3 inches tall in his black combat boots. Though he looks good for his age, he has worn under slept eyes and his black hair is peppered with grey from long trying days like this. The Officer has grown old from all the senseless violence that riddles society like a plague, such as today's stabbing of two juveniles over the color of clothes they wore.

Groups of onlookers and news vans have assembled behind the yellow CRIME SCENE tape that Police had hung up using trash cans, trees, vehicles and anything else sturdy to keep the tape suspended at waist level with its bold black letters to ward off passage DO NOT CROSS. The meddling news reporters are pleading for information and Officer Alvarez who is an authorized spokesmen for the department, walks over. He ducked under the crime tape and gives a simple statement to calm their frenzy.

"All we can say is there are two teenage victims who have been stabbed and taken to the hospital in serious condition." The warm air of his breath can be seen under his moustache as it mixes with the frigid air. He ignores their pleas for more details and turns back around, ducking under the crime tape to join the three other Officers convened at the corner of Columbia Drive and Santa Clara Avenue SE. He tunes out the reporters as they simultaneously bid for more information, joining the huddle of Officers again to the faint sounds of, "Do you have anyone in custody? What hospital? How old are the victims? Is this gang related?"

As the Officers finish piecing together the puzzle, a worried looking couple appeared amongst the crowd of onlookers and news reporters. The lady stood out, catching all of the Officer's attention when she waived her hand vertically and shouted a desperate plea at them, "Por Favor!" Judging by the couple's frightened demeanor Alvarez deduced that they might be the parents of one of the victims. When their son didn't arrive home after school and they heard about an attack from neighbors, the couple showed up to the taped off streets, frantically looking for their boy. Unaware that both victims in question had already been transported to the hospital.

It seemed like the folks might only speak Spanish so Ofc. Alvarez again broke off from the other Officers and steadily approached the worried couple. He lifted up the yellow tape and allowed the couple to duck under in order to gather information from the concerned pair, away from the reporters. As an eager reporter tried to chime in with a question, Alvarez looked at the reporter with an intense stare and shook his head no at the immaturity of the timing, before leading the couple away once they cleared under the tape. "You try and talk to them and I'll put you in the back of my squad car," he warned.

The tall chubby man was in a grey mechanics jumpsuit and the petite woman dressed in a red coat over a blue housekeeping uniform from the Eldorado motel. They couldn't have been much older than he was. The Officer attempted to speak in English, but could tell Spanish would be more comfortable for the two. After introducing himself, he asked the parents their names and for the name of the boy they were looking for and his date of birth. With a small palm sized notepad and plastic pen, he jotted down every detail.

He further confirmed these were the parents of one of the victims by asking the mom what clothes her son left the house in that morning, which she replied red sweatpants and red Chicago Bulls hoodie. Realizing, the Officer put his notepad in his chest pocket. This was always the hardest part of being an Officer, so Alvarez quickly inhaled a deep air into his nose as he closed his lips tight and clasped his hands together. . . before exhaling the heartbreaking news to the parents.

The Officer let the couple know that their son and his friend had been walking home in all red clothes and were jumped by four older teens wearing a different set of colors. But for the investigation he didn't reveal that the other gang's colors were black and silver. He leveled the information upon them honestly, that although the boys were last seen alive, their condition was bad. Rendered speechless, the mom covered her mouth with both hands in shock as her eyes welled with tears of disbelief and the dad shook his head repeatedly while saying in agony, "No No! Mi hijo no." Not my son. It struck a chord in the Officer who was a father himself of similar age and before they could ask any questions, he provided all the information he could privy, knowing that they should get to the hospital as soon as possible.

Officer Alvarez explained that Police had a pair of eyewitnesses who stated that the two boys were walking on a sidewalk and approached by another group, then some words were exchanged and the attack began. Their son and his friend were fighting back and held their ground for a brief instance, but they got cornered in the brawl and were both stabbed by one of the attackers with a butterfly knife. Alvarez spared the parents the harsher detail, that the outnumbered boys each had their arms held and that they were both violently stabbed several times in a matter of mere seconds causing deep wounds.

The Officer knew what would happen next, but in all his experience he had to do it and pointed across the street to where both boys had dropped next to each other on the concrete sidewalk. The sight of the blood caused the parents to weep in horror and the mother collapsed into her husband's arms, clenching onto his shirt. There was never an easy way to do this. Looking around the father began to take notice to all the evidence labeled. All around he saw Police had placed 14 small yellow tent style plastic indicators for points of evidence, numbered in black on both sides from 1-14.

Joseph explained that the tall fence to the cemetery had prevented any escape for the boys. They had to stand their ground to a group of older, dangerous and careless criminals. With both boys bleeding and collapsed on the pavement, the attackers ran off in different directions when a witness walking her dog yelled at them and then ran to a neighboring house to phone 911.

As the victim's parents listened in horrified shock, the Officer explained that although their son was badly injured, he had helped his friend who couldn't move or yell for help. Their son mustered up all of his strength and will to bravely crawl 15 feet into the street to wait for someone to pass by. The first car to drive up saw him in the middle of the street and stopped to help the boys. Luckily the driver was able to administer some well-trained first aid to both youngsters thanks to a former service in the Air Force.

A crew of five Firemen responded shortly after. Upon seeing the blood loss and wounds of the teenage victims, the first responders didn't wait for an ambulance and loaded up both juveniles in the fire truck to transport them to University Hospital nearly two miles away. As the Firemen raced past traffic to the hospital, they applied pressure to their wounds. Both teenagers had remained semiconscious. They arrived in critical condition and were immediately admitted for surgeries in the trauma center.

Upon hearing this life altering news, the parents were devastated. Through tears the mom was able to identify the other victim and how to locate his family to the Officer. He radioed the information out for Detectives and dispatch. A couple minutes had passed by now so the Officer told the parents the names of the two lead Detectives working the case. He explained that Police already know who two of the attackers are and where they live. Adding that fellow Officers were already hunting them down to get to the other two suspects, so that all four and anyone else involved would go to jail for a long time. Shivering, both parents were appreciative of the Officer's honesty and despite their son's bad influences outside of home, they could tell the Policeman cared as he gave assurance of pending justice.

After delivering the tough information, Ofc. Alvarez embraced the worried couple with one arm around each of their shoulders in a hug of strength. They found solace in seeing that Ofc. Alvarez was visually upset over the crime and genuinely determined to help them. Having observed the mother wearing a wooden beaded rosary underneath her housekeeping garment, he asked if he could lead the parents in a short prayer calling for protection of their son and his friend.

After praying together, the Officer gave the parents his little rectangle business card with his department logo and contact information, but not before writing the two lead Detectives names with their phone numbers. Ofc. Alvarez also made sure the parents knew where the hospital was and had transportation to get there. As he lifted the crime scene tape for them to leave, his cold stare backed off any anxious reporters from approaching. Distraught and in tears, the victim's mother pulled the Officer down by his shoulder to her level. Over the yellow tape she told him thank you and gave him a kiss on his cheek. Then the father shook his hand and kissed the top of Alvarez's hand in a very touching moment, endearing to the Officer.

Officer Alvarez walked back to the other Officers to wrap up the scene so that he could get back to working the streets. Alvarez had been hoping to swing by his house for a quick visit to his own family and to grab a sandwich to go. Thinking just maybe he could ease his mind about the harsh crime before returning to the station, to process his photos and write his full report. He knew it was only a matter of time until the next crime scene happened for him to photograph. The cold sunny day was busy for Officers and the weekend night was sure to be the same.

4:01PM

While the sun begins its slow descent into nighttime, Officer Alvarez left the crime scene in his black and white patrol car towards the Main Police Station Downtown after deciding that he won't have time to head home for a break. The Officer was driving in a beat up 4-door Plymouth Volare that had been on the force as long as he had, they had both accumulated many miles. Most of these cars were long gone from the department's fleet, but this one had somehow managed to stand the test of time and although not the prettiest, it ran well.

The patrol cruisers long body was painted midnight black with a white roof and had a large decal of the departments Police badge in gold on the driver's front door. A chrome spotlight on the driver door rested to the left in front of the Officer, for easy reach and night use. On top of the white roof was a thin metal brace mounted horizontally with two spinning lights, one on each side, topped by round red plastic covers making the lights look like two cherries on top of the front doors. In-between the two red lights, rest a large silver megaphone-style siren, facing forward that doubled as a Public Address loud speaker.

The street veteran Officer rolled up his window halfway and drove towards the sunlight as it began its slow fade down to the desert floor off in the horizon. He drove down Stadium Blvd in-between the University's big football stadium and the Minor League baseball stadium. Passing University Avenue, he looked to his left at the large empty parking lot of The Pit basketball arena as he neared the Interstate. It would be faster to get on the highway, but he liked to make his presence known in the community and decided to cruise the back roads into Downtown a couple miles away.

After driving under the highway, he turned right, heading North into the rough South Broadway neighborhood. Just passing through on a routine patrol, he was looking for any new graffiti to document and listening to his Police radio for any calls of distress. Throughout his decade on the force, he has frequently worked this neighborhood and knows every nook, cranny and dead end. He continued North towards Downtown along Broadway Boulevard as Police Officers and Dispatchers squawked out 10-codes on the radio.

Cruising about 30mph towards the Downtown skyline a mile away in the distance, he came across a group of small children playing on the sidewalk in front of a store who waved at him. As he passed them, he turned on his Police lights and blared his siren a couple times, watching their delight in his rear-view mirror, producing a smile of his own. He loved their innocence as he remained on Broadway and crossed Pacific Avenue. On his right he passed a brown adobe church with twin 3 story high bell towers and attached to a private school. To his left were a few small houses and businesses. Alvarez had learned to keep his head on a swivel and maintained nearly a 360-degree watch of his surroundings, glancing all around for trouble.

As he continued patrolling, he passed a local tire shop on his left at 803 Broadway SE on the corner of Santa Fe Avenue. Santa Fe Ave was basically a dead end to his left, it was being used as a dirt parking lot by the tire shop and had enough room for a garbage truck to head into the alley behind the business. Glancing to his right Santa Fe Ave had no streetlight and led into a neighborhood along the highway. All seemed quiet when the veteran Officer suddenly slammed his brakes and came to a halt as he snapped his head back towards the small family-owned tire shop.

Looking back to his left across two lanes of opposing traffic, Ofc. Alvarez noticed a black-haired Hispanic man running in the opposite direction for some unknown reason. It was still broad daylight and in all the Officers experience he knew a person randomly sprinting away from a business was usually trouble. Running in jeans and a brown flannel shirt unbuttoned with only a white under shirt when it was 35 degrees cold outside was a red flag and so he decided to pursue. The tall slender man with long sideburns was quickly cutting through an empty dirt lot next to the tire shop.

The Officer could visualize the man's route and see he was headed towards the dirt alley behind the tire shop that led back South towards Pacific Avenue just down from where he passed the children moments earlier. Driving with his left hand the Officer spun around his steering wheel to the left, completing a U-turn while keeping his eye on the running man as he simultaneously picked up his Police radio with his right hand. He pressed the gas pedal to the floor as he saw the man disappear into the alley behind the tire shop. Alvarez knew there was basically only one way out of the alley and that was to run southbound back to Pacific Ave.

4:04:31 South of Downtown Albuquerque, near the railroad tracks.

Alvarez left off his top lights and kept his siren off in case the man hadn't seen him he could maintain his element of surprise. Deciding in a split second to continue back South down Broadway towards Pacific rather than enter the dirt lot to go behind the tire shop to chase the man down the dangerously narrow and unpaved alley. The Officer had a short race, maybe 10 seconds at most to reach the mouth of the alley on Pacific Ave. He sped down Broadway to turn right onto Pacific to try and arrive at the alley opening before the middle-aged Hispanic male could escape it. Why is the man running the Officer thought?

The long-legged suspicious man in the brown flannel may or may not have seen the Officer as he is running in the dirt alley behind Broadway and heading South towards Pacific Ave. Called Barelas Street, the narrow alley was built for a single garbage vehicle and was lined with high brick walls that would be hard to jump. With adrenalin coursing through his veins Officer Alvarez raced South on Broadway towards Pacific, he peaked right through a few adobe buildings catching glimpses of the alley, but had lost track of the running man.

If the man reached Pacific Ave first, he could continue South down the alley or head West down Pacific with only three streets separating the alley to the Railyard. It would be easy to jump through people's yards then vanish to another part of the city by crossing the rail tracks. The Railyard divided quadrants of the city so the Officer knew he had to be quick to cut off the man or he could completely lose him from the SE to the SW Area Command on the other side of town.

Officer Alvarez floored the pedal and only applied his brakes to turn right, skidding smoothly onto Pacific Ave, facing West towards the sun. The Officer had no sight of the fleeing man, but he immediately noticed a blue 4-door sedan parked on the right side of Pacific, facing forward into the sun with the passenger side doors right in front of the alley exit, the engine running. Alvarez shielded the sun from his eyes with his microphone as he steered with his left hand and cautiously approached the vehicle from behind. He held his car radio and looked around while he waited for the air to clear, as Officers chirped off around the city.

He saw the vehicle was occupied by a lone man in the driver seat with dark slicked back hair covered by a black bandana wrapped around his forehead. The man was wearing a dark blue flannel shirt. When the Officer looked into the man's rear-view mirror, he connected eyes with the driver for a second and the young man's eyes opened wide with worry. Alvarez too had his eyes wide open looking down the alley for the running suspect in the brown flannel as his brain synapses fired, instantly linking the blue sedan and driver to the fleeing man in the alley.

4:04:39 Pacific Ave SE and Barelas Street Alley.

Noticing the blue sedans windows were rolled down, the Officer concluded in an instant that the vehicle had to be freshly parked, as it was too cold to sit in a car that day. His micro thoughts knew the mysterious driver surely must be freezing in the cold desert air wearing only a dark flannel. Alvarez knew the car was out of place and had a gut feeling the worried eyed driver wasn't enjoying the scenery of weeds and dumpsters in the alley or hanging out in the cold. The Officer put his radio near his face while he looked for the make, model and license plate number on the vehicle. He eased his brakes to position himself diagonally behind the car, angling his cruiser 1'oclock to block the mouth of the alley to his right, with the blue sedan in front to his left at 11'oclock. Only seconds had passed since he first saw the running man.

Being cautious, the Officer kept his own car out of park and applied his foot on the brake with about a foots distance from his bumper to the alleys brick wall, thus blocking an alley escape, but leaving enough distance to maneuver the vehicle out if he needed to give chase. Deciding it better to wait for backup, he saw no movement in the alley as he peered right, causing him to fear that the suspect might have noticed him and been athletic enough to jump the 7-foot walls into the backyards of houses towards the Railyard. The Officer pushed the button on his radio and raised the microphone it to his lips to update his location and situation accordingly, but kept his eyes on the man in the car.

RADIO TRANSMISSION #1 "225 Adam P.D."

Operator: "225 Adam?"

Nearly 15 seconds had passed since he first saw the running man, something was fishy and Ofc. Alvarez kept his hand on the radio now that he had the air and he continued to look around for the first suspect in the brown flannel, but he zeroed in his focus on the blue Ford LTD when he observed the driver reach around the interior.

RADIO TRANSMISSION #2 "I'LL BE OUT WITH ONE AT..."

BOOOM, BOOM, BOOM loud shot after shot rang out in succession toward the Police vehicle, shattering glass and piercing through metal. All the Officer could do was raise his left arm up to protect his head as he dropped the radio to try to un-holster his pistol with his right hand to return fire. BOOM, BOOM, BOOM in seconds more bullets slammed into the side of Alvarez's bullet proof vest. BOOM! He instinctively pressed his right foot hard on the brake pedal as violent gunshots continued to ring out and the Officer absorbed defensive wounds to his left arm. BOOOM, BOOM, BOOM, click click! 10 bullets in all were fired toward the Police cruiser's front seat.

Wounded and keeled over in defense, when the firing stopped, he could hear a couple more dry clicks of the weapon right above him, indicating the suspect(s) trying to execute him, but they had used all their ammo. One bullet missed the squad car and struck the side of the brick wall along the alley, five bullets rattled into his door or dashboard and five struck the Officer in his arm and vest. He knew his level III vest stopped some of the bullets, but Officer Alvarez was badly injured as the blue sedan sped off. He didn't have the chance to put out a description on the suspect(s) or the vehicle as it fled and his foot came off the break causing his car to idle into the brick wall, stopping its momentum with a small crash as he slumped over in pain.

Unfortunately, when Officer Alvarez raised his left arm, he exposed the non-plated ribcage portion of his body armor and a bullet smashed under his armpit, through his ribs and into his left chest near his heart. It was a natural reaction anybody would have made in that situation because it was most important to protect the head. His fastened seat buckle had prevented him from accessing his gun and he never even had a chance to un-holster and return fire as he sat taking punishment for doing his job. The radio called out for him. Injured, he bravely used his all his strength and managed to give a grim response through clenched teeth.

Operator: "Location? 225 Adam?"

RADIO TRANSMISSION #3 "I've been shot. I've been shot."

The dispatcher and those listening could hear the faint sounds of Spanish "ponle el pue…" Then they heard on the radio the faint sound of "bullshit." The radio dispatcher asked everyone to check their mikes then asked the Officer for his location again. Officers across the city had their hearts drop into action as anyone who heard the call stopped everything and rushed to find the scene. Sirens activated across the city. Seconds after the shooting stopped, a call came out on the radio that a tire shop at 803 Broadway had just been robbed. The radio sounded off with concerned members of his unit.

Almost 60 long seconds passed before the 1st backup unit arrived with two Officers who confirmed everyone's biggest fear, calling out "Officer Down." They started to attend to the injured Officer right away and apply pressure on his wounds. A nearby ambulance overheard the radio transmissions and arrived shortly after as dozens of Police flooded the area. Police cars sped off in all directions hell bent on finding the culprit(s) as Alvarez was rushed to the nearest hospital.

Within 5 minutes after shots fired, every working Officer, Trooper, Sheriff and Federal Agency in the State had an All-Points Bulletin out for a blue sedan as described by witnesses near the Railyard who gave various accounts describing one or two suspects with dark hair, possibly Hispanic. Detectives canvassed the neighborhood and interviewed the tire shop owner to get a better description of the first suspect. While whole departments looked for the shooter(s), Officer Alvarez fought for his life in transport to University Hospital which luckily has one of the best trauma centers in the country and was less than three miles away.

⚖ ⚖ ⚖

Chapter 01

Love and Boxing

JOSEPH ALVAREZ grew up in El Paso, Texas as an only child and graduated from Stephen F. Austin High School in 1976. His parents were devout Catholics who prayed for a large family. They tried for years to have more children, but couldn't conceive again due to complications from their first-born son.

His mother Carmen grew up on a small farm outside of Lerdo, Mexico where as a girl she worked by trade as a bread baker and seamstress as well as tending to various animals. She originally worked chopping sugar cane fields as a child, but nearly lost her left leg one day when her machete ricocheted into her bone and she bore a large scar on her shin thereafter.

His father Damacio (duh-moss-e-o) was tall with a lean physique. He was a distinguished WWII Veteran from the mountains of Alamogordo, New Mexico. Spending his days after the War as a travelling cigarette salesman for the Philip Morris Company, he nomadically roamed along Route 66, frequenting its neon light motels from Los Angeles to Chicago. He later became an Accountant for White Sands Missile Range after using the Montgomery GI bill to obtain a degree in Applied Mathematics from New Mexico State University in the city of Las Cruces.

A first generation American from Mexican parents, he had embellished on his Military Enlistment stating that he was Italian so that he could avoid some of the mundane jobs often given to Mexican-American Soldiers early in the War. Such as cooks and dishwashers. "*Dino*" joined at 18, shortly after his oldest brother Cruz had taken shrapnel to the skull and was taken prisoner by the Nazis. With two paragraphs of Italian in his arsenal he signed up to fight the Axis and was assigned as a B-24 left waist machine gunner. On a crew of 11, he successfully completed 42 missions over Europe in 1944-45, earning several Air combat medals for his tireless efforts on the .50 cal. All five of his brothers miraculously survived the War, two earning Purple Heart medals for their injuries. Dino had collected pounds of FLAK pieces that just missed on various missions.

JOSEPH'S PARENTS met in 1956 at an open-air bullfighting ring converted for the night into an outdoor boxing arena in Juárez, Mexico. Her oldest brother Jesús was crowned tournament champion at 168lbs after beating out a field of nearly 60 competitors in front of more than 40,000 rowdy spectators. The sounds of excitement reverberating as men in top hats smoked cigars and cigarettes, placing wagers on the bouts. Dozens of young girls in multicolored dresses collected the wagers and wrote out slips while stadium vendors sold meat filled tacos and bottles of beer. Many women and children could be seen scattered throughout the smoke-filled crowd.

Amidst the chaos of the crowded arena Damacio, who everyone called Dino, was introduced by his friend to an entourage of 6 beautiful sisters. The sisters were all in attendance that night to see their brother compete. A quarter German, but only Spanish speaking, the Mendoza sisters were all tall and beautiful with almond skin, sandy blonde hair and green or blue eyes. With blond hair and light eyes, they received as much attention by the surrounding crowd as the bouts did. Looking like a version of Ava Gardner herself, green-eyed Carmen was the only sister with darker burgundy hair so she stood out even more. She appeared rather shy, the only kin who didn't seem to enjoy the pugilists in the boxing ring as she kept covering her eyes or looking away as blood and spit spattered in all directions. Dino couldn't take his eyes off her.

For over a year Dino could only see Carmen while accompanied by a family chaperone, which always included at least one of her four older brothers. The brothers all had piercing diced-green eyes, rough tan skin and over their curly brown hair they wore light colored cowboy hats to go with their snakeskin boots. Each brother carried their own pistol nearly everywhere they went, tucked away.

Dino looked comparable to a tan Humphrey Bogart on those dates with his top hats, variety of freshly tailored suits and his long coats in the winter. He always kept a cool demeanor and would let the brothers drive his red and white hardtop Chevy Bel-Air, giving each a pack of smokes before every date. At first the brothers didn't like the sharp dressed smooth-talking Mexican-American because Carmen was the baby at 18 years and was 11 years younger than this tall man courting her. Before long, the brothers would come to argue over who got to chaperone because they enjoyed those smokes and loved that fancy 3-speed car. She had learned enough English so that they could converse privately from her brothers and every once in a while, the brothers would be occupied with a smoke just long enough for the two lovebirds to sneak a kiss.

At the tail end of the Great Depression, Carmen's father Roque had "disappeared" while working as a *Bracero* to take apart railroad ties in California back in 1942. Her mother Bonifacia was left alone, struggling to manage the family farm with 11 mouths to feed and nobody to answer where her husband was. A few years later Boni learned from rail workers that a rail foreman had forced her husband to continue working at gunpoint one hot afternoon after he incurred a hernia lifting heavy tracks and that he likely died from exposure. He had been sending money back for the family to come join him in California and they learned of his mysterious disappearance from an unsigned letter in the mail in an unknown person's handwriting.

Eventually the aging widow sold all the livestock and moved the big family from their large hacienda outside Lerdo to a small, but modest house in the crowded city of Juárez in 1947 when Carmen was only 10 years old. Carmen suffered hearing problems after once having been dropped on her head as a baby by an older cousin carrying her. Her left ear required advanced medical care including a hearing aid, so the family chose to head towards the U.S. border to seek treatment and find work. The young beauty was very self-conscious about her hearing and kept the hearing aid concealed from Dino for weeks, until he noticed one day while they were out buying winter blankets at the busy Juárez street markets or Mercado's. "So that's why you choose to only hear me when you want to," he playfully joked as she covered her ear with her luscious hair. She gave him a dirty look with a coy smile, but in this moment, she fell in love with him even more and vice-versa.

AT THE TIME SHE MET DINO, Carmen and her two oldest sisters Esperanza and Concha were the only family members permitted to work in the United States of the 10 living children in their family. It was all thanks to a kind wealthy Jewish family in El Paso, the Norton's who fixed their papers and had the 3 sisters stay as live in maids for nearly 7 years. The sisters shared a large room, but lived handsomely, having never owned new dresses, eaten steak or been on a vacation before living with the family of five. This family also made sure Carmen had state of the art hearing aids from Dr. Schuster. The Norton's really took care of the sisters and treated them with kindness. The Mendoza sisters taught the 3 small Jewish children how to speak fluent Spanish and one grew up to be a medical doctor practicing in Miami, Florida.

For years Carmen's oldest brother Jesús had worked by farming chile fields and boxing in prizefights to support the family. On Valentines Day 1957, Dino asked Jesús for Carmen's hand in marriage and with his blessing Dino proposed to Carmen that night in front of the live alligator's enclosure at San Jacinto Plaza in Downtown El Paso. Carmen confided that she had dreamed of this moment since she was a little girl, "Except I never imagined alligators in the background," she winked and they laughed before they kissed in overwhelming joy.

On a hot day in the summer of 1957, the wedding took place in a beautiful catholic church in Downtown Lerdo. Picturesque mountains surrounded the desert town and the ceremony was large and splendid with a beautiful backdrop. Nearly 100 guests attended, including 6 of Dino's 8 siblings and all 10 of Carmen's living. She had lost one brother Federico Roque when she was 6 and he was 7 after he fell down an outdoor water well while the two played with several cousins and friends in the small village of Pedriceña, Mexico. Little Carmen ran over a mile to the nearest Church to summon a priest for help on the hot and dreadful day.

As it turned out Damacio was the youngest in his family also, in fact his oldest sister was 28 years his elder and he actually had four nephews that were 3, 4, 7 and 9 years older than he was. Everyone laughed at his tales about growing up if somebody wanted to fight him, he would size them up, then have one of his nephews take care of it and afterwards they would treat him to the cinema. His family was very impressed at the beautiful bride and her family all knew Dino as a good man. Right before they took their wedding picture Dino presented Carmen with a key to her new house and the world has never seen a happier bride.

Three nights after the wedding at their housewarming party in El Paso on Wickham Ave, Carmen spilled a mound of soil onto her new carpet from a plant that her sister Lupe brought her. As four of her sisters began to fuss and argue about how to clean it, Carmen calmly opened her coat closet right next to her beautiful oak front door and grabbed her new General Electric brand vacuum cleaner. She plugged it into an outlet then flipped the switch on to suck up the soil. Her sisters were startled, one even jumped up and ran out of the room, it was the first time they had ever seen or heard a vacuum cleaner wail before. After the excitement they calmed down to curiously see the soil was gone. They all began speaking a mile a minute, pleading with their own boyfriends or husbands to have one themselves.

One year later, Joseph Anthony Alvarez was born with big beautiful brown eyes at the William Beaumont Army Medical Center in El Paso on September 11th, 1958.

Chapter 02

Dreams Shattered

DESPITE BEING AN ONLY CHILD, Joseph grew up raised with dozens of cousins and also lived right across the street from Logan Heights Park near Fort Bliss Army Base. The 4-acre park was primarily a huge grass field with a small sandy playground on one end that included a 3-story tall steel-barred rocket ship with a ladder running up the middle. Built during the space race of the 1960's, there were three enclosed levels to the rocket ship. On the third platform was a long metal slide from the top level down to the sand, that scalded many legs in the summer. Joseph spoke English and Spanish fluently and got along with the military kids and the other mostly Spanish speaking kids alike. He would only come indoors to eat and sleep if he wasn't in school or church.

Logan Heights could be a tough neighborhood after housing projects were built across the park in the late 1960's, so Joseph had trained with his uncle to box golden gloves, winning the El Paso city championship all 3 years of middle school at straw weight. As a reward his dad bought Joseph a red Yamaha 650cc all-terrain bike and red helmet 3 months before high school, with the promise that he would hang up his boxing gloves for good. Joseph reluctantly agreed, but had his dad hold onto the keys until he finished his last scheduled fights in California.

A week after being presented the motorcycle Joseph traveled with family to visit some of his relatives now residing in Los Angeles and won a small but competitive tournament at the Main Street Gym Downtown. He was victorious in four fights in two days, narrowly winning his last 2 bouts. Despite the victories, his face was too swollen and his head too dizzy to visit Disneyland the next day with his cousins. The *sweet science* prodigy decided that indeed his gloves would go in a closet back home in El Paso and he would learn how to ride that motorbike while deciding what sport to pick up next.

Joseph's new motorbike was huge for his 5.9 110lb frame, too big, but he had strong wrists from boxing and he was growing fast so he was able to ride it well enough to have permission from his parents to keep riding. With only a few days left in the summer before he started high school, Joseph rode out his red Yamaha for the first time away from his neighborhood one late afternoon with a neighbor boy who had a yellow Honda dirt bike. Alfredo who lived a few streets over, was going into the 10th grade and had curly dark brown hair, tan caramel skin and stood almost 6 feet tall at a muscular 160lbs. Alfredo's dad was a fellow Veteran and good friend with Dino and the young boy dreamed of being a Hollywood stuntman as he rode up the Alvarez driveway to ask Joseph's dad if the two boys could ride together. Joseph was surprised that his dad was agreeable as long as Joseph wore his helmet, giving his son a wink and a head motion to ride off into the city.

The two adventure seeking boys filled up their gas tanks for 42 cents a gallon at a Conoco station on Alabama Street. Then Alfredo asked Joseph if he wanted to take their bikes stunting on some huge dirt ramps in the mountains. Alfredo was very popular in high school already so Joseph didn't want to look like a geek and agreed to follow. The older Alfredo didn't wear a helmet and he sped off with his curly brown hair flowing against the breeze and tan skin glistening with sweat in the hot summer sun. Joseph tried to keep up.

The boys traveled for nearly a half hour North of the city into the parched desert and pulled up to an area at the base of the Franklin

Mountains that had "No Trespassing" signs posted from Ft. Bliss Army Base. Alfredo's dad was still an Officer in the Army and the older boy told the apprehensive Joseph, "Don't worry! Nobody is out here past Five o'clock...I've been here a bunch of times before. This is where the tanks romp around and test out their cannons in the day, you'll love it and we'll just stay a half hour." Then his neighbor sped into the restricted area on a path towards some giant dirt hills in the distance. There were miles of cactus all around.

Joseph watched for a moment then kicked up his clutch, twisted his hand to rev and followed. Hitting jumps along the way with rushes of adrenaline invigorating his body, Joseph was learning how to ride well by watching and copying Alfredo as they climbed nearly 30 large hills with tank tracks visible all around them.

The boys raced around and jumped their bikes for a half hour. They stopped to talk between some mounds when all the sudden they could hear a loud diesel engine approaching not far off. Both boys looked at each other frightened and killed their whining engines while hopping off their bikes instinctively. They grabbed their handle bars and ran while pushing their bikes to hide behind a dirt mound, just in time before a camouflaged Army Tank roared over a hill and slammed down to the area where they had just crossed. They had hidden themselves behind a large hill mere seconds before the Tank rumbled the ground screeching to a stop. The boys didn't say a word as 3 soldiers hopped out, trapping the two boys about 30ft away behind the hill. They sat stunned while the burnt orange sun faded into the mountains, slowly bringing about darkness.

Nearly 30 long minutes passed as the boys sat behind one of the dozens of dirt hills listening to the 3 soldiers curse about a poker game debt, brag about "banging some Mexican prostitutes" and then bark about how they hated El Paso and its hot weather. Alfredo laid down on the dirt and army crawled to the edge of the hill to sneak a few peaks at the tank crew while Joseph sat nervously on the ground in silence with his eyes wide open. The boys could hear as the soldiers received a radio call and the driver mentioned aloud how they all had to stay put for a while. Then the soldiers imagined out loud that if they "Found any illegal Mexicans out in the desert tonight they could kill them and the Army would never know." Joseph was thirsty and freaking out when he saw how nervous his fellow Hispanic friend was.

After a few minutes Alfredo suddenly stood up, turned around with his index finger over his own mouth vertically, indicating for Joseph to be quiet and he made a hand motion for Joseph to get up. He whispered to Joseph, "I don't think they have guns and two of them took a walk while the other one is taking a dump, they left their tank wide open, now's our chance to get out of here." Joseph shook his head no, but Alfredo gave him a look that reminded Joseph they both needed to get home plus they were dehydrating rapidly and only 15 minutes or so until complete darkness. The boys quietly stood up their bikes and devised a plan, they waited until the first two soldiers were out of sight then on the count of 3 Joseph and Alfredo simultaneously kick started their bikes and took off the same way they came in.

As they sped from behind the hill towards the city they passed the parked tank, surprising the wide-eyed soldier who was squatting behind it with his camo pants down to his black boots, holding a roll of toilet paper and a folded-up newspaper in hand. Then Alfredo suddenly veered right, took aim and did a few small circles around the soldier purposely kicking up a bunch of dirt, dust and rocks onto the soldier's wet butt and sweaty legs, just as his 2 buddies appeared running down a hill to the sound of motorcycles in the restricted dunes. With Joseph leading the way, the boys sped off, but had over 2 miles of hills back to safety from the now furious Tank crew.

Both boys stuck together, but could only go about 30 mph maximum because they had to weave in and out of the giant dirt hills that were too tough to climb quickly. Adding to the difficulty they had to avoid the thousands of desert cactus surrounding their route out. The Tank however had no problem powering over the large hills going its full speed, surpassing the dirt bikes abilities and gaining the advantage. It was like a scene out of a War movie and unfortunately for the boys, the wet butt they had rocked was the driver and he intended on squashing the fleeing bikes under his tracks for dead. The roar of the tank grew louder.

The angry tank easily powered over the hills and as it gained on them, Alfredo's bike stalled out in between hills and he had to dump the bike, but managed to jump off onto his feet running. Alfredo gathered himself and lifted the bike as he got back on and began desperately trying to kick start his yellow Honda. Joseph kept speeding ahead before slowing to a stop and looking back, realizing he was alone. Alfredo had flooded his engine trying to kick start it too much and he was left for dead. The tank was now only two hills away from enacting revenge. Joseph's heart was beating with fear.

In a split second 13yr old Joseph sped back over to Alfredo and the 15yr old instinctively hopped on with Joe as the massive tank got so close they could hear the gears grinding and screeching so loud that they couldn't hear the red Yamahas engine they were riding. The boys sped off and Alfredo looked back as his yellow Honda bike was destroyed under the steel monster like a recycled soda can. His bike was shattered into pieces just before the hills ended. After coming out of the hills they were home free on a straightaway where they easily outran the Tank crew, who were probably wishing they could end the joyride with a single cannon round.

It was a long ride back to Logan Heights, the bright sunny day had turned into a chilly dark night as the boys rode home silently in stunned disbelief. Joseph dropped Alfredo off at his home on Kemp Avenue and quickly sped out of there before Alfredo would have to explain to his parents what happened to his bike. Before Joseph left, as Alfredo made his death march into his house, he turned and said, "Thanks for coming back man, see you at school." Joseph just nodded his head up slightly to acknowledge, still too stunned to assemble words about what they had just experienced together.

After that crazy day, they became best friends for the next 3 years before Alfredo graduated in 1975 and joined the Army, just weeks after America withdrew its troops from Vietnam. He was first stationed in North Carolina and ironically became a Tank crewmember himself, possibly assisted by his knowledge of their maneuverability. Alfredo sent Joseph's parents a picture of him on top of an M1 Abrams Tank that they proudly placed on their refrigerator. Joseph would smile and shake his head at the irony of the photo every time he looked at it.

In high school, Joseph's smooth chiseled face, v-frame, curly jet-black hair and sporty bike made him quite popular with the young ladies around Austin High School. Standing 6.1 and weighing 150lbs his senior year, he was a talented three-sport athlete who excelled at the 1500m in track, played first base four years on Varsity baseball and was a midfielder for his high school soccer team. The straight A's athlete made the local paper often and was respected by the whole town. Locals especially became fans when Joseph turned down a partial track scholarship to the University of Texas at Austin, instead opting to play baseball for his hometown University of Texas at El Paso on full scholarship.

Joseph graduated high school and joined the UTEP Minors baseball team just in time for America to celebrate its bicentennial on July 4th, 1976. He continued to live at home, making Deans list every semester and averaging a .320 batting average over his first two years of college ball. He had garnered the attention of a few professional scouts who began to make house visits and attend every Miners home game to see the prospect. His parents and family were so proud.

March 14th, 1977. 5319 Wickham Avenue, El Paso Texas

KNOWN AS A HEAVY SLEEPER, Dino Alvarez had once slept peacefully in a bunker through an entire German bomb raid in South England during the War. So one night back in March of 1977 with his mom visiting California, Joseph stole his sleeping dad's car. Joseph took the keys off his dad's nightstand, crept out of the house and quietly rolled the green sedan out of the driveway by placing the car in neutral and with the driver door open he used his left leg to push the car into reverse then using gravity he coasted down the street before starting the engine. As Dino slept, Joseph picked up some teammates waiting down the street to go celebrate in Mexico after crushing rival New Mexico State 11-2 in Las Cruces earlier that day. Six players piled in the family car and headed for the border around 11pm.

After a night of debauchery, Joseph snuck back into his driveway at 4am with the headlights off only to see Dino seated outside sipping coffee and puffing a cigarette in the moonlight, waiting for his Buick to be returned. His dad was scolding the then 19yr old for driving drunk because Dino had lost an uncle to a drunk driving accident in 1933 that claimed four other innocent lives. Joseph was equally embarrassed as he was drunk. All was almost chalked up to "boys will be boys" when upon inspection, his dad noticed that the Buicks rear license plate was missing. Infuriated, Dino got behind the wheel and drove Joseph 20 minutes back across the border to where the car had been parked in Juárez. They searched for several minutes when an old man approached the two to sell them a license plate that would get them into the United States "no problema." Dino traded the *Viejo* two packs of smokes for his Texas plate back, as the sun rose above the tan and green mountains in the near distance. That week was the only time Dino dutied his son chores while Joseph was in college.

February 18th, 1978. UT-El Paso Baseball Practice Field.

STILL UNDECLARED to what his college major was, in his junior season Joseph was struggling at the plate, hitting .247 after 14 games and he lost his First-Base job to a left-handed Freshman from Houston, TX. The night that he learned he was moving to the outfield, Joseph and the other two juniors on the team went out to Juárez to blow off some steam on a Friday night. Tom Gesford and David Maddux picked Joseph up in Tom's single cab white truck. The teammates sat next to each other and were all upset at the Freshman being moved to 1B. The three Juniors parked in Downtown El Paso and walked across the free bridge to chase and get chased by women in Juárez for a few hours at a place called The Tequila Derby. They had a doubleheader vs. Rice University the next day and stumbled through border patrol around midnight. "U.S. citizens," they shouted proudly to the Border Agents as they were waived through the turnstiles, still jubilating the night.

On the way home they took some side streets and back roads to avoid any potential Police. About 5 minutes into El Paso the driver and starting Centerfielder Tom fell asleep behind the wheel of his Chevy pickup and blew a stop sign on Dyer Street at McKinley Ave. He t-boned a lady and her two young kids in a polar white Mercury Comet station wagon, instantly killing the mother and injuring the children. Joseph was hammered drunk, but watched the entire accident unfold before his head slammed into the front windshield smashing an indent into the glass.

When he opened his eyes, his head was bleeding and his friend's unconscious, the driver pinned onto the horn as it buzzed the whole neighborhood. Joseph hopped behind the driver out of the window and was the first to get out to check on the family, he knew instantly the mother was gone. He had enough sense to get the two kids out of the car and safely onto the side of the road. Joseph went to flag down a car for help.

Police arrested all three young men at the scene and they went to the hospital in handcuffs to get patched up before heading to jail. The El Paso Tribune printed the front-page story on the Sunday paper a day later and all three players were kicked off the team, the driver Tom was charged with vehicular manslaughter and driving while intoxicated.

Ashamed, but still loving, Damacio went down to the hospital and paid the widow father of the children $7,400 cash that he had saved gradually and hidden over 20 years for Joseph to eventually use as a down payment on a house. He even insisted on giving the grief-stricken dad a ride to the bank. Upon returning from the children's wing of the hospital where the widow's kids were being treated, he walked into Joseph's bedroom and for the first time ever closed the door behind him.

With his head bandaged and heart pounding Joseph sat up in his bed. Dino looked his son deep in the eyes and told a depressed Joseph that his first job started Monday at the A&W stand that their neighbor owned. He firmly told his son, "From now on you are going to pay for everything and earn everything and you are to continue college on your own." That was it, his dad got up and walked out. The words, "On your own," were echoing in Joseph's head over and over throughout that sleepless night.

Tuition payments weren't cheap for a green 20yr old who had never worked a day before and soon Joseph had to take on a 2nd job as a part-time janitor at U.T.E.P. His Tío Jesús, who had also posted his bail for public intoxication the morning after the crash, grew up with the head Custodian at the University and helped his beloved nephew get the job. Joseph had 12 hours of classes a week and worked 62 hours, 40 at $2.38 an hour and 22 at $3.60 an hour.

Many students and faculty would whisper about the handsome janitor Joseph and it seemed like everyone on campus knew what had happened. Saying high to some familiar faces resulted in strange glances when he connected eyes with them. Before long, the two work schedules, a full-time course load and all the *chismosos or gossip* became too much for him and he began to fall behind. He even started missing some classes, highly unusual for a guy who had perfect attendance since kindergarten.

ONE DAY IN APRIL OF 1979 while sweeping a popular corridor at the University in his blue janitor jumpsuit just 2 hours before an important exam, an exhausted Joseph found a recruiting flyer on the ground. It was for the Albuquerque Police Department. Along with A.P.D. across the top and contact information on the bottom, it read, "Serve Your Country in an Exciting Career! Paid training, full benefits, 21year retirement and promotions available." With broom in arm, it all seemed like divine placement and Joseph thought maybe this is how he could pay back society for that careless night. Albuquerque was only 5 hours from El Paso he figured and he had visited once as a kid remembering that he liked the city. As fate would have it, he also scooped up a loose dime as he swept, which he used to call the flyers 505 area code number from the nearest rotary dial pay phone to set up an interview and testing arraignments. The recruiter told him he was lucky because he was the last interview they were accepting this year and he would have had to wait 9 months to apply again.

Joseph was very excited when he hung up the phone. Then he walked two steps and felt immediate regret. What had he just done? Joseph had scheduled the interview on the same day that the Major League Baseball's California Angels were to host open tryouts at the Dudley Dome, home of their AA minor league team the El Paso Diablo's. Did he really want to give up his dream to be a Policeman?

Chapter 03

Naked Idiots

May 21, 1979. University of Texas at El Paso, Downtown campus.

ABOUT 18-24 MONTHS AWAY from a Philosophy degree, Joseph finished his 6th semester at U.T.E.P. with 3 C's and 1 D, his first ever, placing him on Academic probation for the upcoming semester. As summer began, he told a white lie to his folks saying he was going to New Mexico to visit Alamogordo for a few days to clear his head. His older cousin Pasquale lived on his own in Alamogordo. Joseph had phoned Pasquale ahead of time asking him to cover his story if his parents were to call or ask, simply telling his cousin he had met a girl from Albuquerque and didn't want his folks to know yet. Pasquale said, "Sure bro, hey ask her if she has a sister."

Joseph got some time off from work and spent hours debating whether to attend the Police interview or trying out for professional baseball. He spent a whole day swinging a bat and perfecting his timing at a local batting cage. Ultimately though he still felt a sense of shame in El Paso and rode up to Albuquerque on that red Yamaha with only $30, a sleeping bag, small suitcase containing a water canteen, 4 cans of beans, can opener and a .22 revolver his uncles secretly gave him on his 18th birthday. When he rode passed the "*Dudley Dome*" he felt nauseous and couldn't even look over at it.

He arrived two days before the interview he set up with A.P.D. and camped next to the Rio Grande River in the forest or *Bosque* of Albuquerque's scorching South Valley. He parked his bike against the giant stump of a cut down cottonwood tree and set up a nice little campsite 10 yards away next to the river in a patch he cleared. He collected many small sticks and placed them in a circle around his campsite so no water snakes would bother him.

The night was hot and humid so Joseph took off his shirt, but there were so many bugs biting his flesh he had to wear the shirt on his head at the neck hole and had a hard time sleeping as he sweat profusely. Not knowing that he was around a tough *barrio* or neighborhood, he awoke the first night to see two bald *cholos* or gangbangers dressed in black trying to steal his cherished Yamaha. Only 10 yards away he hollered out to them. When he did, the taller skinny one wearing a Raiders shirt produced a switchblade while the other short and stubby one in blue started trying to kick-start the bike.

The taller teen with the knife picked up a baseball-sized rock in his free hand and threw it just wide of Joseph's dodging face. BOOM! Joseph fired one shot into the river and then pointed his revolver right at the idiot with the knife. Joseph transferred the gun to his left hand still aimed at the youngster and with his free hand Joseph reached for a small rock next to the base of a tall Cottonwood tree. He returned the favor and threw the little rock with pinpoint accuracy right into the back of the bike thief who grunted in pain and hopped off and tried to run. A Bernalillo County Sheriff picked up two naked teenagers early that morning walking home covering themselves with their hands, their clothes in the Rio Grande forever.

Over the next 3 days Joseph passed all the required tests and signed all the necessary paperwork to begin the 24-week Academy set to commence 2 1/2 months later on August 1st 1979. The Albuquerque Police Department had recently been accused of not hiring enough Spanish-speaking Officers in the 1970's to meet the demands of the growing population and the recruiters were happy when Joseph walked in the door able to read, write and speak both English and Spanish fluently. He proved to have exceptional writing ability and after meeting with recruiters, Joseph had been told that he was the last of 46 Cadets admitted to the Police Academy Class of 1980. When asked if he had a criminal history, he was honest about his arrest and a few traffic violations he had picked up. They could tell he was remorseful about that dreadful night. Since he had only been charged with a class C misdemeanor, he wasn't disqualified. He was very grateful, but also very nervous for the opportunity.

At the time Joseph signed up to join the Albuquerque Police, the growing Department had roughly 540 Officers working in conjunction with 170 Bernalillo County Sheriffs covering a large jurisdiction of 187 square miles from the East Mountains out West to the wild desert with the State's largest and most diverse city in between. The A.P.D. pay structure and hierarchy of the Department at that time was Mayor > Chief > 4 Deputy Chiefs > 12 Captains > 20 Lieutenants > 35 Sergeants >70+Detectives > 380+ Union Officers. Different Department Divisions included PATROL, SPECIAL PATROLS, HOMICIDE, SEX CRIMES, ARMED ROBBERY/BURGLARY AND AUTO THEFT, JUVENILE, POLICE ACADEMY, PAWN SHOP, GANG TASK FORCE, TRAFFIC AND MOTOR (CYCLES), K-9 UNITS, EVIDENCE, FIELD INVESTIGATORS, MOUNTED HORSE PATROL, CIVIL LITIGATIONS, INTERNAL AFFAIRS, AIR PATROL (1Cessna), BOMB SQUAD and the VICE UNIT which worked NARCOTICS, PROSTITUTION, and UNDERCOVER STING OPERATIONS.

Everybody worked alongside one of the country's premier Special Weapons and Tactics or S.W.A.T. teams, deployed primarily for barricaded subjects and hostage rescue situations. There were civilians employed by the city who worked Police Dispatch and Radio Communications as well as the Transcription department, used to type up Police reports or audio recordings for court. Additionally, both Police Officers and civilians were staffed to serve as ID technicians, to help process criminals with mug shots and fingerprints. An Officer always paired with a civilian. The department was fascinating to Joseph and he dreamed of becoming a Detective someday.

Before he returned back to El Paso to await the Academy, Joseph stopped by the University of New Mexico to research the city he would soon call home. Despite almost being robbed on his first night, he had a nice impression of the places he saw, but really didn't know much about the city he agreed to work, live in and protect. He went to the campus library to read the local tribune and use a microfiche to find information. Joseph noticed that Albuquerque was just like any other major city in that the media covered what was happening in Washington D.C., the local government invested in the Stock Market in New York, regular people watched the movies and TV shows of Hollywood and Albuquerque cheered all the other major cities sports teams. Joseph had noticed a lot of Dallas Cowboys gear around town, which was his favorite football team and figured that would help for easy assimilation.

The mayor of Albuquerque in 1979 was David Rusk who was considered an international expert in Urban Planning. Mayor Rusk's father Dean Rusk was the U.S. Secretary of State for the Assassinated President John F. Kennedy and for his successor Lyndon Baines Johnson, from 1960-68. His son David might have followed in his father's Diplomatic steps, but he was married to a foreign national from Argentina and this wasn't permitted in the Foreign Service in those times. David Rusk was only Albuquerque's second modern day Mayor after Henry Kinney served as the first from Dec 1st, 1973 to Nov 31st, 1977. Before that the city was run on a City Manager system for decades that transformed into a 9-member City Council when Kinney was elected its leader.

Joseph also learned that in Spain, the pueblo of Alburquerque is near the Portuguese border and is more or less the center of Spain's cork tree industry, used to make bottle corks for wine or olive oil. In antique Spanish, Albuquerque means white oak cork tree and in old Arabic it translates as father to oak cork tree. When the Spaniards controlled the western half of the U.S., the future States of Texas, New Mexico, Colorado, Utah, Nevada, Arizona and California were all called New Spain from the late 1500's until 1821 when Mexico took over the land until the Mexican-American War from 1846-48 ceded the land to the U.S. In Santa Fe, the Palace of the Governors is where all the important land and resource decisions were made amongst the Spaniards controlling the New World.

Viceroy was the title of the Spaniard named Don Francisco de la Cueva, who was in charge of New Spain from 1653 to 1660. Back in Spain, he was the Duke of Alburquerque and when he arrived to control New Spain, a provincial governor Don Francisco Cuervo y Valdes named the farming settlement along the Rio Grande "Alburquerque" in the Duke's honor, a member of the Bourbon Monarchy. 70 years before General Washington's United States declared its Independence on July 4, 1776, Albuquerque officially became a city in 1706 and has since been nicknamed the "Duke City" and is also referred to as "Burque" on the street and by gangs, after the extra R in the original name. Some say the first R was dropped in the late 1880's when a train station agent couldn't pronounce it and started writing the city's name without the R.

Joseph was getting tired in the library doing research, but he wanted to learn all he could about the rich history of the area.

Albuquerque is seated in Bernalillo County and is the largest city in New Mexico and has the largest municipal Police Department in the State. In 1979 it was the 36th largest American city with roughly 320,000 residents. The Duke City is home to the Sandia National Labs for government weapons research and also to the Kirtland Air Force Base, including its Nuclear Weapons Center manned in 1979 by the 1606th Air Base Wing that would share airfields with the local airport. Sandia also housed the Atomic Energy Commission and Strategic Task Force for Atmospheric testing of the Stratosphere, until they were disbanded under International Nuclear agreements. The University of New Mexico also makes Albuquerque more modern than other parts of the mainly rural State.

Located only 275 miles North of the large U.S.-Mexican border cities El Paso and Juárez, many neighborhoods in the southern half of ABQ have strong ties to Mexico or Latin America. In some areas not only business signs, but even the billboards can be found advertising in Spanish. This influence can be found in its culinary as Albuquerque is famous for spicy food. In New Mexico and Albuquerque there is a standard question asked when ordering many types of food, "Red or Green?" This is for what color chile you would like on your food, if you ask for Christmas, they put both. The chiles are a spicy vegetable and can be served in a variety of ways and Scoville.

Central Avenue, part of Route 66 for 17.4 miles, split right down the heart of the city and connected the University East to the mountains and West to the desert. West of U.N.M was the Downtown and a little further West the Spaniards had set up the Old Town starting in 1706, using their traditional style of a central plaza surrounded by a church, government buildings and businesses on all four sides. The twin towered adobe church was originally named San Francisco and later changed to San Felipe de Neri. With two brown adobe towers topped distinctly by white Crosses, a beautiful thick wall surrounds the property with various archways to allow entry.

In 1975 Paul Allen and Bill Gates founded and headquartered a micro-computer and software company called Microsoft in Albuquerque's war zone at 199 California Street NE 87108. By 1979 they headed to the West Coast and the largest building in Albuquerque and the State of New Mexico was the 18-story National Building Downtown on 505 Marquette Ave NW. The Main Police Station was down the street at 401 Marquette and stood 3 stories tall with 1 basement floor. Most of Downtown was built between the 1880's and 1920's before skyscrapers. The city skyline was practically non-existent, but the mountains to the East were part of the Southern Rockies and they rise to peak at almost 11,000ft, making the surrounding area prime real estate. However, the majority of the land in front of the mountains was home to the Sandia Indian Reservation and remained undeveloped, leaving its natural beauty.

Sandia is 1 of 19 such autonomous Native American Pueblo communities in the State with their own distinct languages, laws, and Tribal Police forces. There is also the Navajo Nation and 3 Apache Tribes in New Mexico. The 19 Pueblos are Acoma, Cochiti, Isleta, Jemez, Laguna, Nambe, Ohkay Owingeh, Picuris, Pojoaque, Sandia, San Felipe, San Ildefonso, Santa Ana, Santa Clara, Santo Domingo, Taos, Tesuque, Zuni and Zia. The Pueblos range from a few hundred tribal members to several thousand. The ancestral

Pueblo People of Chaco and Anasazi date back thousands of years. The Clovis people hunted the land even further back.

Being at a high altitude of over 5,000 feet and surrounded by dirt, the Spaniards learned from the Native Americans the best resource for building was to dry mud into thick bricks to imitate their adobe architecture. They also learned dry farming the 4 sisters, corn, squash, beans and sunflowers. There is legend of a famous indigenous musician Kokopelli who used to travel the 19 pueblos spreading seeds and playing his flute to attract rainfall for the crops to grow. The rainbow a symbol of abundance. 9 months after he left many babies were born.

Joseph exited the Zimmerman Library at U.N.M. just after noon and took a long cruise through the city before he left, until his return in a few months for the Academy. Old Town was beautiful and many Native Americans displayed their pottery and turquoise jewelry there on the sidewalks around its main plaza and he bought his mom a beautiful necklace. The large population was spread-out, keeping Albuquerque simple and aesthetic, but the city was definitely different to say the least. From the blend of Native American elements, the adobe architecture and spicy food, to the ethnic makeup of people and the southwest style of clothes, it was unlike anywhere Joseph had visited before.

As Joseph left Old Town, he cruised South on his motorcycle to leave the city. On his way out he must have spotted 20 low-rider cars in various paint schemes and in different parts of the city. It wasn't like the low-rider's made up every other car, in fact there were very few in comparison to the general population, but even seeing one was a culture shock to Joseph who had only seen a couple before in Los Angeles when visiting his cousins. His favorite low-rider was a blue ice cream truck with orange fire flames on the front and tiny white wall tires with gold spoke rims, a gold exhaust pipe and a double swirl of gold chains for a steering wheel. It was so ghetto fabulous that Joseph couldn't help but follow it for a little bit and buy an ice cream when it pulled over, opting for a Mississippi Mud Pie. To Joseph, Albuquerque was very different from El Paso, but similar enough in its rich tapestry of culture that he thought that the transition should be normal when he returns.

EVERY DAY THAT SUMMER in El Paso, Joseph filled a backpack with rocks and ran up and down the steep Sugarloaf Mountain near his home in preparation. Joseph had struggled with the decision to become a Police Officer because he knew he was close to finishing his degree and in his heart, he wanted to play baseball, but mainly he was afraid to disappoint his parents. His dad was the first in his family to graduate college with a Bachelor's Degree, earned and paid for by the Montgomery G.I. bill after battling Nazi's over Europe. His mom was a very smart lady, but had a poor upbringing and never attended school after the 8th grade when she began working full-time.

Both of his parent's dreams were for Joseph to go to college and use his brain to make something out of himself. When the time came, Joseph again fibbed to his parents and said that he and some friends were getting their first apartment closer to campus and that he would still visit on weekends after a while. His father handed him $20 and said, "Be careful Mijo! And you always know where your room is." His mom would cry every night for the first month he was gone.

The only person who had known Joseph's intentions ahead of time was Father Henry, who the young man had known his whole life since his baptism, first Holy Communion and his days as an altar boy. The tiny 75yr old Priest from Colombia

invited him for a blessing and prayer three days before he left. Afterward sitting on a wood bench outside the Church, Father Henry tucked a $20 bill down Joseph's front pocket and said, "Here buy some good Champu, for you don't lose your hair like me," he joked while rubbing his own head and smiling, before presenting him with a pocket bible and sincerely telling him to, "Never lose your faith, it will always guide you."

THE NIGHT BEFORE LEAVING for Albuquerque, Joseph went to Juárez and visited his aunts and uncles. Tío Jesús knew something was going on, but wasn't exactly sure because Joseph had quit his janitor job months ago. His stoic faced uncle took him aside to give him a jump rope and an American $20 bill, telling him in Spanish an advice he had said to Joseph only once before, "If you ever get in a fight, never lose your feet or you can die on the ground."

Joseph spent the night in a guestroom, getting serenaded occasionally by the howls of Coyotes under the Mexican moonlight. It was hard to sleep with his mind racing and he replayed many moments of his life until that point. The whole world stood still in that room, but everything was moving for him.

He had a huge breakfast of migas and tortillas before leaving, equipped with some sound advice, $360, a sleeping bag/clothes, jump rope, his .22 revolver and a recently acquired switchblade in pocket. Joseph rode the five hours back up to Albuquerque. He never looked back.

Chapter 04

Wild Wild West

July 23rd, 1979. Albuquerque Police Academy, 5900 Jefferson Avenue NE.

SEVEN DAYS BEFORE THE ACADEMY officially began, the 46 Cadets met in plain clothes for a meet and greet orientation along with their 3 main Instructors. The Cadets sat in brown metal folding chairs placed into a giant circle around a conference room at the Fraternal Order of Police Lodge and Union Hall, where they're Academy would be held. It was a very diverse group of 41 male and 5 female Cadets. The Instructors partnered the Cadets in 23 groups of two and they were given 5 minutes to talk before each pair would introduce one another, specifically where they are from and what they did before the Academy.

Joseph was paired up with a young Spanish looking Cadet who had tough eyes and a scowl on his face, his black hair shaved bald to reveal a mean looking scar on his head causing him to look more like he was a gang member than potential Police Officer. He was about 5.8" 140lbs to Joseph's 6.1" 150. Joseph had to move his chair over to sit next to him and saw the bald Hispanic Cadet's cold stare observing him. After sitting for 10 seconds of silence Joseph said, "Hey I'm Joseph from El Paso and I worked for UTEP!" The Cadet just did a little expressionless nod so Joseph said, "And you are?" Which was answered by a quick faint whisper of, "Jimmy Zamora from Tierra Amarilla." Joseph smiled and said, "What? Excuse me?" Very unenthusiastically the Cadet repeated his information.

Joseph asked, "Is that in New Mexico?" A very cold "Yes" was all he got in response from Cadet Zamora.

When it came time to introduce themselves as the 12th pair, Jimmy went first. Not being able to go on much and feeling a little devious when it was his turn, Joseph introduced his partner as Jimmy Zamora from Yellow Dirt, New Mexico. Zamora's eyes snapped towards Joseph with a look of death at his translation of Tierra Amarilla. Joseph's face was cool with a hint of amusement.

As for the rest of the class, there were two more Texans, one from the city and one from the country, a baby-faced kid from Las Cruces, a welder from the Navajo reservation in Arizona, a Mormon musician from Utah, a private investigator from L.A., an 11th grade German teacher from Denver, a young mother from Boise, Idaho. Only one Cadet was from back East via New Jersey and the rest of the Cadets were from New Mexico. Most of the Cadets were from Albuquerque and hailed from various family and ethnic backgrounds, but the majority of the Cadets were Hispanic or White males in their early 20's. There were three Black Cadets, five females and 20 Hispanics (two females). Joseph was one of only five Cadets who spoke Spanish fluently including Jimmy Zamora and Ken Williams, one of the Black Cadets who grew up in Albuquerque's South Valley and made everybody laugh when he explained that he learned Spanish to survive middle school.

From 1975-1980 Albuquerque Police were mandated by the Citizens Police Oversight Agency or C.P.O.A. in a lawsuit settlement to recruit more Hispanic and minority Officers to match the demographic makeup of the city. Hence Joseph sweeping up a recruitment flyer in El Paso. Some of the other areas the Department recruited were the Indian Pueblos, Northern New Mexico and southern cities near the border like Las Cruces, Deming and Alamogordo. Even though this new class was almost half Hispanic, the Department fell short by 1% of the agreement and was fined $1,000 by the C.P.O.A.

The 47th Cadet Class of 1979-1980 had three main Instructors, all three males born and raised in Albuquerque each with dark hair and mustaches, two of them wearing wide framed glasses. All three of the Instructors had been on the force for over 10 years and had each been involved with thousands of different crimes in their tenures. The Instructors fully understood human nature and in one of their introductions the brawny old salt said something that stuck in Joseph's memory forever, "You never know what factors into a person's life or what secrets lurk in people's minds to make them commit crimes or how desperate people are not to go to jail. You will encounter lies so convincing the liars themselves will believe it. Don't trust anyone until you have completed your investigation into why you got called out to this person. Record your suspicions and always follow your gut instincts, no detail is too small."

After the introductions the Cadets were explained the uniform and dress policies then given a list of basic expectations including, "To be in peak shape, be sharp in the classroom, perform in various field scenarios, memorize Police codes, laws and Due Process, to drive good and to be able to defend against danger right down to the last 10 seconds." The room seemed puzzled then got serious as the Cadets were told by one Instructor that, "Historically around the globe when a Police Officer has heroically fallen to gunfire there have often been about 5-10 seconds before they bleed out and die where many were able to return fire in their last breaths." Class was suddenly in session and reality hit a lot of the Cadets, who sat with eyes wide open and fear on their faces. Joseph raised his hand to ask the Instructors, "How many Police Officers have died in Albuquerque?"

All the Instructors conferred for a few seconds and then one said, "Nine total in the line of duty, but don't worry they don't shoot Cops here, that was all before 1960 in the Wild West days." Then Joseph asked if they could describe each scenario. With only 10 minutes of required attendance left, one Instructor looked annoyed at the question by taking a long look at both his wristwatch and a clock on the wall. Instructor Bartram seemed to realize how interested the class was in the question and he gave a quick profile on the department and the history of Law Enforcement in New Mexico.

The Instructor explained how, "In the 1800's the New Mexico Territory had swapped hands 3 times by centuries end. While Spain, Mexico and the United States fought for the land taken from the Native Americans, the territory turned wild with gunslingers, outlaws, crooked politicians and intolerant lawmen. New Mexico was a haven for trouble and young men like Billy the Kid went around shooting themselves in and out of havoc, including the murders of 7 Lincoln County, NM Sheriffs and a U.S. Marshall between 1878-1885." The Instructor continued, "Hell Albuquerque's first police chief Milton Yarberry was hanged for murder back in the Cowboy days and they sold tickets in Old Town to watch the gallows. He had found his old lady out with another man, confronted the fella to a fight and that ended with him tried and sentenced to death for murder. The cowboy from Arkansas and once wanted in Missouri busted out of jail after, but was eventually caught up North and put on a train full of deputies that brought him from Santa Fe to Albuquerque for his execution."

Everybody's eyes got big with interest, the Instructor continued "Meanwhile the land was run wild with grey wolves, packs of coyotes, jackrabbits, roadrunners, scorpions and lots of snakes. The mountains have been home to black bears, bobcats, cougars, mountain lions, lynx and other wild cats. The skies give flight to hawks, eagles, falcons and every other football team you can think of." The class laughed and the Instructor continued by saying, "And don't think those animals aren't out there still, ready to eat you for dinner. So be careful if you venture into the mountains or desert." There was a rolling chalkboard in the large room and the Instructor wheeled it to the front as he began to officially answer Joseph's question.

On Saturday November 20, 1886 Albuquerque lost its first two Police Officers when City Marshal Robert McGuire and Deputy Marshal E.D. Henry were killed in the line of duty. It all started when a posse of law enforcement had gathered to look for two suspects Ross and Johnston, wanted for robbery and cattle rustling. As the posse split up into various search parties, the two Marshal's McGuire and Henry fled South and arrived on horseback to Cutinola's dancehall. There they interviewed patrons and learned that the two suspects were renting a room across the dancehall.

Sneaking up to the small adobe hut with a door on the left and a small window in the front, Marshall McGuire peered into the room and was able to see the two suspects were inside with two disreputable women. Straight of the front door on the left side of the hut was one suspect on his bed and across the room to the right was the other suspect on the bed with a woman. The Instructor drew a crude diagram.

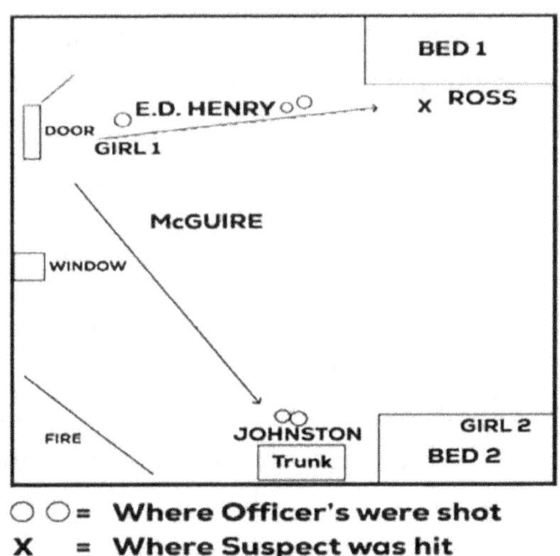

The Marshalls hatched a quick plan to enter and double checked that their pistols were loaded and cocked ready. McGuire would cross the room and go after the suspect further to the right, and Henry would follow and go after the one on the left in front of the entrance. They went to the front door to kick it in, when coincidentally one of the prostitutes opened the door to throw out two buckets of water. Startled, she screamed in Spanish and their cover was blown. The lawmen improvised and ran into the building, but the door was partially blocked by an additional two buckets on the wood floor, causing just enough delay to alert the men entirely. As they struggled to open the door and enter the adobe hut, both suspects reached for their pistols.

McGuire stumbled over the buckets and one of the women, but quickly fell onto suspect Johnson and the two began struggling. The door flung back closed and didn't open fully for Marshall Henry and he entered late. Smoke filled the room as both suspects opened fire and struck the lawmen multiple times each. E.D. Henry fired once then died instantly. Deputy McGuire, despite being wounded, was able to fight to disarm Johnson while firing shots at Ross who managed to flee out the door. When McGuire needed to reload, Johnston too was able to escape and now both suspects had fled on foot, but Marshal McGuire had managed to hit Ross in the back before crawling to his partner.

McGuire too, died in the hospital a week later from his injuries, but was able to identify both men to a Judge before he succumbed. Suspect Johnston was never caught despite bounty rewards for his head. Dr. J.F. Pearce the coroner took 3 bullets out of Henry and tried to ship his body by horse carriage back to Henry County, Ohio, but passage was denied halfway and the casket sent back due to the cholera pandemic. Eventually he was put in the ground in an unmarked grave.

Ross was arrested the next day following a massive manhunt. At 7am the Mayor and Sheriff had set out with teams on a bloodhound trail. He was found at an adobe brothel and authorities surrounded the building, waited for his companion to come out then followed her back in with pistols to her back. She was a young Black lady with no record. Charlie Ross was on her bed with a gunshot wound to his back. Upon recovering, Ross escaped two different jails and was never brought to justice. He was last seen in Bernalillo, New Mexico selling horses, described as full of swagger, wearing his pants in his boots and donning a white Chihuahua cowboy hat.

ON JANUARY 06, 1912 New Mexico became the 47th State to join the Union and on that day, Albuquerque lost their 3rd Policeman. 50-year-old Officer Alexander Knapp, of Eastern European descent, was a 10-year veteran of the department and had seen his fair share of saloon fights, bar brawls and rough customers. He was a burly man himself, over 6 feet tall and 200lbs with a tough looking mustache and jawline. Ofc. Knapp was walking around downtown unarmed, when he saw a drunken man in a cowboy hat and a long coat, stumbling out of Ricodartis Saloon on 216

North 3rd Street. A bartender from this particular bar had just been killed earlier that week by a drunk with an iron bar over a dice game dispute.

Tonight was special, Statehood was being celebrated and the Officer initiated friendly contact as the man started to bother around some closed businesses. Ofc. Knapp offered to escort the man home, but the drifter became feisty and belligerent, refusing to answer any questions or identify himself. Pleasantries were over and Officer Knapp handcuffed the man, placing their hands in front and then grabbed him by the arm to walk him towards the jail cell in Old Town to sober up for the night.

Suddenly as they walked, the drunk fired a .25 caliber pistol from a vest pocket inside his coat, striking Officer Knapp in the chest so hard he spun 180 degrees. Hurt and stunned, Knapp didn't let go of the man's left arm as the drunk tried to shake loose to getaway. Knapp was able to wrestle on top of the man where they fought on the ground. With his life on the line Knapp was able to use his forearm to choke the man out unconscious. He took the man's gun, preventing another shot and blew his gold whistle until help arrived. Civilians and lawmen took Knapp to a local hospital.

Before he died 9 days later, he was able to identify the shooter to a judge and lawyer who convicted the paroled man from the Minnesota State Penitentiary to 10 years in New Mexico's. Hardly long enough for Knapp's widow, 30 years his bride. The night of the shooting Chief Thomas McMullen arrived in his 1910 Studebaker department vehicle and had interrogated the drunk thoroughly, that was something the drifter would remember and liken to forget. As a result of this tragedy, it became department policy to search detainees or suspects immediately before continuing an investigation or transporting them. Perpetrators hands would additionally now be cuffed behind their back for escort. It also became policy to always carry a pistol on duty.

Although the United States was officially in control of New Mexico in 1912, the State still maintained strong influences from its past. Most towns, mountain ranges, businesses and city streets were named in Spanish and the State still bordered Mexico in the Southwest corner. In 1916

Mexican revolutionist Pancho Villa and a band of his men raided the Southern New Mexico border town of Columbus, in what was a major indication to the United States to increase border security for the entire country.

Columbus was a quiet town of about 700 people with no defenses. In the middle of the night, Villa and his men arrived on horseback and couldn't have planned worse. They had unknowingly raided the town while it had a visiting detachment of 350 U.S. Army Soldiers from the 13th Calvary just passing through. Awoken by explosions and gunfire, the soldiers sprang into action and killed nearly 80 of Villa's men after firing 20,000 rounds and losing 8 Army soldiers and 10 civilians themselves.

After the Battle of Columbus, U.S. President Woodrow Wilson sent 110,000 soldiers to be spread along the border and 5,000 troops rode down into Mexico to try and catch Villa. Led by Army General John Pershing out of Ft. Bliss in El Paso, the expedition had partial successes by deterring future attacks, but yielded no Villa. General Pershing did however bring back over 500 displaced Chinese workers into New Mexico. These Chinese people had assisted the soldiers in the arid Mexican desert, saving the General and his men from dehydration and nursing many back to health. They were granted official permission to work in the United States on Army bases despite the national Chinese Exclusion Act that barred such immigrants from living or working within the country. Shortly after, General Pershing went on to be the top U.S. commander in World War One.

The new recruits were all ears as the knowledgeable Instructor went past their required time. In 1926, the famous mother road of the United States, highway Route 66 was commissioned, connecting Chicago to Los Angeles and roughly 480 miles ran through New Mexico. It was built just in time for greatly depressed Americans to flee from the Dust Bowl in the Midwest States during the 1930's and head out West in search of work. Route 66 created businesses along its stretch in New Mexico and Albuquerque's section of "The Mother Road" was known for its Native American arts and crafts, its neon light motels, trading posts and tasty local cuisine. Not only was the highway important to supporting Albuquerque's growth, but the Railyard was also the only stop between Illinois and California that could repair locomotive trains. With the highway and railroads importance, Albuquerque became a crossroads for industry and began to modernize. Electric cable cars ran up and down 4th Street to accommodate the growing foot traffic.

Many New Mexicans fought in World War I and even more in World War II. The day after the Japanese bombed Pearl Harbor in Hawaii, New Mexico's main military recruitment center at 215 Central Avenue in Downtown Albuquerque had young men lined up for literally almost a mile out the door to enlist, up past Broadway. While many New Mexicans saved countless lives serving as Navajo Code Talkers and as Soldiers, Sailers, Marines or Nurses in both the European and Pacific campaigns against the Axis, the State lost hundreds of brave men to their Japanese captors during the Bataan Death March in the Philippines. Santa Fe, Ft. Sumner and Lordsburg were home to Japanese internment camps and after the Bataan news made it to New Mexico an angry mob assembled with weapons and wanted to kill all the Japanese citizens in the Santa Fe camp, but were convinced to calm down by the Sheriff's posse.

With the Manhattan Project successfully producing the Atomic Bomb in Los Alamos (then the Secret City), New Mexico gave its most significant and worst contribution to the world in 1945. The invention ultimately led to the end of World War II with the devastation of the Japanese cities of Hiroshima and Nagasaki by these nuclear bombs. German scientists Albert Einstein and Robert Oppenheimer, amongst others, contributed to the creation of these bombs. Einstein himself was never allowed at the site because he was suspected of being a possible spy for Germany and couldn't obtain the necessary top-secret clearance.

During the Manhattan Project a middle-aged married couple from New York City, the Rosenberg's, had spied for Russia and smuggled atomic information out of the Secret City into the hands of the Soviet Union. The communist American couple accelerated the creation of Atomic Weapons around the world and helped thrust the U.S. into what became the Cold

War and a post-nuclear era with the constant threat of total annihilation from enemy states with nuclear capabilities. Mr. Rosenberg was an engineer and smuggled secrets out of the project and drove with his wife over an hour down to 209 High Street NE in Albuquerque to meet with Russians. The Spy House. Due to this espionage the Rosenberg's were executed at Sing Sing Prison in New York for their treasonous espionage and New Mexico opened its own F.B.I. Field Offices in Los Alamos and Albuquerque. Both were offices that would grow with the State.

After World War II, the baby boomers came to the Duke City by the thousands via Route 66, and so came the film industry. A lot of great Hollywood movies and of course Westerns were filmed in the State. The legendary actor John Wayne was famously rumored to have once ridden his horse into the El Dorado Hotel in Oldtown Albuquerque during a set break. "The Duke" ducked his head and rode the horse into the main lobby then ordered a beer for his horse, which they of course brought out in a giant bowl. Despite being mini-Hollywood, the State remained very poor and rural. Santa Fe and Albuquerque make up a majority of the population and much of the wealth has been concentrated amongst their elite. Then the Police Instructor wrote a rough population history on the board.

The historic population for Albuquerque was about:

7,500 in 1900. ***25,000*** in 1930. ***200,000*** in 1960.
10,000 in 1910. ***35,000*** in 1940. ***250,000*** in 1970.
15,000 in 1920. ***100,000*** in 1950. ***300,000+*** by 1979.

In the 1940's there was a shootout in the Main Police Station between two Chief's and a Detective who recently joined from the U.S. Indian Service. The deputy chief was drunk and confronted the Chief, over not liking his personal schedule. Words were exchanged and guns were unholstered at point blank range. As bullets flew and narrowly missed, nearby Detective Paul Shaver put an end to the drunkard with a head shot to the cerebellum. Shaver would go on to become Chief from 1948-1971 and grew the department from about 25 to nearly 400 Officers in his tenure.

When the city doubled its population in the 1950's, the Albuquerque Police Department lost four Officers over the course of the decade. On Wednesday August 5th, 1951 a drunk driver killed 2-year veteran Officer Donald Redfern. Ofc. Redfern was conducting traffic where signal lights had gone out on 2nd Street during a flashflood when a car skid through an intersection at 50mph into the Officer, violently smashing his vital organs and sending him flying down the road 47 feet. The car kept sliding sideways and eventually stopped by smashing into 2 cars as the Officer lay dead with a broken neck. Tire skid marks measured over 150 feet. Civilians surrounded the drunk driver, an airman from nearby Kirtland Air Force Base. In a military tribunal he was charged and sentenced with manslaughter.

Patrolman Donald W. Redfern. End of Watch Aug 5, 1951. Age 27.

Then the Instructor said, "Now remember what I was saying when I told you that you have to be prepared to fight down to the last 10 seconds?" The class all shook their heads yes before he went on to elaborate. On December 1, 1954 a rookie A.P.D. Officer Eugene Casey located a vehicle on 124 Arno Street SE suspected to have been used by robbery suspects wanted for questioning. Using his squad car radio the Officer called for backup and fellow rookie Officer Frank A. Sjolander arrived at the elongated one-story boarding house. The Officers were in the Academy together just months before and walked up some steps into the yard and made their way to the entrance where there were 3 steps up to the front door. It was 1:37am.

As they knocked on the door two suspects swung open the front door with .45 caliber pistols in hand and began shooting at the two Officers. Both Officers were hit, but both un-holstered their .38 revolvers to exchange gunfire, getting in a shootout that wound up leading them out in front of the boarding house. Both Officers were hit five times and returned six shots each. Before Sjolander bled out, he shot and fatally wounded one of the suspects, a parolee of the Deuel Vocational Institution out of Tracy, California. The second suspect fled and got to the Rio Grande and swam across, but was later found at 1234 Lopez Rd. SW, by a raid of 35 Officers when the department had just over 90. A third suspect inside the house emerged and stayed to call for help on Officer Casey's car radio, the Officer instructing him how to use it. Officer Casey was into bodybuilding and his peak physical condition certainly helped aid his recovery. He spent some extensive time in the County Indian Hospital after surgery and carried a bullet near his spine the rest of his career. Casey likely thought of his fallen partner every day for the rest of his life, remembering vividly how as Sjolander was loaded into an ambulance he spoke his last words, "I can't breathe."

Officer Frank Sjolander Jr. End of Watch Dec, 1 1954. Age 27.

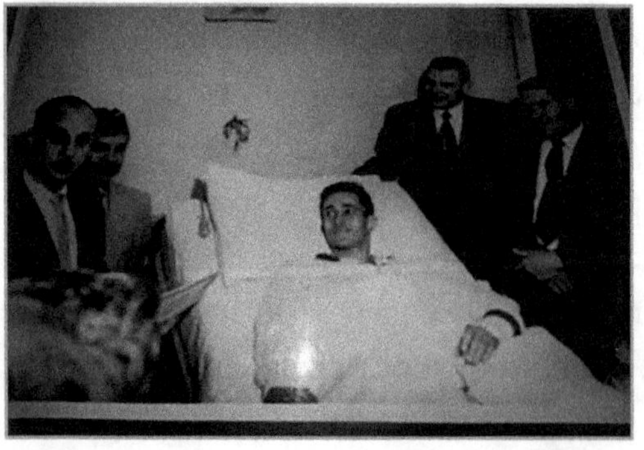

Ofc. Casey in the hospital.

On September 30, 1958 a 6-year-veteran Officer Richard Armijo was responding to the scene of a car accident Downtown. Armijo was riding in a department issued 1954 Harley Davidson Motorcycle. As he rode through the intersection of 2nd Street and Coal Ave SW with his Police siren and light engaged, a white vehicle smashed into his side and sent the Officer flying onto the street causing severe internal bleeding. The car's driver had the green light, he thought the sirens were behind him and he didn't see the motorcycle until it was too late. It was ruled an accident with the 24-year-old UNM student being sober and incredibly remorseful as well as really shaken up, especially when learning the Officer had a wife and 3 daughters devastated by the event.

Officer Richard Armijo. End of Watch Sept, 30, 1958. Age 31.

Officer Armijo's Harley motorcycle was actually repaired and reissued to Officer Max Oldham of 2842 Aliso Drive NE. Then just 5 months after Armijo died, on February 21, 1959, 2nd year Officer Max Oldham was riding on the 600 block of Lomas Blvd NE when a speeding car heading on the wrong side of traffic slammed into the Officer's motorcycle head on. The Officer lost his white crash helmet at time of impact and was hurled through the air, his cycle driven back nearly 50 feet into a vehicle. The 59-year-old wrong way driver was found drunk and unconscious, practically unscathed. He was charged with manslaughter. Oldham had a wife and daughter and his parents had a baby brother who eventually became an officer in San Marino, California.

Police Officer Max R. Oldham. End of Watch Feb 21, 1959. Age 22.

The Instructor then got a little emotional talking about the next Officer as it was a friend of his who died in November of 1971. Sergeant James Bundy was the lead Detective of Violent Crimes, which included Robberies and Homicides before the Department split up the two in order to dedicate more attention to each. Bundy was a tall strong man, who was working overtime and as he left the Main Police Station Downtown, he collapsed in the stairwell while walking with three other Officers. They immediately administered C.P.R. and got him transported to St. Joseph's hospital. Bundy who was very dedicated to his profession had died of a heart attack.

After explaining the fallen Officers heroics, the Instructor saw they were 19 minutes over the scheduled time and finished by reminding the gut checked Cadets to pick up their workout uniforms before they left and that they started their training on Monday at 6:00 am sharp. As some Cadets tried to get up, he shouted them back to sitting and exclaimed, "Hey everybody, that means if you arrive here at 5:55am then your late!! Get it?" "Yes sir" all the Cadets answered. He reminded everyone about elevation and hydration before dismissing. The 46 Cadets of the Academy recruit class of 1979-1980 were all issued two types of training uniforms after the orientation.

For physical activities they were given grey sweatpants and a matching sweatshirt with their last name stenciled in black across the chest. Cadets provided their own running shoes, underwear and socks. For classroom activities the Cadets were to wear short sleeve light blue dress shirts with navy pants, ties and captain hats. Cadets provided their own black belt. If they survived the Academy and earned graduation, then they would be issued a formal black uniform to commence their ceremony and two regular black uniforms to begin their job.

After the orientation let out, some of the new recruits stuck around and grabbed a beer at the F.O.P. Lodge with Joseph. The Fraternal Order of Police. He came back every day that week to eat lunch, swim laps in the pool and to shower there. Every day he met a new veteran Officer or Retiree and listened intently to their stories. He loved the camaraderie and was excited to begin.

Chapter 05

Old School Police Academy

CADET JOSEPH ALVAREZ moved into a small 3-bedroom 1-bath hole in the wall near the Academy with two other recruits he met at orientation. Juan Hernandez from Albuquerque and Drew Banks from Lubbock, TX. Juan was 23, he was a quiet man, but strong and slim about 5.9 160lbs with black hair. He wore thick Elvis sideburns before the 3 bachelor's shaved their heads bald and shaved their faces completely.

Juan's parents helped him move in and loved speaking to Joseph in Spanish, asking him to teach Juan and Drew some Police commands in Spanish. The proud parents would always keep the 3 young men's fridge stocked and had them over for huge dinners on Sunday's.

Fresh out of the Marine Corps, Cadet Banks was the old man of the recruit class at 29. He was also the biggest, standing 6.4 and 230lbs of solid rock with a short dark-brown flattop. His forearms and biceps were comparable to Juan or Joseph's calves and thighs. In his size 14 boots he stood nearly 6 feet 7 inches.

The Cadets felt immediate solidarity in the reasons they were all there, to make a difference helping people and to fight crime. The 46 Cadets would meet at the parking lot of the Academy in the darkness every morning and start the day with a run at 6am in their grey sweat pants and sweatshirts with their last name in black letters traced across the chest.

Drew Banks was an immediate leader and led all the daily class runs with funny and vulgar cadences he learned how to make in the Corps. Everyone got a kick out of his booming Texas twang. Banks would run alongside the flock of 45 chanting things like, "Well I don't know why the hell we're here....but three more miles and we earn some beer..." Then the class chimed in unison, "Just three more miles until we earn some beer." Or Banks, "Forget this job we ought to just quit....but filthy rapists make us sick..." Then the class, "But filthy rapists make us sick." It was something everyone picked up on that really united this class from the beginning, he had dozens of the cadences in his repertoire.

Nowadays modern Police Academies have a lot more tools and resources to teach Officer safety and have to try to be more politically correct for the cameras. With insurance liabilities running high, instructors tend to teach strictly by the book with the advent of codes like the use of force continuum model that are used today. Modern Officers are under a microscope for any little thing, but these times were far different. For example, Joseph had never used the word negro before, he certainly heard it growing up in 1960's West Texas, but his father didn't like it or tolerate it after being called negro and nigger a few times in the military for having dark skin.

In training Joseph was a little taken back to learn the department called out Black suspects as NMA (Negro Male American) or NFA (Negro Female American). Hispanics were called SMA or SFA for Spanish and Natives were called IMA or IFA for Indian. This was 15 years after the Civil Rights Act of 64, but these descriptors were a protocol the department would follow until someone changed the Standard Order of Procedure or S.O.P. Joseph was impartial to race, but wondered if the other Officers in his class and on the department would be too, in a country that was still healing from decades of racism and segregation.

This Police Academy was the old school when Cops had limited resources and had to be a different kind of tough than today, preparation was different. The Academy prepared Cadets to handle situations with no bulletproof vests as they were not issued, but could be purchased and worn on an Officer's own dime. They wore a heavy black leather utility belt around their waist that was close to 30lbs with all its tools. Police were still issued six-shooter revolvers with drop pouches to reload and the only other tools on their person were an 18inch hickory club or nightstick, 14inch steel flashlight with four D batteries, one set of black steel handcuffs, a cassette tape belt-recorder and an 8oz canister of pepper mace. There was nothing light or compact in those days, no ASP flip out batons, lightweight Glocks or high-capacity ammunition magazines, no cell phones, lapel-cameras, tasers, spike strips, computers, Internet or mini tape recorders, even the old school cuffs were heavier.

An optional preference of some Officers in the old school was to carry a short thin slapper stick or a blackjack slapper in their back pocket, which was a 6–10 inch leather strap filled with lead on both sides. They could be folded in half and easily put in their back wallet pocket for quick access, it was then held by either side to thrust a concussing slap onto anybody, usually to counter those who resisted with violence. The Academy didn't teach it, but the slapper was used regularly until mid-decade when it became banned as it was deemed too much of a liability by the damage it inflicted.

In 1979 the department issued a cowboy style Smith & Wesson Model 10 pistol, it was a dark steel grey .38 caliber six-shot revolver with squared wood grip handle. It came with a black leather holster that was indented for a revolver. The holster had a button snap to secure the weapon in and prevent anyone from grabbing it from behind, yet the Officer could quick draw the gun by pushing it out of the holster down and forward to bypass the snap, something an average criminal wouldn't know how to manipulate.

Officers carried 12 bullets, six loaded in the gun and if they fired all those, they would push a lever with their thumb then twist their arm to flip out the pistol's revolving chamber and dump out the spent bullet casings using gravity. While they are emptying the first six bullets' casings, they were trained to cup their free hand under a black leather drop pouch on their utility belt. Then they would unsnap a button, dropping six bullets out of the pouch into their free hand to be reloaded one by one. If practiced enough, the bullets should all drop into the hand facing the same direction for easier loading. Depending on the situation an Officer might only be able to reload 1,2,3,4, or 5 bullets before having to fire again, but they were well trained to speed load all 6. Gun safety was taken very seriously and in just their third week of training a major accident occurred that let everyone know why guns needed to be secured at all times.

ON AUGUST 17, 1979 some four hours Northwest of Albuquerque, the Police Academy in Farmington, NM was conducting training exercises to safely diffuse different scenarios involving mock suspects. The Farmington Cadets had been in the Academy for a few months and were wearing full uniform and issued a gun loaded with blanks. The first scenario was a call out of domestic violence, no further information as it very common for Officers to arrive to a call with little or no information and assess the scene upon on arrival. A Cadet was to call out on the radio that they had arrived at the address and had one male in sight, finding Lieutenant Owen Landdeck participating as an upset husband who walked out to his front yard. The Cadet approached with caution when suddenly the Lt. playing the suspect pulled out a weapon.

As Lt. Landdeck pulled out his gun, the Cadet un-holstered his revolver and fired 2 blanks at the training Officer. Only the gun had accidentally been loaded with live ammunition and the rounds struck the Lieutenant in the chest, one bullet passed through his body and struck another training Officer. Landdeck wasn't wearing a bulletproof vest at the time and despite every effort to revive him he died at the scene while the other Officer luckily recovered from their injury. The Albuquerque Police Instructors told their whole Cadet class what happened and everybody was completely shocked, it was terrible news. Albuquerque Police wore a black ribbon across their badges for the next month as a reminder of the tragedy and to honor the Officer who gave his life teaching others how to be prepared for anything, including the unknown.

Lt. Owen Landdeck, Farmington Police, NM. EOW Aug 17, 1979. Age 40.

Gun safety became such a strong emphasis for the Cadet class after the Farmington tragedy. Every day they counted bullets and did weapons safety checks often. At the gun range, the Training Officers would load random blank bullets into their "empty guns" and if you were issued an "empty gun" you better check it to be loaded first. Nobody made a mistake after Juan Hernandez did the first day they implored the accountability technique. They made Juan run miles until he threw up and then, he had to run some more. His whole day was spent running, but it taught him and everyone else a lesson.

After week six of the Academy the Cadets began to ride on-duty often, pairing with veterans to gain real experience. They were to observe and assist if needed. Cadets riding along with Officers were instructed to never draw their weapon unless their Training Officer did so or in an obvious emergency situation. A few Cadets who were still very amateur with their firearms were not allowed to even carry, but only observe in Field Training until they advanced their firearm training.

When Cadets rode with veterans not only were they responsible for their own revolvers, but also each patrol car was issued one shotgun and Cadets were responsible for the bullet count. They carried 12-gauge Remington's in those days with an 18" steel barrel, a wooden pump action bar to load and fire the six rounds in the gun. On the wood butt of the shotgun fit a black elastic sleeve with 6 shell slots for 5 additional red buckshot shells and 1 green slug shell. The buckshot contained dozens of lead bb's and depending on the distance of the shot would spray out in a small, medium or large circle, while the slug round is a single large projectile that can basically go through a car engine at close or medium distance.

For ride-a-longs, the Cadets were issued some new gear for emergency crowd control. All Albuquerque Officers and Cadets rode with a two-tone, blue on dark blue riot helmet to be carried in the trunk of their vehicle at all times. The riot helmet offered no face protection, but could protect your head in a motorcycle crash, it was secured on by a single leather strap worn under the chin. Some Officers had tear gas rounds they could insert into their shotgun barrel as a special load, bought after violent student riots at the University in 1970 protesting the Vietnam War and Kent State massacre.

The Albuquerque Police Department had used radio communication in their cars since the 1940's to coordinate against crime and portable hand-held radios carried on an Officers person since the 1960's. Original car radios known as one-way, were to receive calls only. After the shooting of Frank Sjolander and Eugene Casey in 1954 the department began to purchase two-way car radios for all of its fleet to receive and make calls as the two-way helped save Casey's life by getting information out to help him quickly. By 1980 most Officers carried a personal handheld radio, but A.P.D. still hadn't secured funding yet for every Officer and they often had to double up radios until they were made available to each.

Up until the early 1980's some Cops on foot patrol or in remote areas were still issued two quarters during their briefing to call for backup by using 10 cent payphones that charged to call 911 and were located all over the city. The early model hand-held radios weren't great and even a few times in the mid 80's Officers still had to find pay phones to use in order to call for assistance due to poor frequencies and bad reception. The radio was a great tool, someone can physically outrun an Officer, but it's very hard to outrun dozens of radios directing communications. Many have tried and very few have succeeded.

Not only did Albuquerque Police cars not have computers yet in 1979, but the department also lacked funding for security cages in the vehicles to separate the front and back seats. Prisoners in transport rode in the front passenger seat next to the Officer. Secured only by a seatbelt, if a prisoner acted crazy or got violent, they often received a forearm across their throat to choke them until they complied, sometimes until the offender blacked out as Officers were constantly attacked while driving in those days. Officers could use the prisoner's seatbelt for leverage to assist the choke or if forced they might even throw some punches, pushes or elbows to protect themselves while they pulled over. In those times, a few disorderly prisoners spent their rides handcuffed in the trunk for the Officer's safety, or because they crossed a line like continually spitting on an Officer, but the Academy didn't teach this method of restraint and of course you certainly wouldn't find proof of such an instance occurring in any Police report.

Aside from not having cages yet, all four doors of the Plymouth Volare squad car could be manually unlocked from the inside and the windows could be rolled down manually, making it easier for anyone riding in the front or back seats to exit. Officer safety was very vulnerable compared to modern day where the Officer controls the vehicle, is separated from the suspect and there is no ability for a criminal to unlock the back doors from the inside or unroll the windows in the back. Besides their gun, which almost always commanded respect, the old school cop's best resources were their savvy, squad car radio and each other serving as backup or partners. Their training was designed to make them street smart and tough, using the resources they did have.

ONE DAY OF THE ACADEMY involved each Cadet having to fight against three other Cadets with no rules for one minute, essentially experiencing what its liked to be "jumped" with the key objective being to protect your holstered gun from leaving your utility belt. If the three opposing Cadets un-holstered your wooden training gun used in the drill that meant you were dead in the scenario. Although everybody had grown a deep respect for one another, no rules meant no rules and when Joseph was up against the foes, he felt himself catch a jab in the head and a hand reach onto the butt of his service weapon. As he was swarmed and about to lose control of his wood gun he didn't hesitate to protect and reaching down he ended up broking the pinky of the biggest of the three who had their hand on the gun, leaving them in complete agony. Then

Joseph knocked down a feisty female Cadet with a stiff left cross on the jaw and kicked the last man standing in the nuts who keeled over just as the minute was up.

His training Officers were impressed as they sent the three riling Cadets to the triage to get patched up and recover. The female Cadet refused treatment, she was tough and aside from a little blood in her gums she was unfazed by the strike. Joseph had defended himself with the most ferocity out of the class, but only because when it was Drew Banks turn to be jumped nobody even bothered to get within striking distance of the giant. The three would-be attackers spent their entire minute avoiding him while the rest of the Cadets watched laughing as he tried so hard to get a hold of one. He desperately offered his gun, placing it on the ground and walking back 10 feet before time expired.

Most Cadets lost their wooden gun within 30 seconds, but one Cadet Steven House was a martial arts badass and stood out as a defensive expert who didn't even have his gun touched by his three attackers. He was so good that the Instructors let him assist in many drills after that and one time even take over the class for almost an hour to show some great defensive strikes and ground-fighting tips. Standing about 5.10 150lbs, he proved the effectiveness of a few simple moves during one Instruction by disabling an attacking Drew Banks in a variety of holds, repeatedly getting the class giant to tap out or have a limb broken. Steve House also helped the Instructors show the class how to apply proper chokes or choke holds to disable someone fighting. He also showed some techniques to get out of a choke while protecting your gun.

The Cadets were partnered together to test the new moves and Joseph was paired with Jimmy Zamora. Joseph choked Jimmy's carotid artery first and the smaller Cadet tapped his hand on Joseph's arm to indicate the effect had worked so Joseph released. When it was Jimmy's turn to choke, he applied the choke so hard that Joseph instantly couldn't breathe and while he tried to break free, he realized it wasn't possible and he went to tap out. Next thing you know Joseph woke up in a daze on the ground with two Instructors above him, one saying, "He's alright," while the other told him to, "Breathe, breathe...you passed out there." He took a moment to gather his senses and then saw Jimmy Zamora back in line looking cool with a hint of amusement on his face.

ANOTHER TRAINING DAY involved Cadet-boxing matches with 12oz gloves and held on wrestling mats where the Instructors stated to the class that it was either, "Volunteer or be voluntold," who you were going to fight for one, three-minute round. The training Officers put the gloves on Drew Banks first and asked for a volunteer. Everybody's eyes went panning around each other, wrought with anxiety. Outweighed by 80+lbs, Joseph didn't want anybody else to get picked by the Instructors knowing that his roommate had candidly sworn the night before to knockout whoever he had to face. Joseph was the only one willing to go against the behemoth, Banks barely fit into the gloves and headgear.

Banks smiled at the volunteering toothpick, until the bell sounded and a super-fast combination from Alvarez tagged Drew in the nose, then another causing his nostrils to bleed. For 3 minutes Cadet Alvarez hit the brute with 10 punches to Banks every one landed. When Banks connected the whole class would collectively "Oooohh," as Joseph's head snapped back. Boxing wasn't Banks strong point, but he was a high school wrestler and Marine Combat Veteran who knew how to fight and throw a solid punch. Nobody expected that out of Alvarez, to take that punishment several times and still be hooking punches back so fast. When the three minutes were up everyone was applauding and even the Instructors got in on the cheers.

Both men wound up with concussions, Banks with a slight one and Alvarez with a weeklong nasty headache that made him nauseous enough to vomit a couple of times over the next few days. The day after they boxed both men got dizzy back in the classroom when the Instructors turned off the lights and put on a manually operated slide show projector showing photos of fatal traffic accidents. It was hard to concentrate. Mutual respect established forever between the boxing buddies.

ALVAREZ CALLED HOME ONCE A WEEK and about six weeks into the Academy he let his suspicious folks know where he really was.

After the 8th week they drove up to have dinner with him along with his mom's brothers Jesús and Isaac and his dad's nephew Pasquale who was still looking for that sister from Albuquerque of the girl Joseph had made up months before. They were all proud of their "*peloncito*" everyone rubbing his bald head and even though his mom couldn't stop crying she was so happy that her son was now a man. When she went to the bathroom of the restaurant Joseph told everybody the story of the cholos by the river from his first night in town and showed the guys the switchblade he confiscated, much to their pleasure.

After dinner to end the night, everyone including his mom had a shot of tequila in toast to his upcoming graduation in 4 months. When his family piled into the mean metallic green 1974 Buick Skylark, Damacio had a quick heart to heart with his only child. He said with a tear in his eyes and a lump in his throat, "Mijo I know you are ready for everything that comes with this job, but you're going to see some terrible things that will haunt you forever and I just want you to know that you can always tell me anything. I understand." Joseph realized this was the first time in his life that his father openly mentioned or at least implied the scars of war to him. "Gracias Papa, Yo sé" he thanked his father with a hug and acknowledgment.

The truth set Joseph free and he was able to really focus on his new career after the visit from his parents, it was invaluable to him to have their support and it strengthened his will. Good timing, as two months into the Academy Cadets began to ride along regularly with veteran Officers to gain real experience. Joseph began to fully embrace the change in his life and his persona began to evolve.

The young man was no longer a kid, he was now a Policeman and the world looked different to him and at him. He began to watch people around him everywhere he went and notice everything taking place around him. Suddenly he could recognize the prison tattoos on a gas station attendant who he hadn't paid any attention to previously. Joseph noticed the bruises on a lady's arm in line at Walgreens as hand prints from a bad person. He noticed a young man drawing pictures of block letters and suspected him correctly as a possible gang member by looking at his style of writing. His viewpoint was changing and so was the world around him.

The world and American culture were completely evolving during Joseph's time in the Academy in late 1979. In New York City the N.B.A. introduced the 3-point line 20 feet from the baskets, the National Hockey League now required helmets, Disco Demolition night was held in Chicago's Comiskey Park to end the era, a new retirement savings plan called 401K began to take shape on Wall Street and the McDonalds chain introduced the happy meal for children around the nation. It had been almost a year, but San Francisco was still healing from the Assassinations of Mayor George Moscone and City Supervisor Harvey Milk who were killed by former Policeman and City Supervisor Dan White. With the upcoming census New Mexico was in line to gain its 3rd seat in the House of Representatives, having had 2 since 1940. In Asia, China began its one child only policy and in the Middle East the Iranian Revolution had left the country in a power vacuum.

Then on Nov 4, 1979 the whole world watched as the U.S. Embassy was taken hostage in Tehran, Iran. More than 50 Americans were taken hostage at the Embassy in Tehran by a crowd of over 500 student protestors who breached the gates, many with guns, after realizing the Guards weren't going to risk using lethal force to stop them. The Americans at the Embassy were tied up, blindfolded and paraded around in front of international media. President Jimmy Carter and the State Department had their work cut out for them, as the Iranians demanded the return of their former leader who was granted asylum in the U.S.

As the Iran Hostage Crisis took place the Albuquerque Police Instructors decided to dedicate a day to demonstrate crowd control by bussing in nearly 60 elementary school students who after a tour of the Academy were fed cake and ice cream. The Instructors then put the sugar-crazed kids in the giant rectangular conference room with the Cadets, but not before giving all the kids 2 small bouncy balls each that worked surprisingly well on the hard grey carpet and laminate wood dance floor.

Next thing you know Joseph was breaking up two little boys from fighting atop the center stage and he looked down as Drew Banks got bit in the leg by a girl in blond pony-tails and Juan was cornered with six boys throwing balls at him as he bobbed and weaved his head. Kids were crawling all over Cadets in every part of the room, chairs and tables were getting turned over by the tornado of energy as Banks was screaming "10-83, 10-83" the emergency sign for Officer in trouble. For some reason all the kids instinctively left Cadet Steve House alone. It was the most exhausting 10 minutes of the Academy. Luckily there was a large playground outside, as well as the Academy obstacle course for the Instructors to send the kids out to unwind before any of them got loose inside the building to cause any further damage. Officers would go on to find bouncy balls for months to come, sometimes at formal events a random ball would appear.

While the Iran-Hostage crisis continued to boil tension in Washington D.C, former actor and the Republican Governor of California Ronald Reagan won the nomination to run for the White House against Democratic President Jimmy Carter. Reagan was very adamant about freeing the American hostages from Iran during his campaign. International media covered the crisis daily and it was a major topic of the campaigns for Presidency. The country and world were indeed changing drastically, as was the life of Cadet Joseph Alvarez as he transformed from civilian to public servant.

The Albuquerque Police Cadets got a few days off for Christmas and Joseph went down to El Paso to spend the time with his loving family. After a giant all-day feast with three turkeys and nearly 40 cousins, aunts and uncles, the house cleared late that night and Joseph's dad went to sleep while his mom finished putting the house in order. Sipping eggnog and watching It's a Wonderful Life with Jimmy Stewart on December 24th 1979, Joseph watched intently as his movie was interrupted by breaking news on the TV as the Soviet Union invaded Afghanistan and began what would lead on to become a decade long war. Joseph attended Midnight Mass with his mother, saying prayers for the people of Afghanistan. As the service let out, unbeknownst to him, tragedy struck back in Albuquerque.

Around 1:00am on December 25th a young mother from Mexico was holding her baby while cooking menudo in her kitchen on 915 Walter Street SE, Apartment C a one story casita. In the living room of the small apartment a Christmas tree sat in the corner as her husband was watching TV and calmly drinking a beer on their couch when suddenly a loud explosion blasted through the kitchen window. Shotgun pellets sprayed the mother in her face and along her right arm carrying the infant. The baby was murdered instantly in her arms. She was just cooking for Christmas and now her life was tragically altered as she lay in her hospital bed recovering, while Detectives interviewed the grieving father. Police found no motives for the attack, this was an innocent family and they speculated that the gunshot was most likely intended for a neighboring apartment in the drug-laden area.

It was very disturbing news to the whole Department and the Cadets were further reminded why they chose this noble field when they heard the horrible news after their Christmas holidays. They realized how spoiled they were to have this last Christmas break as civilians, because responding Officers, many with kids and their own families had to work that night and see such macabre. Shift supervisors did their best to schedule off the Officers with family, but typically everybody worked a 4-hour shift on Christmas as crime stopped for no one and Officers routinely have to miss important holidays moments with their families.

The Academy was moving along swiftly for Joseph and he was really trying to absorb as much knowledge as possible to ensure his safety, he gave up any free time he had to study laws and procedures. His head was constantly buried in a book and on his two off days he would volunteer to ride along with Officers. He was gaining a lot of experience and one day Banks saw him reading a civil penalty code book and asked him, "Hey man don't you have a social life?" Joseph paused reading for a second to ponder, then replied, "More than ever before," as he lifted the book up. Joseph truly loved learning how to help protect the community and the job gave him such purpose. "Such a Virgin" Banks said shaking his head in astoundment before walking away.

Juan Hernandez knew a great place out in the desert for shooting and on days off he would load up his roommates in his old Ford 351 Cleveland pickup truck to go practice firing. These trips to go blow up the barren desert helped Joseph, Juan and Drew become three of the best shooters in their class along with Jimmy Zamora who was an avid hunter/outdoorsmen and Steve House who was lethal from any range. The three roommates were excellent at shooting skeet as well as other target shooting.

As final evaluations began and Graduation was on the horizon, Juan and Joseph found out that one of the Cadets who was top of the class academically had one thing holding her back. She had repeatedly shot below the mandatory 70% on the final target course, in fact she shot way below on one occasion at 52%. Most Cadets were shooting in the mid 80's and many were above 90%. Upon discovery, Juan, Joseph and Drew took her out one Saturday and Sunday, letting her shoot nearly 250 rounds each day. The guys had even secretly taken donations of ammo and money to buy bullets for a .38 special that an Instructor let them check out for the weekend. The roommates were really supportive and tried to just relax her as much as possible because she memorized the motions to un-holster and could reload with ease, but her aim was all over the place.

Unfortunately, she didn't pass the shooting portion and was cut from the Academy after being given the final shooting test three times scoring a 61, 65 and finally a 62. It was really sad to everybody knowing how tough she was and how much she had dedicated to the profession, she clearly was on the fast track to Detective if it wasn't for the shooting requirements. She went on to become a 911 Dispatcher and moved up the ranks to Supervisor, her inside knowledge proving invaluable to the department's radio communication.

In the weeks before graduation the Cadets of the 47th Academy were assigned to ride along more often with veteran Officers. The Cadets were armed and in full Cadet uniform and many saw a good variety of action, a couple even saw dead bodies. Joseph loved every minute out in the field. If it hadn't been for the driving portion he failed twice before passing, Alvarez could have finished at the head of the class. Four Cadets quit during various points of the Academy, one was released for repeated errors and one failed the shooting portion. 40 of the 46 Cadets survived the Academy and earned their actual uniforms, which were all black cotton with blue department patches stitched on both arms below the shoulder at the biceps. The Cadets earned a small first aid patch on the left arm that was really meant to signify to other Officers they were Rookies since all Officers were trained in basic medical assistance.

The Rookies were given a long sleeve and short sleeve uniform shirt, both versions had square chest pockets. In front of their right shoulder was a silver whistle on a chain that could extend to their mouth and across the top of their right chest pocket was a thin gold-plated nametag, displaying their first initial and last name in black. Joseph was proud to see "Joseph A. Alvarez", it also read below "Since Feb 1980." Their chrome plated brass Police badge with blue enamel writing and light blue seal of the great State of New Mexico will be pinned over their heart pocket at the ceremony. With its eagle wings spread on top, Joseph was assigned number 222, probably from an Officer who retired.

The black cotton pants they wore had two front side pockets and two rear pockets that were very big or practical for carrying various items. The formal uniform had a gold whistle instead of silver and was long sleeve instead of short, but eager to join the streets and with nice weather, the Class of 1980 voted unanimously to wear their short sleeve with the gold whistle for the ceremony. It was also to be worn with the formal attire of white gloves and the departments black Captain style hat.

Joseph had the largest family presence at the ceremony inside the historic Kimo Theatre downtown on Central Avenue, almost 30 relatives and Father Henry had caravanned up from Texas and Mexico to support. Cameras flashed from friends and family as well as various media outlets that were invited. The Cadets all took a solemn oath to defend the Constitution of the United States and the State of New Mexico before being called up individually. When Chief Bob Stover pinned Joseph's badge at the ceremony, he was cheered on like a rock star causing the tall craggily faced Chief to give him a strange scowl of approval. After Jimmy

Zamora became the last Cadet to have his badge pinned and he returned to his seat, the Cadets all earned the right to throw their hats in the air together in solidarity, they were now officially Police Officers.

After the ceremony the Alvarez and Mendoza families threw a big BBQ celebration in Roosevelt Park on that brisk, but sunny day February 1st, 1980. They had rented a local mariachi band for the occasion and as the quartet serenaded the crowd, the young Officer's cousin Pasquale became Joseph's 1st honorary arrest for spilling Tío Jesús's beer. All the guests laughed as he placed the handcuffs on his cousin, the irony Joseph thought was that his uncle was the one breaking the law drinking in public, but today was a special occasion. Everyone was so proud. His mother could hardly let go of his waist all day.

When Drew Banks showed up halfway into the fiesta, the whole party got audibly quiet and everyone stared at the giant man who was almost 6.7 in his Police boots. Some of the kids playing stopped and stared. All eyes were on Banks lumbering in when he lightened the mood by walking over to Dino and Carmen and saying, "Mom, Dad I'm so glad you could make it." Then he lifted the pair off the ground in a bear hug. The crowd gave him the biggest 'grito' of approval you've ever heard as the patriarchs laughed with joy in the giant's arms. It was understood now that Joseph had another family that would help keep him safe.

As the Graduation celebration wound down, Joseph's father and his Tío Rosalio or Rosy, presented him with the finest gift of the day. It was a heavy box meticulously wrapped in newspaper, the weight of the gift puzzling Joseph as he sat down to unwrap it at a concrete picnic table with concrete benches on both sides. When he saw the gift, his eyes began to tear up and he shook his head side-to-side in disbelief knowing how expensive and meaningful the present was. His Uncle and father were holding back their own tears.

It was a Second Chance brand ballistics shirt, an early form of the bulletproof vest. At $4.33 an hour there was no way Joseph could afford the nearly $300 protection. He wasted no time and undid the buttons on his Police shirt handing the uniform to his mom so that he could try on his new armor. He placed his arms through the sleeves and his head in-between the fixed elastic shoulder straps and as it dropped down to his waist, he fastened the velcro straps snuggly on each side to connect the front and back. It wasn't the level III armor issued in today's world, it was a level II with panels sewn in front and back to hold Kevlar pads, the chest protected by a double soft armor pad up front. Joseph knew how lucky he was, only a handful of the Cadets from the class owned one.

After the park celebration his family and Father Henry all stayed the night at the Downtown Inn on Route 66 and went to church in Old Town the next day with Joseph before leaving. He was anxious to get started and after they left he headed right to the Main Police Station to get in a workout before selection day.

Chapter 06

Fight or Flight

FEBRUARY 3RD, 1980. A.P.D. ROOKIE ASSIGNMENT DAY, DOWNTOWN CIVIC CENTER.

THE 40 CADETS WHO SURVIVED APD's Class of 1980 were stationed throughout the city depending on where the training Officers and top brass felt they could best serve and learn. All Rookies were placed on a probation period for a minimum of 3 months and up to 10 months, where they were partnered with veteran Officers and routinely evaluated. Depending on their performance an Officer could be "Cut-loose" to ride on their own after any proven period of time or depending on the needs of the department.

Cadet Alvarez was assigned to the SE Area Command and to ride with Field Training Officer Ted Keoppinger during the swing shift Wednesday-Sunday 2:30pm-11pm with a 1/2-hour briefing to begin and they were told they could request a 1/2-hour unpaid lunch at any appropriate time. Ted was a sharp 9-year veteran of the department and was a seasoned warrior dating back to a Vietnam tour in 1968-69 when he was 18. He was over 6 feet tall, skinny with thick wrists and ruggedly handsome, his brown hair mixed with patches of grey and white. His older brother was a Lieutenant with the Department and his dad had retired with the Bernalillo County Sheriffs in 1974.

The SE Area Command had a reputation as being really busy, which is a political way of saying dangerous. It was also a large assignment with the area concentrated, but not limited to 402 miles. Starting East of the Downtown railroad up over 9 miles towards the State Fairgrounds to the East Mountains and from Interstate 40 running 6 miles South past the University of New Mexico down to the Airport, Sandia Labs and Kirtland Air Force Base. With the University, Air Base and National Labs, you had some of the most expensive real estate in the country minutes away from some of the worst pockets of neighborhoods in the country. A mix of everything.

A beat that never sleeps, the SE Command included organized gangs operating out of areas like the Warzone, Martinez-town, San Jo(se), Los Pa(dillas), South Broadway, Barela's and Kirt-town amongst others. The SE Heights or Warzone was an area known for a lot of dope houses and was filled with violence, prostitution, robbery and every other vice. Home to thousands of trailers and low-income apartments it was the underbelly of the city. East Central Avenue is not recommended to tourists.

Created by Police, the moniker Warzone was known by the public for that area of town. Although the actual government issued name was the International District due to the high volume of immigrants who had settled from all over the world, mainly Mexico and some large groups of Thai and Vietnamese refugees who came after the war. You could practically find a joint for Pho or Menudo on every block. The "Juaritos Maravilla" street gang brought in a lot of drugs to the Warzone from Juárez and they had strong ties to cartels.

AFTER GRADUATION Juan moved to his parents' guesthouse and Drew moved in with a New Mexico State Policeman in the suburb Rio Rancho out in the middle of nowhere. Joseph found his own Westside apartment on 47th Street and El Rincón SW near lower Pat Hurley Park, his first time ever living alone. It was a tiny studio apartment, clean but drab. One of the only furnished apartments he could find within his monthly rent budget of $225.

Preparing for his first shift Joseph had butterflies in his stomach as he loaded his gun and triple checked his equipment while waiting for his Field Training Officer to pick him up. They had only spoken on the phone once for 30 seconds. He nervously looked out his small kitchen window when right on time he saw the Police cruiser pulling up. Joseph grabbed all his things and headed out the door.

Before so much as a hello, the first words/advice Ted Keoppinger gave Joseph when he picked him up, was to move the hell out of that neighborhood. "Once they find out a cop is staying here, they're gonna steal everything including your guns and maybe worse, like your life. If that's your motorcycle I would park it inside your apartment when you leave." The doe-eyed Joseph looked at him and Ted motioned with a head movement saying, "Go on." Slightly embarrassed, Joseph exited the vehicle and wheeled his red Honda inside the apartment, nervously feeling timed as his superior waited looking on.

Ted then took Joseph for a tour of the lower Pat Hurley neighborhood where Joseph was living, driving up and down many streets, eventually heading West until they hit Coors Blvd SW. In the course of 20 minutes Ted had pointed out nearly 30 known gang, drug or just problem houses and explained where all sorts of different criminal activity had happened in just the last 12 months near Joseph's apartment. Joseph was impressed at how in step with the community Ted was. Their first official action stopped the tour when they were flagged down by a lady in a Samon's hardware store parking lot. She looked frantic, but had just been locked out of her car for some time. Ted gave Joseph his first lesson, in opening a window with a slim jim tool he kept in the trunk.

A slow evening, Ted must have stopped at 10 different small businesses and gas stations that first day and night. Every time Ted parked the car, he pointed for Joseph to remove the keys from the ignition to hand them to Ted which Joseph found to be a little odd, but caught on quickly and did it without being asked to at most stops. Inside each store the workers were all very friendly with Ted and as customers entered or exited Joseph noticed a lot of strange looks, almost fearful, that many people gave the Officers. He also noticed a lot of people saying hello to them.

Towards the end of the night as if Ted could read the Rookie's mind after one encounter he said, "The people who say hello to us are rarely the ones you have to worry about. You can read a lot about people just by their eyes and expressions." The shift had been calm, the Officers assisted on a few calls and checked on another stranded motorist, but Joseph got the feeling this was all just an orientation. That night Ted drove him back through the Pat Hurley neighborhood and when dropping him off he gave Joseph directions to his house to meet before the next shift.

Too close for comfort, but not really able to afford much else, Joseph left that small adobe apartment the next day after talking to the landlady. She was cool about it and gave him his deposit back and he paid for a week. He moved to the Sand Piper Apartments on Montgomery Blvd NE where a few other Rookies had moved to, including Steve House who lived in the upstairs of the same building as Joseph. LESSON LEARNED, "You're a target now so don't shit where you have to eat," as Ted had eloquently explained it best the night before.

For their second shift together, Joseph rode his motorcycle from his new apartment to Ted's house a couple miles away on Carolina Street and met his wife and two young kids. His wife was very sweet and packed both Officers a sandwich and snack, she said to Joseph with a wink, "I'm going to make you one every night so make sure he gives you one or I'll lock him up and throw away the key." Joseph smiled and tried to resist the future grub, but thanked her for the awesome gesture. She gave her husband a big kiss and then looking the young Rookie deep in the eyes added for Joseph to, "Keep my Teddy safe." Ted replied sarcastically, "Honey not in front of the rookies." She smiled and Joseph let out a small chuckle before he grabbed some supplies Ted had waiting by the front door for him to carry, as Ted kissed his daughter and son goodbye and they begged for him to stay home.

Green with inexperience, the Rookie asked his Training Officer why they had packed 2 gallons of water in their trunk along with a bag filled with dried fruits, first aid gear and extra supplies including a surplus of ammunition. "Great question and I expect one day you should do the same, being out here surrounded by desert." Keoppinger responded to the question by explaining that before he joined APD in 1975, he had previously served 3 years as a Doña Ana County Sheriff's Deputy in the southern part of NM. It was a county he was impressed Joseph was familiar with, naturally as it bordered El Paso and ran along 50 miles of Mexican border.

ONE LATE NIGHT in Doña Ana County, Keoppinger had turned off his lights and sat on the side of Interstate 25 along the southbound lanes waiting under the moonlight for any lawbreaker. After just a few minutes, he was passed by a speeding blur and he followed in pursuit. He had to climb to nearly 105mph to catch up to the vehicle to initiate a traffic stop on what was a speeding black GMC truck. The moment he turned on his single top light and siren, the pickup killed their lights and veered into the desert. Off road they tried some moves to lose the trailing deputy, but mostly headed South. The pickup led him on a 10-minute chase down bumpy dirt paths for nearly 7 miles to a spot just a few miles North of the NM-Mexico border. His radio communication had cut out in no man's land and he was alone in an unknown location.

What Ted didn't know was that they were tired of fleeing and had lured him out alone in the desert for reason he would soon find out when suddenly the fleeing truck stopped some 50 yards in front of him. Four occupants hopped out and started spraying high-powered rifle rounds toward the Officer. Still rolling in drive, Keoppinger ducked down as his windows exploded into pieces and his car started getting turned into Swiss cheese from the gunfire. Using a mental photo, that he had noticed moments before the shooting, he had luckily angled his cruiser up onto a little dirt mound with some weeds on it. This provided just enough cover when he exited his vehicle so that they couldn't shoot under his car as bullets struck the undercarriage and deflected away from him. The sound of rapid gunfire reminded him of Vietnam as bullets hailed onto his car and the desert around him.

He then explained to Joseph how he always grabs his keys out of the ignition when he parks and how this saved his life that night. His vehicle was being annihilated and with the keys Ted always instinctively grabbed, he was able to stay low and quickly unlock his trunk to get his shotgun out. They shot towards his trunk as it flung open upward with the keys inserted and he was amazed that he wasn't hit yet while quickly reaching in to grab the big gun. He then rolled over and crawled across cactus and weeds in retreat back to a safer spot behind a tiny mound of dirt as bullets whizzed by and pelted the sand near his every movement. Ted described seeing cholla cactus and yucca plants being shredded by bullets all around him, dust everywhere.

The black truck had turned off their lights and Ted's lights had been shot out, leaving him in the cold darkness of the desert with only a partial moon barely providing any light. Staying low he then moved to another small mound, angling himself to a slight flank where he was able to fire off 5 shotgun rounds and 6 more bullets from his pistol towards the area where he had last seen the light from their muzzle blasts. They returned a barrage of gunfire back at his last position but he had already crawled and rolled across more cactus to a new position where he laid face first in sand, grimacing from a body full of pricks. Ted attempted to protect the top of his head by extending both arms forward to rest the shotgun butt in front of him.

He was expecting them to drive off, but they kept him pinned down for nearly an hour as the night grew colder with a howling wind piercing his ears. They shot sporadically, a couple shots every minute or so. Although freezing, the adrenalin caused him to sweat profusely and he thought he was going to die of thirst, his mouth growing increasingly parched from not having any water and taking in puffs of dirt. The gunmen would shoot then wait, shoot some more, wait. Ted would return fire when he could, but had to be very careful about exposing himself. Luckily, when they were yelling at him or talking loud amongst each other he could kind of track their position without seeing them and he carefully retreated far away.

Keoppinger explained that the bag he packed in his Albuquerque squad car was full of ammunition because in his Doña Ana firefight he had fired his weapons down to literally his very last bullet. He had saved 1 bullet for the first gunman that tried to approach him, thinking if they realized he was out of ammunition they might try to execute or kidnap him. He watched helplessly from a distance as they rummaged through what was left of his vehicle and took turns pissing on the driver seat. Ted figured that maybe he had temporarily disabled their vehicle, because they eventually drove off and most likely escaped into the Mexican sunrise with ease.

Ted wasn't so lucky, his vehicle had been destroyed by their bullets, including his car radio and antenna. His personal radio was rendered useless by the amount of sand it consumed. A search party assembled to find him, but had no idea what direction exactly he could have gone. Tired and fatigued Ted had to march over an hour in the freezing arid desert to Interstate 25 to flag down help from a semi-truck, nearly succumbing to dehydration. He kept checking himself for injuries and had no idea how he survived relatively unscathed, except for a large intake of cactus spines across his legs, stomach and back that took a team of nurses over 4 hours to get out collectively.

After the shootout Ted did spend two nights in the hospital and couldn't return to work for a week from the dehydration. State Police counted over 90 rounds from 5.56 caliber weapons that had struck his vehicle and estimated the suspected drug runners of firing nearly 400 of these high-powered rounds compared to his 14 shotgun shells and 23 revolver rounds fired. What a story. Joseph gained so much respect for this Officer who had not only survived the Vietnam War, but also a major firefight in the domestic War on Drugs and criminals. LESSON LEARNED as Ted said it best, "Better to have supplies and not need them, then need supplies and not have them."

Joseph knew that riding with Ted was going to be a great learning experience. The first two shifts on duty were fairly calm, mostly just assisting other Officers, becoming familiar with the blueprint of things and putting into practice the S.O.P. policies he had learned throughout the Academy. He assisted on 6 calls each night, which he would learn was the general average for a standard shift. Joseph talked to Drew Banks and Juan Hernandez after their first nights to find out how things went. Juan's F.T.O. had turned off the lights to a busy intersection and made Juan conduct traffic for an hour in the freezing weather both nights. Banks ended up having to stand over a dead motorcyclist for over 2 hours in the cold and described it as pretty nasty. Joseph felt pretty lucky that his experience wasn't as harsh, thus far.

On his 3rd night as an Officer, Alvarez and Keoppinger responded to a possible stabbing call in their vicinity on Zuni Road between Pennsylvania and Dallas Streets SE, no further information available. Joseph's adrenalin instantly amped up as Ted sped towards the nearby address in the Warzone. Upon arrival on the dimly lit street, from the vehicle both Officers saw a man laying on a sidewalk, his clothes and the ground were stained by a large amount of blood. Keoppinger drove up to the curb a few feet away and pointed his spotlight on the man on where they could see blood pumping out of his abdomen or chest, the blood producing steam as it mixed with the frigid air.

Both Officers looked around and exited the vehicle with guns drawn. The Officers approached the man and Keoppinger asked the Native American male with long black hair, "Who stabbed you?" They could see the man's breath as he replied, "Fuck you pigs," and then died right before their eyes. The man was laying on his back facing up with his arms across his body attempting to stop the fatal wounds to his upper abdomen that had pierced his spleen. Within a minute his blood coagulated on the cold sidewalk as backup units and rescue arrive.

The rest of that freezing night was spent at the crime scene with Detectives, knocking on doors and canvassing the area for clues. The homeless man ended up being only 27 years old and his loving family identified his body a week later, the case cold and unsolved to this day. LESSON LEARNED, some people are sworn to the streets and genuinely hate or distrust the Police, in this case they would rather die before accepting their help or giving up information. Joseph went home late that night and replayed the image in his head dozens of times. Some last words, he thought as he struggled to fall asleep.

TED KEOPPINGER was very familiar with gang zones and he would constantly position their vehicle in bad neighborhoods with their lights off so they could just watch and wait. Within a week after that first stabbing, the pair responded to Alvarez's first call of shots fired. They were parked off Central Avenue on Florida Street SE and watching a known drug house while eating Giovanni's pizza slices when they got the call. Only a few streets away Keoppinger rushed deeper into to the area known as the Warzone.

They were the first to arrive at the El Pueblo apartment complex at 6020 Kathryn Avenue SE. Ted turned off their headlights and cherries on top before they parked in the pitch-black parking lot. BOOM, BOOM two loud shots were fired as they exited their vehicle. Both Officers drew their weapons and reacted by getting low, Alvarez took cover behind a nearby dumpster and Keoppinger behind his driver door so he could peak forward. BOOM BOOM BOOM, 3 more shots rang out and Ted could make out the action was coming from the left building on the 2nd story of the multiplex.

The stairs to the building in question were nearly 15yards away across the open parking lot. There was a lone staircase to the left, with the shooting likely occurring at one of first apartments at the top of the stairs. Alvarez was terrified and genuinely reconsidering the job as he was glued behind the dumpster with bullets flying in unknown directions. Joseph had the radio and shouted out. "Shots fired 6020 Kathryn." Keoppinger shouted to his Rookie, "Sounds like a shotgun stay low." Then Alvarez saw

Keoppinger running into the open parking lot towards the gunshots and carefully heading up the left stairs to go up where the gunfire was blasting. Eyes wide-open Alvarez took a deep breath, glanced up to heaven and followed as fast as he had ever run in his life to the bottom of the stairs, realizing he was the only backup.

Joseph was about to follow up the stairs, before BOOM another round was fired. Keoppinger had realized it was from inside the apartment located directly at the top of the stairs. Ted yelled down to Joseph, "Cover the east side of the building, shield your body and watch the top windows." "10-4," Joseph shouted in acknowledgment. Ted dangerously ran past the apartment suspected of shooting and banged on a neighbor's apartment at the end of the balcony to try and protect or warn any occupants, the light was off and it appeared nobody was home. Ted eased back along the balcony and used his hickory club to smash out the lone front window of the suspects apartment while retreating back safely in front of the neighbors. His angle protected him from direct fire. "Police," he yelled with his pistol pointed down the landing at the apartment's door and window. Ted instantly established a dialogue with the occupant(s). Joseph could hear a raging man's voice while he was taking safe cover with his gun aimed at the windows on top. He noticed one window was broken and he kept his gun fixed on it.

With Ted talking to the man, some glass was heard being smashed inside the apartment, but no shots were being fired. Turns out some drunk husband was firing his shotgun into his ceiling and out his back window into the air because his wife wanted to leave him. As more and more units arrived, no further shots were fired and the drunk surrendered peacefully. Joseph was very impressed at the line of 4 Officers behind him on the front wall of the building, all communicating with him to find out the situation and then deciding for 3 of the Officers to assist Ted at the stairs and one stayed with Joseph.

When it was all over Joseph went into the apartment to see the scene of destroyed drywall, damaged furniture and empty beer cans. The arrested man had medium length brown hair and Keoppinger pointed out

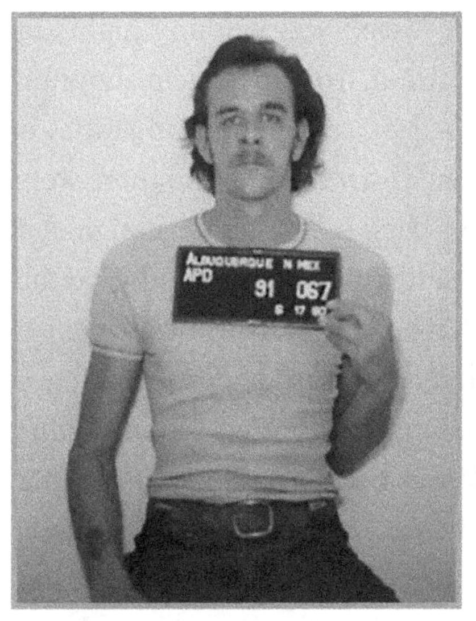

his aryan prison tattoos to Joseph and how the man had sawed off his shotgun barrel to an illegal short length. His wife, a known prostitute, was found hiding naked in the bathtub, his name tattooed across her left breast. She had barricaded herself in their only bathroom and was laying down hiding in their filthy bathtub while he shot up the place and yelled at her. Joseph could hardly understand how the man could allow his wife to work the streets, but didn't allow her to leave him or how any woman would stick around such a dirt bag.

Ted was practically yelling at the supervisors on scene about how dangerous the situation was because he didn't have a radio up there while his Rookie covered the back below. He was making a strong case for two-man units to have individual radios and how when needed one Officer can keep theirs off to avoid interference between the two. Joseph was impressed at how much sense Ted made and had voiced his displeasure in a way that couldn't be argued. It was a good thing Joseph had his pistol aimed on the back windows and watching the backside of the apartments when backup arrived, he was on probation and showed courage to a lot of veterans including Ted who told the ranking Officers how, "The kid was right with me at the stairs but I ordered him to cover the rear because the suspect was still firing and I was in a safer position."

LESSON LEARNED, Police must run into the eye of danger and place themselves in harm's way to keep society safe.

When they arrived to work before the next briefing, Joseph was surprised to get commended by several Officers that he didn't even know, cheering him about sticking with his partner. It was uncommon to get in a shootout or deal with live firing so news spread when it happened. The department might get 25 unique shootings involving Police each year. SWAT might get half of those, but Joseph was working nights in the Warzone, increasing his odds Rookie or not. This apartment shooting been a very serious event and he could tell by comments and stories it was good things played out the way they did. In the briefing there were no computers to pass along information back in the day, a designated spokesperson Officer from the previous shift stuck around and gave the lay down. The night shift didn't always have the wildest stories either.

In Joseph's 3rd week riding with Ted, the dynamic duo responded to a domestic dispute near San Pedro Drive along Kathryn Ave SE, but didn't have any details as to parties involved. It was below freezing outside that night and they discovered a young black female out in front of a tan adobe house, dressed only in her red bra and panties. She was shaking, crying and told the Officers that her boyfriend was belligerent drunk and had kicked her out for turning on the heater. Then their hearts sank and blood boiled when she said the boyfriend was alone inside with their 3month old baby son. "What's your boyfriends name?" Ted asked. "Martin" she replied, "Martin Alexander." They quickly gave her a jacket and let her into their patrol unit then marched toward the situation, up 3 cement steps leading onto a small square porch lined with white wrought iron railing on both sides. The whole neighborhood appeared to be sleeping, it was just past 2'oclock that night and both Officers should have been home hours ago but the night was too busy and they kept taking calls to help out.

Alvarez opened the black screen door outward and kept it open with his body while Keoppinger pounded on the wood front door and rang the doorbell once. As the front door opened both Officers tilted their heads back and looked up at a giant man standing almost 7 feet tall with his big round afro, he was in his late 20's with a tough looking beard and standing only his grey boxers. Reeking of booze, he greeted the Officers, "What the fuck do you want?" Joseph tensed up, but always smooth, Keoppinger gave the drunk a chance, "Hello sir! Albuquerque Police! Are you Martin?" The man didn't reply so Ted continued, "We're just checking on your son's safety can we step inside for a moment sir?"

The 6.6 200lbs man hadn't exactly broken any laws yet, but he was unfit to be alone with a baby on such a cold night, it was a child safety issue so all bets were off. "Dat bitch call you again? Man get the fuck outta here," he said as he attempted to slam the door shut where Ted was standing and turn around. The bottom of Keoppinger's foot met the door and his fists met the man's nose repeatedly as the Officer entered the home throwing hooks and then going to wrestle the man down. Alvarez didn't have time to be shocked and he pounced on the giant man who started pushing and sending punches back at the Officers. Joseph latched onto a swinging arm and slipped in a nice left jab that had no effect on the guy, but he managed to grab a hold of the fighting man's Afro to help tackle the drunk onto a wood coffee table that obliterated under the weight of the three men, Ted on bottom. Chunks of wood and wood shards were all that was left of the piece of furniture as the three men continued their fight on the floor. The Officers struggled for a long minute to cuff the man who was very strong and agile despite being heavily intoxicated.

Luckily the baby was sleeping peacefully in a backroom, but the man was charged with two counts of interfering with an Officer of the peace and one count of child endangerment for being so drunk in care of an infant and refusing a safety check. After she put on clothes, they were civil enough to let him get some clothes on before they left the residence. Before they drove off, they gave the wife a resource packet on Domestic Violence help and phone numbers to get a ride. Ted was a sweetheart of a man, but TWO LESSONS LEARNED, it doesn't matter how big a guy is you have to be ready to fight and also that nothing is more important than the safety and welfare of children.

AFTER THREE WEEKS ON THE FORCE, Alvarez had seen a large sampling of many different crimes, both violent and basic. He understood why he and many other Officers carried their guns 24-7, even off duty in Church. Crime was so random it was best to be prepared at all times. People lived normal and safe lives because the men and woman who wore badges sacrificed everything to keep things that way, dispatchers, EMT/Fire and medical workers included in the team. Most citizens slept peacefully in their homes or apartments and went to work while Police Officers were out protecting their properties, responding to murders, burglaries, domestic violence, rapes, kidnappings, thefts, assaults, and every other crime imaginable, including many so heinous that they are unimaginable.

The first person that Joseph handcuffed by himself was a 57yr old naturalized American from Mexico, who had almost beat his petite Vietnamese wife to death. It was almost surreal for a 21-year-old to lock away a man almost three times his age, but that was his job and swift action had to be taken. All it took was one glance at the victim to realize why this older man's freedom was being suspended. Joseph was sworn to protect, right down to following up with the case day by day and after nearly two weeks of recovery in the hospital Joseph and Ted personally transported the wife to a shelter house, her face and arms still heavily bruised.

One of the most important things he learned with Ted, was to always protect yourself, both physically and legally. Whatever arrest Ted made he always had Joseph sign the affidavit as a secondary Officer and then he would get a Sergeant or a Lieutenant to record their statements from the crimes and then the superiors would log it with a signature before notifying a Captain or a Chief. He was adamant in teaching Joseph to strictly follow the chain of command. The city had a lot of politics and criticism involved in its history and civilian overviews were appointed to look for any little mistake. Police really had to write solid narratives and have separate statements recounting their version of the same crime in order to make sure they triangulate each other's stories. If people ever wanted to accuse them of corruption or coercion, every Officer had a tape recorder on their belt to record proof otherwise.

Chapter 07

Blondes and Brunettes

JUAN HERNANDEZ AND JOSEPH worked the same swing shift 2:30pm-11pm those first four months with their Training Officer from Feb 3rd to July 3rd 1980, but had different beats or sections of town. Drew Banks was assigned to Northwest side graveyard and had become completely nocturnal. All 3 had Tuesdays off and would usually grab a beer together those nights at Pink Molly's cantina on San Mateo NE. The three Rookies would compare battle stories and BS about life and football while showing off their moustaches. One night the three Rookies all showed up to the bar in jeans and a white t-shirt, the typical outfit of a broke bachelor. Banks joked outside in the parking lot, "Go home and change busters, we ain't gettin no lady's looking like the three stooges!" Then they drew toothpicks to see who was the designated driver. "Damnit," said Juan.

Inside the bar they ordered drinks. Two Budweiser's and one Dr. Pepper with cherries. Joseph sipped his brew and asked his buddies, "Can you guys believe Reagan is boycotting the summer Olympics in Moscow this year?" Squeezing a cherry into his drink and shaking his head Juan replied, "Yeah man, uncool we already missed Lake Placid this year working! Those sneaky commies lucked out, might as well hand them all the summer golds!" Then Drew chimed in, "Speaking of luck out, at least y'all look bigger in your vests, mine hardly fits." Banks joked seriously while scratching his chaffing shoulders from marks left by a hand me down vest he got from an old Marine buddy of his, who was 5.9 compared to Banks 6.3. Joseph smacked Banks on the shoulder with a backhand to let him out of the dimly lit booth and said to his massive compadre, "Well that's what happens when your parents mix steroids in your baby food there, Earl Campbell."

They all smiled as Joseph got up to fetch a last round of drinks since they had a movie to catch. A grinning Banks sat back down and grabbed Joseph at the arm, temporarily stopping his journey to tell him, "Hey man ask that pretty redheaded bartender if the drapes match the curtains? Better yet invite her to the movies with us. I'll take her to Raging Bull why y'all share popcorn at Empire Strikes Back." Juan looked at Banks with a scowl and then flipped his bottom lip down and told Joseph, "Hmm…sounds good to me, ask her Joe! And I like extra, extra, extra, extra, butter, just so you know, that's four extras." The three amateur comedians smiled and Joseph blushed when the pretty bartender asked, "What are you having handsome?"

Juan and Joseph would meet up a few times every week for Brenda's Coffee after their shifts, at a diner near the Sandia Mountains named Carrows at the corner of Wyoming and Montgomery Boulevards NE. The 24-hour restaurant had been robbed at gunpoint three times already in 1980 by April, all occurring during the late hours so management spread word that Police could eat free breakfast and coffee from 10pm-6am. Well that quickly became the safest place in town after hours. Cops came in and out, positioning themselves facing an entrance or exit as they tend to always do. People would see Police cars in the parking lot and would feel safe to stop in and thus the free food initiative worked as business picked up and crime stopped at the restaurant.

Carrows became quite the popular hangout as it was licensed to sell beer and wine until 2 am. Brenda was a very pretty young waitress who had gorgeous long legs, she was tall with blond hair and sharp green eyes and distinct deep sultry voice. If an Officer ordered Brenda's Coffee, like a code at a Harlem speakeasy, she would go in the back and pour the Officers a coffee mug filled with beer, no matter the time. Brenda was really cool to the Officers, who appreciated her special cups and they always tipped her well. Even if you weren't in her section, you just had to get her attention when she passed by.

The Police graveyard gangs were grateful for the free 'comida' and left generous tips to all the waitresses, some even bought the delicious pies displayed under the front counter. It helped that Carrows seemed to only hire pretty waitresses with 8-14 of them on staff at any time, each wearing the latest perms or blowout hairstyles in fashion. The almost 30 waitresses in total employed at Carrows wore white long sleeve shirts partially buttoned up the front to expose their cleavage and tucked into their black miniskirts to make the shirts extra tight. They also work black heeled boots up to their knees, leaving their thighs exposed. Each waitress wore a yellow ribbon tied around their necks to the side and this particular Carrows hiring manager only hired women size 10 and under, they actually had to show him a tag at the interview.

EILEEN STALLA was one such waitress, a young 5.5 blond haired blue-eyed college student size 1. Joseph liked her sun kissed lips that complimented a light tan on her creamy skin and the pink and white saddle shoes she wore apart from the other gals in their dark boots. She always greeted him with a nice smile and kind words. Although young, Eileen was one of the managers and was rumored to have calmly asked each of the 3 Carrows robbers if they wanted any food to go while she emptied the cash drawer. Legend was that one masked gunman told her, "No thank you mam."

In May of 1980, Juan began to date one of the pretty Carrows waitresses a petite brunette named Rosalinda. Rose as everyone called her was a beautiful young North Valley girl from Albuquerque with a strong pitched voice with a slight Spanish accent that complimented her caramel skin, dark hair and midnight eyes. She had a cake business on the side and would make the Cops free cakes if she ever found out a birthday or special occasion was coming up. Juan had fallen for Rose at first sight and several other Cops managed to claw their way into dating some of the other blonde and brunette beauty's working the popular hangout.

Rose started dating Juan and always tried to convince Eileen to go on a double date with her or a date with Joseph, who had grown quite partial to blondes, which he had rarely seen growing up in El Paso. Of German/ Prussian ancestry, Eileen had long beautiful fine hair, great legs and resembled Joseph's Hollywood crush, Farrah Fawcett. Eileen was originally from Cleveland, Ohio and had moved to the suburb of Rio Rancho, New Mexico in high school. In high school she rode a city bus 40 minutes to Albuquerque everyday with the other RR teens, graduating from West Mesa in 1976. She was very nice and quiet, having been independent and living on her own since she was 17. The bright-eyed beauty did have a wild streak in her though.

Eileen lived with a tall auburn-red headed college roommate named Marlene near the University of NM, where she worked on-campus and the two often hosted parties at their run down two-bedroom apartment in the student ghettos. One night too many strangers showed up to their party so Marlene and Eileen devised a plan to get everyone to disperse without looking like squares. Marlene had this portable crank record player and a Cheech y Chong record that played a police siren during one skit. They went into Marlene's bedroom and kicked out some potheads before locking the door, then they snuck out the window with their plot in hand. Eileen stood outside the front door holding and cranking the radio to play the police siren and Marlene ran inside the party, dramatically slammed the door behind her and with wide eyes began frantically yelling "COPS, COPS, it's a raid." Stupid as it was, the plan actually worked and you never saw so many young adults rush out of a sliding back door so fast. 30 people in less than 30 seconds scattered into the night in all directions.

Eileen walked in the front door shortly after with the radio in hand and the good-looking pair of roommates looked around then began laughing uncontrollably. They were even more joyous realizing they had hit the party jackpot. Several bottles of booze were left behind including an unopened Jack Daniels fifth and they also found mirrors with coke lines and a rolled up $10 bill for snorting, a bag of weed, a rolled joint, a deck of cards, cigarettes, even a few more dollars were abandoned. Needless to say, Eileen wasn't exactly in the market for a cop boyfriend.

Chapter 08

A Loony Tune

JULY 4TH, 1980. ALBUQUERQUE, SE AREA COMMAND POLICE SUB-STATION, GIBSON BLVD.

RIGHT AT THE END of their 5th month of training, all the Rookies from the class of 1980 were assigned a new Field Training Officer, shift, and beat. Joseph was assigned to graveyard in the North Valley and with 9-year veteran Officer Allen "Al" Byrnes. Al Byrnes was 31, a firm man he stood about 5.10 180lbs with wavy brown hair and a 1000-watt smile. He wore large tinted glasses, a bushy copstache and always carried a guitar in his trunk next to his shotgun. He had a deep distinct voice, boisterous and was a very funny man, but also very cunning in knowing how to speak to people to solve crimes or disputes. His wife always packed Joseph a sandwich and invited him to dinner at their families Restaurant that weekend in Cedar Crest, Molly's. She smiled when Joseph accepted and asked "But where's Cedar Crest?" She would invite him often.

The NW and North Valley command included the beautiful cottonwood forest and mansions along the river, including acres of lavender fields, corn, horses, cows and a buffalo farm on Rio Grande Blvd with about 40 in the herd. The area was also comprised of pockets of violent gangs such as Brew town, 14th Street (bloods), Los Carnales Locos, Duranes and downtown Wells Park boys, amongst others. Joseph's first night with Al Byrnes was on the 4th of July, which was always a wild night due to the explosives and heavy drinking around the city. Al had been in the North Valley Command for 3 years and he really knew the lay of the land, often arriving to scenes first despite being farther away than other responding units. Byrnes gave Joseph a crash course in the North Valley gang warfare as he took Joseph on streets the rookie never knew existed. He felt like Sancho Panza on a quest every night.

Joseph quickly learned that Ofc. Byrnes kept tabs on all the gangs in the city and kept a lot of informants in his back pocket. Informants he usually gained after arresting them then reducing their criminal charges in exchange for cooperation with investigations or information and in some cases, Byrnes kept a little pocket change to hand off for info. Snitches would be the street term and they had to be kept discreet because in gang land known snitches didn't have a long-life expectancy. A lot of times Al used treehoppers, which were gang members who switched crews, usually after catching charges and they would turn against their old cliqs to get out of trouble, having intimate knowledge of the former gangs' tactics and hangouts.

In the early hours of that 4th of July night as they drove down 2nd Street, Al chirped the cars siren to catch the attention of a driver in a white Ford truck next to him, once he caught their eye, he motioned for them to put on their seatbelt. When the driver did, Al sped away from the truck and told Joseph, "Bigger fish to fry Joe, bigger fish to fry." Then Al turned left on El Pueblo Road and told his Rookie, "Let's go check on some intel from a little birdy before the night gets too busy." Al drove a mile then headed South towards downtown and gave Joseph a tour of the beautiful farms on Rio Grande Blvd as they drove to see an informant that wanted to speak to him.

THE TWO OFFICERS arrived at Bubba's gas station on Rio Grande Blvd NW near I-40 and approached the large machine car wash attached to the side. Joseph felt like such a hick, he had never seen or been through a machine wash before he only knew they existed from movies. Dusk was setting and Joseph was interested as Al paid $1.00 and all kinds of gadgets and lights lit up as they began their entry. While Al inched the car forward and soap washed the front hood, a pretty young lady hiding inside the wash opened the back door behind Joseph and hopped in, then ducked down.

She kept the door open just an inch so that water wouldn't pour in, but she could still open it to leave, obviously knowing Al had had removed the inside door handles so the back doors can only open from the outside once shut. The Officers could smell stale cigarette smoke mixed with hairspray, from her black hair with big 6-inch bangs curled up high in the front. She almost looked pretty, but Joseph couldn't tell if she was 18 or 30 from her stressed out face. She was wearing a purple shirt with a huge yellow image of Tweety Bird and tiny white shorts worn with red Chuck Taylor shoes. She had big hoop earrings to go with her valley girl accent and she gave Joseph a sharp look of uncertainty as she crouched before saying, "Mr. Al you have to help me, my boyfriend is loco, he flipped a switch..he's going to kill me I know it." The girl took heavy sniveling breaths.

Al looked at the carwash timer and said "You've got 3 minutes to tell me what's going on, everything!" The girl had huge eyelashes and beautiful dark brown colored eyes, but Joseph also saw her ugly trek marks on her arms and neck from heroin use. The girl continued, "Did you see three nights ago that they found that man lit on fire and bit by a dog?" Joseph and Al perked up, they knew exactly what she was talking about and Al said, "What do you know about it?" The tweety girl was pale and crying as she continued, "Me and my homegirls Holly and Mar got dropped off here at Bubbas and they told us to get somebody to buy us liquor for a house party!" Al stopped interrupted for a second, "Your boyfriend told you?" She nodded, "Yeah Vestro and his boy Eightball."

Tweety went on, "Anyways we found this older guy and told him we would fuck him and suck his dick for a 30 pack and a bottle of rum." She started crying as the timer read 1:22 seconds. "Then we had him drive the three of us back to the party on Hudson and told him to come inside so we could get down, then they jumped him and started stabbing him as he walked up." She looked green in the face now and Al asked "What happened next?" She continued, "Then I thought he was dead and they let their two Pitbull's sic him for like five minutes, they were eating his face and everything while everybody watched laughing." She was pouring tears out as she spilled the story. "That's when they took him to the mesa and burnt him in his own trunk, but we heard he survived on the news and now I think they are going to kill us."

Only 20 years old, Gloria Rascon aka Tweety, hadn't slept in days and makeup ran down her tired eyes. Al gave her a McDonalds coupon booklet with ten $1 dollar vouchers and said, "Here Tweety get your kid some food and I'll be by to pick you both up tonight at your grandma's around 8pm. I'm going to take you somewhere safe for a while." Then to make sure the vigilante didn't take off hiding, Al added "And they have methadone nurses okay! They'll take care of you and also feed your son, everything! It's going to be alright Okay, but if you bolt, I'll have you subpoenaed and I'll be pissed off if we have to kick in your Abuelita's door." Tweety agreed and as the timer expired she hopped out before the Police car was exposed as it exited out of the carwash.

Joseph couldn't believe that Al solved this high-profile crime that was all over the news and Detectives had talked about in two different briefings. The victim had lost parts of both ears and sight in one eye and had a long road to recovery before he could return back to his family life, although would likely never play ball with his 10-year-old son again. Al went inside Bubba's and was able to confirm a purchase for a 30 pack and bottle of Rum the night in question at 8:36pm. Later that night the two Officers were tied up with Sheriffs in arresting her boyfriend Sylvestro Garcia and tracking his henchmen as well as the other girls with Gloria that night. So Al had a female Detective in an unmarked unit pick up Gloria and her 5-year-old from her Abuelita's on Griegos Road, to drive them to a secret 30-day shelter across town.

Al sent his recorded conversation with Gloria to the Transcription Department who used typewriters to print the conversation and Joseph helped with a supplemental report. Sheriffs were able to triangulate her story when they found a receipt in the victims partially burnt car from Bubba's, for a 30pack of Milwaukee's Best and a bottle of Ronrico Rum, time stamped 8:36pm. 21 days later, a grand jury subpoenaed Gloria to testify and her statements would go on to convict 5 members of the Brew Town gang to at least 10 years a piece for attempted murder, assault with a deadly weapon, arson, and various other charges stemming from their arrests.

The case would go on to help rewrite the laws for animal cruelty and assaults involving animals. The pit bulls were seized and put down by lethal injection and the house on Hudson Drive actually yielded a pretty nice heroin bust for the Sheriffs who served the search warrant along with A.P.D. and Federal Agents from the A.T.F. Gloria was subsequently relocated to Arizona, where she went on to work at a casino and actually cleaned up her lifestyle. She sent Al a picture of her son every school year with no return address, the back of the photo always marked with the year and the simple but powerful message, "Thanks for saving our lives."

While riding with Al Byrnes, Joseph really furthered his abilities as an Officer. Joseph was becoming better every night at detecting crime. Al would tell him, "You can never be overly suspicious, so follow your hunch...Always. If you see something I don't, then call it out and we're there!" Joseph was crafting his skills on how to read people, on how to decipher fact and how to interview witnesses, victims or criminals on a case-by-case basis. Most importantly, Joseph learned new examples on how to follow law so that prosecutors would have an advantage over defense attorneys in trial.

For example, Al taught Joseph well on when to read Miranda rights, sometimes when you were detaining someone for questioning it wasn't necessary, other times you read them right away. This was very important in obtaining information legally. Al taught Joseph clever ways to ask the same question three times in a different manner so maybe a person fibbed the first two times but three times was hard even for liars. If any of the three answers to the same question varied the Officer could prove the person wasn't being truthful.

ANOTHER HOT EVENING, on their second night together, the pair was riding North on 2nd Street around midnight, Al lecturing about auto burglary when Joseph emphatically said, "Stop." Al's ears perked back like an alert horse and his eyes snapped to where Joseph was pointing. Joseph said "Possible 10-15." A young Hispanic woman in overalls with a sports bra underneath who appeared to be pregnant and a young Hispanic man shirtless in dark pants seemed to be arguing across the street. Al pulled over and turned off his headlights. They looked like a couple and the two Officers watched intently as the male looked like he was making jokes, as the female tried to walk away, they observed her laughing a little. "Maybe it was nothing," Joseph said. Then suddenly Al turned on his lights and siren to investigate when they saw the man pull her by the arm to prevent her from walking further.

The arguing couple spotted the patrol car as it climbed over a median and made its way onto their side of the street, the car parking in the opposite direction of traffic and the two Officers getting out. Al had Joseph separate the female party while he had the male half place his hands on the front of the Police car. While Al frisked the young man at the front of the car Joseph asked the female a series of questions.

First, he asked, "What's going on tonight?" She responded in a concerned tone, "Nothing I'm just trying to go home." Joseph then asked, "Did he hit you?" She quickly replied, "No, not even I just want to go home." Then Joseph asked, "Where are those marks on the back of your neck from?" He shined his light with a quick flash to where he was referring. She didn't say anything and looked at her boyfriend then just shook her head no like she didn't know what the Officer was talking about.

Al had found a small metal marijuana pipe on the boyfriend and was placing him in handcuffs then calling out on the radio they had one in custody. Ofc. Byrnes placed the man in the backseat of the car on the passenger side, secured him with a seatbelt then shut the door and came to talk to Joseph away from the female. Joseph explained what she had said and that she was nervous when asked about the marks on her neck. Al walked over to the young lady and asked her name. "Stephanie" she said.

Joseph realized in that moment he didn't even ask her name and watched in awe at the master of interrogation at work.

Al asked the young mother to be, "How many months are you?" She replied, "Almost five." Then Al said, "And he is still hitting you?" She said, "No it's not even like that sir." Al insisted, "C'mon that's not what you told my partner, he said you have marks on the back of your neck." The girl's eyes got wide and she began to cry out loud in sad confession she said, "We were up the street and he was drinking with his friends. I'm tired and wanted to sleep. Then I told him I was leaving and he grabbed me by the back of my neck because I wanted to go home to my parents. But please I don't want him to go to jail."

Officer Byrnes said, "Stephanie, don't you worry okay you didn't do anything wrong, we will take you to your parents, but he's going to jail for the marijuana pipe and those marks on your neck. He can't be doing that to you and the baby." Her tears and protest tried to grow heavier, but Al kept her breathing calm while they waited for an ambulance to check her out. Joseph looked up to see a small traffic jam in front of them from rubberneckers, there was hardly any traffic out, but the lane near them was stacking with onlooking vehicles.

As the ambulance arrived, she repeatedly told her boyfriend that she loved him and would bail him out. At one point she was starting to get so hysterical that she began to hyperventilate and the E.M.T.'s wanted to transport her to the hospital, but Al came over to help her control the breathing. What an intense and upsetting energy. She was taken to her parents by another unit just over a half hour after Joseph first spotted her. The gal was stunning, had a job and came from a hard-working family, the boyfriend not so much. It was a lesson in love so to speak for Joseph and while it was hard to comprehend, Al summed it up back in the car perfectly after they left the young guy at the jail. Al said, "Scary isn't it Joe, but that's the reality we deal with. People don't always want our help and we can't be quick to judge her. Who knows what she's been through in life, all we can do is hope it doesn't happen again."

After a month riding together, Joseph was really starting to make progress as a Police Officer and Al decided to let the Rookie take the wheel for the night. Al said, "Listen Rook, from now on we are going to alternate nights driving, but one thing I want to make very clear..." Joseph eagerly listened as Al said, "...The Police car is one of the most dangerous places to be in. The vehicle is a target for criminals and we are often responding at high velocities. With that being said, anytime we go over 60 miles per hour you put the bright lights on so we can see ahead of where we are going, otherwise the normal lights can't catch up to the road." "10-4" Joseph acknowledged.

Those warm summer nights, over many cups of coke and hot coffee, Al repeated over and over that if a Police Officer makes one mistake an entire prosecution can be thrown out of court and a serious criminal can walk free. Byrnes schooled Alvarez on how to write excellent reports, record everything possible, how to secure evidence and follow leads. In one month of riding with Al Byrnes, Joseph saw many different crimes solved by skilled Officers and he soaked everything up like a sponge. By the fall of 1980 there seemed to be a giant spike in white-collar crimes especially check fraud in the North Valley and a lot of gang warfare around the city over drug territory. It felt like every night Al placed their car in an action zone, or maybe it was the city growing so fast that crime grew quickly with it too.

Chapter 09

The Smoking Gun

SOME WEEKDAYS Al Byrnes would pick up Joseph in the middle of the day so they could assist high volume crime areas instead of experiencing a slow night, depending on the crime trends. Al Byrnes mainly kept to his NW beat, but he also patrolled the whole city and always seemed to position himself in the right place at the right time. Joseph noticed that Al always took these perfect coffee breaks or short lunches at the right time and location. Their radio would sit quietly while they ate, then as soon as they would pay the tab and get back to work the radio would squawk off and something was happening in the area Al chose to eat. The guy had a knack for positioning himself in the thick of things and Joseph counted on things to get wild every time he rode with Al. Some of the other Rookies were amazed at the stories Joseph would tell and the action he was seeing.

September 10, 1980. Loyola's Family Restaurant, 4500 Central Avenue SE. 7:00pm

One evening there was an ominous overcast about the city, so to escape the grey gloom Al took Joseph to one of his favorite diners from his old beat, Loyola's in East Nob Hill. Murals of chile ristras and hot air balloons over yucca plants adorned the walls as Joseph ate a sopapilla burger with green chile and Al had huevos rancheros smothered in red chile, both ordered coffees. As they settled the score at the counter in the front, the radio toned, followed by a Dispatcher announcing an Armed Robbery in progress at a shoe store on Wyoming only 5 blocks up from their location. "C'mon Joe, they're playing our song," Al told Joseph as they rushed out the door.

The pair hopped in the car and sped out of the restaurant lot onto Central Ave and East towards the call as the robbery dispatch announced another call of the 211 robbery suspects, "Two NMA's fleeing in a silver sedan, possibly heading West on Central." While doing 70mph Al only braked to slow down through intersections checking left, Joseph was trained to announce clear on the right side as they zoomed forward. As Dispatch re-announced the suspect's description and direction, Al and Joseph could hear faint gunshots in the approaching distance as they neared the suspect's last known position. "Get your spare set of keys out and get ready to open the trunk and grab the shotty when we pull up if you can," Al instructed Joseph.

With the mountains in the background, they came up quickly to Wyoming Blvd and slowed down, screeching their tires and jolting Joseph to push his hands onto the dashboard in reflex. Past the right side of the intersection, they could see a dark-haired man was laying down bleeding next to a motorcycle in the exit of a strip mall parking lot. Al sped to the middle of the intersection closer to the downed cyclist. "See those casings!" Al pointed down to the parking lot exit for Joseph to see this was the shooting they heard.

Several pedestrians got the Officers attention by pointing South on Wyoming Ave and Al told Joseph, "Forget the shotgun, hop out and secure the scene, don't touch the casings." Al called in the shooting victim with the car radio as he pulled next to the downed motorcyclist. He told Joseph, "Turn on your radio and wait for backup, I'ma chase these bastards." Al slowed down and Joseph jumped out with his gun drawn. Byrnes peeled out and sped to where the people pointed down Wyoming Ave, before Alvarez could even close his door, which the momentum took care of.

A large group of bystanders were standing on a nearby sidewalk, many of whom were crying as Joseph approached the downed Motorcyclist and took a knee while holstering his weapon. Joseph rolled the muscular man onto his back and recognized his face from somewhere, as blood soaked the ground from two bullet wounds, one in his chest and one in his neck. "Sir can you hear me? Back up everyone back up," Joseph shouted to the crowd as they neared the bullet casings, the man was fading in and out of consciousness. "It's Officer Chacón," one of the ladies yelled through tears as Joseph remembered exactly who this was, Alvarez felt nauseous as he turned ghost white holding his off-duty comrade. Al Byrnes had already called in the shooting and his pursuit, but Joseph knew what he had to do. Without hesitation he feverishly announced on the radio!

"Officer Down Wyoming and Central repeat Officer Down at the intersection of Wyoming and Central. Northeast corner by Winchell's donuts."

Joseph ignored the radios request for repeat and he administered first aid and C.P.R., using a knife he carried to cut off his own sleeve to make a tourniquet for the neck. One of the robbed workers Brian Iwanski was quick to assist. The large crowd wasn't helping until a former Army doctor who had been shopping nearby came to intervene. The doctor taking lead as Joseph assisted with first aid. Officer Chacón tried to say something to the man, but it was already too late as the area swarmed with rescue ambulances and dozens of Police Officers.

OFFICER PHILLIP "PHIL" CHACÓN had been volunteering at a shelter for battered women on 8900 Central Avenue NE. Two young girls, who stayed at the shelter, came in to tell adults that some men in masks were robbing a Kinney's shoe store across the parking lot outside. Chacón overheard the girls and excused himself from a presentation he was leading. He had made several arrests off duty before and the former Chief Bob Stover had once joked, "I'm going to have to start giving him 8-hour lunches." Despite being in civilian clothes and unarmed, Chacón ran outside, hopped on his personal Honda motorcycle and sped toward the shoe store not far from his location.

An experienced rider, Chacón zipped across the small strip mall and sped up to talk to two college age workers in front of the shoe store just as their 911 call was dispatched on the radio. The shoe store workers pointed to a silver sedan across the parking lot and told the Officer that those men just robbed them. Chacón took off to catch up to the sedan in his speedy bike and with its maneuverability, accompanied with some traffic congestion from a red light slowing their exit, he was able to block their pathway right in front of a Winchell's Donut House, East of the busy intersection of Central and Wyoming. Many witnesses stated that before Chacón even identified himself as a Police Officer, through their open windows, the driver hit his brakes and the passenger stuck out a handgun and fired two loud shots. Officer Chacón was hit in the chest and neck and toppled off with his bike staying upright onto its kickstand.

The armed robbers had shot with no hesitation, then sped past the Honda bike and the downed Officer with no remorse, to flee South on Wyoming towards Zuni SE. Al Byrnes was able to locate a silver sedan on Zuni Drive SE shortly after. Al had called in the vehicles license plate and suddenly all these undercover cars came out of obscurity and 7 units helped Al surround the 4 door Cadillac. Department cars he didn't know existed. As soon as the sedan pulled over one Detective ran up and jammed a shotgun right into the back of the driver's head.

Turned up, it was just a 54-year-old Black male coming home from a hard day's work. Al felt really bad because he immediately realized this guy was clean and that so many resources diverted away were wasting precious time. A couple Officers tried to quickly apologize for roughing him up, but the old man rubbed the top of his neck area and said, "It's okay fellas, y'all get back to work and catch the real guys and we'll call it square." The old man respected the Officers mutually and they respected his advice and that's exactly what they sought out to do.

As time passed into the night, the Police realized they would have to hunt down these suspects and every Officer on the department was on board to do so. It was the first time the department had lost an Officer in 26 years to gunfire and Chacón left a wife and two young children behind. It was the worst day of Joseph's career and Al felt really bad for the Rookie, but even worse for the brave fallen hero and his family. Officer Chacón became the center of all news in the State. Subsequently Joseph and Al were separated and would spend hours giving statements to different investigators. The same story over and over. Joseph felt an emptiness in his heart and nauseous all night long, a distinct stillness that would persist to plague him for days, weeks, months and years to come any time he thought of Chacón.

The day before the shooting Officer Chacón had filmed a TV program introducing the new Chief E.L Whitney, a segment called "Ask the Chief." It was a gutsy call, but they aired the spot posthumously because they knew that Officer Chacón would have wanted it that way. Joseph attended several fund-raisers for the fallen Officer at the F.O.P. (Fraternal Order of Police) Lodge and Police Academy. It seemed like everyone thought Joseph did a fine job at the scene, but Joseph felt sick to his stomach every time the street warrior veterans commended him. Up until then he had felt like the luckiest Rookie, but now just wished he didn't have to ever set foot in the Warzone again.

The next morning, for the first time Joseph considered quitting or maybe calling in sick that afternoon. As he contemplated his career path, his phone rang and like clockwork the timeless Al called and let him know the department was giving him three days paid time off. Joseph really needed to clear his head and process what had just happened. Everybody wanted to talk to him and he just wanted to become a hermit. News of the incident had made the news in El Paso and he received a call from his dad checking up on him. It was the first adult conversation he had ever really had with his father. Dino was well versed in losing colleagues he had never met, but loved like a brother just the same. Joseph's experience was unique, but he was not alone.

After the massive funeral, Al took Joseph to visit the fallen Officer's family. Joseph knew he had to be strong for the lovely young widow when she bravely asked him to tell her what he saw that day. This wasn't the same as telling investigators, he felt like crying looking into her eyes and was struggling to give his detailed version. He left out anything gruesome, but she held his hand with both hers and asked him to continue before Al explained what else happened from his viewpoint. What a brave woman Joseph thought, to sit there and listen with such composure. They left the beautiful family's home and Al made Joseph eat a burger from Wendy's because he looked so pale and couldn't answer Al when asked the last time he ate was.

From that day forward, Joseph vowed to be a better man and aspired to be like Officer Chacón, a great leader in the community and one day a great family man like he was.

Officer Philip H. Chacón. End of Watch Wednesday, September 10, 1980. Age 36.

Chapter 10

The Committee

BACK IN 1976, an innovative thinking Albuquerque Police Detective Greg MacAleese, thought up an idea to catch criminals, using their own neighborhoods against them. The idea became so successful, especially with cold cases, that hundreds of Departments would follow the model to solve crime in years to come. Crimestoppers was intended to keep informants confidential and offer rewards for their successful tips. People could dial 842-Cops and their number would be scrambled three times by one machine, keeping them confidential even from the Detectives who answered the phone.

Informants could give anonymous tips, then leave any address marked to any name and if a tip was successful, a money order would be sent in various agreed upon sums. Many people simply had the check left blank and would make it out to themselves when it came. The very first call a Detective answered, helped solve an 18-month-old gang rape that they aired on a News segment as their first "Reward for information leading to an arrest." In June of 1980, Albuquerque hosted a highly attended convention for Detectives from Departments around the country to help develop a similar model, with Las Vegas, Nevada being one of the first to follow suit.

In the Officer Chacón murder investigation, the two shoe store workers were frightened young men and neither could positively ID either of the two members they saw, since they had worn ski masks. It was very quick and scary for them, the robbers exiting in under 2 minutes. When Phil Chacón had talked to both store workers on his motorcycle, they had just come outside and were able to point out the back of the silver sedan. Both witnesses swore that it was just two Black male suspects in the sedan.

There weren't a whole lot of Black people in Albuquerque, so Officers and Detectives canvassed the Black community for two days, offering rewards and especially concentrating pressure on the ghetto areas. They set up a roadblock on Broadway and Stadium Blvd for over 40 hours, another roadblock was set up 3 miles South on Rio Bravo and Broadway SE for over a day. Police knocked on every single door in the primarily Black neighborhoods. Officer Chacón was well known in the community and people cooperated, but it certainly made a few people uneasy. That's when the Crimestoppers tip came in.

On September 12th of 1980, a dime was dropped into a payphone, giving a Crimestoppers tip that would help lead Detectives to the group responsible for Officer Phil Chacón's murder, two days after the shooting. The committee was a group of about 10 young Black males from the South Broadway area and the Kirtland Addition near the highly guarded Kirtland Air Force Base SE. Their neighborhood in the Kirtland Addition made up an eighth of the Warzone and even the Black Officers on the department referred to it as the Black ghetto or skid row. The committee members grew up in the same neighborhoods and had gone to elementary, middle, and high school together before most of them dropped out or were kicked out of school. A couple attended U.N.M. and most came from decent families with no criminal history. The group's alleged ringleader had recently been under military investigations in Ft Ord, California, Ft. Riley, Kansas plus Camp Howze and Camp Casey in Korea.

On Sept 12 1980, Van Baring Robinson and Reginald Walker were both charged with the armed robbery and murder of Ofc. Chacón. Van Robinson of 6601 South Sangamon, Chicago, Illinois, had a clean record, no priors, except some military investigations for misconduct in Korea and California. Reggie Walker had previously been charged on June 19th, 1978 for auto burglary near U.N.M. Walker was a student there himself so he was given a fine of $75, ordered to remain in college and sentenced to 4 years' probation. A couple months later on August 29th 1978 he was charged with assault and battery after allegedly hitting his girlfriend Sharon Goodloe in the face and taking her wallet. The couple never showed up to court on that charge and despite subpoenas mandating their attendance, the charges were dropped.

Robinson and Walker formed the committee in July 1980 on Dan Avenue SE. The other members were 18-23, locals who grew up from Yale Blvd SE over to Cornell, Stanford, Columbia and Princeton Drives, but these men or the neighborhood were hardly Ivy League. Van Robinson's foster brother, Barry Foster, owned a sedan that matched the description of the getaway vehicle, but was painted the wrong color to what had been identified to Detectives. His sedan was blue and they were looking for a silver car. Although depending on the sky, the grey granite façade of the Sandia mountains reflects various hues of blue, silver and grey throughout any given day.

Some of the committee members had prior incidents with Police, others remained completely anonymous. Based on physical descriptions it was hard to distinguish the committee members apart from each other in those days, other than their heights and weights. Whether light skinned or dark, on paper they showed up in the system as Race: Black, Hair: Black, Eyes: Black.

None of the committee members would talk without a lawyer present after Police went on a 24-hour mission of raiding their known addresses. This stirred up the gang and got their neighbors on alert. The members purposely cut their hair the same, wore similar clothes and shared each other's vehicles, housing and often their women, making them hard to distinguish even by their own neighbors. The group controlled the nickel and dime marijuana trade in their neighborhood and Detectives surmised that the committee had wanted to expand up in the drug game and needed capital to do so.

John Maruffi, Clarence Kraemer and Joe Polisar were the lead Detectives investigating the committee and they learned that the committee was a lot more sophisticated than they had initially suspected. It was hard to get the committee to talk, their girlfriends and members of the community provided for much of the information gained. The three middle-aged Detectives learned that the committee trained themselves how to fire handguns and assault rifles so they could commit organized armed robberies together. They targeted low-key cash businesses, like the Kinney's shoe store that was robbed in connection with Chacón's death. Detectives suspected that 3 of the committee members would rob an establishment at a time, 2 entered the business and a lone driver parked outside in a getaway vehicle. The shoe store workers testified that there were only 2 masked robbers in the store who fled in the "silver" sedan and Detectives hoped for a witness to put 3 men in the vehicle to connect to an informant's statement about their Method of Operation, for the courts.

Detectives applied pressure to the committee members and their neighbors with random daily visits sometimes at 6am or into the late night. Soon Detectives heard more rumors that their tactics were perhaps more sophisticated than just having two or three robbers doing quick stickups at a business. The committee was thought to use an extra decoy vehicle that would circle around the crime, maybe even two vehicles if the heist was a big enough score. The decoy vehicle(s) driver would allegedly be unarmed and the decoy carried a police scanner and had a walkie-talkie to communicate with the getaway driver who had one as well. In a worst-case scenario for the committee, the decoy was trained to break any law in order to draw the Police towards them, even if it meant ramming a squad car to protect the getaway car with the money.

They were also suspected of possibly using another decoy tactic moments before robbing a place, by calling in a fake crime from a payphone to lead Police away from the real crime area temporarily. Police might respond to a false call of a person wielding a knife at a park 2 miles from a store that was being robbed simultaneously to the fake call, giving the robbers extra time when Officers in an area's attention were occupied. Detectives investigated the 911 calls preceding the shoe store robbery, but found their findings fruitless. All they had were allegations and circumstantial evidence.

The three lead Detectives investigating the committee were confronted with a lack of physical evidence against the group or any one member and had to release them until more facts could be presented. Their lawyers cited harassment, but their own neighborhood was cooperative after the shit storm rained down and Police quadrupled their patrols in the areas known to house the committee members. Honest people were tired of having their doors knocked on because of criminal suspects. Police knew all they could do was persist until a lead broke.

Detective Maruffi began to stakeout the shared apartment on Dan Avenue of the two committee founders Walker and Robinson, who he was certain were the shoe store robbers and gunman in the murder of his friend. Maruffi even had a released felon, Gene Green, become his informant for money and move into the apartment next to the suspects. Green became friends with Robinson and they started doing little burglaries together. One evening they attempted the armed robbery of a Jack in the Box restaurant that was literally across the street from where Chacón was murdered. Police arrested Robinson for the attempted robbery and Gene Green walked with his full testimony against Robinson.

Undercover Detectives would sit out for hours to try and catch the unemployed Walker breaking any law in their presence so they could interview him again. However, no Police witnessed when Walker's landlady was robbed in broad daylight and she told Police that Walker had appeared shortly after and gave chase to the robber. The informant Green however gave a statement that Walker had bragged about robbing the landlady then pretending to help her. Walker was arrested for the landlady robbery and he started singing like a bird to avoid jail time.

Reggie Walker stated that Barry Foster's car was used in the shoe store robbery and killing of Ofc. Chacón. Then Walker told Police that he himself was the driver and Van Robinson was the shooter. He also stated that Foster, owner of the vehicle had intimidated anyone from talking with the threat of death. This was a breaking development. A search warrant was issued and Police impounded Foster's car, but it didn't match the shoe store workers description of a silver sedan. After combing through the blue sedan, Detectives told Foster he could come get his car out of impound. They didn't tell him that he had been indicted by a Grand Jury for intimidating a witness and when Foster arrived to get his car, they arrested him on the indictment and found a vile of cocaine on his person. Then Foster started singing whatever tune he could to get out of trouble.

The committee members Reginald Walker and Barry Foster now turned snitches on each other, but ended up jerking Detectives around and recanted their statements later, claiming Police had coerced them into giving planned statements. Tricky lawyers. Walker's plea bargain was dropped and he had to be relocated to Tucson, Arizona while they awaited trial. Van Robinson was convicted of the murder, but had the decision appealed and overturned by the State Supreme Court, due to the alleged coercion from Officers and a lack of physical evidence. It was a low blow to Detectives who had worked so hard and followed so many steps to catch these suspected murderers.

All the committee members wound up in and out of jail and they were all dead from street violence or overdose within the next 15 years before any of them saw 40. Officer Chacón was honored with a Police substation and Park in the Warzone, where he spent so much time helping the community and laid down his life in the ultimate sacrifice as a guardian of the nation.

Chapter 11

"Half mine!"

ON THEIR NEXT SHIFT after Officer Chacón's funeral, Al noticed his Rookie was still rattled and needed a pick me up. Al Byrnes loved coffee and the pair would frequent Carrows often to relax so Al took Joseph there on their midnight lunch. The night was slow and Al noticed that Joseph had been eyeing the cute blonde haired blue-eyed waitress Eileen. "So are you gonna talk to her or do I have to?" Blushing, Alvarez realized how serious Byrnes was when he called Eileen over to the table, which wasn't in her section. As she came over Al said, "This is Joseph, have you two met?" Then he politely excused himself to go to the bathroom. All Joseph mustered up was "Hi," as she stood at the end of his booth. Eileen thought, "Well he is handsome, even if he is a Narc," and she chatted with the soon to be 22yr old that she had seen around.

They talked about Rose and Juan and then Joseph asked her about the robberies at Carrows, "Is it really true you offered the robbers food to go?" Eileen looked shocked by the question, "Noooo!" she said, "It was a whole Pie." The two laughed and before she left to go check on her tables, he told her she had a beautiful smile and asked for her phone number, to which she obliged on a paper napkin. They smiled at each other again on his way out of the restaurant. Back in the car he showed Al the napkin and Byrnes gave him a pat on the knee for understanding the assignment.

"Cheerio! Well done lad, well done." Al said in a makeshift British accent. They smiled.

Their first date was a disaster! Joseph stood Eileen up for nearly 3 hours at a local restaurant. After a busy shift, Al Byrnes had let Joseph borrow his personal vehicle and Joseph was heading home to change clothes. He was supposed to meet Eileen near Downtown for breakfast at 8am. Al had a CB radio put into his silver 1976 Nova hatchback and Joseph listened to it just louder than Queen on the radio. Turned out that on his way home to change for the date, he had responded to a domestic violence call and was the first Officer to arrive so he got caught up.

Joseph pulled up to Gabby's Family Restaurant located at 2039 Fourth Street NW, a place he had suggested. This was years before cell phones and Joseph was really surprised that she was still there, highlighting a childhood education textbook after 3 hours and who knows how many cups of coffee. He was supposed to meet her off duty, but lucky for him he looked good in uniform even after working 12 hours. He apologized several times, explaining what happened until finally she grabbed his nervous hands, looked him in the eyes and said, "It's okay, I understand. You can make it up to me next time." In this moment he fell in love with her.

Joseph and Eileen began to date steady every day despite his initial tardiness. She drove a brown Datsun hatchback and would always meet him somewhere like the Little House Café or Frontier, or go to his apartment. Eileen was beautiful and his first girlfriend ever really. They both worked graveyard and usually spent mornings falling asleep in each other's arms to the Price is Right or soap operas like All my Children.

On Joseph's days off they would go out on the town to dinners, visit the zoo, hang out on benches at different parks and walk the La Luz trail at the base of the Sandia Mountains. Eileen carried seed and loved to feed birds along the Rio Grande, especially the cranes along Corrales Road. They were always on beautiful walks together and memorable dates. She once took him to Santa Fe and they spent the whole day walking art galleries around the plaza and along Canyon Road. In Albuquerque she organized a tour of what was left of the shuttered Alvarado Hotel downtown that Joseph drove by curiously every day, an absolute architectural masterpiece. They saw the Rosenwald Bros. building before it was renovated. Another day they went to the Luna Mansion in Los Lunas, had lunch and then visited the Harvey House in Belén. She was the best friend he ever had, her company was full of exciting adventures.

Around the time Juan proposed to Rose in early November of 1980, Eileen learned she was pregnant. Joseph bought the nicest ring he could afford and proposed 3 days in a row before she finally said yes. She wanted to make sure he wasn't just marrying her for the baby's sake. The night she said yes on November 06, Joseph went on duty with Al. It was a slow night and overwhelmed by his new world, Joseph randomly burst out sobbing on a frontage road, telling Al that he was going to be a father and could barely afford rent, let alone a good ring.

Byrnes pulled over into a closed gas station and lightened the mood by saying, "Hey, hey relax kid! That babies half mine, we're in this together!" They stopped and talked for a good 15 minutes next to a leaded gas pump. The conversation really cheered Joseph up and focused him on manhood. Joseph called his parents the next day to tell them he was engaged and on his next day off he borrowed Drew Banks truck to move Eileen into his apartment so she could save some money.

Eileen knew he was a great guy, but when Joseph took her to meet his parents in El Paso for Thanksgiving 1980, she realized how little she knew about her fiancé. At Joseph's parents' house on Wickham Ave, he had a whole small den full of trophies and pictures enshrined for him. Eileen learned he was in a Church choir his whole life, was an Eagle Scout, played sports and had even more than once had a family ask for his hand in their daughter's marriage. He was quite the interesting guy and she was in for quite the culture shock when they headed to Juárez for the Thanksgiving dinner at Tío Jesús's house.

THEY CROSSED THE BORDER into Mexico and Joseph reassured her she didn't need a passport to get back in. The city was absolutely beautiful to Eileen, the streets were busy, the air perfumed like a steakhouse and baked bread. Cars honked and moved about all around. Hundreds of different colored houses and buildings windows shined back into the mountains glare. After a busy 30-minute drive Eileen and Joseph pulled up to the one-story house hand built by his uncle, high in the Sierra Occidental Mountains. She saw a parking space was reserved for Joseph on the crowded dirt road with an orange cone marked with duct tape Josef and Ayleen. She had never seen her name spelled like that.

The house was on a corner of two unmarked streets and had a wrap-around porch overlooking both hilly streets. That night dozens of cars lined the curbs along both sides of the two streets. As Joseph exited the vehicle some small children kicked a soccer ball to him and he flicked the ball up with a lift of his ankle and bounced the ball on his head four times before returning a kick on the ground to the smiling sender. Eileen was smitten. Past the front porch they walked through a small white-stucco atrium decorated with taxidermized Gila Monsters and Rooster feet hung up on the walls. Tío Jesús had killed four Gila Monsters in his time on the chile fields, mean as they were. Three were displayed when you walked in the atrium and he used one to make a pair of boots.

As they entered the lovely home, dozens of his family applauded Eileen and many who were sitting literally stood up clapping from different rooms and everyone was smiling as they began lining up to meet her. Tío Jesús greeted them first and kissed her on the forehead repeatedly as he ushered her across dozens of smiling faces over to a waiting chair in the busy kitchen. She sat down surprised, but was shocked when the table next to her had a cooked cow head on top of a dish, charred up waiting to be savored. Carmen could tell Eileen was kind of overwhelmed and quickly looked for some American records on a player under an archway leading to the bedrooms.

When Carmen first got her hearing aids when she was younger, she taught herself English by listening to Beatles records. Naturally, she played an entire side of the White Album while Eileen was welcomed. Nearly 50 people welcomed her, adults, children, babies and elderly, the line just kept going and Eileen couldn't comprehend how Joseph remembered everybody's names. The music was barely audible in the chaos of excitement, but a nice gesture.

The house smelled really good and was toasty from so many personalities gathered. Dozens of women prepared side dishes in the large kitchen and dining area with both a fridge and a large separate flat freezer in one corner. Eileen found a crowded section of counter to help cut some carrots and potatoes, braving the language barrier and orchestrated movements to share the sink. An older blond lady showed her young daughter how to chop onions and garlic. Some small boys placed silverware on several tables that were lined up like a horseshoe around the larger of two living rooms and the children set up their own trio of tables in the smaller room.

At dinner Eileen stuck mainly to mashed potatoes and turkey, but tried a little of everything, including menudo, which she faked liking. The rounds of food and dessert never ended. As the family gathered around the 25" TV to enjoy the Cowboys blow out the Seahawks 51-7, Eileen won the family over by offering to help with the dishes. She was royalty that day so they didn't let her, but they appreciated the beautiful *güeras* sincerity. Eileen learned that a goodbye in Mexico can take some time, especially when Joseph invited everyone to his wedding, before they left to spend the night back in El Paso. His parents hadn't told anyone yet and the party ended like it started for Eileen, with 50 people lining up to see her, this time to congratulate.

Driving across the border, the Border Patrol Agent looked at the two for 2 seconds and waived them through without question. On the route back Joseph was afraid it was too cold, but she was from Cleveland and placed the back of her hand on the window, pressing her face against her palm as a pillow on the drive back. When his parents came an hour later Eileen was already sleeping under two blankets in Joseph's childhood bed and Joseph stayed up with his dad for a half hour.

When they awoke in the morning, it had surprisingly snowed an inch outside. They marveled at the scene as Carmen fixed everyone breakfast. She served up delicious turkey omelets smothered in homemade salsa with sides of refried beans and hashbrowns as they drank coffee and orange juice. Before they left his parents, Joseph ran across the street to Logan Heights Park and had a quick snowball fight with some neighborhood kids, who had never seen snow in El Paso and wouldn't again for years after it melted before noon.

WITH BOTH THEIR WIVES PREGNANT, Rose two months ahead of Eileen, Juan and Joseph passed their probation period and were cut loose to ride alone on December 3rd, 1980. This was the last time the Rookies would be assigned somewhere without formally bidding first. Juan and Drew Banks were assigned to the Westside swing shift. Alvarez was assigned to graveyard 11pm-8am Tue-Sat and they wanted him in the SE Area Command, particularly in South Broadway because of his ability to speak Spanish.

Driving alone was very different than having a partner. The decision making had to be just as fast, but now it was all inner thought processing a crime before calling it out, before he could confer with his partner. The biggest advantage of having Rookies being cut loose was the extra warm bodies patrolling the streets at the lowest pay in the department. They weren't part of the Union yet and for the holidays they wouldn't have to be paid *Time and a half.* To the Rookies the disadvantage was not having the extra set of eyes riding along and having to simultaneously drive, observe and communicate alone in an instant while waiting for backup to arrive. Multitasking was something incredibly difficult to manage, but knowing how to use your resources could save lives every night so it became like clockwork to Joseph.

His training had resonated deep and he was realizing more and more that his every waking second was now spent observing the world from a new set of highly trained eyes. Not only did he have a hawk like approach to patrolling, but his writing ability as well as his vocabulary and voice command had also improved tremendously and he was very adaptable to the tones needed for different scenarios. He was really lucky to have had two high-quality training Officers in Ted Keoppinger and Al Byrnes to prepare him right, although he would go on to make his share of Rookie mistakes.

Joseph made a big mistake to start his 1st night riding alone. Joseph had very steady nerves, but was highly alert and very nervous that first night he set out to patrol alone. During the Officer briefing, his palms were sweaty as he listened in with anticipation. He left the Police station with the eye of vigilance ready to spot anything, hoping his months of training had prepared him well. Then a couple miles from the Police station something caught his attention and his sight tunneled in. It was his first time initiating a traffic stop alone, pulling over a brown Pontiac trans-am for a possible Driving While Intoxicated after having witnessed the car cross its lane two times. There were three occupants in the vehicle and Joseph called out his location "Mary-Adam One Four, Got three at Broadway and Lead."

His adrenalin was coursing through his veins as Joseph approached the individuals, then he realized that he was actually at Broadway and Iron Street. He had called out the wrong location by 2 streets over. Now he was alone and had already committed his approach to the car and its three occupants with nobody knowing where he really was as he started talking to the male driver. Keeping his eye on the female passenger in front and male passenger in back he was nervous and ready for anything. Turned out just to be some young teenagers that needed a warning to drive more carefully, they were free to go after he ran their information and they came back with no outstanding warrants. Luckily for Joseph the veteran Officer who backed him up was able to find him and didn't say anything about the bad location he had called out, but it was a scary mistake he didn't plan on ever doing again.

The rest of his first night riding alone was relatively calm, he assisted on all 6 of his calls, but really benefited with some experience when Officers confiscated a cache of tools used by a serial burglar. Joseph wrote down a description of each tool as a veteran Officer explained how each was used to the Rookie. It was incredible to Joseph how thieves figured out weaknesses in systems and exploited them.

Joseph's 2nd night riding alone was a warm Thursday evening and started off with a call about a pedestrian being hit by a car. He was the third Officer to arrive to the gruesome scene, finding out the victim's right leg was mangled and would most likely need to be amputated. The driver stayed on scene and cooperated. For almost an hour Joseph had to conduct traffic to divert drivers away from the spot of the accident as it was photographed. What a terrible accident.

He left and after just a few minutes driving and awaiting the next call to come in, Ofc Alvarez called in that he was reporting suspicious activity.

The moment he exited his vehicle, the incident had all the warning signs of trouble. Joseph had observed several men drinking at South Broadway Park and radioed for a backup unit. The park was dark and the moon was hidden behind clouds that bitter cold night, not exactly a usual time or ambiance to be hanging out at the park. He approached the men with his flashlight and began to ask everyone for an identification card. Joseph explained it was illegal to consume alcohol in the park. He had everyone pour out their beers while keeping an eye on all six subjects as they produced identification. After taking everyone's ID card and matching their face with the picture, he saw his backup arriving and explained to everybody to hold tight while he ran their information, if they checked out, they were free to go with no tickets for the drinking.

The backup Officer walked up to Joseph and the group, Alvarez realized it was a fellow Rookie that he knew well from the Academy, the two Officers conferred in secret a few yards from the group. Officer TJ Martinez grew up in the neighborhood and told Joseph that one of the men Candido "Candy" Maldonado was wanted by a warrant for failure to appear in court. He also told Joseph that Candy was probably going to run when they went to arrest him on the warrant. They radioed in the other five men's information and everyone turned up clean. Officer Martinez stood behind the group close to Candy Maldonado and when Joseph handed the first one their ID back, Ofc Martinez told Candy to put his hands behind his back and the young man took off to run. Both Officers reached for the running man and Martinez got a hold of his white shirt. As the Officer tried to yank the young man back, Candy was able to reach his hand down and jerk Officer Martinez's knight stick in a way that manipulated the Officer's momentum and caused him to be thrown right into a muddy puddle of lawn water.

The troublemaker took off sprinting with Joseph just missing him by inches, now following in hot pursuit as Ofc. Martinez quickly gathered himself and radioed in the foot chase. Despite Officer Alvarez being a former track star, Candy quickly gained a 20ft lead that was growing. Joseph was built to last though and after about 120 yards the suspect slowed down and eventually just gave up when Joseph drew his weapon and ordered him on the ground. He was quickly taken into custody as Ofc Martinez appeared trailing, soaked from the waist up and covered in mud.

A Sergeant named Simballa arrived to the scene shortly after and commended the two Rookies. When Simballa arrived to the park, the other men had remained because the two Officers had their Id's still. Martinez certainly earned his uniform pay, but Joseph got the arrest credit and got to take the bad guy to jail. The two Rookies laughed that they would remember this night when they were old retired men, it was both of their first foot-chase.

On his fifth shift riding alone, Joseph responded to a dispatch requesting assistance in front of the University of New Mexico on Central Ave and Stanford SE. The famous singer/songwriter John Lennon had been assassinated earlier that day outside the Dakota building in New York City and about 25 local students had set up an impromptu candlelight vigil on a large sidewalk on the North side of Central across from the Frontier Restaurant. A few of the students turned instigators with political protest signs against the Reagan administration saying they lacked gun control. The protesters were drawing attention from passing pedestrians as well as motorists and in reality, the Police wouldn't have minded, everybody loved the Beatles, but the group had obstructed traffic repeatedly by walking onto the street. They were given two warnings and wouldn't receive a third. Al Byrnes was one of four Officers on the sidewalk observing the students when Joseph arrived. Joseph approached the group of Officers several feet from the crowd and he walked up to hear one of the Officers say he was ready to pepper spray the kids who apparently had refused repeated commands to move back 15 feet.

As Joseph joined the group Al smiled upon seeing him and gave him a wink as he left the huddle and walked over to the back of his patrol car to open the trunk. Al grabbed his shotgun with tear gas then moved it aside so he could open up his case. He strapped on his light brown Gibson guitar, grabbed a black triangular pick and then closed his car trunk and started strumming "Imagine" by Lennon on his guitar. Al was able to capture the rebellious fan's attention and began walking them away from the street.

Joseph walked up to a smiling Al as the other Officers laughed at Byrnes best trick yet. Joseph was smiling too as he approached the lime lighting Al and just as Al made a slight mistake Joseph said, "Hey hey relax old man, this baby's half mine! Were in this together!" Al's smile grew wide as Joseph sang the words to "Imagine" in his beautiful Choir voice and the crowd couldn't believe the two Officers combined skills. The Officers managed to sing the whole song from the top and when they finished, the gathered mass applauded for an encore, almost as loud as the other Officers, who had been recording the whole duet to play during their next briefing. Some of the protesters even thanked the two-man band, it was pretty entertaining.

A couple weeks after the Lennon assassination, with Joseph and all the Rookies working the holidays, Eileen's parents flew in on Christmas Eve from Hawaii with her kid sister Laurie for the wedding on December 30th, 1980. Eileen's older sister hadn't been heard from for years and her only brother was in the Navy abroad and sent a nice check for the wedding. Her parents had traveled with a four-year old Laurie to Kona, Hawaii for their 20th anniversary in 1975 and literally had only been back to the mainland once since. They left everything that didn't fit in their suitcases behind, including their house payments in Rio Rancho, NM to 17-year-old Eileen and her younger brother David. Instead of enjoying High school, she was working three jobs and raising her tough brother two years younger.

The day before her family arrived, she confessed to Joseph that her high school sweetheart Robert had died in a motorcycle accident when they were seniors and she never fully recovered until she met Joseph three years later. They had been engaged for five weeks when tragedy struck and she just wanted Joseph to know the truth in case anybody mentioned him. She nervously awaited Joseph's response and he said "If our baby is a boy we should name him Robert!" Eileen burst out crying and wrapped her arms around him, kissing him over and over and telling him how much she loved Joseph.

The parents of the bride and groom were getting along great during the wedding rehearsal. Both dads had served overseas, hers in Korea, and they welcomed each other as family. Dino was a reserved man who rarely went out, but he was laughing and having a good time with her dad Harvey. The two dads took off to the local V.F.W. after dinner and left the wives to chat. Carmen needed to do some shopping and nervously asked Elsie if she wanted to go to Juárez. Elsie was so excited, to Carmen's relief and delight. They had such a great time shopping for hours down near the Plaza de Armas in Juárez.

FOR THE ACTUAL WEDDING Joseph wore a white tux with white bowtie and Eileen wore a beautiful white gown with lace arms and an elegant four-foot train. The medium sized church was full and it seemed like half of A.P.D. and half of Mexico showed up to their wedding, compared to her small contingent of a dozen family and friends. At the wedding reception someone asked Eileen what it was like to be a mixed couple with Joseph. She said "Mixed? Because he's catholic and I'm protestant?" She had a big heart and was shocked that they meant Hispanic and White, she hadn't even thought about it until that moment. Only a few select friends had known she was 4 months pregnant at the wedding, but Carmen figured it out days later in her El Paso garden. It dawned on her that Eileen didn't toast champagne at the reception and she called Joseph to confirm. Joseph explained that he didn't want anyone to even have the chance to judge how he knocked her up before marriage.

The newlyweds postponed a honeymoon and opted to put a down payment on their first place nestled in Academy Hills, part of Albuquerque's fast-growing NE Heights. On January 4th 1980, they finalized on a modest 1200sq ft. stucco built in 1976 with 3 bedrooms 2 baths, a nice kitchen, brick fireplace, 2-car garage and on .25 acre with a big backyard for a dog one day. They moved on a cul-de-sac with five other houses owned by an all-American cast including a fireman and his wife who owned a video rental store, a couple that worked at the airport as a mechanic and reservationist, a reverend for a Christian church who was married to a social worker with three small children, a nurse from El Paso whose husband was a Retired Air Force Major and now a Engineer for the Bureau of Indian Affairs.

After Joseph carried her through the threshold of the front door, he called Eileen "June Cleaver" and rubbed her baby bump calling it his little Beaver as she compared him to "Eddie Haskell" and ordered him to his room. "No way I'm Poncherello" Joseph joked moving his forehead up and down before giving her a kiss. A hummingbird zipped around an old feeder and butterflies danced from flower to bush in the back yard. Life was good.

Chapter 12

Cuban Dismissal Crisis

AS A YOUNG ROOKIE OFFICER, Joseph Alvarez would quickly learn his importance to the department's veteran Officers by his ability to speak and interpret Spanish. In 1980 the Cold War was still hot in Cuba 20 years after the U.S. embargo began against the country for allowing Russia to house and point nuclear missiles at the U.S. during the Kennedy presidency for 13 days. With the Cuban economy down, people on the Caribbean Island began to up rise against the Castro dictatorship. To quell more uprising, the communist country announced to its citizens that anyone who wanted to leave was free to do so. Immediately the United States began accepting Cubans as political refugees and granting them asylum or even U.S. citizenship, angering the Cuban government.

Within a 6-month period in 1980, over 100,000 Cubans fled by boats to Mariel Harbor in Miami, Florida. In cunning political fashion during the mass exodus, Cuban President Fidel Castro freed many of the country's mental patients and scores of criminals from the prisons, sending them to Mariel Harbor also. Instead of only hard-working Cubans and families looking to escape the Communist regime, thousands of questionable characters were also unleashed to the wild and the plan backfired in Washington's face. What history tends to forget about the Mariel Boatlift is that many of those freed prisoners also wound up in Mexican ports. From Mexico many traveled to El Paso and then found their way up to the lucrative drug market in Albuquerque.

Pretty soon many of these Cuban criminals embarked on a drug war to take over neighborhoods in Albuquerque and clashed with local gangs. With most of these new criminals undocumented, Police were caught in a deadly crossfire game of cat and mouse. Obviously, Police wish they could prevent crime before it happens and in some cases, they are lucky enough to do just that. However, in their line of work, Police normally respond and are left to figure out what happened and who's responsible for crimes after they occur. They are generally left to piece together the puzzle after the fact. Crime never stops so Police Officers work tirelessly 365 days a year-round the clock in any weather and often for humble pay to protect 99% of the population from the 1% that are capable of anything. That's 100 bad characters out of every 10,000 good citizens.

Crime always evolved and Police had to adapt to help prevent further trouble in their communities. In the case with the Cubans, Joseph became invaluable to the department in his ability to interrogate in Spanish and he quickly started receiving many requests to interpret for Detectives in what were often violent crimes and shootings over drugs. Suddenly Albuquerque Police had an influx of dangerous new criminals and around 200 shootings happened during the 1980's involving Cuban syndicates. He gained a lot of experience interpreting for Detectives and learning from their techniques, particularly how to probe by asking the right questions and the way they controlled their demeanor to prevent anyone from reading their next move in this strategic game of crime solving. South Broadway became a hotbed, and with his first child on the way, the Rookie Alvarez became a seasoned veteran in homicides and shootings in a matter of months. This wasn't the first time Albuquerque had problems with the Cubanos though, the State of New Mexico actually had an ongoing legal battle with the Cuban government.

November 8, 1971. Near Laguna Pueblo, New Mexico.

Back on a cold night in the desert 9 miles West of Albuquerque, a New Mexico State Patrolman Robert Rosenbloom was driving eastbound towards the city. Raised in Upstate New York he was 6 feet tall and slender, driving comfortably in a white 1970 Plymouth Fury, unit #245. He was returning from Gallup, NM near the Arizona border where he had delivered a scientist to testify in a court case. Working overtime, Rosenbloom was driving home tired and pulled over to stretch then run a little radar.

In his car he was alert when he noticed a green sedan speeding with a California license plate. The State Police had in recent months discovered dozens of stolen vehicles with California plates passing through New Mexico. Rosenbloom pulled out to initiate a traffic stop for the speeding and as he caught up, he requested a check on a green 1972 Ford Galaxy, California license plate 824-EDH. When he turned on his top lights, the car pulled over up ahead.

Rosenbloom approached the vehicle occupied by three young Black males, one wearing a beret sometimes associated with Black radical groups. The young driver hopped out of the vehicle to speak to the Trooper. Something was suspicious about the man's demeanor and the Officer asked for the driver to retrieve his keys and open the trunk of the vehicle. The driver complied and when he opened the trunk the Trooper looked inside. As Rosenbloom discovered a cache of weapons, BOOM Trooper Rosenbloom was struck by a .45 caliber bullet in the neck sending his body into a violent spin as he unholstered to fire back.

The former Army veteran and 9-year Policeman was wounded, but managed to exchange back some shots as a hail of bullets flew towards him. As the Officer fired off a third shot, he was hit in the chest above his armor plate and he was knocked unconscious by the impact. A car on the highway had been passing by heading East around the time of the shootout, seeing the Trooper on the ground, the motorist pulled over up ahead. The concerned citizen waited a moment in the cold desert night, then decided to turn around to check on the Police car after seeing the green 1972 Galaxy flee past him, presumably towards Albuquerque.

At 11:11pm a voice came over the Officer's radio informing the department that one of their Officers was injured and needed help. Several minutes later Sgt Charlie Hawkins arrived and found Rosenbloom 20ft from his vehicle, faced down with a flashlight in his left hand and his hat rolled down a small embankment off the road, the Officers service weapon missing out of his holster. Officer Rosenbloom was dead at age 28, just one day after his wife and he had closed on their 1st mortgage near his upcoming post in Las Cruces, NM; achieving their dream of providing a home for their young daughter and son.

New Mexico State Patrolman Robert Rosenbloom.

End of Watch Nov 8, 1971. Age 28.

The civilian from Greeley, Colorado who passed the shooting and called for help was able to give a description of two Black males, having not seen the third. He saw one man dressed in Army fatigues with a black beret and the other wearing normal clothes. With only a vague description of the suspects, Police all over the State set up a search and roadblocks for the vehicle.

About the time Rosenbloom was discovered, back in Albuquerque on Coors Blvd and Bridge Ave, Bernalillo County Deputy Sheriff Chuck Dubois saw what he thought was a Green Buick speed past him over 120mph. He gave a short chase, but the vehicle quickly disappeared at that speed somewhere near Gun Club Road SW. A minute later Dubois quickly presumed it to be the Green Ford after hearing the call about Rosenbloom's murder and he helped give a general sense of what direction the suspects might have fled, narrowing the dragnet for over a hundred Officers. A Police Cessna took to the sky with a spotlight to comb the desert.

The F.B.I. and State Police were investigating every detail and made sure the newspapers put out the story that next morning with composite sketch drawings of the two suspects who had already been identified as Michael Finney, 20, of San Francisco and Ralph Goodwin, 24, of Berkeley, California.

Early the next morning the abandoned rental car was found in a vacant dirt lot off Tapia Blvd SW near San Ygnacio Road. Investigators combed the vehicle and found camping gear, survival supplies and lots of revolutionary and radical literature. They found writings of Mao Tse-Tung, Che Guevara and of the Republic of New Afrika out of Detroit, a U.S. group of Black separatists aimed at creating their own republic in the southern States. Police also found hand writings from the suspect Michael Finney, a known member of radical groups at UC-Berkeley including their chapter of the Republic of New Afrika.

Police were able to trace the rental car back to a Hertz Agency in San Francisco, the car was rented with a credit card in the name of a Mrs. McFearn of San Francisco where she worked for the U.S. Postal Service. She claimed the rental car and her credit cards were stolen, but she hadn't filed a police complaint yet. The rental car was conspicuously scheduled to be turned into New Orleans, Louisiana on Nov 27th laying further suspicion to Mrs. McFearn. At the same time Police were discovering a 3rd suspect existed due to a fingerprint they lifted off a beer can in the backseat.

News spread all over the State about the murder of Patrolman Rosenbloom, people in the South Valley were particularly on edge after learning about the abandoned car found in their part of town. The following morning a young boy was walking home from church and kicking a dusty suitcase in a dirt lot. When the boy arrived home, he told his mom about the suitcase, she knew of the investigation nearby and called Police about the piece of luggage. The boy had been kicking a suitcase loaded with explosives, political manifestos and over 300 rounds of ammunition. It was about this time when the beer can fingerprint came back to Charles "Charlie" Hill, 21, a former student at UC-Berkley whose mother had residence in Albuquerque at 1724 Arno Street SE.

Police found her to be a nice hard-working lady who was completely shocked, she fully cooperated with authorities allowing them to come check her residence anytime they wanted and giving names of Charlie's friends in Albuquerque. Authorities searched every connection to Charlie Hill they could and roadblocks were set up to stop every car at a few major intersections in town and every major route leading out of town. The first thing Police did after Rosenbloom was discovered was shut down the exits to the city which they planned to do indefinitely. This went on for days, many citizens lives were slowed down, but everybody was very understanding as this was a town that largely supported the actions of its Officers. People would bring snacks to the Officers, Sheriffs and Troopers who were posted for hours at these checkpoints.

Unfortunately, a lot of criminals took notice to the concentrated Police presence, did the math and figured correctly that response time would be a little slower to an armed robbery with Police saturated at the checkpoints and in other known areas. Leading to almost two armed robberies in Albuquerque each day these roadblocks were set up. Meanwhile back in San Francisco, Michael Finney's family was notified of Rosenbloom's murder. Finney's father was a very honorable man, he had been the San Francisco Police Departments first Black Officer back in a time when Civil Rights violence was at an all-time peak and he surely endured a lot of opposition and intolerance, sacrificing so much for his children. Things were rough all over.

Back in Albuquerque unbeknownst to Police the three men had buried themselves under dirt that first night as the Police Cessna flew overhead nearby with its spotlight scanning the ground. They remained buried for nearly 3 weeks living on minimum supplies until they were able to make a call back to some friends of Mrs. McFearn in San Francisco. From that point they were moved and hidden continuously under the cloak of darkness until they while they put a plan in motion. They were moved about between three apartments in the city. All three apartments had at some point been visited from Police Officers investigating the death of a Policeman, but each time the men were sweating it out in one of the other apartments. Knowing the Police were close, they devised an escape while staying primarily at the 3400 block of Gibson SE, a small complex of 21 units that Police had checked twice.

Ralph Goodwin aka Antar Ra and Michael Finney had witnessed a lot of racism in their lives, ultimately taking up their perception to advocate with groups like the Black Panthers of the Bay Area then the republic of new afrika who had for years been in confrontation with Police in Oakland and Berkeley. Goodwin and a large group of radicals had armed themselves to the teeth once and made a small group of four Oakland Officer's retreat from a rally. Both men also intently watched news across the country about other confrontations involving Police and Black groups, causing a deep disdain for law enforcement. Charlie Hill was a relative unknown to investigators, a young man with no record now wanted for murder.

For 20 day's the Policeman's killers lay in hiding when on Sunday, Nov 28, 1971 a tow truck driver was called after midnight to pick up a car. Upon arrival the wrecker looked for the car when he saw who he assumed was a stranded individual. The individual quickly hopped into the wrecker with two others holding weapons. The driver was forced at gunpoint to drive the three men to the airport, through a gate and onto the runway. ABQ International Airport Security Officer Joseph Parra was making rounds that dark morning as over 40 passengers boarded from the runway onto TWA Flight 106 headed for Chicago. From a distance Parra saw three men running toward the ladder and knew something was wrong. He ran in full sprint to try and board, but was stopped by a flight attendant who told him three armed men had boarded and not to embark or someone might get hurt. Parra stopped three remaining passengers from boarding and took them to safety as the plane's door shut behind them.

The first of several Police cars to arrive on the scene quickly pulled near the aircraft which was still sitting outside Gate 3. Parra said the jetliner Captain J.B. McGee wanted the Police cars to stay away from the plane as he taxied, for fear of exciting the armed hijackers. The aircraft departed the city at 1:55am, about 10 minutes after the hijackers boarded. There hadn't been much Parra could do, but observe. He was a gun aficionado and able to identify the makes and models of the weapons he saw. The Security Guard gave a detailed account of a .45 caliber, a .38 special and a steak knife with a serrated edge. Rosenbloom's .38 special was missing.

Airport worker Ronald Simpson, 30, from Los Angeles had just finished fueling the 747, he was checking with the pilot when he saw a tow truck pull alongside the plane and three men hopped out and ran toward the ramp. Simpson tried to run out but was ordered at gunpoint to board the plane, close the door and sit next to the stewardesses in the first-class section. Testifying that Goodwin had a .45 caliber in his right hand and a briefcase in the left. He heard one of the men ask a stewardess if anyone could board the back, she said the back steps were up, but they could lower them to let passengers off. That's when the men ordered the pilot to head for Cuba.

This plane was now bound for La Havana, other skyjackers had done this in recent years and remained in asylum on the island, protected from extradition. By this time the military scrambled fighter jets to escort the flight and all three hijackers were charged with Air Piracy in a federal warrant issued by a U.S. District Judge. Their bond was set at $100,000 each. Four hours later the plane arrived in Tampa, Florida to refuel and let the passengers who didn't work for the airlines off before the next 90-minute leg.

When they finally made it to Cuba, the authorities weren't exactly pleased to have incoming criminals. They placed all three of them in jail while diplomatic missions were sent to persuade their release back to the U.S. Joining dozens of other skyjackers, all three men would sit on that island until their dying days and every New Mexico Governor tried for over 50 years to get them back for justice. The investigation still open and records closed to the public as of 2025, with Charlie Hill still living in Cuba.

There were many good Cuban families that were outstanding members of society, business owners, hard workers and scholars. Most families that immigrated to New Mexico come to chase the American dream and work hard to be successful. Like many cities, the people who testified against criminals were neighbors and community members protecting each other from the bad element. However, that bad element always lurked and often gave bad reputation to their people and they were feared amongst their own for intimidating witnesses and attracting immigration authorities.

Chapter 13

Unassailable

A GOOD POLICE OFFICER must be unassailable in their work and have a strong mental fortitude. With the Crack Wars raging and destroying communities, Alvarez's Rookie class wages started at $4.45 an hour to get shot at, spit on, cursed out, give chase and witness things so terrible that like all other violent jobs, they were susceptible to develop Post Traumatic Stress Disorder. Joseph himself had nightmares of Phil Chacón and his grieving family on occasion. They were given lots of tools for the job, but each Officer was left alone to process their own situations on a constant basis. It was wild in the big city how you could be at a murder scene for one hour then guarding a school play the next hour.

Police can't leave room for error or let emotions cloud their judgment because not only can it get them in trouble, but mistakes can cost them their life or allow defense attorneys to free dangerous criminals. Joseph Alvarez was very safety conscious and a very meticulous Officer when he wrote his reports and interviewed victims, witnesses or criminals. He studied law and court cases to ensure he was on top of his game and that he was adapting appropriately to the changing times. When faced with lawyer tricks, he did very well against defense attorney's cross-examinations. As a Rookie, both of his Field Training Officers had taught Alvarez to be lucid and record everything possible. Details. They also taught him to treat all people fairly to gain respect from the community.

To ensure his creditability and safety, before every shift Joseph counted his bullets, checked all his equipment and once every couple of weeks he would take apart his guns and clean them if needed, ensuring that he was a well-oiled machine. To keep the smells out of the house, Eileen surprised him with a carpenter's bench one day, placed in the garage with a little station for oils and polishes. Every other night he did a quick polish on his boots and ironed his freshly washed uniforms.

He kept a moustache to the edge of his lips and shaved the rest of his face almost every morning and twice a month he got his hair faded at a barbershop in the Warzone. His vehicle was immaculate and he gave a brief inspection of his tires and looked under his hood for car bombs or rodents before patrolling every night. He checked his car fluids regularly and always scheduled necessary maintenance to do his part to help keep the city fleet running. The only time Joseph's patrol car was ever dirty was if drunks pissed themselves or threw up in it, which happened on numerous occasions.

Joseph maintained a network of relationships with Officers and Sheriffs around the city and always kept tabs on the Uniformed Crime Reports around Bernalillo County. This was a great way to keep his eyes on the lookout for patterns or trends, for new scams in surrounding cities or even other States. He also got to know 911 Dispatchers, Doctors and Nurses in the E.R., Ambulance Drivers, Drug Counselors, Probation Officers, Shelter workers, Lawyers, Teachers, good Media reporters and anyone else who worked against crime.

Alvarez truly enjoyed Police work and never sought recognition, he just wanted to help victims and prosecute criminals accordingly. He supported small businesses and many supported him, happy to have a Patrol car out-front in exchange for a little meal. Ofc. Alvarez always offered to pay, but he appreciated every comp to help with the mediocre wages he and other Officers earned amidst such great sacrifices to their personal well-being. With long hours and low pay, the job really took a toll on Officers physically, mentally and fiscally.

To begin the New Year in January of 1981, Officer Juan Hernandez had witnessed 2 suicides occur right before his eyes, 2 weeks apart. The first one really rattled Juan when a young teenage girl jumped off a bridge into the freezing Rio Grande, the second time was equally dramatic as he was the first Officer on scene and the one negotiating with a man to put the gun down as he pointed it at his head. Then in an instant the man made a bad move with his hand, lowering the gun forward and forcing all 3 Officers present to take his life. The man's last words "Shoot me." When the Chief arrived, Juan turned in his shield and gun forever, 2 bullets missing.

When Joseph heard, he traded shifts with another Officer to free up a three-day break and took a silent Hernandez down to El Paso in Eileen's Datsun for a few days to go see Father Henry and shop in Juárez. Father Henry always had the right words and really helped the shaken young man see light through the darkness. His time as a cop was over.

Juan remained close friends with Banks and Alvarez throughout their careers. He ended up growing out his Elvis sideburns again and getting one of the most dangerous jobs known to man, as a middle school bus driver. Hernandez settled back into civilian life and often joked that he wished he still had his pepper spray and handcuffs for the kids.

Eileen and Rose spent just about every day together during their pregnancies and Joseph would join Juan and them on his days off. Rose taught Eileen how to cook enchiladas and Eileen taught Rose how to make grape pies. When they both needed to take off maternity time, they started selling breakfast burritos together around the Police stations and courthouses to supplement their households, Drew Banks being their #1 customer. Sundays were the best days, everyone was off and the couples alternated hosting weekends at each other's houses, usually barbequing something tasty. They talked about everything from politics and sports to education and Hollywood while usually taking in a football game or two.

One Sunday Eileen surprised both men with matching "kiss the Chef" aprons to accompany them at the grill, Rose joked that "When the baby's come those cute Aprons are for the mommas." "My thoughts exactly," Eileen agreed. Rose grew up in a bilingual house and whenever they parted, she always told Joseph in Spanish, "God Bless you and Eileen and God

Bless the American hostages in Iran." It always reminded Joseph about the day after the hostage crisis began and Juan was being pelted by the kids with bouncy balls in the Academy. Joseph smiled at the thought of his dear friend now having to deal with similar energetic youth on the school bus daily.

After much debate, many analysts believe that the Iran-hostage crisis and its tense negotiations to free the U.S. hostages was the platform that helped Reagan defeat Carter in the winding days of the election on November 4, 1980. On January 20th, 1981 the tall handsome Republican Reagan took his oath and the country began a new era, on this same day the American hostages were set free after 444 days held captive. The Americans flew back Stateside and Iran was left in a war with Iraq. People celebrated the release across the United States, Drew Banks and Joseph met up for a cup of Brenda's coffee after their shift with some other Cops to toast the Americans freedom and the new Commander in Chief. "Hail to the Chief" everyone toasted.

After they celebrated the new era, privately in a booth Drew got very serious and gave Joseph a flyer, "In a few months I plan on transferring to Washington State to join the Spokane Police Department or their State Patrol. They both pay more than double and their benefits are much better. You should think about it, they are hungry for certified Officers and they say we come from one of the best Academies out West. They even asked me if I spoke Spanish because they pay more for Bi-lingual." Joseph opened his eyes shocked, he didn't know what to think. Just then a couple buddies joined the table. The rest of his evening Joseph was smiling, but in deep thought.

As Joseph left, he agreed to keep the secret until Banks was surely headed up Northwest. He went home that night and couldn't sleep thinking about the proposal as he lay next to his pregnant wife. Money was tight and the job was very difficult and had grown increasingly dangerous.

JIMMY ZAMORA wasn't your average Rookie, he had 4 kids and 1 on the way, so if anybody knew the pinch of money it was Jimmy. No matter when, even with family in tow, Jimmy was known to pull over and watch a Police Officer who was conducting a stop alone. A second set of eyes and another gun always helped. He understood how dangerous being a city Cop was, his Rookie experience had been wild and eventful like Joseph's. On their 365th day as Police Officers, Jimmy was off duty that night in his patrol car and went to the Dog House on Route 66 between Old Town and Downtown. With its signature dachshund neon light with wagging tail, it was a great place to get fed well without spending a lot of money, so he could afford to feed his family usually once a week there. The car hop in roller-skates brought out his order for six and a half. With food in tow, he headed back to his house in the North Valley.

A quiet evening cruising home, his patrol car smelling like delicious onions and chili when a loud tone beeped and the Police radio squawked off about an Armed Robbery in progress at a grocery store on 12th and Mountain. Jimmy stopped the car, he was on 12th approaching Mountain and now looking at the grocery store. He reached down and pushed in the knob to black out his headlights. With no traffic or people in sight, he waited as the tone sounded off and dispatch called out the Armed Robbery again with no answer. After nearly 30 seconds that felt like 5 minutes in slow motion, Jimmy called in that he was off duty and putting himself on duty.

With Officer Chacón in mind, Jimmy flicked out the chamber of his revolver to double check that it was loaded, spun it back in and put his car in drive. He opted to keep his lights off to stay camouflaged in the darkness of the night. Jimmy crept his vehicle around to the corner of the grocery store building so that he had a good vantage point of both streets before parking his car and getting out. Jimmy was in black Police pants, but not in uniform with only a white t-shirt. He had a badge, handcuffs and gun all clipped onto to his pant waist, but he did not have a flashlight or pepper spray.

Acting quickly, he exited away from his vehicle and maintained his element of surprise by walking tactically with his gun drawn, hidden behind his butt as he located the entrance. He moved past the front door along Mountain Street and hugged along the one-story building to the back parking lot, a more likely escape route. Jimmy watched the back doors and checked for a trailing accomplice. The business was open for sure and Jimmy knew the area well enough to recognize that the lone car in the parking lot was the owner's and he also knew it was closing time.

The small family-owned grocery store was a former hacienda family home turned business, the former yard was now paved into a back parking lot. The lot was almost completely dark and barely lit by a small porch light. Jimmy was starting to think and worry about backup not arriving or arriving and mistaken him for the criminal, when suddenly the back door flung open and its bells on top chimed. Jimmy raised his weapon and saw the suspect exit in dark clothing. By chance the shadowy figure missed Jimmy, walking away fast in the other direction, but he wasn't running so Jimmy easily stalked after him. It was perfect luck. "Albuquerque Police, hands up-I will shoot you." Zamora called out cocking his pistol. Jimmy extended his free arm out and grabbed the young man's clothing with one hand and said, "Don't move."

It was a young Hispanic man who couldn't believe his bad luck and he started to plead, "Please bro just let me go," and he kept trying to walk away, kind of feigning that his hands were in surrender, but slowly fidgeting them. BOOM, BOOM Jimmy was shot and the force spun his body and almost dropped him then BOOM the robbery suspect shot him in the stomach as dollar bills flew and scattered from the wind. Jimmy connected eyes with the store owner who was holding a rifle and had shot Jimmy from behind the first two times. He fired two more shots at the fleeing thief when Jimmy looked at him and just said "Police Stop!" and the squinty eyed proprietor did just that. As the shop owner leveled his gun down Jimmy used his adrenalin to chase the suspect through the parking lot along the side of the building back towards 12th Street. Something was wrong and after a short sprint Jimmy began to falter and took a long heavy blink. Everything was dark.

After shooting Jimmy once, the suspect took just a half second to try and gather some flying bills before ducking blasts from the shop owner. Now he was running towards downtown in the direction where Jimmy had originally come from with his hot dogs. In foot pursuit Jimmy reached as far as the first house down 12th from the grocery store and he stumbled into the trunk of a car parked in the driveway, the suspect was up two houses. Jimmy took a long blink and began to collapse. He did his best to rest his pistol onto the car's trunk and propped himself up as his blood smeared onto the car. Before collapsing down Jimmy yelled out one last time "Stop! Police!" The suspect kept running further and further. Jimmy unloaded his pistol into the night and did his best to drop down towards the sidewalk behind the trunk. His body was in so much pain and then he felt this rush of relief, the universe was telling him to fall asleep and it would all go away. He closed his eyes.

Both Jimmy and the 23-year-old were taken to the same hospital, unfortunately the young man didn't make it. Jimmy had other plans for the universe and falling into the sidewalk helped him get aid a minute faster, which is a minute faster to the hospital and a minute faster to life saving surgery. He refused to fall asleep, he knew he wouldn't wake up and fought to stay awake all the way to the E.R. nearly 15 minutes after being shot twice in the back and once in the stomach. He had focused on breathing, not trying to talk. The E.R. Doctors administered anesthesia to finally put him to sleep for 6 hours of surgery.

Joseph, Juan and Drew went to see him at the hospital like all his other Academy classmates and friends in the department. Jimmy swore to them all, that not falling asleep saved his life. He would carry a bullet in his back the rest of his life and returned to duty 4 months later and became an accomplished Undercover Detective. Needless to say, he didn't exchange Christmas cards with the shop owner after that. Jimmy showed more care in the proceedings for the robber then the shop owner. He had hunted his whole life and he had snuck up on the kid so perfect to take him into custody, he did everything correct and it all went sideways by the forces that be.

ON MARCH 30, 1981 there was some great news as Juan and Rose introduced their first baby into the world, Juan Jr. Everyone was so happy. Drew Banks came to the hospital in uniform and brought cigars to distribute for the welcoming. Juan had grown back his sideburns and was ready for his toughest job yet.

In the hospital waiting room, Joseph and Eileen watched a newsflash interrupt the TV soap opera. The new President Ronald Reagan exited the Hilton hotel in Washington D.C. to a crowd of people who were waiting in the light rain to catch a glimpse of the leader before he entered his waiting black limousine. A cameraman captured the jeering crowd as the President waived casually and then BOOM BOOM, Shots rang out towards the heavily guarded President. BOOM BOOM BOOM, his Press Secretary James Brady took a bullet in the head, a D.C. Police Officer fell next to him when he got hit in the neck and a chiseled Secret Service agent in a light blue suit shielded the President and then fell to the sidewalk shot in the abdomen as other Agents rushed the President into the passenger side of his bulletproof limo.

BOOM a bullet ricocheted off the bulletproof limo and caught the President just under his chest as he entered the limo door. 6 shots fired in less than 2 seconds as Police and bystanders pounced on the shooter as he continued squeezing the trigger while the limo sped off with the wounded President and the other 3 injured men lying on the sidewalk. With people on top of him, the shooter kept dry-firing his weapon after all the bullets were spent. His name was John Hinkley Jr., a 26year old White male with a history of mental problems.

Hinkley Jr. was trying to impress the actress Jodie Foster whom he was stalking and in love with. A few video cameras caught the whole scene including a famous image of a Secret Service Agent with an automatic Uzi securing the aftermath. Joseph and Eileen watched the news and waited on word for the four injured men who went into surgery. Joseph remembered his mother crying in their kitchen listening to the radio when J.F.K. was assassinated. Eileen too thought of JFK, also remembering Bobby Kennedy and the riots in Cleveland after Dr. King was assassinated. Luckily President Reagan and the 3 brave men all survived, but the D.C. Officer had nerve damage and was forced to retire. Press Secretary Brady was confined to a wheelchair and became a strong advocate for gun control.

The Secret Service Agent returned to work and eventually became a Chief of Police in Oak Park, Illinois. The President survived by a matter of inches and seconds, thanks to the quick reactions and sound decisions of all around him. He would return to his duties only weeks later and begin a new era of Reaganomics, changing the landscape of the United States and Global politics.

April 19, 1981. A.P.D. Southeast Area Command. Graveyard Shift.

Then one night it happened to him, the unthinkable. With only a month left in Eileen's pregnancy, Joseph was shot at for the first time in his career. It was a chilly Spring night with a full moon, but the sky was dark, covered by thick dark clouds stretching as far as the eyes could see. The full moon always seemed to stir up craziness and veteran Officers had mentioned this to Alvarez on more than one occasion. Joseph had once heard a Lieutenant say it was the barometric pressure. Whatever it was, full moon nights definitely seemed to cause all the coyotes to howl.

Alvarez was patrolling up and down Broadway Boulevard in a marked cruiser, when he spotted a group of about a dozen young Hispanic, Black and White males shooting dice and drinking out on a sidewalk near San Jose Street SE. Although they were brazenly breaking multiple laws in full public view, Joseph knew better then to go jack up a group so large by himself. He knew they saw him because several looked at his car, but he was looking for bigger fish to fry, deciding to let it go and told the group on his loudspeaker, "Go home!" Then he drove past them and planned to return in 10 minutes…if they hadn't got the hint, then he would call it in. The group was on his right peripheral when suddenly SMASH a loud thump and broken glass on his car causing him to instinctually duck down and swerve into the empty lane next to him.

One of the gambling men had thrown a 40oz beer bottle onto the roof of his squad car after he had already passed them. The bottle exploded into several pieces, denting his roof and causing a splash of beer down the front windshield. Joseph quickly flicked the lever to turn on his wipers and flipped on his Police lights, circling back to the group while calling for backup. He positioned his vehicle 15 feet away facing all the subjects with his bright lights on. Nobody ran, these were tough guys. "Everybody show me your hands," he commanded on the PA speaker atop the roof as he flicked on his spotlight to create a photonic barrier and searched for a guilty faced culprit by shining 3,000 lumens into most of their faces. Then as they attempted to shield their eyes a couple flipped him off gesturing obscenities, making him realize that they didn't look very remorseful and ought to be taught a lesson in conduct.

Albuquerque Police carried the shotgun locked in the trunk in those days before cages separated the front and back of vehicles and Joseph exited with only his six-shot revolver to deal with 11 suspects. "Which one of you geniuses threw that? I'm giving you one chance to come forward or all of you are going to have problems tonight?" Joseph shouted his authority with his gun aimed. In a neighborhood where snitches get stitches or snitches get lead, the gang bangers all started laughing it up. A tall skinny guy took a step forward and Joseph warned, "Don't you fucking move another step, I'll shoot you first," Then one in a silver and black Raiders hat threw up his arms, blocking his friends and taunting the Officer by manipulating his hands and fingers into gang signs and saying, "Shoot us A, find out what happens." Then the 5.3-tattooed gang banger yelled his set, "South Side Locos." The air was cold and tense.

Based on appearance and demeanor, Joseph's first instinct had actually been that this short little loudmouth kid with tattoos appeared to be the most capable of causing problems and he was spot on in his assumption. The Officer didn't balk at the gang signs and threw his own gang sign with his off hand, tapping his heart twice and temple once while cocking his pistol and pointing it at the aggressor. The tension increased at the audible sound of the spinning metal preparing to deliver destruction. "Step it up guys," Joseph radioed in to other Officers then he addressed the group, "Keep your hands up and don't try anything, all of you can thank loudmouth here for the bad time you're about to have!" Joseph was surprised that none of them ran, probably because the neighborhood was all dead ends backing up the train tracks, he thought.

The young group acted awfully brave, shouting obscenities and telling him to quit wasting their time…until 4 other Police units stormed in within a minute of each other and the punks were all thrown up against a wall and searched as a couple more units came to check for additional back up. Joseph was furious about the dent to his car. "Real smart guys, I saw what you were doing and I let it go, but one of you had to be a badass right? Had to look cool in front of your boys," Joseph said loudly to the group as he kicked one's feet wider and frisked him.

They all were on their way to spend the night in jail for illegal gambling, loitering and a couple for drug paraphernalia. "We were just break dancing," the same loudmouth punk from earlier bellowed as a young Officer removed his Raiders hat and his white cord of a belt that extended out extra-long to hang to his thigh with *SSL* sewn in black Old English letters on the strap and a metal buckle with a letter D cut out for the first letter of his last name. One officer couldn't resist "What's the D for… dumbass?" His partner chimed in with a chuckle "No no, it's for dipshit… now watch your head dipshit" as they put him in the back of a squad car. The jokes were only funny to half the people there.

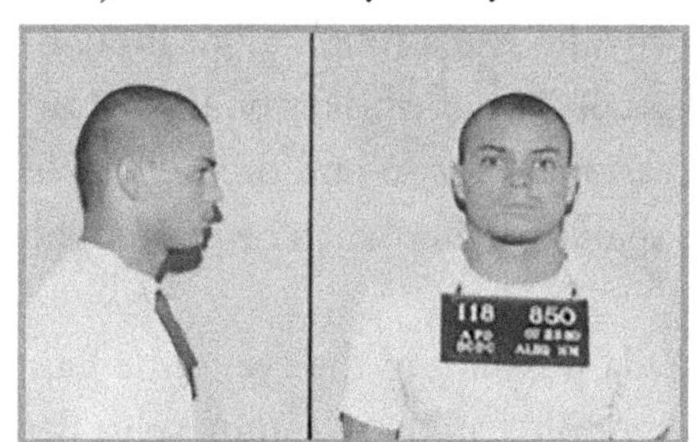

Joseph had wasted over an hour jacking up the gambling punks before continuing his beat. He drove to a gas station with a machine car wash, but it was closed because of freezing weather so he used the hand-held windshield cleaner in-between the gas pumps to clean up the beer best he could. The young Officer continued to patrol the streets as the night grew colder and things were relatively calm for a couple hours. Later around midnight with temperatures nearing 0°, Officer Alvarez was drinking a tall paper cup of coffee from another gas station and heading West on Gibson Blvd, just patrolling for any signs of trouble. A giant BOOM sounded behind him and he instantly realized it was a gunshot as a bullet struck with a whiz into his front left fender 4 feet in front of his seat. All Joseph could do was duck towards his console, put the gas pedal to the floor and bail off Gibson to turn right onto Carlisle Blvd while calling for backup. His engines roar drowning out all other sounds to him.

Radio Transmission "Shots Fired, Gibson and Carlisle...Shots fired"

A sea of lights began to accumulate in minutes as two dozen Officers and Sheriffs responded and scoured the area for over an hour. From a bullet fragment the hypothesis determined it was likely a .22 rifle fired from an unknown yard or rooftop, the culprit and casing never found. In the span of 3 hours his car had acquired a dent and a bullet hole. He wasn't sure if it was random or if he was targeted by the south siders and he would never find out. The department saw about 25 Police involved shootings per year where a Cop was shot at or fired their weapon and it is a traumatic experience always.

When he arrived home from the long shift, Eileen took one look at him and asked if he was okay. Joseph was as angry as he was shaken, but he never told Eileen that story, she would've been mortified and was 8 months pregnant. She always knew when he had a tough night though, that night he wasn't smiling and drank a tall glass of whiskey on ice instead of his normal glass of water or an occasional beer to end the night. He had to really concentrate to steady his shaking hands when he poured the glass and took his first sip.

That year another Officer Greg Avila was shot in the eye in the East Mountains when he pulled over a biker. Approaching the motorcyclist the man was angling his wheel then twisted his left handle bar and a shotgun round exploded out into the Officer. The motorcyclist rode off. Avila lost vision to one of his eye's, but continued a career with the department. He had previously been shot in the line of duty in 1976, taking four bullets. Before that he was Navy Combat Corpsman in the Marines, serving in Quang Tri, Vietnam.

If you look at the history of the United States it is an inherently violent nation. While the vast majority of people are peaceful citizens, every generation has had a history of violence involving arms, not just in Wars, but domestically. Gun ownership is a right, but so many millions of guns leads to bad people owning them too. News reporting of shooting murders is not uncommon across all 50 States and coupled with readily accessible firearms, the U.S. is a world leader in gun violence.

The Second Amendment of the Constitution allows citizens the right to bear arms, but all too often guns wind up in the wrong hands. Small crimes are misdemeanors, serious crimes are felonies. If convicted of a felony a citizen loses their right to vote and their ability to own a gun or carry one. Not many felons turn up at poll sites on Election Day, but all too often felons in possession of firearms are routinely found. From its inception, the United States has always had a problem with armed criminals who plague society. Of course, many parts of the world suffer from the same affliction.

On May 11, 1981 the legendary reggae singer Bob Marley died in Miami after an infection, he had previously survived 2 gunshots in 1976 during an assassination attempt in his homeland Jamaica. Days after being struck in the chest, Marley gave a moving concert despite concerns from his doctors, friends and family. 2 days after Marley died the Pope John Paul II was critically shot in the Vatican City while waiving to a crowd in St. Peter's Square. The Pope was hit 4 times, it was a miracle that he survived the bullets from the Turkish assassin's attempt. The Vatican Security Chief and some nuns were able to subdue the gunman, who had also shot a Jamaican lady and a woman from Buffalo, NY. After recovering, the Pope actually met and forgave his shooter in person while calling for peace and tolerance across the world.

May 20th, 1981. Gibson Blvd and University Blvd SE. 2:22am:

"Mary Adam one-two, calling Mary Adam one-two" the Police radio squawked as Alvarez pulled up to an intersection. Alvarez was waiting for the traffic light to turn green and radioed back, "Mary Adam one-two over." The dispatcher announced, "Your baby is on the way proceed to Presbyterian hospital...copy!" "Ten-Four COPY THAT," Joseph said with the biggest smile on his face. He always appreciated the 911 Operators and their genuine love for the Officers they helped coordinate and protect. Joseph excitedly turned on his Police lights and floored the pedal heading North as the Officers in his unit sent quick congratulations over the radio.

Joseph pulled up to the 4-story hospital in record time and none other than Al Byrnes was waiting in front of the E.R. entrance, "What took you so long?" he greeted Joseph with a big smile. Al gave him a quick handshake and hug, then took Joseph's gun belt and uniform shirt, leaving Joseph in black pants and a white t-shirt to help deliver his baby. Al took Joseph's keys off his belt and hopped in to park Joseph's car to clear the hospital's emergency entrance. Joseph walked in and he didn't have to ask anyone where to go, he spotted Rose and Juan smiling ear to ear with their baby, they had driven Eileen there. As a beautiful tall brunette nurse named Barbara led Joseph back to get cleaned up and in scrubs, Joseph asked Rose to call his parents in El Paso.

Joseph was fresh off 6 hours on duty and stayed up the next 12 hours of labor, he never left her hand once except when his parents came in to kiss the couple halfway into the wait. Joseph, half exhausted and succumbed by emotion, partially fainted when the head of the baby began to emerge. Nurse Barbara, who was working overtime, caught him and rushed a smell stick to his nose. He snapped out of it just in time to see his beautiful baby son Robert Damacio Alvarez be born at 7:24pm on May 21st, 1981. Sweating at the brow he kissed his wife repeatedly while the doctors cleaned the baby and then let Joseph cut the umbilical cord. They were both so exhausted as he kissed her again and again, telling her "I love you Angel, you did so good," while they shared tears together. She told him, "Congratulations Daddy," as the midwife handed her their gift of life. They both just smiled and talked to the baby for several minutes.

Half an hour later Joseph entered the waiting room with an enormous smile. He told his family and friends, "It's a boy!! 19 inches long 7lbs 6oz all 10 fingers and toes." Everyone cheered and he hugged his parents then Rose and Juan and everyone else in the room including Al's wife before quickly heading back in. As he entered back through the double doors Barbara met him, but she wasn't smiling and stopped him with her hands up and eyes wide open. Something was wrong!

Chapter 14

"How's the Baby?"

"WHAT'S WRONG?" Joseph asked Nurse Barbara with his eyes wide open as his heart dropped into the pit of his stomach. She firmly told him, "The doctors are with her now, there's some bleeding they need to look at as a precaution." Joseph wanted to rush past the tall Nurse, but he couldn't move as he started to panic and said with a swallow, "But I…but I Just saw her! Everything was fine, I…I…just saw her." He did a sign of the cross with his right hand and then snapped out of his disbelief and said, "The baby! How's the baby?" Barbara grabbed his hands and assured, "The baby is fine, here let me take you to see him while I go check on Eileen." She put an arm around him and led Joseph down several doors over to the newborns, having to support him as he kept looking back to where his wife was. "Can you get my folks please?" he pleaded. She reassured "Of course Joseph, please stay calm and I'll get back to you every chance I can." He took a deep breath and nodded okay in wide eyed confusion. Barbara left him with, "You need to stay with the baby right now, I'll be back."

Barbara had only been an RN for 6 months and the young lady handled herself with great poise when she entered the waiting area to get Carmen and Dino. Barbara didn't want to startle anyone so she had to fight back the tears and put on a smiley face calling the Alvarez's in. Once past the double doors she let the folks know Eileen was in the Operating room, so she needed them to support Joseph and she would check with all of them every chance she could. Her blue spocks were smudged in small stains from a long night as she led his folks to the newborns were. Carmen and Joseph couldn't control their emotion when they saw each other and they began reciting prayers in Spanish. As they hugged, Dino was strong for both of them as all 3 embraced.

Barbara learned that Eileen had suffered from severe hemorrhaging and was losing a lot of blood. The doctors were performing a transfusion, but feared they would need more blood as their supply was low. Without even being told, Barbara rushed out to the waiting room and leveled with everybody, asking for blood type A negative. Al Byrnes had returned with his wife in civilian clothes and was the only one. Barbara prepped him to donate, when he heard it still might not be enough, he got on the radio that he carried off duty.

Within 7 minutes, 4 more Officers with A- blood had rushed to the hospital when they heard an emergency dispatch for donors. Some of the Officers had never even heard of or met Joseph before as the receptionist assigned them nurses to draw their blood. Joseph learned of all the support from a passing nurse and he wanted to come out and thank everyone just as soon as they put the babies to bed and after he heard more from Barbara. 20 minutes passed when she kept her word and checked on Joseph and his folks, updating them with the truth. She told them bluntly to, "Please pray! She has lost a lot of blood and the Doctors are operating to do all they can." Stunned, Dino led his family out to the waiting area where several friends and Officers were and led everyone in a group prayer for Eileen. Dino hadn't been to Church since Joseph's first communion.

Everything seemed like slow motion to Joseph, it was surreal how fast he went from a storybook life experience to clinging for hope. With the waiting area filled up, Barbara appeared from the operating room. Barbara didn't even need to say a word. She could barely look Joseph in the face as she shook her head no in front of everyone. The air was sucked out of the room as everyone went silent, except for Joseph and his mother who cried out "Ay Dios Mio," as she collapsed to the floor passed out. There were no words to express how bad everyone felt. This tough man had just lost his whole world and as his deep eyes poured tears like a waterfall, Joseph howled into the moonlight. Every cop, friend and nurse welled up in disbelief. This just wasn't supposed to happen, Police Spouses have a hard enough job worrying about their loved one on duty, but it's hard to imagine the opposite scenario.

For hour's, Officer after Officer showed up to the hospital to provide support and some of the toughest Cops in the country were reduced to tears. Not only because half the department knew the waitresses from Carrows, but just the thought of what Joseph was feeling made his fellow Officers feel terrible. It made all those Cops value their own families just that much more. The Chief was at a conference in Denver when Eileen died, but shortly after she passed a Deputy Chief had even showed up to the hospital. Joseph recognized him approaching, as the tall grey-haired man made his way down a white corridor lined with patient rooms and sat on a hospital bench next to a pale Joseph, whispering towards his ear, "Hey Joseph, sorry I couldn't be here sooner, I um…" he paused and cleared his throat. "You know I became a widow earlier this year…raised three wonderful boys with my Sandra." The acting Chief paused momentarily in reflection and then added, "Look I know no words or anything can make this easier, but I want you to be strong and be with your family and cherish your new son!"

His eyes dry from exhaustion, Joseph listened as the Chief continued, "You let the department take care of everything we can and take as much time as you need to enjoy your son and recover from this deep pain okay." The Chief looked at Joseph and remembered his own pain before finishing, "I'm truly sorry for your loss son," he said with a pat on Joseph's knee. Joseph could barely muster up a head nod and a long blink in thanks. "Now you try and get some rest okay. My doors always open," the acting Chief said before he got up to offer his condolences to Dino and Carmen, who had just spent a half hour on the phone with Eileen's parents in Hawaii.

Part II

Chapter 15

The Beat Goes On

MAY 21ST, 1981

FOR THE FIRST TIME in his life Joseph didn't have any energy after his wife died, yet he couldn't sleep. His grief was consuming his every thought. Baby Robert was being kept at the hospital for 72 hours to be monitored as a precaution. Finally, after being up for almost 48 hours straight, Joseph fell asleep for almost an entire day in a room at the Crossroads motel across the street from the hospital. He was in a real bad state of hot flashes, tossing and turning for hours when he just felt this soft voice speaking to him in his dream, "Joseph I love you, take care of Robert." He awoke in tears and head to toe in sweat.

His dad was in the room watching his son sleep and came over to hug him, greeting Joseph gently, "Buenos Días Corazon." Joseph's mind was racing and he began to speak, "She's gone dad, she's gone!" Dino interrupted softly, "Shhh, shhh my son, God is taking care of her now," Dino reassured as he caressed the back of his son's head and Joseph clung to his father's jacket. Dino hugged back and then said, "Now let's get you cleaned up, I have some clothes here. Let's go see my grandson." His dad always knew what to say when things got tough and Joseph realized he had the ultimate obligation waiting at the hospital. While Joseph took a long shower, his dad went and got some coffee, muffins and bananas at a nearby gas station. It was a sad hot shower, mostly spent seated down.

Joseph had lost a few pounds in the stress and looked terrible until he ate a little to bring the color back to his face. His dad brought him blue sweat pants, a white t-shirt and a grey windbreaker jacket. After he dressed, the men drove across Central Avenue that cold sunny morning to pick up baby Robert. Joseph asked the front desk for Nurse Barbara and was disheartened to learn she had turned in a letter of resignation. A few minutes later when the Nurses gave him his son, Joseph was just overwhelmed at the blond little angel who bore his mother's beautiful blue eyes and fair skin. He instinctively held the baby the same way the nurse had.

The whole walk out of the hospital people paid attention to the handsome men and the newborn. Dino drove his son and grandchild in the backseat of his Buick back to Joseph's house where Carmen was staying with Eileen's parents Harvey and Elsie and her kid sister Laurie. On the drive back Damacio broke the silence, "He is just like you son, you never cried...well unless you were hungry," and right on cue the little sleeping Robert let out a tiny cry. "Hahah see, tiene hambre."

May 25th, 1981. Albuquerque Old Town, Villa de San Felipe Catholic Church.

The funeral was huge, Joseph didn't even know what to expect and was deeply moved by the support. Leading up, he didn't have to do anything, but attend. Her parents weren't Catholic, but loved the idea of having the funeral in Old Town. More than a hundred Police Officers, some from different departments all showed up in full formal uniform with white gloves and their sharp dress hats. Joseph brought the house down when he shared a eulogy while holding baby Robert, hardly a dry eye was left in the service. Nobody had expected Joseph to speak, it had only been 4 days since the tragedy.

"Hello everyone, I want to thank you all for coming from the bottom of my heart! Say hi Robert" he held up his baby to the crowds' awe and managed to smile before continuing. "I wanted to just share with you all a little note Eileen left me the night she passed away when I was 10-8," he said fighting back tears. "It reads: Sweetheart come to the hospital and bring diapers, Robert is on the way." Joseph struggled to finish the note, "Love you-Leenie.... P.S. fix the sink already." Everyone laughed for a second and many wiped away tears as Joseph and baby Robert stepped down. People could only imagine the tough road that lay ahead.

The Police motorcade was superb, shutting down traffic for miles to a cemetery in the village of Corrales where people bid their farewell with hundreds of single pink roses covering the casket. At the cemetery Joseph met Eileen's brother David who stood out in full Navy dress uniform. Uncle David accepted Joseph's invite to stay for two days to meet his nephew Robert before leaving back for the Philippines. Joseph had a full house, all four grandparents and his brother-in-law. The time was well spent and the two really got to know each other a little bit. David told Joseph and family a lot of funny stories about his sister growing up and asked him to pass them down to Robert in time someday.

⚖ ⚖ ⚖

It took a week after Eileen's funeral before Alvarez realized how addicted to adrenaline he had become. Every day and night he spent off the job was torturous, the call to duty beckoned. He needed the job to help with the grieving. Working a full-time job and raising a baby alone wouldn't be easy and his mom offered to move in with Joseph. He always kept her offer in mind and told her she could visit anytime for as long as she wanted to. After Eileen's family and his own parents left, Joseph would invite different Police Officers over for breakfast, lunch and dinner as the community had overfilled his kitchen. His buddy's wives would hold baby Robert, giving Joseph a break to keep up on the current affairs of Bernalillo County and A.P.D. through conversation.

After everyone left, he realized how overwhelming being a parent is when he was alone with the baby. Joseph had done nothing but build a distinguished start to his career before his wife died. Now he couldn't build a baby crib. He would be devastated, lonely and lost at times. The boy was beautiful like his mom and Joseph would sweat at the brow holding him realizing he was totally responsible for this tiny human. Eileen would have been the best mom, she would have helped him figure out all these new tasks.

Luckily his community of friends stepped in with multiple assists, daily. Rose with her baby and a group of Cop's wives all created a calendar to help the young widow see who he could call on certain days. Joseph never had a problem finding babysitters, he had problems finding ones that would accept any type of payment for the arduous task of infant care. Infant milk powders were expensive and someone took up a collection to get him a variety of supply. His neighbors on the cul-de-sac were always on stand-by too, everyone had enjoyed the young couple and felt so bad for Joseph and baby Robert.

June 1st, 1981. 1st Precinct Downtown Albuquerque, 4th and Roma.

10 days after burying his wife Joseph woke up and checked on his baby. Little Robert had grown so much in that week, getting longer and putting on weight every day. As Joseph buttered toast, he turned on the radio and the second song to come one was Eileen and his song. The same song had been playing when Joseph arrived late to their first date, he held back tears as he turned up Sonny and Cher's, 'The beat goes on.' By the end of the song baby Robert had awoken crying for food and this moment snapped Joseph back to duty. Joseph couldn't stay away from Police work on bereavement any longer and he just buried his pain deep inside in order to move on.

He found a sitter with one of the wives in his unit and showed up to work a few hours early at 8pm on a Tuesday night, looking to get in a workout at the Police gym before his shift. He was still in plain clothes when he heard of a special evening briefing led by a Sergeant Tanner from Sex Crimes. Curious about the nature of the special briefing Joseph delayed his workout and sat in. Sgt. Tanner had a thick New York accent and Joseph paid strong attention to her, grabbing a small writing pad and pen from his gym bag to take notes.

Geraldine Tanner was a petite lady, but had a strong bravado with sharp eyes and long hair. Her dad had been a highly respected Sheriff, now retired. The moment she spoke, she commanded everyone's attention. Most citizens would never know, but there was a serial rapist terrorizing the city on and off for the last 5 years at least. Detectives had finally connected a possible piece to the puzzle. The Sex Crimes Detectives had a very good idea who the suspect was, but hadn't been able to link the man to any specific rape scene. Raised near Downtown near the Wells Park Community Center on Mountain Road NW, the suspects name was Jonatan Leo Raimondi aka John Lee Raymond or Johnny Lee. 28 years old, he was a 5.9 light-skinned Hispanic male, 170lbs with short curly black hair and no tattoos or visible marks. Sgt. Tanner passed around different mugshots of the devilishly handsome suspect and his cold black eyes with the typical glaze of a weirdo.

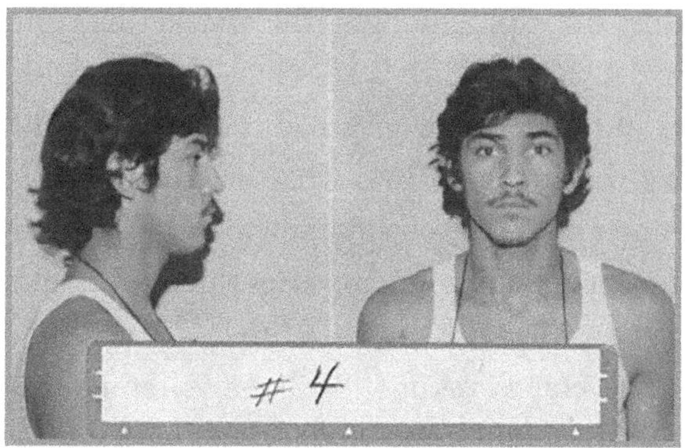

Johnny Lee had been caught 4 times from 1979-81 stealing Chevy pick-up trucks thrice and an El Camino once. Each time, he had been caught with a black ski mask, gloves, flashlight and keys shaved down to fit the trucks he stole. Similar to Johnny Lee, the rapist used stolen Chevy trucks twelve times and twice an El Camino using skeleton keys to break in and committing the filthy acts in the bed of the vehicles. The steering columns were never busted open and the windows never broke into at the rape scenes or in any of Johnny Lee's stolen trucks. "Coincidence? I think not," Sgt. Tanner continued with her thick NYC accent.

All 14 of his victims were tall and skinny, aged 17-31 and with long hair, either dark brown or black. They had all been attacked late at night and in no particular pattern, just randomly around the giant city. Similar to the rapist, each time Johnny Lee had been caught in the stolen vehicles it was late at night and he was arrested in different parts of the city. What was happening were the innocent females had walked by the shadowy figure of a young soft voiced man with the hood of his truck open, he was asking for help to hold a flashlight that he shined at them as he approached and pounced. A nefarious tactic.

It had been too dark and violent for any of the victims to make a solid identification on the masked animal. He would leave the young women in the bed of the trucks, naked and beaten unconscious every time, never leaving a fingerprint once. Sergeant Tanner explained that they had a lot of physical evidence against the rapist though. The attacker had left behind black hair at 3 of the 14 scenes, a size 9 1/2 converse shoe print was left behind at five scenes and three of the girls had collected his skin in their nails while scratching the attacker. "And what size shoe do you think Johnny Lee wears?" Tanner asked the group knowingly. "Nine and a half," she confirmed, "And we logged him in converses three times and a pair of Nikes once."

D.N.A. wasn't adequately developed yet in 1981, but Sgt. Tanner had convinced a judge to allow the hair samples and victim's nails with skin as evidence with no statute of limitations to match their owner(s). After the J.F.K Assassination and into the late 1970's, scientists had begun a lot of research into matching criminals to more types of physical evidence left behind at crime scenes, far beyond Latent Index fingerprinting. Many Officers and legal professionals knew how forensic science was evolving far beyond the Sherlock Holmes days. The Judge in the midnight rapist cases felt the research would breakthrough sooner than not and his decision to apply no time limit to link the evidence to the criminal was a 1st in the State. Other Prosecutors in the Southwest followed the precedent eagerly in the years following. Everyone progressive was waiting for Scientists to do their part and break the Genetic Code, so old and new evidence could be tied to the correct criminals.

The media had spread fear across the entire county of Bernalillo about the "midnight rapist," but it was impossible to warn everyone. There was no computer database back in 1981 to triangulate crimes, so different types of Detectives shared leads and maintained close working relationships to tie together crimes such as this villainous rapist and Chevy truck thief. Sergeant Tanner finished the briefing by telling everyone; "One of you's bring him in on something…anything. Jaywalking for all I's care. Then let us handle the rest. If we can't get a confession or he can produce solid alibi's then we can at least get his hair on file for later if I have to pluck it off his skull myself." This tiny Detective had the hair on his arms raised. She was fascinating to Joseph and he wished he could pick her brain for an hour.

As Joseph got ready in the locker room, he heard a few Officers berate Tanner, they didn't believe one piece of hair could be linked to a specific criminal. Ofc. Burt said, "Hair I've actually heard of, but finger nails, what the hell is that nutso Sergeant thinking?" Then Ofc. Ernie followed, "Yeah Some Detective." The Officers looked at Joseph for confirmation and Joseph just threw up his hands and shook his head like *not sure Pals, but maybe*. In his own mind however, Joseph was fascinated at the before mentioned possibilities of new types of physical evidence to help Police and Prosecutors.

From his days as a new recruit in the North Valley, Joseph knew that a lot of old Chevy Pickups were worked on at the auto garages along 4th Street from Candelaria to Menaul NW. He also knew that particular area always had problems with stolen trucks, parts and vehicles in general, plus Johnny Lee grew up not too far away under I-40. Al Byrnes had made Joseph pretty savvy about where to find auto burglaries. It was a slow night so Joseph radioed in a midnight lunch break and headed over to his old beat to grab a bite and see if he could stir up some trouble. It was a cold Monday morning at 1am when Joseph drove past a man crossing Indian School Road dressed in a black hoodie, black pants and black gloves which actually was normal attire in winter for some people.

Zooming in on the man, Joseph caught a shining glimpse of a large key ring attached to the man's belt loop. The key ring was the kind school janitor's use with dozens of keys bunched around in a hooped circle or the kind professional car thieves use at late hours crossing streets. Alvarez noticed the keys as he passed him going 30mph. He continued along not wanting to alert the suspicious man because he was afraid to lose him in the dark if he took off running. Driving and glancing over his shoulder, the blacked-out figure furthered Joseph's suspicion as he ducked behind a small picket fence in someone's front yard after undoubtedly seeing the patrol unit. Continuing along, Joseph watched carefully in his rear-view mirror and signaled right, pretending to turn off the street and out of sight to appear oblivious to the hiding man.

In an instance Joseph turned off his headlights, circled back and carefully drove back towards the hiding man, quietly turning back on the street with a wide turn and then heading on the wrong side of the road using an angle to have parked cars up ahead block his approach. Knowing his vehicle, he gave one tap of the pedal to get the speed he wanted. Rolling forward he radioed in his location then turned off the radio. Approaching about 50 ft away to where the man had hidden, he dropped the car in neutral and shut off the engine to eliminate its sound, using its forward momentum to roll closer towards the front of some cars parked on the street. He cracked his door open before tapping his break to come to a quiet stop in front of a vehicle about 30 feet behind the hiding suspect. Joseph exited onto the dark street and stepped up the curb without shutting his door completely or audibly placing the car in park, by leaving it in neutral.

The man was on the other side of a 3ft wood picket fence that split two front yards. He was facing away sitting in a fetal position in between two bushes leaned back on the fence, his short breaths seen in the cold.

Joseph carefully snuck up behind the suspect from the neighboring yard and pressed his gun muzzle onto the back of the man's cortex over the fence, cocking back the hammer. "Put your hands out or I'll splatter your fuckin brains all over this yard," Joseph demanded. The suspect, clenching his black gloves, slowly extended out his sweaty hands and dropped the filthy mitts. With his free hand, Joseph reached to his hip and twisted his radio back on with his thumb and index finger, surveying how he would take the man in custody.

"Slowly lay flat on your stomach, arms to your side," Joseph said as he stepped over the fence while using his left hand to grab the suspect's jacket, his gun pointing dead ahead. The suspect put his perspiring face on the dry yellow grass, the cold blades almost breaking skin as he remained silent while being mounted. Joseph placed a knee firmly across the antsy man's back then Joseph let the suspect feel his strength by controlling his wrists with some pressure before patting down his waistband, pants and jacket. Joseph's gun was pressed onto the back of the man's head still as he removed the suspect's flashlight and ski mask tossing them to the grass then jingled his set of truck keys and asked, "Johnny Lee Raymond, who are you raping tonight?" The flattened-out suspect's eyes got huge with worry. "Nobody!" said Joseph with aggressive punctuation as he holstered his gun and transitioned to close handcuffs tightly onto the sicko's wrists.

Johnny Lee hadn't broken any laws in Joseph's presence, except one, which would require a little creativity to help pin. Now Joseph had to cleverly find a way to convince the homeowner to file trespassing charges against Raimondi for being in the front yard. If the owner said no, Johnny Lee could walk free to terrorize young women again and he could easily disappear to violate another city. If he went down for the trespassing, Police could take Raimondi Downtown and submit his shaved keys, flashlight and clothes for evidence, collect hair off of him to put on file and question him about the rapes he was suspected of. By law Joseph couldn't inform the homeowner of the rapes or that this extended far beyond trespassing. Now in a neighborhood where people prefer to mind their own business and not get involved, Joseph had to be unassailable in this delicate legal situation. Without showing any bias, he needed to somehow convince the homeowner to press charges against the suspect.

The homeowner was a middle-aged father of 3 who was reluctant to sign a trespassing affidavit, but Joseph explained that it was best for his wife and children's security by showing him the black gloves, ski mask, flashlight and ring of keys from the suspect. For all the homeowner knew those keys could have been for homes instead of trucks and Joseph played that angle. Right on cue the mom walked out to the porch with a toddler daughter in her arms, they had both awoken by the Police lights and Officers knocking on their door. Joseph said to the daughter, "Don't worry Angel, we got the bad guy he can't hurt you, you're safe now." The daughter smiled at the reassurance and the dad was convinced, opting to press charges for criminal trespass to protect his family.

When she heard how Joseph coaxed the trespassing charge, Sgt. Tanner with the New York accent was ecstatic and very impressed by the young Officer when listening to his audio recording. His arrest led to an eventual confession to knowing one of the rape victims, stating they were mutual friends, only the victim didn't know him or have any connection to him previously and thus he pinned himself to the crime. Sgt. Tanner personally thanked Joseph and brought his whole squad some good coffee, cookies and donuts at their next briefing while handing out flyers of loose sex offenders last known hangouts. Joseph really admired her attention to details. His comrades all gave Joseph a high five or pat on the back for the snacks and congratulations on busting the perp. Privately while reviewing Joseph's report with him, she let Joseph know that if he took the Detective exam, she had a spot on her roster for him anytime.

Chapter 16

Boiling Point

IN AUGUST OF 1981, a young Florida businessman named John Walsh and his wife fell victim to child abduction outside a Sears department store in a shopping mall. The crime made national headlines and Joseph was deeply disturbed when he read that the 6-year-old child Adam had been found gruesomely beheaded. Nothing could explain this tragedy. The most beautiful kid. Mr. Walsh would go on to become the country's most successful advocate for missing children and for capturing America's Most Wanted fugitives.

A week after the tragic news of Adam Walsh and with an infant himself, Joseph would contribute his own local security measure for children's safety while at the Sports Stadium watching a AAA baseball game between the Albuquerque Dukes and Colorado Springs Sky Sox.

After the Pacific Coast League games, children were allowed to line up on the first base side and then let onto the field for a run around the bases before the grounds crew took apart the infield. Dozens of kids lined up, little ones to older ones, it was adorably funny. Joseph smiled until he noticed that the 'fun run' kids were left to wander the crowded stadium after touching home plate and entering the stands. The kids were directed near his section on the 3rd base side and most of their parents were coming from the other side of the stands as the children exited into the large crowd unsupervised. He saw one scared little girl crying because she was lost temporarily.

It was baby Robert's first ballgame and although off duty, Joseph was showing his badge on his hip and stopped all the remaining kids running up the stairs before they could exit section 126 over the 3rd base dugout. He had all the children sit in the last row of seats until they could identify their parents, many of whom shared Joseph's same concern and had hustled over. Several were thanking the Officer for his safety concern. After the last kid reunited with their folks, Joseph found the Dukes head of security and made sure they took the measure into their own hands permanently.

Also in late August of 1981, a new cable television channel was introduced called Music Television or MTV and it began to influence generations of followers. The channel showed rock music videos and the first video shown was "Video Killed the Radio Star," by the Buggles and it was followed by "You better Run," by the great Pat Benatar. Joseph couldn't afford cable and didn't have much time to watch TV in general, but within weeks of MTV being launched Joseph noticed a lot of the youngsters around town began to follow the channels trends. Almost overnight teenagers and college students in Albuquerque began to wear bright colors, big sunglasses, t-shirts under suit jackets, skinny ties, mismatched socks, loose shirts exposing one shoulder and stone washed jeans. One night standing in the parking lot outside a Manzano High vs. Eldorado High basketball game, the game let out and hundreds of rival students poured out of the gymnasium. Joseph must have counted 20 different versions of Madonna alone and a half dozen Michael Jacksons. There was enough hairspray in that parking lot to burn a hole in the ozone layer.

On October 6, 1981 Joseph was warming up milk in the kitchen to feed baby Robert, he had moved his small TV onto his kitchen counter to where it could be viewed in the little dining room and in the kitchen. With baby in arm, he sat down in the lonely dining room and watched a breaking news story. The President of Egypt Anwar Sadat was assassinated by high-ranking members of his own military. They killed the President during a Military parade in Cairo and in front of many news reporters and dignitaries. The Vice President took a bullet to the hand as well, but was expected to survive and succeed Sadat. The whole assassination was caught on video and Joseph saw the wild assassination shooting on the television right after it happened. He was asking other Cops the next day if they had seen the shooting images, but there was no way to get a hold of the video after that and see it again so he followed the aftermath in print. Former Presidents Richard Nixon, Gerald Ford and Jimmy Carter attended the funeral, but there was a conspicuous absence of Arab leaders.

Raising a child alone was the most exhausting job Joseph had ever worked. His mom and dad would drive up on many weekends, often with family and sometimes Carmen would stay a week to help out. Joseph had no problem finding a baby sitter, many people knew his situation and helped him out beyond words. Being a father and member of such a tight knit community really matured the Officer and his job took on a whole new meaning. Before, he had felt like his job was to arrest bad guys, but now he realized it meant to protect your community and loved ones. Every night when he left Robert in the caring arms of someone, his whole goal was to return to his son. His own safety became paramount to ensure the upbringing of his son, the legacy of his mother Eileen.

In November of 1981 Joseph kept finding reckless out of control drivers. That month he arrested 8 drunk drivers for D.W.I., including 3 on thanksgiving night. You name it men, women, teenagers, seniors, people were driving drunk like it was totally casual. One guy he pulled over was heading straight towards a bunch of kids playing football up the street, his Blood Alcohol Content was measured at 2.6%, more than 3 times the legal limit of .08. "Dis is bullsshit, guna take me to gel…and I got work in the morneen," the drunk contested slowly, as the crowd of kids watched on. Alvarez said, "Well that's your fault for being a danger, you should have thought of that before you got behind the wheel." Afterwards securing him, Joseph tried to reach a family member of the arrestee by pay phone, but nobody answered and the car was towed to the city impound. The bill would be $70 to get the car out, for Joseph that would mean working 20 hours and he thought about the economic strain this drunk driver had just put on his family. Then he thought about what would have happened if the man had plowed into the kids in the street playing football and he collected his dime back.

Despite all the extra things Joseph did for the community and the department that went unnoticed, he truly enjoyed his job and didn't want any recognition. His morale was a little low though, because of many factors, mainly from being lonely and trying to raise a son while being overworked and underpaid. Even though he had two fast track promotions already, Cadet to Patrolman 2nd class to Patrolman 1st class, it was still hard to make ends meet. He was married to his job, but had little to show for it financially. He was dedicated to attending meetings, volunteering at schools and checking on people's welfare on his own time when he could. None of this paid and it wasn't like he could get a second job with all his responsibilities.

Earning less than $5 an hour take home pay was almost as bad as being a janitor and cook in college, only this job was dangerous. Making the pay more insulting, he learned from his mom that his cousin Pasquale had spent the summer of '81 in Los Angeles and caked $11,000 detailing cars at a Mercedes dealership. Joseph wouldn't make that in a year. The worst part of it all though was that Joseph missed his son's first steps, first words-Dada and Coke, and by winter he was in serious jeopardy of losing their house. Two of his fellow friends from the Academy had felt the financial pinch as well and decided to move on to other departments. Drew Banks had put in his resignation to transfer over to Washington State and Steve House was leaving for the Titusville Police Department in Florida in a few months.

If it wasn't for the gals at Carrows feeding him constantly, he might have withered away with empty pockets. Then right before the holidays of 1981, the city and Police Department decided to take away the $50 a month clothing stipend for Officers and disguise it with a substitution pay raise of .25 cents an hour across the board for all Officers. The clothing stipend was untaxed and they all stood to lose roughly $15 a month after taxes on the weak "pay raise." Joseph was on a strict budget and he felt the effects of the loss of the clothing stipend when he had his electricity turned off for a day because he was $12 short two months in a row. Then he got a $25 reconnect fee added. He felt ashamed to his wife, like he wasn't taking care of Robert like she told him. He had reached his boiling point and was ready to explode.

⚖⚖⚖

One night during a briefing, Ofc. Alvarez overheard mention of a young Officer in need of housing. Joseph had never met the guy before, but people vouched for him so Joseph contacted him and ended up taking on a roommate. He charged 1/3 of his rent. The young Officer Richard Smith was a really good guy and he helped Joseph out a ton with all the aspects that troubled him, from talking about the job to organizing his personal life. Sometimes Joseph would even come home and saw leftovers marked "eat me" and beer marked "drink me" in his fridge from his kind roommate who didn't drink, but knew Joseph enjoyed a cold brew at night to help settle the nerves. The guy was a godsend, he even brought diapers home a couple times and routinely did the dishes. It was also nice to have someone to go to the shooting range with and talk about crimes in different sections of towns. Richard taught Joseph to always do his 2 hours paid shooting with the 50 round monthly allotment early in a week of each month to all but guarantee accrued overtime that week. Water bill.

Meanwhile, Joseph became very involved with the ongoings of the Police Union. He knew the plight of a struggling Officer and was willing to fight for more rights. At one Union discussion about unpaid lunch wages, he brought baby Robert along and one of the Union board members used the dad and son as an example while addressing the contingent of 30 Officers. Gesturing at Joseph and Robert the union Teamster said, "We got Cops over here who don't even see their families enough, but are forced to bring them here because the city wants to ignore our requests and make us fight for what's right." It was so true and the sentiment touched many

Officers personally as they looked over at Joseph with baby and worried about their own expensive holiday's approaching.

Luckily for Joseph, Officer Richard Smith stayed for 4 months from late November in '81 to late March of '82. The time really gave Joseph a chance to catch up on his bills and relaxed him. Officer Smith was unbelievable, he even decorated the yard with luminarias on Christmas eve and made Biscochito cookies for Christmas marked, from: Santa.

An ensuing lunchtime lawsuit filed by the Union was successful and would secure that Officers received an allotted lunch time, paid while on duty.

Chapter 17

Knockout Kings

FROM THE BEGINNING, 1982 would prove a tough year for Joseph, he kept getting in dangerous situations by default as he seemed to be a first responder to many intense situations. January 1, 1982 didn't welcome Joseph to the New Year very kindly. It was a terribly windy day, with dust kicked up all over the city. Joseph was driving down South on Coors Blvd towards Barcelona Drive SW in response to the need for a Spanish interpreter at the scene of a home burglary. Before he arrived to the original call, Joseph was driving past Arenal Road and saw a man across 4 lanes of traffic in a dusty parking lot using a black slim jim or lockpick to break into a parked Cadillac. Ofc. Alvarez radioed in the scene as he pulled a U-turn to investigate.

The heavyset young male car thief was in black pants and a white t-shirt with black gloves on his hands. He stopped breaking into the car to look up at the approaching engine noise. Seeing a Police cruiser with its lights on headed straight for him, the man darted off, dropping his skinny metal burglary tool. The Officer turned on his siren and raced forward. Alvarez was closing in on the portly young man, but as Alvarez pulled up near the Cadillac the man had enough time to jump over a chain link fence into a huge dirt field where a housing development was being constructed. Sand was blowing everywhere on that windy day, but

Joseph was hot on his tail, parking quickly, exiting his vehicle and then jumping the fence with ease in pursuit.

The running man was short and stubby and despite the lead he had, he was no match for the former track star and slightly younger cop. As Joseph ran, he realized he hadn't given the best directions to his location for responding backup and he might be on his own with all this sand obstructing the view of the vacant lots he was running through. He caught up to the '*gordo*' and the man turned around and put up his dukes like he wanted to box the lone pursuer. Upon seeing fists Joseph instinctively spear tackled him. The man swung and missed as he flew backwards under the Officer.

The tackle turned out to be a bad idea as the two crashed into a partially hidden pile of bricks, a laid down ladder, buckets, and some other construction debris previously unnoticeable due to the waves of dirt in the air. The tackle rattled Joseph's whole body. Ofc. Alvarez was injured and started pouring blood from his face. He somehow twisted his left ankle badly and needed stitches over his right eye and under the right side of his chin. His uniform was thrashed and his badge had even been warped to the point that he would need a replacement issued.

The suspect wasn't in much better shape, his mouth was bleeding and he was missing chunks of skin on his arms and back, but he managed to get up and limp off gingerly, taking off into the sandy field. Joseph was hurt bad and he laid down, unable to put weight on his right ankle. He rolled over in pain to reach for his gun and thought about shooting the fleeing felon in the leg, but knew that was a bad idea. His radio reception was useless in that part of town. As he yelled, "Stop" sand swept into his mouth from the wind and he was left with a mouthful of little rocky particles.

Luckily construction workers working on a structure had witnessed the chase and had come down their ladders to surround the man. When the fat car thief tried to escape and get tough with them, one of the workers knocked him out with a right cross, which was later described in the Police report as "subdued the suspect."

Two of the workers came over and spoke Spanish to the Officer, but half in shock from the pain, Joseph was tucking his chin into his neck to stop the flow of blood and didn't want to speak. They got the hint that something was wrong and one ran in the distance to flag down help, using the Officers radio in his parked car. Another construction worker took off his flannel shirt and used a boxcutter to tear off a piece of sleeve and handed it to the Officer. Joseph padded it under his chin, the wad of shirt burned his leaking cut for a moment, but made the blood slow and helped Joseph snap back into his senses. Dust was sticking to all the blood on his face and black uniform.

The first backup unit to arrive was Bernalillo County Sheriff Deputy Bobby Foster who was about 6.5 in his tan uniform. Sheriff Foster was a hulking man, the former 3-time light heavyweight champion of the world who had twice moved up a weight class, having gone toe to toe with Joe Frazier and Muhammad Ali in the 70's. Foster had a perfect V frame and he ran over to handcuff and search the still barely conscious suspect. Squinting his eyes he could see through the dirt storm in the distance that Joseph was down and Foster got up and told the construction workers in Spanish to keep holding the cuffed criminal, which they gladly and forcefully obliged.

The Sheriff was strong as an ox and carefully picked Joseph up with ease from under the legs with his right arm and supporting Joseph's upper back with his left arm. Joseph moaned loudly, "I think my ankles broken." Foster had hands so big that he held Joseph's lower left calf while supporting his wounded ankle still, as he carried him across the dusty field to his squad car to call for an ambulance to step it up. The tall Sheriff kept one eye closed as wind pounded them and both he and Joseph were sweating from the energy they exerted by the time they reached the fence. Sand stuck to their hair, faces, and arms, not to mention both men were not enjoying the dirt sandwich with extra pebbles served up by the dusty desert. Sheriff Foster had parked next to an opening in the fence not too far from where Joseph parked and they didn't have to jump over the fence like Joseph and the car burglar had previously.

Foster laid Joseph in the backseat of his Sheriffs car and carefully helped remove Joseph's left boot, causing the wounded Officer to writhe in pain for a few instances. Foster then went to the front seat and grabbed his full drink from Blake's Lotaburger and laid a green bandana on the ground outside his driver door. He emptied the white cup onto the green cloth, wasting the drink and capturing the little cubes of crushed ice for a makeshift poultice. Foster wrapped up the ice and tied the soaked bandana around then placed it across Joseph's swollen ankle to cool off the swelling. Joseph sat up with the sticky ice pack on his ankle as Foster gave Joseph a first aid kit to patch himself up in the back of the car while help came.

Then Foster made his way back across the windy construction site to get the criminal, getting blasted in sand along the way. He grabbed the heavy dazed criminal by the left leg and dragged him through the dirt field using only his right arm, with his left arm shielding his eyes from the relentless waves of sand. Only the construction workers and the semiconscious criminal witnessed this extraordinary feat of strength, dragging a heavy man like that using only one arm for 100 yards. Once back at the patrol vehicle, the pudgy criminal looked like he had slid into home plate 20 times as the Sheriff secured the man against his tire while he checked on Joseph in his backseat.

Awaiting the ambulance, Joseph was concerned the man might run again and offered Foster his keys to place the subject in his patrol car to which the Sheriff simply replied, "It's okay he knows better than to go anywhere." Joseph had never met the Sheriff before, but knew who he was and he joked with Foster as the ambulance and more units arrived, "Hey Champ does this mean I get your autograph?" With dust in is teeth, Foster figured, "Probably several of them."

Later, laying up on a gurney he thanked Foster with a handshake and said he owed him a coke and a Lotaburger. Foster joked back, "Thanks Meat, but I'm a Vegetarian." Joseph smiled because they both knew the hulk had a cold burger in the front seat awaiting him when this was all over.

Joseph had to spend the night in the hospital where it turns out his ankle was only badly bruised, but the pain came from incurring Achilles tendentious. Doctors estimated him to be unable to run for 3-4 months, but the next day he returned to the construction site in an ankle brace and crutches with donuts for the whole crew of workers and had an apple fritter for the knockout king. That day was a bright sunny day with totally clear skies, free from any dirt storm and Joseph got to shake each one's hand. They spoke in Spanish and the guys were all pumped with excitement recalling what they saw to the cool stitched up Officer before he left.

AFTER A RECOVERY DAY and with his body all beat up, Joseph went to a Claims Validation Officer and had to be reassigned for a few months while his ankle and Achilles healed. He got a desk job as an ID tech at the main station's booking. He would be processing fingerprints and taking mugshots amongst other clerical duties. Other Officers were always around so the crutches or ankle brace to stabilize his Achilles didn't handicap him or put him in danger if a suspect being processed decided to get squirrelly.

The ID tech job was really interesting because he got to process so many different faces and types of criminals. He saw the whole gamut of criminals, teens to grandmas. A big city like Albuquerque had 400,000 innocent people moving about on any given day, but also about 5,000 criminals operating in various insidious ways, day and night. Seeing so many faces and reading what they did, Joseph got a feel for the trends and data that went into the Uniformed Crime Reports that Police collected for FBI statistics. A lot of burglaries and domestic violence seemed to be a large bulk of offenses in the city. Processing was very rewarding professionally because he learned more about criminal behaviors and patterns, but being behind the scenes could never compare with slapping the steel on the wrists of the criminals himself.

One thing about being off the streets that he did like was that the Department gave him an unmarked take home car and he was actually able to make it home on time to relieve his babysitters for a change. He really got to spend some quality hours with his son Robert, who taught his dad everyday about providing. The demands of being a Dad were so hard, especially on crutches, but the second that baby smiled at him, just for him, all the sacrifices made sense. Aside from the extra family time, another great perk to pushing papers was that Joseph used this desk job time wisely and signed up for every type of training he could fit into his weekly schedule. Additionally, he was able to get a handle on scheduling himself for court and billing the department accordingly, earning his appropriate overtime from there on out.

On slow nights he had moments of downtime where he was actually able to read newspaper articles for brief moments to catch up on politics, sports and the recession that was being combated by Reaganomics. The world seemed so distant to him now, he realized that his existence was so defined by his work against crime. Things that used to matter took a backseat to keeping his eyes peeled for trouble in the city he now called home and loved.

In February of '82, Joseph couldn't believe his eyes one day reading the local paper at the Police station. Ozzy Osbourne, the lead singer of his favorite band Black Sabbath had been arrested for defiling a national monument when he pissed on the grounds of the Alamo in San Antonio, TX. Joseph was smiling in disbelief, this one was so good he actually cut the article out to show his cohorts. "Man, why couldn't he have pissed on something in Albuquerque" Joseph joked in his head, "I would have got to process him." Cops have a funny sense of humor. Then suddenly while reading the paper, Joseph received word that the Chief wanted him in his office. Joseph got a little jolt of anxious tension, but knew it was probably nothing and calmly checked on everyone at his post then excused himself to head to the top floor. Still in crutches, even the simple task of walking was now slow and methodic.

This was only the 3rd time ever that Joseph was called to the Chiefs Office directly, but the first time by the new Chief Sam Baca. His first Chief visit was September 11, 1980 after Officer Chacón died and because he was first on scene the Chief wanted to talk to him. His second Chief visit was in May of 1981 when Joseph returned to work after his wife died and Chief Eloy Hanson offered condolences. It had been a while, but Joseph knew this was a good opportunity to network with the boss in charge. Joseph took the elevator up and was happy when an attractive young lady from Evidence joined him briefly from his basement floor to the 2nd. Then he continued up to the top floor and exited stage left.

After 4pm the Chief's Secretary went home, so Joseph knocked and heard the Chief say, "Come in." He opened the wood door with mystery, entering quietly to hear the Chief say, "Go ahead and shut the door behind you." The corner office faced East and South, overlooking downtown and with a good view of the Manzano Mountains and a great view of the Sandias. To Joseph's right were a sleeper sofa and a television stand, with a little kitchen area behind it with only a microwave, small fridge, and a coffee maker. Left of the kitchen was a private bathroom and the door was open, revealing a sink, toilet and a standup shower.

In front of Joseph, a giant oak desk with two leather wood chairs in front for guests and the Chief sitting behind it in a nicer rolling leather chair. Behind the Chief were two windows perfectly framing the Sandia Mountains in the distance. The Chief was on his desk phone and he covered the mouth of the yellow phone for a second, pointing with his chin to tell Joseph "Grab us both a coke will ya, then have a seat?" Joseph carefully walked to the mini fridge and grabbed a couple bottles then found the bottle opener on top. He went and sat down at the desk with the sodas and the Chief gave a head nod in approval.

While Joseph waited for the Chief to get off the phone call, he remembered in the Academy that the media tried to portray the shower and kitchen installations in this office as frivolous government spending by the old outgoing Chief Bob Stover. They tried to make a big deal about it, but the Chief's wife explained the reality of the office to the News in a live statement outside a City Council meeting. A female reporter wearing a wedding ring said something to the effect of what do you think of your husband's new office paid for by taxpayers.

The Chief's wife was walking to her car and caught off guard, but took umbrage and went from casual to fiery, she swung back with, "Do you know what it's like to spend the night in your husband's office sharing a couch bed after eating TV dinners at TWO AM because you haven't seen him in a week. You think he wants to shower at work, are you kidding me?" The reporter tried to say something smart, but the Chief's boss cut her off and continued, "And that's our microwave from home, our fridge, OUR TV that you're complaining about!! The only time he watches that thing is to see the news, in case he has to waste his time and respond to any absurdities created about this hard-working department from news people like you!" She walked away from the wide-eyed reporter and the news never showed the statement again or brought up the office renovations after that.

When Chief Baca finished his phone call that had something to do with federal funding, he asked Joseph, "How's the ankle? Heard you twisted it up pretty good." Joseph explained that it was okay and his Achilles was getting better. "Good, you've been a fine Officer since joining us and we need you back on the streets in good time." Before Joseph could thank the praise, the Chief continued with the heart of the matter. "So that car thief you tackled is suing the department and suing you for some dental work."

Joseph caught himself exhaling in protest, "Tsssuh" just like his own Dad did on occasion when he disagreed with something. The Chief said, "I know, I know. Don't even worry about it though you've got a strong counter suit and I don't even know why the hell his lawyer is trying, but I thought I'd give you the heads up myself. We've already got our lawyers working on it and they suggested that its best for you just to represent yourself since you'll still be on crutches. We'll get everything prepared and be sitting in the courtroom if you need an assist." Then another call came in for the Chief and Joseph excused himself remembering to take his drink, which was quite hard to carry and not spill on crutches.

Joseph successfully countersued a few weeks later. Aside from his recovering physical appearance, his mangled badge was all the evidence the Judge needed to rule in his favor. Those were not easy to warp. Ofc. Alvarez remained an ID tech for nearly 3 months until his ankle and bruised Achilles recovered. That week another Officer Chris Martinez won a ruling from the city to install cages in squad cars. Just like he had many times before, Ofc. Martinez was escorting an arrestee to jail. Driving on Carlisle Blvd., he was turning on to the freeway watching out for oncoming traffic when the handcuffed suspect pulled up his legs and double donkey kicked the Officer in the head. Perfectly timed it. Knocked out, the Officer's vehicle accelerated and crashed down into arroyo injuring both himself and the suspect, totaling the vehicle. Cages were installed in the months to come and all cars were finished being outfitted while Joseph was recovering his Achilles. Now prisoners would sit in the back and Officers were up front protected by a cage barrier.

On April 3rd, 1982 Joseph officially hit the streets again. He had never been so happy to see a Plymouth Volare patrol car. First things first, Joseph took the car to a cop buddy Duke Oliver's house who had a hose and buckets to clean the car while Officer Oliver cleaned his Police motorcycle. Joseph cleaned out the filthy cop car that was previously used by an unknown smoker and chip aficionado as he vacuumed out various types of snacks. While he cleaned, Joseph put baby Robert and the other Officers son on the roof to play with the red light covers as Oliver's wife looked on.

Cleaning the backseat, Joseph reached his hand into the gap slit between the cloth seat and cloth chairback to find something wedged down there as deeply possible in the crevice. Pressing up against the seat to get a good angle he carefully scissored his index and middle fingers together and struggled to pull out something. He showed his fellow Officer and they were both equally shocked at the discovery, a small plastic bag of cocaine. They radioed in an on-duty patrol unit and filled out a report before tagging the anonymous bag into evidence after no prints were found on it, other than Joseph's partials from grabbing the bag before he knew what it was.

HIS SECOND NIGHT BACK he was down at the jail to interview a prisoner in Spanish. Police have to turn in their weapons and duty belt into a locker at the jail lobby before they enter. Only a tape recorder went in, no pens allowed. After trying to interview an uncooperative inmate, Joseph was buzzed through a door into a normally secure room and walked right behind a prisoner in an orange jumpsuit that was trying to fight two guards. Unarmed, Joseph instinctively reached down and put the man in a standing choke from behind using both arms. The little guy bucked and scratched up onto his face so Joseph sunk the choke in tighter to pinch the carotid artery. Holding on and squeezing onto the man's throat with his right forearm and elbow under his chin while pushing the back of the man's head forward from behind with his left arm until he felt the man go limp.

Both guards jumped on the man's arms and Joseph let the man gently fall into their custody, the guy was out. They brought him to the floor and laid him down. 15 seconds passed, 30 and the prisoner still wasn't conscious or breathing. Joseph was starting to sweat and suggesting resuscitation. 45 seconds, Joseph assisted in the attempts at getting the man conscious. "You guys have a doctor here?" Joseph asked panicked as they smacked and yelled. The guards weren't as concerned, but played the part as they slapped around and shouted at the man. Joseph started to yell for more help. Finally, the jail prisoner took some shallow breaths. Joseph exhaled as well.

It was really scary the more he thought about it that night. His hands were shaking all night recalling the sounds of agonal breathing. He couldn't sleep, couldn't watch TV. Joseph just sat for a good while in his living room and thought, while his little guy slept. Looking into his mirror after midnight, he stared deep into his own soul for longer than a minute. He reached down to put away a toothbrush and saw his hand still trembling a little. The inmates last name had been Alvarez. Splashing some water on his face with both hands, he then dried his hands on a towel, turned off the light and went to bed. He slept the best he could.

April 17th, 1982. 8th Street just off Bellamah Ave NW.

On the same day Canada officially gained its independence from the United Kingdom, Joseph ran into his 2nd bad news Johnny from Wells Park. John Lee Tapia was a troubled 14-year-old with no parents raising him. Johnny's dad was in jail and he never met him, thinking for the majority of his life that his father was dead. When he was only a child, his mom had been kidnapped by her boyfriend and was chained to the back of a truck right before Johnny's eyes. The young kid yelled for help to people, but nobody believed the kid's wild story, that was until she was found by Police the next day, brutalized and murdered.

Also, as a child Tapia was on a city bus that fell off a bridge 40 ft into the icy water of the Rio Grande. Not many people survived the bus crash and Johnny had tried to help a pregnant lady with another small child that had been sitting next to him, but they both perished drowning before his eyes. The kid was as tough as they come and wise beyond his years. Officer Alvarez ran into Johnny Tapia when he was dispatched to the call of a disturbance in progress in the 1500 block of 8th Street NW.

Ofc. Alvarez pulled up to the address of a small brown 1-story adobe with a square front yard lawn surrounded by a 4-foot-high chain link fence, its gate right in the middle. He noticed two men in red and brown flannel shirts inside the confines of the fence, standing finishing a cigarette in front of the residence on a little front porch with a window on each side of the front door. Joseph had been called to this same address as a Rookie when the same two men got into a bloody and violent fistfight with each other and broke their mom's television. This time the young Hispanic men were pointing down the street like victims and were adamant enough to come down from their porch and open the gate to point down the sidewalk as Ofc. Alvarez stepped out of his vehicle after radioing in his location status.

Alvarez looked down the sidewalk and saw a light skinned teenage boy 9 houses down, walking away in black shorts, a white tank top undershirt and with short brown hair, including a rat tail he grew on the bottom of the back of his head. Joseph hollered out to the boy to "Get back over here," and the boy turned around, shrugged his shoulders and started walking back towards the Officer very slowly. Ofc. Alvarez recognized the boy when he got a little closer. Joseph knew some of the young boy's troubled history and that his primary sanctuary was Amateur boxing for the Police Athletic League, where he was a local star.

As Johnny Tapia walked towards the Officer, Alvarez questioned the two brothers while keeping an eye on the approaching youngster. The two brothers were in their early 20's, but apparently they had a younger 16-year-old brother who had pissed young Johnny off something awful and Tapia wasn't about to leave until somebody in the family fought him. The brothers stated that Johnny refused to leave and stood on the sidewalk threatening the family and intimidating them. Ofc. Alvarez asked, "Did he ever step onto your property?" The older brother pointed inside their yard and said "Shit yeah man, he came right there." Then Johnny appeared saying "Don't lie A, all I did was touch your fence," then Tapia looked at the Officer and said, "I put that Sir I never walked in!" Ofc. Alvarez raised his hand then brought it down in a lowering motion for the young man to calm down then looked at the younger brother, "So did he step onto the property?" The younger brother glanced at Johnny and then put his head straight down saying, "Not even!"

Obviously there was more to the story, but Joseph preferred "I put that Sir" over "Shit yeah man" and he then told the brothers, "Well I suggest you invite your little brother to go to down to Johnny's gym and box Johnny with gloves before they end up meeting on the street with fists!" The two brothers and Tapia got big eyes and surprised looks from the Officer's comment. Johnny smiled at the brothers until Joseph said "As for you Mr. Tapia, I'm issuing you a 365-day written warning for trespassing and if you come on this street near this home again you go to jail no questions asked." Joseph spent 10 minutes gathering info and writing out the 1-year no trespassing ordinance. He gave both parties a copy as well as keeping his own. Then Joseph told the brothers, "Thank you Gentlemen good day" and he looked at Johnny and said firmly with a gesture to his vehicle, "Now you, get in my car." Johnny Tapia lined up at the back door of the cruiser and put his hands on the vehicle to be frisked, but was surprised when Joseph unlocked the front passenger door and hollered "Get in!" Joseph walked around to the driver side and the teen hopped in suspiciously after the Officer did. Ofc. Alvarez took off driving after reminding Johnny to put on his seatbelt.

Nothing was said between the two until they turned onto Lomas Blvd heading East looking at the mountains and Joseph began, "Listen kid, you got a lot of talent and you don't need to be out here hustling and bustling with these losers. Okay! Apply yourself and keep your fights in the ring, these idiots out here are killing each other every day over nothing, just because." Joseph lectured and looked at the boy, but he said no more as he pulled into a Burger King. Joseph asked the kid if he wanted something and Johnny humbly shook his head no. "Well come inside anyway, before I get you on with your day." He took Johnny inside and ordered them both a Whopper with fries and a drink.

He handed the boy a free auto trader publication while they waited for the food and Johnny checked out some cars silently. They didn't say much as Johnny scarfed the food down like it was his last meal. As he finished his fries Johnny finally spoke, "You got kids Sir?" Alvarez replied, "Yeah…I got a baby son, he's almost two." Then Johnny looked down and said, "Oh cool well…when he gets older if he ever needs a boxing lesson," then Tapia didn't say anything else and got up to ask for a drink refill before they left. In the Police car Joseph reminded Johnny to put on his seatbelt then drove him over to his trainer's house in the North Valley. His trainer was always glad to see the kid alive.

Johnny Tapia would go on to win National Golden Gloves as an Amateur before becoming a Professional and 5-time world champion boxer who captured titles in 3 weight divisions from 115-126lbs. All covered in tattoos, his nickname was Johnny "Mi Vida Loca" Tapia and despite his many successes, he lived "my crazy life" having lots of rough times with drugs and violence outside of the ring, including surviving attempted murders and overdoses. No matter what, he remained loyal to his city after every bout and people loved him for how authentic he was. Win or lose he always kept it real and said, "I love you Burque." He rarely lost and constantly gave performances that were nominated for Fight of the Year globally.

Chapter 18

The Four Corners

THERE IS ONLY ONE PLACE in the United States where the borders of four States connect into one point. The area is known as the Four Corners and includes converging points from SE Utah, NE Arizona, SW Colorado and NW New Mexico. The Four Corners area offering a peak into four beautiful States, where beyond the tourist monument their landscapes remain virtually untouched and desolate for millenniums. The area is also known for its cold winters with huge snow-storms. Home to part of the Navajo Nation, which is the largest Native American land preserve in the country. The reservation stretches over 25,000 square miles from Arizona and into parts of Utah and New Mexico. Back in 1982, the sovereign land had around 90,000 tribal members with laws enforced by their own Navajo Tribal Police. The Diné are a proud and beautiful people.

In Albuquerque's tough South Broadway neighborhood at the stoplights on Broadway Blvd and Trumbull Ave there were 4 liquor Bars near the corners of the busy intersection. Smack in the middle of the hood, the four bars were a haven for trouble making. The bars became the most popular hangouts for Black folk to get a cheap drink and after a while, hardly anyone other than some Mexicans from the same area neighborhood would go there anymore. The bars were always packed, especially on weekends when there could be over 50 people in each one of the four medium sized bars. The drinking age was only 18 in Albuquerque at that time and there were always a lot of youngsters mixing it up with older men at "The Corners" bars, the nickname given by local law enforcement.

Adding to the popularity of The Corners were street vendors who brought the intoxicated patrons out onto the sidewalks and parking lots. Different hot dog vendors, taco carts, and other food vendors came down to the busy intersection to sell, especially on weekends. The enchilada burrito guy made a fortune and always had a line all night. The Corners had been popular now for a few years and the parties kept growing with the population. A few times in the 1970's Officers were outnumbered and attacked inside and outside The Corners bars.

Other times after that, Police had to watch petty crimes occur right before their eyes while they waited for additional units because it was too dangerous to respond alone to any of the bars. Sometimes criminals got away in plain view, there was nothing Police could do without numbers. Every time Police entered one of the bars it seemed like something crazy happened, so Police stopped entering the rowdy bars on busy nights without at least 5 Officers in riot helmets.

ONE COOL APRIL NIGHT Joseph and another Officer Mike King, responded in their cars to the front of the NE bar of The Corners, the Palomas Bar, in reference to a fight out on the sidewalk. When the two Officers arrived, there wasn't any fighting taking place. The Cops asked people walking around the area about the reported fight, but of course nobody saw or said anything. Ofc. King was 23yrs young and strong, one of the big guys on the force he stood tall in his boots 6.4 200lbs. He had some grey action growing prematurely in his brown hair, but not his mustache.

Finished wasting time, the two Officers hopped back into their patrol cars and parked across the street. They maneuvered facing opposite directions with their driver windows next to each other so they could guard each other's backs and talk while they kept an eye out for any fights or trouble. They were parked next to the Elks Lodge, another of The Corners bars. The bars were busy, but nothing exciting happened as the Officers kept their eyes peeled and chatted with their lights off. Both Officers were fascinated by the newly installed computers in their console and shared a couple tricks with each other. Alvarez showed King how to enter license plates without having to radio it in to a dispatcher. Joseph always had pens to write information down, sometimes on his hand if he needed to and King showed him how to record a note into the system.

Under the cloak of darkness, the Officers were just about to leave when Ofc. King spotted two suspicious Black males under the light of a taco stand and nudged his chin up for Joseph to take a look back. Sure enough the two suspicious men exchanged money and what appeared to be a small plastic bag with something white in it. Officers King and Alvarez witnessed the possible hand to hand drug transaction from across the street.

The one young man who had the drugs and took the money was wearing a distinctive orange muscle shirt with gold necklaces and rings, he also had a full beard and freshly cut Afro. Within a couple seconds the man who bought the drugs disappeared into the darkness and the suspected dealer in the orange shirt went back into the Palomas Bar as Officer King radioed for at least three backup units with riot gear. "Shit" Joseph said, "Now we have to go in there if he doesn't come out soon."

They both drove back across the street and parked in front of the Palomas bar at 401 Trumbull Ave SE. As they waited, the two Officers kept an eye on the lone door in the front and the emergency exit on the side of the bar as they suited up in their battle gear. Awaiting the calvary, they snapped the leather straps under their chins on their two-tone blue riot helmets while they devised a plan.

Four Units arrived within minutes with five additional Officers totaling 7 now, including another giant, none other than Drew Banks who had only three weeks left with the department until he transferred to Washington State Patrol. Some of the Officers were eager to enter the well-known bar and the others were saying things like, "Here we go again with these damn Corners bars." An ominous feeling of a fight brewed amongst the 7 Officers as mingling patrons had seen them now. There was only one Black Officer, Kenny Williams. He had graduated the Academy with Joseph and actually spoke fluent Spanish having grown up in Albuquerque's South Valley where he joked it was necessary to survive middle school. Williams gave advice to everybody saying, "Let's be cool, but you guys watch out last time I was in here things got rowdy, let me try talking to them."

There was one superior Officer, Lt. Ed Griffin and the calm elder statesmen instructed everyone on a game plan to minimize the threat of violence. "We're going to form a wall, hand on the guy in front of you. Kenny and I will lead, the plan is to convince the orange shirt to surrender and try to get out of there without incident. This would be ideal, but if we have to extract and in the event that things go sour, crack anyone who crosses the line and fight back-to-back." He partnered the Officers to make sure everybody had someone to, "Watch their SIX." Once the entry team of 7 was all geared up, they entered the bar to go find the orange tank-top wearing drug dealer.

When the Officers walked in the bar with their helmets on and hickory sticks in hand, the massive bouncer at the entrance wearing all black moved aside and rested his right arm on a cigarette machine and lifted his left hand to allow entry. He shook his head knowing this could go bad as they entered into the main room. There was a long wood bar to the left with 3 bartenders and 20 occupied stools while dozens of small round bar tables with stools were occupied to the right. In the back were restrooms, 8 pool tables in two rows of 4 and racks of pool cues and stools lining the walls. With over 50 people moving about, The Police formed a horizontal wall for intimidation. Ofc King was on the far right and unplugged the loud jukebox, killing the sweet voice of Marvin Gaye and drawing the attention of the patrons.

Officer Alvarez easily spotted the orange shirt over behind the 8 pool tables in the back of the bar. Alvarez pointed and said, "Look Mike he just shoved an eight ball into the corner pocket! No pun intended." The

6 other Officers smirked at the comment as Ofc. Williams pointed his nightstick and motioned with his free index finger at the suspect in the orange shirt to come towards them and across the room announced, "YOU in the orange, come over here and save everyone else from any trouble." Hundreds of eyes flashed to the young man and he knew the gig was up and reached down to grab his drugs out of the corner pocket. The Officers walked toward him and he slowly approached in between two pool tables toward the Officers with a look of defeat.

Only he was playing coy and bolted towards the bathroom that was behind him to flush the evidence. Joseph had the best path through the pool tables and he sprinted towards the bathroom and all the Officers ran in file behind him. As Joseph made his way past the pool tables, he felt a hard smack on the back of his helmet and he witnessed skinny wood shards from a pool cue fly out in front of both sides of his face. Alvarez maneuvered into a duck and spun around to kick somebody's ass, but it looked like Mike King and Drew Banks had things under control.

Officer King doubled as a professional kick boxer in his spare time and he had the tall man who busted the pool cue over Joseph's helmet bent over a pool table by the back of his neck. The crowd didn't like that and bottles began to fly at the Officers as King tried to handcuff the man, who was resisting by pressing his weight on top of his clenched hands. In an instant, dozens of men and women hurled drinks and heavy napkin holders toward the 7 Officers while a few others started throwing punches at the Officers and a few more began swinging pool cues. Forget the drug dealer, the fight was on for all the Officers and it quickly became like a wild bar fight in a movie scene.

Thuds and broken glass sounded off in all directions, luckily the Officers were suited up after hearing stories from these bars that were now living up to their reputations. Fists and bottles were flying everywhere and anybody who approached the Officers was fair game for a whooping. Ofc. Alvarez used one arm to swing his billy club and hit a home run into the ribs of a young dark skinned Hispanic looking man from behind who had raised a pool stick, but released the weapon and now doubled over in pain. Joseph didn't have time to cuff him so he stiff armed his head into the side of a pool table and kept a lookout as chaos erupted all around.

Ofc. King ducked a flying bottle as he bent the original pool cue aggressor over onto the pool table determined to free the criminals clenched hands to cuff him, even if it meant breaking the man's wrists. While King freed one of the man's hands, he checked his rear and literally threw a high kick into the temple of a 6-foot-tall rushing man in a blue flannel, knocking the youngster unconscious on top of the pool table like something out of a Bruce Lee movie. Joseph looked over as King had 2 men on 1 pool table, then pressed the conscious man's face smack down into the pool table to finally free his hands. SMASH! Caught looking, a bottle clipped Joseph's helmet and shattered loudly in a wall behind him.

Joseph's ears rang and he had no idea who threw that particular bottle, but then Joseph focused on 2 men smacking Drew Banks in the back, one with a glass pitcher wearing grey and the other with a beer bottle in beige as Banks was attempting to cuff a different aggressor. Alvarez ran forward and used his billy club to smack the beer bottle out the tall man's hand in beige. He followed up with a thrust to his stomach and as the bottler reached down to grab the nightstick, Joseph cocked back with both arms and came down onto the man's leg with a club so hard it sent the man to the floor in agony, scooting away under a billiards table as Joseph tried to grab his ankle and keep an eye out.

Ofc. Banks was still struggling to cuff his resister and protect himself from the other attacker in grey, who dropped his glass pitcher, turned and clobbered Joseph with a haymaker to his mouth from the Officers blindside as he just grabbed the ankle of the bottler under the table. Ofc. Alvarez stumbled back a few steps then shook off the pain and saw the man who punched him reaching forward towards his holstered gun. Joseph dropped his nightstick and turned his body as the man's hand got onto the gun handle. As they struggled, he reached down inside the pocket of the man's blue sweatpants and grabbed the man's testicles, jerking them into a twist. The man raised his hands, closed his eyes and yelled like a horror movie victim as his knees buckled from his testicles pain and he desperately grabbed Josephs arm. Joseph squeezed again and the man surrendered in agony and he placed handcuffs on him.

Chaos was everywhere for a solid minute when many people could hear one of the Officers Brichetto, use his lead slapper to smack onto the forehead of a man who had snuck behind the Officer and was trying to choke him out in between two pool tables. A lady screamed at the thump from the Officers slapper, her shriek so terrifying that just about everybody looked over as the man fell to the floor unconscious, his body a pretzel underneath as the side of his head leaned on a pool table and his forehead lumped up like a golfball. By that point everybody was grabbing their things and running out the door.

After a long minute or two, most of the bar patrons had exited the fiasco and three of the Officers finally made their way into the bathroom and opened the door only to find the original orange shirt suspect wasn't there. There was a small rectangular window in the bathroom, but it seemed impossible he could escape it. He was gone, somehow sneaking past all 7 Officers during all the mayhem. The 3 Officers in the bathroom turned around and joined back in the aftermath of the fight as it winded down to handcuffing anyone they had seen fighting. Every Officer arrested a person that they had witnessed attack an Officer in some fashion.

As the Officers walked the 6 men and 1 woman out, they saw the giant bouncer in all black still leaning on the cigarette machine. Only below the bouncer he had added an unconscious drug dealer next to his left foot, it was the man in the orange shirt and he was literally snoring bubbles into his own spit and blood coming from his lips. When they booked the dealer downtown, he got charged with refusing to obey, tampering with evidence and intent to distribute. The man from Palatka, Florida had his charges reduced to a probation violation because they never found any money, drugs, or paraphernalia on him despite seven Cops plain view witness of his actions that led to the brawl.

The fighting had lasted 73 seconds in total and the Officers were in the bar for less than 10 minutes. Yet when the Officers gathered outside afterwards, a few of their cars had been spray-painted with graffiti and one squad car had its driver mirror punched out and two tires slashed, adding insult to injuries. The Officers all secured the detainees in their vehicles before attending to their variety of pains. Lt. Ed Griffin went back inside and yelled at the two bar owners for a minute, thanked the bouncer and then returned outside to check on each of his troops as they finished reading off Miranda rights. Lt. Griffin went around inspecting them, himself with a torn shirt and a pretty nice scratch across his cheek after stumbling over a stool wrestling a guy and then getting whacked by a flying pool cue as he stood back up.

Joseph was fine, sporting only a fat lip that he was checking on in a mirror and spitting out a little blood from his gums. Ofc. Williams had a blood-stained shirt from a bloody nose that was still dripping onto the parking lot before he plugged it with a napkin. Ofc. Williams had arrested the only girl because she threw a bottle that clipped his nose and then broke a beer bottle intentionally and pointed its jagged edges at the Officer. She undoubtedly had a broken wrist after the smackdown he gave her forearm with his hickory stick for holding the lethal weapon. He had lectured her a solid five minutes when she complained about her wrist and being cuffed, he made her realize he was seconds away from shooting her dead for her attack.

Two of the Officers sustained minor cuts on their arms and Banks on his neck from the bottle or pitcher. Ofc. Brichetto from Toledo, Ohio was covered in salsa and had a shiner under his eye that would quickly turn black and purple as he cracked a joke to his Lt. in his Bugs Bunny voice, "You know, I knew I should of made that left turn in Albuquerque." The guys all laughed as Griffin told them all what a fine job they did. Ofc. King only had a bruised knuckle, some beer on his shirt and under his moustache a huge smile at his motley crew.

The Officers began talking as they gathered themselves from the adrenaline dump. Drew Banks walked over and thanked Joseph for covering his back by one armed hugging him across the shoulder while smiling and telling Joseph, "Man I'm going to miss days like this Joe."

Then Banks asked, "Hey is it true what they say about Black guys, did you get a hand full of meat with those nuts you grabbed." Joseph gave him a scowl, then Ofc. Williams honked his groin at the remark and said, "Why don't you come over here and find out." Banks calmly replied with his index finger upward, "Only if you buy me dinner first." All 7 of the Officers started laughing hysterically before many either lit a cigarette or threw a dip of tobacco in their mouth to decompress. The battle buddies joked for weeks to come every time they thought about that good ol' boy comment from Banks and Ofc Williams doing a Michael Jackson crotch grab in response.

10 minutes after the fight, an ambulance drove up to check on the Officers. The medical team of three must have thought the Cops were crazy looking, even more when they took some Band-Aids, but waived off any assistance for themselves, instead insisting that the detainees get checked out. Police Field Investigators came out and photographed the damaged cars as well as the injuries of all the Officers and those arrested, each covered in beer and with a nice story to tell. The Fire Department arrived to write some code violations to the bar on bequest of Lt. Griffin after the debacle.

A week after the bar brawl Joseph saw Mike King at a Circle K in the "hood" and they both grabbed some coffee and chatted. Joseph still had a slightly fattened lip and asked Mike about his black eye. "Is that from the fight at the Palomas?" "Nah man that's from training," as Mike then proudly shared some info, "Hey Joe I talked to anybody who's anybody and they say we have the craziest Corners story of all. My Sarge told me that the Chief told L.T. that our Kung Fu crew probably shouldn't go into those bars anymore." Joseph smiled and said sarcastically, "You think he just meant the Palomas Bar because you know there's three more at The Corners!" King was getting ready to leave and gave Joseph a pat on the shoulder and said, "My kind of guy Joe." Then King said goodnight to the clerks on his way out while Joseph went into the back to use the employee only bathroom. Like many gas stations they took care of the Police.

Despite countless incidents, The Corners bars remained unruly on most weekends. Many of the drunk patrons were known to leave the four bars to go puke, piss, panhandle, and pervert the surrounding neighborhoods. It was so bad that a local Baptist preacher and several small business owners met with Officers and City Councilors to try and strategize a way to protect the community surrounding the bars. In June of 1982, two months after the pool cue fight, the City of Albuquerque funded a special project to curb the four corners' bars behavior. A special sensor was funded and installed on top of a street pole on Trumball Avenue just East of Broadway Blvd and The Corners bars. Any patrol vehicle could drive up below the sensor and angle their cars spotlight up to shine into it. The sensor would then trigger from the lumens and shut down the power for almost an entire city block.

The next time Joseph got called to the Palomas Bar was in August of 1982 when the Fire Department ordered the bar shut down because of occupancy violations and electrical hazards. Nobody in the bar thought to respect the Fire Department, but the Firefighters knew about the new sensor and momentarily left the bar to summon Police to use the spotlight sensor. Joseph arrived alone and after a quick chat with a Fire Captain he drove up Trumball Ave, parked and angled his spotlight to shine the sensor. He was impressed as all the lights went out for more than 10 streets in different directions, including The Corners bars, all four of them. Ofc. Alvarez sat for minutes and watched the bar patrons scamper out into the darkness, yelping about like confused coyotes.

A Fire Captain let the other 3 bar owners know that the lights were shut down because the Palomas Bar refused to comply. After that loss of business, the 4 bars maintained an accurate count of those who entered, in order to never exceed the occupancy limits imposed by the Fire Department. By the end of the summer of '82 the drinking age was raised from 18 to 21 in Albuquerque to help keep all the "Peewees" away, helping reduce crime amongst young people.

That summer in Hollywood a terrible accident happened on set. Joseph's favorite actor growing up Vic Morrow was killed with two young child actors. The Jersey Shore native was filming a Vietnam flashback scene, when some pyrotechnics exploded into a lifting helicopters tail and the four rotary blades inverted. It was a horrible situation for the actor and the poor kids on the ground who were chopped up and died instantly. The film industry had to reexamine strict child safety procedures after that.

Chapter 19

The Eye of Vigilance

ON SEPTEMBER 11TH 1982, Joseph turned 24 years old. A few weeks before he had planned ahead and traded shifts to treat himself to a night off work and some of his Cop buddies promised him a night out on the town he'd never forget out. He was all excited that morning, waking up early and making himself a pot of coffee to accompany a giant omelet with bacon. While his infant son slept, he was enjoying the worry-free day and reminiscing in his youth by laughing hysterically watching Loony Tunes. He missed his family, he missed home and he really missed Eileen.

The night before, Joseph was gifted a tactical fanny pack by Al Byrnes and his wife to carry his pistol, badge and handcuffs when off duty. He practiced quick drawing dozens of times in a mirror with its drawstring opening the zipper to reveal his gun. Then his mom called him at 9:00 o'clock sharp, waking baby Robert up. Robert was crying a little louder than usual and after a quick happy birthday song of *Las Mañanitas* from his parents, Joseph promised to call her back, but hung up to go check on the baby. Joseph knew something was wrong immediately as his boy ran a fever. He bundled up toddler Robert in a blanket, put on his fanny pack then grabbed his mini duffle bag of diaper and supplies to head for the Emergency room.

While 2-year-old Robert was being treated for dehydration from diarrhea, Joseph used a hospital phone to call his friends and cancel the evening to take care of his son. As he dialed, he suddenly heard a commotion of nurses and a bunch of loud yelling in the waiting room. An unruly man being admitted into the next room was fighting with nurses and Joseph assisted in restraining him to the point where doctors had to physically strap his arms and legs to a hospital bed. He recognized the man, but couldn't place where from, when it dawned on him.

It was the first man he had ever handcuffed, for beating his wife half to death. Joseph remembered the kind Vietnamese woman who he and Ted Keoppinger drove to this same hospital that night. Turns out the husband had continued his abusive ways and she had poisoned a jar of sun tea he liked to mix with vodka. He was completely delirious in his tirade and Joseph stood by as he struggled with Doctors who fought to get a tube down his throat to pump his stomach of the toxins. Happy Birthday Officer.

ON THANKSGIVING OF 1982, Joseph took a half hour lunch and ate some turkey tamales with mashed potatoes at the little family owned El Dorado Bakery on Broadway and Gibson SE. He left the bakery and drove a short distance North up Broadway, turning left on Cromwell Ave near the Railyard. He was just cruising slowly and spotted a bunch of teenagers on the lone basketball court at the small Guadalupe Park. Joseph decided to go investigate. He hopped out of his car and approached the kids who met him with suspicion, the tallest one saying, "We didn't do anything." Joseph said "Relax guys I just want to play too." They smiled because they were only 5 and a sixth man meant they could play 3 on 3. Joseph played basketball with the teens for 20 minutes in full uniform, getting schooled in a sport he was never great at. Then duty called as his radio reported someone breaking glass a few blocks down. He high fived a couple of kids as he ran to his car and said he would be back one day for his revenge, the teens all smiling and talking about the radio transmission.

Later on that Thanksgiving night, Joseph was on a routine patrol with his ever-watchful eyes looking for trouble. The night had grown cold, he could see his every warm breath turning into little clouds as they mixed with the cold air. His shift would be over soon and driving slowly he looked over next to the basketball court at Guadalupe Park where he had just had fun hours before. Something caught his attention. He pulled his car up to the park facing North on the wrong side of John Street SE, stopping his car and turning off his lights. What first appeared to be the breaths of a young man now looked to be clouds of smoke and then he saw a lighter spark up and a young black haired Hispanic male take a hit of a glass pipe. Ofc Alvarez radioed in that he was investigating a subject.

He then rolled down his window, angled his spotlight at the man and flipped the switch on, the bright light shining onto the man who was some 25 feet away sitting down smoking his pipe. Ofc. Alvarez still had his Motorola car radio in hand, the cord extending over the Officers console, he heard his backup partner radio in just as the man stood up, dropping his glass pipe onto the grass below and he began walking towards the Officer. Wearing a long dark jacket, hair over down his face the man appeared a little off when Joseph saw his bloodshot red eyes. Suddenly from out of his jacket pocket the man raised his right arm and produced a hidden ax, raising it up into a throwing motion.

Joseph dropped his car radio, unbuckled his seatbelt and drew out his pistol. The man was within 10 feet of the Officer and could easily throw the ax into the window as Joseph screamed, "Put it down right now, I'll kill you!!" The man's eyes grew wider and he looked angry and puzzled as Joseph pleaded again louder, "Put the ax down, don't make me kill you." The man didn't budge. "Put it down now!" Joseph said as he realized he had accidentally cocked his pistol in the quick draw from a seated position, now he had a hairline trigger ready to shoot his gun centered on the man's chest. Then it happened.

The man dropped his ax and complied with Joseph's orders to step away and put his hands up. Breathing hard, Joseph opened his door, but waited for another unit to arrive before stepping out and handcuffing the man. The young man was high on PCP and went to the park to smoke marijuana where he ended up with charges of possession of marijuana, drug paraphernalia and aggravated assault on Joseph. His ax shocking both a Sargeant and later a Lieutenant who came to check on things. The Lieutenant took Joseph over to the park so he could slowly release his cocked pistol lever, pointing the gun towards the ground when he did. It's was very nerve-wracking to un-cock a live round under his Lt's flashlight.

The incident at the park and its aftermath ate up more than three hours of Joseph's time. Upon further investigation into the man at the park, they interviewed his mom and found out he had one older brother who was shot dead by an Undercover Police Officer two months earlier. The Undercover had to reveal himself when witnessing the brother stabbing another man on San Jose Ave SE. The mom thanked Joseph for not killing her only living son who just turned 18, she was actually a really nice lady who broke down talking about raising two troubled kids on her own. Unfortunately for the mom, her son wasn't a kid anymore and would be facing some real jail time. The whole night he couldn't get the high young mans confused face and red eyes out of his mind or the poor mom.

When he finally finished his late night, he hadn't eaten in hours, but had no appetite to eat when he picked up Robert from Sharon Valtierra's house that night who was a former co-worker of Eileen at Carrows and was married to a cop, also named Robert. She always helped Joseph and whenever he tried to apologize for being late, she had no part of it, "There's only one Robert in this house that gives me a hard time," she winked sarcastically. Sharon made him a to go meal, but he couldn't eat and had a hard time sleeping that night, feeling grateful that he didn't have to shoot the man. He replayed the scenario in his head over and over again. After further review he felt that if faced with that same type of situation again he would probably shoot.

Thankfully Christmas was a quiet day that year for Joseph and he was able to catch some football at the Valtierra residence. Sharon and Robert spent the day in their new his and her robes while their three children and little Robert opened up presents. Joseph was happy to be there, but a little sad when his son was crying in his arms and reaching for Sharon then stopped when Sharon took him. It made him realize how much time he was missing with his son. The boy even said "Sharwin" more often than he said "daddy."

When little Robert unwrapped a counting book and an ABC book it was very exciting to see his boy start to count and do his ABC's, but Joseph knew he wasn't responsible for that. Many Police gifted his son presents and Sharon gave Joseph a $25 dollar check certificate to Albertsons groceries. He was really touched, but again a little sad thinking how hard he worked just to struggle to buy food. How could he resist, Sharon's smile was always so big it seemed like her eyes closed. It was a perfect present and he was truly grateful for all the help he had raising his son.

When New Years came around it was all hands-on deck, that night was always one of the busiest for Officers across the country and probably the world. Joseph worked Downtown with a group of 7 other Officers and they arrested 5 people for fighting, 4 for drugs and 1 driver who cruised down the wrong side of Central Avenue in front of all the Officers, nearly hitting Joseph and another Officer who was waving his flashlight at the man to pull over just an hour after 1983 rang in. They all earned their pay that night.

As a rookie Police Officer, Joseph had learned from his Training Officers and Veterans on the force to always carry his gun, badge and handcuffs with him at all times, especially after Phil Chacón was shot dead off-duty. Being a Police Officer was a 24-hour job, 365 days a year for Joseph and he really had to be vigilant at all times and keep his eye out for trouble. Joseph realized how different his persona was on a trip to the grocery store. He began to scan anybody and everybody that he came across, just glancing them over. Just in case.

He had over 3 years on the force now and had seen his fair share of danger. Off-duty and certainly on-duty, trouble always seems to find Police Officers, due to the nature of their profession.

ON JANUARY 17, 1983 Joseph was walking Downtown after a day in court. He was in a suit and tie, but had his gun and badge displayed on his belt to indicate he was a Police Officer in an area riddled with lawyers. He was going to grab a bite to eat before getting ready to go home when a man across 4th Street made strange eye contact with him. It wasn't uncommon for people to look at Police Officers differently, but this guy acted awfully suspicious when he must have spotted the badge from across the street. Joseph pretended not to notice and crossed the street nonchalantly so that he would have to pass the man, all the while keeping his eye concentrated on the unknown subject.

He was a big stocky young Black man who had enormous biceps bulging out of his dark green shirt. As Joseph went onto the street towards his direction, the strong man casually went to a payphone that was near him, picked up the phone and started pressing buttons while turning his face away from the Officer. He started talking to the phone and Joseph just knew something was up because the phone didn't work without money. There were plenty of people around and the second Joseph initiated contact with "Hello I'm" the man dropped the payphone and bolted off leaving the phone dangling by its grey armored cord with Joseph in hot-pursuit.

The young man was fast and Joseph couldn't keep up in his dress shoes as the two ran past 3 streets and the man gained distance before turning off and disappearing into an alley. Joseph drew his gun and cautiously entered the alley, where he caught site of the running man again and kept chasing, the whole-time yelling, "Stop… Police." Eventually the fleeing man began to slow down and Joseph was able to gain on him after nearly 10 streets, finally catching up to him in the alley nearly 13 streets over and a half mile away from where they started. Having holstered his gun to run, that's when Joseph made one of the biggest mistakes of his life.

As Joseph approached the man in the alley, they were both short of breath, huffing and puffing. Joseph yelled "Put your hands up against the wall!" The man listened and looked completely exhausted pressed against the wall. Breathing hard, Joseph cautiously walked up to the large man. He drew out his pistol again as he made commands, but on approach he fumbled the gun down between the man's spread apart legs. The revolver bounced around in front of the man in the foot of space between his body and the wall. As the hulking man looked down at what happened Joseph reached down with his right arm while shoving the man's butt forward with his left arm telling him, "Don't you fucking move."

Right at this life-or-death moment, a light blue Plymouth Fury with white top stormed into the alley, it was a Police Service Aide. They are 18-20-year-olds who help out Police and citizens, but do not carry a weapon or make arrests, however they did have lights on top of their cars. The Service Aide saw the chase a few streets back. Luckily the buff suspect had likely thought that this was a Police Officer and didn't put up a fight for the gun. Joseph handcuffed the suspect and told the PSA to call in additional units. The man was a recent prison escapee out of Denver, Colorado and certainly wanted to avoid going back at all cost. He would be extradited back to Colorado in the following days.

After court and making the off-duty arrest, Joseph picked up Robert from the Valtierra's, who had three older kids of their own. He was so grateful for his Police family and all the relationships he formed. That same night at home he received a call from Eileen's parents who had a 4-hour time difference in Kona, Hawaii. The grandparents had accepted his invitation and he was excited that they were coming to visit him for Robert's Baptism on February 20th after receiving his Christmas letter. They would stay with Joseph from February 20th until February 28th.

Joseph had been waiting to baptize Robert and was pressured by his own family to have the Baptism, normally it occurred with a newborn in his family, but Joseph patiently waited to include the Stalla family when they came back to the mainland. Now he had just one slight problem, explaining to his mom that Father Henry could come, but that Robert was going to be baptized in the Stalla's church in Rio Rancho. He called Father Henry and they flipped a coin over the phone to see who would tell Carmen. "Ooh, say a prayer for me," Father Henry told Joseph when it landed on heads in Joseph's favor.

Just weeks away from hosting the baptism, Joseph couldn't sleep at all that night thinking of how close he came to orphaning his son with the gun fumble. After putting the boy down for the night, he drank a tall glass of whisky on ice hoping to steady his nerves, his hands were shaking as he poured the drink down and watched news of the arrest on the television. *Prison Escapee Caught Downtown.* Joseph was very grateful to the young PSA named Rick Foley, who saved the day.

Foley would go on to become a Police Officer and friend of Joseph, always enjoying when he could find a nice busy meeting to whisper the occasional inside joke, "Hey have you seen your pistol today, I think it fell down in the alley back there." Or he would sneak behind him somewhere and point to the ground and say "dropped your gun." He got him to look every time. Joseph would always be happy to see his friend and just make fun of his Albuquerque accent with a simple mock of "or what" as he greeted him with the question. "Did you get a new haircut or what?" "Gaining weight or what?"

Chapter 20

Tom and Gerry[2]

ON JANUARY 30, 1983, a tall young sandy-blond haired Officer named Tom Tanner was celebrating at the main Police station giving high fives to everyone. He was from the D.C. area and his Redskins just beat the Dolphins in the Super Bowl. When he passed Joseph, he went for a high five, but Joseph put up both hands in halt and responded, "Look you guys got lucky with the short season and all from the players strike." The Officers didn't really know each other and Tanner responded, "Let me guess you're a Cowboys fan?" Joseph smiled and Tanner replied, "See I knew it, why you have to rain on my parade man? Tell you what, you and I are going to bet a six pack from now on when we play each other. I really enjoy a free beer." Joseph smiled and gave him a high five and confirmed the pact before Tanner continued his onslaught of high fives around the Police station. It was the first time Joseph had missed a Superbowl in years, he took a second to reminisce watching Roger Staubach win two as a kid and idolizing him with his dad.

Most Police Departments in the United States offer the opportunity for civilians to ride along with an Officer for a shift, usually for locals who are aspiring Police. Rules and age restrictions vary from each department, Albuquerque's policy was a minimum of 16 years old. Joseph had never hosted a ride along, he didn't even like having to pick up his in-laws in his Police car with Robert. The grandparents thought it was neat, Harvey made everyone laugh pretending to be a prisoner in the back at every stop light to neighboring cars in broad daylight. However, Joseph just wanted them to be safe and Police cars are a magnet for trouble. When they arrived to the cul-de-sac a roadrunner was in the front yard, delighting everyone as they curiously watched it move in controlled spurts from their yard to the neighbors before they parked. "It looks like a little dinosaur," Harvey proclaimed rightfully at the sight.

Having the grandparents over was nice, but Joseph did plan to work graveyard the week they were in town. One night both Elsie and Robert fell asleep early, Joseph was getting ready to leave Harvey alone and bored. That's when he asked, "You want to ride with me tonight at work?" Harvey was a Combat Vet who had seen enough action for one life, but he was game and accepted the adventure. Joseph had asked, but didn't necessarily expect a yes. Robert was a great sleeper, so they left Elsie a note and headed out for a night on the town.

Back then Joseph just had to inform everyone in his unit and dispatchers that he had a ride along, there was no formal process if your Sergeant was cool. Harvey enjoyed sitting in on the briefing. Everybody was very nice to the 49-year-old gentleman in a floral Hawaiian style shirt under his coat, who greeted everyone and said goodbye with "Aloha Ohana!" In the Police car, this was the first time Joseph was able to talk to Harvey just the two of them. It was nice to share stories of Eileen as they patrolled around. Harvey was impressed at how mature Joseph had become in the years since he first met him, watching in awe as he multi tasked driving and the radio.

They had two exciting calls that night. The first when a foot chase occurred Downtown. Joseph knew the area and while most cars responded to where Dispatch called out, he imagined from the direction they were announced running what route they would take. He zoomed his car over 4 streets and waited a moment, he had placed his vehicle right in front of the running man's route who appeared as two Officers gave foot chase behind. It saved all of Joseph's energy and he was able to get out and easily stop the man to allow for the Officers to arrest him. Harvey watched from the vehicle, astonished.

Later that evening they found a stranded motorist way up by the mountains on Tramway Blvd. Joseph and Harvey took her to fill up a gas can and when they returned Joseph even filled up the tank. They followed the lady into a parking lot before she parted, then a moment later in the lot, Harvey pointed out a fight way across the street. Joseph shined his spotlight towards the fight in a parking lot of an office building. A group of 3 cowboys were getting into it with a group of guys and girls, a bunch of cholo's. They were probably road raging and pulled over.

Joseph called in the fight, but then exited his vehicle and got ready to make a long pistol shot when witnessing one of the cholo's reach in the back of a little blue truck and produce a machete. Joseph instinctually left Harvey in the car and started running closer to try and take a better shot. As Joseph ran across four lanes on Tramway, one of the Cowboys kicked in a wood fence and broke off a big piece of board, swinging it wildly towards the cholo's. The machete wielding attacker was kept at bay by the quick-thinking cowboy and when Joseph emerged running in the distance, everybody scattered into vehicles and took off. He just missed getting any license plates and only had vehicle descriptions as four cars sped away. Just then he looked over and saw Harvey had driven the Police car into the parking lot, wearing his Hawaiian shirt with a giant smile on his face. Joseph's thinks he would have been game to chase them, but that concluded their action for the night.

Elsie was upset with Harvey and Joseph when they returned in the morning, ending Joseph's plans to invite him again and Harvey's plans to ask to go one more time. At Robert's baptism all the grandparents were there at Harvey and Elsie's church from long ago, First Baptist in Rio Rancho. Many friends made the drive up the hill to attend, Robert was very popular around town. Those nights Joseph could go off to work very assured with all the grandparents in town staying up and playing board games.

ON FEBRUARY 24, 1983 he went off to work with a grocery size paper bag full of sandwiches from his mom for his squad. That night Joseph was lent out to the South Valley to go help the Sheriff's Department translate a big dispute between two large families that lived on the same street. Joseph had his radio on another frequency when back in Albuquerque a radio transmission called out a dispute at the Tewa Lodge motel on Route 66 in East Nob Hill.

The motel was sleezy now, but built in 1946 for tourists along Route 66, it had a beautiful Native American paint design and thunderbird murals to go along with its iconic 3 story skinny neon sign. Double-sided it had a light up orange trapezoid with TEWA written in white horizontally, sitting on top of vertical white blocks underneath reading LODGE in orange. An orange arrow lights up in the middle and at the bottom a vacancy sign lights up or not to indicate room availability.

A mangy drifter from the Dallas, Texas area was out drinking at El Cid Bar along East Central Avenue that night. Wanted back in Texas in Garland and Ft. Worth, the long haired 5.9 180lbs man with aryan tattoos started a fight with a patron he had arrived with. They were kicked out and he drove back to a room he had at the Tewa Lodge near the corner of Central Avenue and Alvarado Drive NE. The raging drunk turned onto Alvarado, then turning left he missed his parking space and crashed into the motel room #24 where he was staying. He backed up slightly and exited to go into the room. Three unrelated men watched him crash the car and made eye contact with him. These men decided best to enter into their room #25 to get away, the last room along Alvarado before an alley separating businesses.

After arguing with his lady friend and acquaintances, the Texas outlaw went over and knocked on the three men's door #25 a time later and when they opened, he started fighting them. One of the three men inside wrestled him outside and they saw the random drunk go back down to a friend's room #21. It wasn't long before the wild drunk retrieved a rifle in room #21 and appeared outside again, sending the three men he fought running in all directions as his own friends tried to calm him down. He broke the window next to the door at #25, cutting his arm, then the drunk man's friend helped take away the rifle from him as he bled, and they walked the gun back to room #21.

The drunk wasn't done yet and after cursing off belligerently into the night, he went into #21 again and got the rifle back and walked outside bleeding from the arm. Across the street was a busy restaurant, Kap's Coffee Shop and Diner. Built in 1968 it had big windows facing Central and a large parking lot behind it that wrapped around the business. The bad guy walked out into the street in-between the motel and the diner and fired one round into the street. After howling at the moon, the rifle wielding felon walked back into room #24 as patrons of Kap's called 911 and a car passing by the shot when it was fired, stopped at Sambos restaurant up Central to call also.

Officer Gerald Cline, Jerry, had a civilian ride-a-along with him that night and he was the first to radio in he was responding, as the primary. Gerry Tanner called in as the backup Officer. Cline, 11 years on, arrived quickly to the Tewa Lodge, turning at the two-story office along Central and passing a row of one-story apartments on his left. He parked his car in backwards to an alley behind the Tewa, giving a line of vision down the rooms 25-15 towards the two-story office along the busy road. Under his brown mustache, Cline told his young citizen ride-a-along to stay in the car as the tall Officer got out and conducted a search. A sea of cars passing along Central in his backdrop, the area was saturated with Officers and he knew backup was near. A blue car parked on the motel sidewalk was out of place and seemed to have crashed into the building. Walking down the apartments he noticed the broken windows at #25.

Dispatch had called out rooms 24 and 25. The Officer knocked on #24, no answer. He pretended to be looking for some beer, no answer. Just a minute after arriving in his car Officer Cline walked to #25 to knock. As he did a deafening loud shot rang out from behind BOOM. The ride along didn't see the shooting, but saw Officer Cline fall and yell out he was shot. The crazed mangy haired drunk from earlier exited room #24 and hovered over the Officer with a high powered .30-.30 rifle, who was facing up and bleeding from his back and chest. The gunman, with his own arm still bleeding from breaking windows, looked up at the patrol car crazed, holding his rifle level and the ride-a-long opened his door and bailed on foot West into the alley away from the back of the patrol car.

A young married couple had just parked their car at the Kap's Diner across the street to get a late-night coffee. Hearing the shooting they looked up. The couple saw a disheveled man come towards them from the motel across the street and raise his weapon up, bleeding from the arm. The lady ducked down, the husband had just stepped out with his door still open and hopped back in the car while his quick-thinking wife got on the floorboard and reached back to hit the automatic locks to their car. As the husband started the car, he backed out and would have to pass the armed man who stood in front of the car, blocking a forward exit onto Alvarado. Noticing the Police car, the husband rolled down the windows with his automatic button and yelled, "Hey man leave us out of this man."

Across the street Officer Clines ride-a-along had run behind the Tewa Lodge and onto Central to flag down the first Cop he saw to warn them of Officer Down. Lights flashing, the approaching Officer Gerry Tanner called it out and sped up, turning on Alvarado to see Officer Cline down on her left and the gunman running holding his rifle towards an occupied vehicle in the Kap's parking lot to her right. Geraldine Tanner didn't hesitate, she zoomed forward to the Kap's lot and exited her Patrol car in record fashion. Drawing down her shotgun she took a good position and pointed at the man. She would give him one warning and half a second to respond. The crazed man turned and she aimed.

He had thrown his bloody rifle on the couple's hood as the husband parked his car in shock and then the disarmed gunman turned to run behind the Kap's further into the parking lot. The lionheart Tanner gave a short foot chase into the lot, continuing to aim at the man until she ran by the rifle on the hood of the couple's car and told them to stop as they tried to leave. Hearing distant sirens get louder, she aimed at the fleeing man as multiple Police swarmed in. She provided cover as Units stopped the fleeing man before he exited the parking lot. Almost simultaneously

Officers behind her attended to Officer Cline and in front of her they arrested the evil drunk 300 feet from where the downed Officer lay. They had been so close yet so far.

That night dozens of Officers came to secure the scene, including Cline's brother-in-law T.C. Haralson. He would grieve a good man many of days with Cline's widow and three children.

Officer Gerald Eugene Cline. EOW Feb 24, 1983. Age 35.

The News of Officer Clines shooting death was devastating to the community still healing two and a half years after Officer Phil Chacón's murder that happened not too far up the street from the Tewa Lodge. The shooting created really bad press, especially with the city ready to host the men's NCAA Basketball Final Four in 5 weeks. The media was kept at bay during the fallen hero's funeral and the service made everyone feel awful for Clines wonderful family of 3 children and his wife, who was known to be helpful to many Officers on and off duty. In honor of the fallen Officer, flags across the State were flown at half mass and all the Officers carried a black strap around their badge to mourn for over a week, some longer.

In the 1830's Boston, Massachusetts established the first Police Department in the United States as the gangs of New York, Chicago and other cities still needed to be regulated. They wore copper badges and "Cops" derived from street slang to announce their presence. An early tradition brought onto the profession by Boston and still practiced in almost all major departments is to have a bagpipe played at Officers funerals. The Albuquerque Police Department always kept a bagpipe team, paying homage to old traditions, dating even further back in the United Kingdom. Officer Clines funeral was not a happy time. Bagpipes and 21-gun salutes are a powerful tribute to the ultimate sacrifice Officers make and Cline's were very moving.

On March 4th Joseph received an unexpected call from a man speaking in Spanish at his work desk. His mind was thinking in English and it caught him off guard so he asked the man to repeat. The man then spoke in English, "Hey what's wrong with you, have you forgotten Spanish?" Joseph was taken back by the comment and said, "Excuse me, who is this?" It was Father Henry and he told Joseph he had called with bad news. Father Henry was calling from the hospital in El Paso. The aging priest was in distress by the sound of his voice as he said "Joseph, they shot them." Joseph's heart filled with fear as the priest continued, "Right around the corner from your house they shot them both." Joseph had a lump in his throat as he listened. "Yes two young Detectives out here, one in the head named Chuck Heinrich, he's in a coma, but it doesn't look good." Joseph became angry and sad. It happened a couple streets over from his childhood home, occurring in front of the Shamrock hotel at 6101 Dyer Street when they stopped to ask a man for his ID.

The two men then chatted about Chuck Heinrich who left behind a wife and 6-year-old son. He was a Vietnam Veteran and had just been named Detective of the Year. Then they talked about Gerald Cline. Both men were glad to speak to each other, albeit under such terrible circumstances wasn't ideal. Before they hung up Father Henry led him in a prayer and a blessing for the families of the fallen Officers as well to Joseph and all the other Officers fighting to make their country a safer place.

Detective Charles Douglas Heinrich El Paso Police Department, Texas. End of Watch Aug 29, 1985 Age 37. Incident date: March 3, 1983.

With the department still stunned from the loss of a great Officer, the N.C.A.A. Men's Final Four came into town and Officers made sure it went off without a hitch. The first two basketball games on Saturday April 2nd both had attendance of 17,300 in The Pit arena, hosted by the University of New Mexico Lobos. Entering the stadium fans walk down to their seats and the court is nearly 40 feet below ground level. In the afternoon, North Carolina State beat Georgia 67-60 in a gritty game that NC State had trailed with 2 minutes to go. At night, the #1 seeded Houston Cougars, led by Hakeem Olajuwon and Clyde Drexler beat #2 Louisville 94-81. Many sports enthusiasts were considering this the real championship game and Houston was a heavy favorite to repeat as National Champion.

Joseph was one of the lucky Officers to get Chief's overtime and work the Championship game on Monday night April 4. The tournament was great for tourism as Downtown hotels, Old Town and the Pit Arena became a zoo of visitors who spent a lot of money that week. All the National news outlets came and every day dozens of hot air balloons flew both in the morning and afternoon.

The final game was great, the 7-foot-tall Olajuwon and high-flying Drexler were amazing and it seemed like a blowout was in store. As the game progressed N.C. State held tough coached by Jimmy Valvano. With time expiring the game was tied at 52 and N.C. State guard Dereck Whittenburg launched a prayer shot from just inside half court. The shot fell short, but his teammate Lorenzo Charles grabbed the airball and dunked it with .01 second just as the buzzer sounded. The victory dunk and Coach Valvano running onto the Lobos court in excitement, became one of the most famous images in the tournament's history. The city of Albuquerque had really needed the uplift.

⚖ ⚖ ⚖

After the murder of Gerald Cline, the Chief himself commended Geraldine Tanner and the whole department saw how heroic she was in the face of danger. Her superiors saw extreme discipline, a lesser Officer might not have chased the dangerous man alone or could have shot the cop killer in cold blood. None of the compliments or commendations mattered to her, that night was haunting. If it hadn't been for kind words from Clines widow at the funeral, Tanner might have taken a leave and possibly transferred to a civilian job. It also helped that her husband was a highly respected Officer on the department as well, and they struggled through many of dark nights together. It was a one-of-a-kind support net, who better to understand the terrible things they saw then each other.

As a Sex Crimes Sergeant Gerry Tanner was an accomplished Detective. Although only 5.4 and 100lbs, she was as tough as nails. Raised in Brooklyn, Gerry was very beautiful with her long curly brown hair spread all the way down her back and piercing blue eyes, but past those innocent looking eyes was an extremely street savvy investigator. At age 25 she had gone undercover for 3 months as a high school senior to break up a drug ring at Highland High. Gerry was in so deep that she refused two prom offers. Her teachers took her for a regular student and she had to do school work to remain under their radar.

TOM "T.B." TANNER was a blond-haired brown-eyed Detective raised in the Washington D.C. area. After 4 years with the department Tom began to endure pain in his legs while sitting, walking, running, pretty much his whole lower body was experiencing trouble and at 6.2 feet tall, it hurt really bad. The Department sat him behind a desk while he underwent tests to figure out why he could hardly run anymore. Tom reviewed the Departments human resource policies and realized he was on the precipice of being let go because of diagnosis of a degenerative hip condition. Instead of waiting for the imminent, Tom had the Department help foot the bill for college courses relating to his job. He finished a Computer Science Degree from New Mexico Tech in 16 months with previous credits from Georgetown. Before long he became one of the most renowned Computer Forensic Detectives West of the Mississippi, even teaching courses at Langley, VA and Glynco, GA.

Many Officers and city personnel were instrumental in introducing the Police Department to computer technology, but T.B. Tanner and Robert Valtierra were two Officers in particular that standout as having pioneering roles in advancing and developing a solid technology infrastructure. Officer Valtierra was a strong advocate for department wide automation to help store and track data. Starting in the early 1980's, he helped push for grants to secure and allocate funds toward equipment and computers. Valtierra contributed countless hours learning about the advantages and strategies behind computers systems when they were brand new and then remained a technology advocate for the duration of his career.

When computers were first purchased by the city, Officer Tom Tanner was the departments original MS-DOS expert and as the technologies developed, he never missed a beat in remaining ahead of the learning curve. From the early computer days when criminals would try and erase files or data, Tanner used his training to generate formulas to connect a giant puzzle of scattered data bits in order to recover information. Criminals could try to wipe away and erase every dirty little secret from their computer and Tanner would spend hours to recover the lost data to help bring justice.

Thomas Tanner had met Geraldine Ferrara working narcotics and they were both from back East. He asked her to date once he was transferred out. Coincidentally his sister married a rancher in Nebraska named Gerry with a G also and her dad was Jerry. When Tom and Gerry got married in 1980, they had to work different assignments for the duration of their careers per department policy. However, being Detectives they were often in the same building on different floors and would bid to get matching schedules or days off throughout their careers when they could.

Tom and Gerry had their first son around the time Robert was born. The couple learned she was pregnant again in the Fall of '83. Gerry knew this might complicate things and she needed to find a Detective that could be out on the streets as her eyes and ears in the Line of Duty. She began to recruit a Detective she could rely on to report their findings to her so she could help piece together everything back in the office on desk duty. Her Lieutenant knew there was no stopping her, so he ordered that she could only interrogate people with another Officer present. When he had suggested she go on light desk duty with her first child she refused. At one point he ordered her to turn in her gun and badge to take maternity, "Is that it?" She had asked as she complied. When he replied yes, she pulled out her ankle piece and put it in her empty hip holster and walked out.

Chapter 21

Truth or Consequences

JOSEPH HAD NO OTHER CHOICE, but to use his department vehicle for his personal use as he could barely afford gas for the Datsun his wife had left behind. It was dangerous to have a baby in a marked Police car for various reasons, but he had to, economically. He also had to sell his childhood motorcycle for $500 just to help make his mortgage in November and December of 1983. His holiday plans included getting ready to spend Christmas alone with 2-year-old Robert and have turkey TV dinners cooked in the microwave, even though several Officers invited him to their homes. Joseph appreciated every offer, but seeing his friends with their wives and family would have just crushed his lonesome heart.

Luckily though on Dec 19 Joseph was recruited for a special assignment requiring a Spanish speaker to go down to El Paso on December 21st to interview a murder witness. The assignment was a gift sent from heaven for Joseph, the department paid for his gas to go home and enjoy Christmas plus he would earn some overtime money. He surprised his family on the winter solstice by knocking on their door in uniform, holding baby Robert. Tío Jesús was there and it was the first time he saw Robert in person and he kissed the baby boy's forehead nearly 20 times as Joseph hugged everyone. After a half hour Joseph left his son with his family, to go conduct his interview with assistance from an El Paso Homicide Detective named Duane Johnston. He then returned home a few hours later ready to write a report so he could fax his superiors a copy and then relax for a few days.

Carmen surprised Joseph on Christmas Day, pulling off a last-minute Christmas lunch. Just before 9am she sent him out to get a small list of things, everything hard to find on Christmas day. When he came back around 11:00am there was a celebration in his honor with over 30 family members having reconstructed their plans. They had 2 big turkeys and just about every side dish imaginable. For dessert they had pumpkin pies, key-lime pies and dessert tamales where the maize was mixed with strawberries, bananas, or pineapples.

When the first round of food was over all the men gathered around the TV. They were all watching the Christmas commercials and talking about the Sun Bowl the night before where the University of Alabama rolled the SMU Mustangs 28-7. The Football bowl game was held in El Paso every year since 1934, the longest of all college bowl games. Children played and women showed off their new gifts and thanked Carmen for the reunion.

He was lucky to have this Christmas as a holiday, it was the first time since he was in the Academy. There is no cure like family. After the house cleared out Joseph took a small nap before leaving for Albuquerque around 6pm that night. Joseph had to be back to work at 11am the next day and a storm was coming. He had a special bag with an opening for a hanger to place his uniform in. His mom had somehow made his uniform look brand new again and laid it down in his trunk to preserve its crisp linen smell. He kissed his folks goodbye as grandma sang one last song in Spanish to the smiling baby, "Cinco Lobitos tiene la Loba."

THE WEATHER WAS FREEZING that night in southern New Mexico and the wind gusts were so brutal heading North on I-25 that Joseph had to slow down several times when his light bodied Datsun blew into the other lanes. Gripping the wheel tight, he wanted to pull over, but Robert was just a baby. It was too cold. To make matters worse a new hit song came on the Radio by Dexy's Midnight Runners titled

"Come on Eileen." Such a cool song, but Joseph fought back tears at the title lyric and turned off the radio, opting to hear the wind screaming onto his windshields.

A little over an hour into the drive, Joseph, like all the other drivers out that stormy Christmas night, had to stop at a Border Patrol Inspection Station just North of Truth or Consequences, New Mexico. T or C was named after a popular television show in the 1950's and was a quiet lake town home to Elephant Butte reservoir, but I-25 was a lucrative drug route for Mexican traffickers headed to Albuquerque, Denver and wherever else they shipped. Small specks of snow started to fall as the wind howled on the car windows. At the checkpoint there was a blue van and two white cars in front of Joseph and the vehicles were all waived through fairly smoothly after a few questions each, while Joseph kept his baby son warm the best he could in a child seat in the back.

Joseph had been through the Border Patrol checkpoint many times before and he rolled down his window a third of the way and greeted a brown uniformed Agent with, "Hello Sir U.S. Citizen," as another Agent circled the Datsun with a young German Sheppard on a short leash. Joseph looked at the Hispanic man's brown uniform that read Agent P. Tafoya just as the Agent replied, "I didn't ask you anything. Now where are you coming from tonight and whose baby is that in the backseat." Blonde haired Robert sat sleeping and Joseph replied, "Excuse me Agent Tafoya! That's my son and we're heading back from El Paso to our home in Albuquerque." Tafoya must have been in a bad mood or pissed at the mention of his name as he spoke a code into his walkie talkie and then told Joseph, "Step out of the car Pancho, so I can verify that's your baby." Joseph could see his own breath as he snapped back, "You sure you wanna do this pal, its 10 degrees out here and you want to keep my 2-year-old in these conditions?"

Agent Tafoya's brown eyes grew wide and as Joseph thought of his son, before he stepped out, he rolled up his window instinctually and turned the heater up. At these motions, the overzealous Agent drew his weapon and ordered, "Get out of the car now!" Two more Agents were working inside a small station house with windows and were alerted to the scenario. The two came out of a brown door to assist Tafoya and the other Agent's, who's German Sheppard started making attack motions and barking wildly on its leash at Joseph's door. Tafoya kept his gun drawn and opened the door from the outside.

Joseph hopped out of his brown Datsun slowly with his hands up and as the freezing wind hit his face, he kicked his door shut behind him to provide warmth for his son. Then Joseph spoke loudly through the dog barks "Why did you pull your GUN on me Agent Tafoya?" Tafoya snapped back, "Shut up and put your hands on the roof amigo." Joseph did as he was directed, but when he tried to turn for a glance back when Tafoya holstered, Tafoya pushed Joseph's head down by the back of the neck onto the roof of his Datsun. Tafoya began searching Alvarez with one hand while keeping the other on the back of Joseph's neck and Joseph's face pressed on the cold rooftop. It took every ounce of strength not to fight back and keep a level head.

Past patience, Joseph waited for the inevitable discovery. "GUN" Agent Tafoya shouted to his colleagues and the two Agents without a dog rushed forward and grabbed each of Joseph's arms as the K-9 Officer drew his weapon with his right while holding the riled-up dog's leash with his left. Agent Tafoya used his handcuffs on Joseph after the other two brought his arms down. Then Agent Tafoya put Joseph's service revolver on the hood of the Datsun as the two Agents moved Joseph away from the vehicle to continue patting him down and the fourth Agent held the barking dog back as it tried to reach Joseph for a taste.

When Agent Tafoya turned around after emptying the revolver's bullets onto the Datsun roof he said to his partners, "What are you guys doing?" The other two Agents were uncuffing Joseph after discovering his badge in the fanny pack that Tafoya had just removed the gun from. Joseph rubbed the red circles on his wrists and then reached in his fanny pack and grabbed his tape recorder as it spun recording with the red record button pushed in. The K-9 Agent gave his dog a command and it shut up to move on to go search the next vehicle of a small line of 5 cars that had accumulated during the witch trial.

Joseph spoke into the recorder, "What's your first name Agent P. Tafoya?" Then Joseph extended his arm and put the recorder three feet away from Tafoya's mouth. Joseph said into the recorder, "No Response Amigo? Okay I'll find out. As for you two gentleman Agents Bradfield and Granderson, thank you for doing your job. Ill include that in my letter! Now if you'll excuse me Panchito, I have an infant son to take care of." Joseph turned off his recorder and walked past Tafoya to collect his bullets and gun. "You should treat people with respect or you can make some serious enemies in this profession," he scolded the young Tafoya before hopping in his car to head home after wasting 20 minutes in the freeze.

For the next few nights Joseph had an awful earache from the cold wind at the checkpoint. Robert was fine, but Joseph wrote a detailed letter about the bizarre stop and sent a copy of the tape to a Border Patrol supervisor he had known since middle school who was also one of the few men to have beat him in a boxing match in their youth. He got a phone call a few weeks later from his old pal saying that that he contacted the Agent in charge of that office and they disciplined Agent Tafoya accordingly.

BILLS BEGAN TO PILE UP on Joseph and he was working long shifts, often missing those precious moments in a baby's life. In March of 1984 Joseph had to borrow money from his folks and was really embarrassed, especially when they showed up one weekend with a car full of groceries. He was humbled, realizing he was tired of every day feeding his 3-year-old Mac-n-cheese with tuna or weenies in it, oatmeal for breakfast, noodles or cereal for dinner. Joseph was considering everything in his power to provide, including a lateral transfer to another Department.

Drew Banks had left to be Policeman in Spokane, WA where the salary was 4x as much base pay. Banks made the move to the Pacific Northwest almost 18 months earlier and seemed happy when they would talk on the phone. He mentioned more than once that they would hire a Spanish speaker at Detective pay, which Drew said was a nice salary. Joseph thought about how far that was from El Paso and that he would never be able to see his parents on a drive in a moment's notice. But looking in his pantry, he decided that he might as well just inquire.

Late in March, Joseph was making a blanket fort with Robert when he received a frantic call out of the blue from his mom. She was telling Joseph that his favorite cousin Mary Margaret was in an abusive relationship with her new husband down in El Paso. Trying to process, floods of memory rushed to him. As a teenager Joseph had traveled with his Tia Rocha and her 4 kids to Los Angeles, Margie was the youngest. Dozens of family members went to a crowded Disneyland one day and she snuck off, but Joseph followed her. They were soon lost from the group and ended up spending half the day together. She was always fond of Joseph and the only person in the world who called him Joey after he stuck with her and went on all the kiddie rides despite wanting to go on the big rides at the "happiest place on earth." This phone call wasn't how he expected to start his weekend so Joseph called over to Juan and Rose, they happily took Robert to play with Juan Jr. for the evening while Joseph took his Datsun down to El Paso to investigate his own family's well-being.

AFTER ARRIVING to El Paso Joseph found out that his cousin Margie had been married to a carpenter from Mexico who pretended to be nice until he married her and got his work visa for having a wife with American citizenship. He began treating her like a slave, cashing her paychecks and demanding three squares a day, despite the fact that he was lucky to have this beautiful former Miss Juárez 1981. The family all said she looked like her Aunt Carmen and Margie was always a sweet girl. Carmen told Joseph about bruises on her face and body and Margie covering up with lies, saying she slipped or bumped into something. Tío Jesús had begged for Carmen to lure the husband over for a "talk." Joseph knew what that meant and convinced his mom Carmen to give him the address of his cousin and he took a little ride.

When he arrived, Joseph saw a van his mom mentioned in the driveway and figured the husband to be home. Joseph decided to hell with it and knocked on the door, figuring he could just play dumb and say he was there to surprise visit his favorite cousin. After he knocked, he heard a man inside say in a heavy accent, "Shut the fuck up don't answer it, I tell you when you answer it" and then what sounded like a beer bottle breaking violently into a trash can filled with other bottles. Listening in, it was only getting worse and then he caught a glimpse of his cousin through a little opening in her blinds.

Joseph did a perfect Chuck Norris front kick blasting his cousin's thin door open with the bottom of his boot. He entered the house with his gun drawn and sure enough on the living room couch there was a man hovering over his cousin who was sprawled out in a defensive position in her nightgown. She was all covered in bruises on her arms and back, then when her hair moved out of her face Joseph could see her purple eye. "Joseph?" Margie said shocked. Joseph didn't pay her attention and told the man in Spanish to sit down with his hands up. The drunk looked at the gun and listened.

Furious at his cousin's condition, Joseph was amped up and probably breaking a few laws himself. Years of rage had boiled into that room as he scolded the bad husband. Then Joseph told his cousin, "You've got five minutes to collect what you need, you're coming with me." She couldn't believe her swollen eyes, but as the husband commanded her to stay, she listened to one of them. Margie got up, walked towards her husband and told him "I love you." She kept walking passed him to pack a bag back in a bedroom while Joseph cursed out the husband, pointing his gun at the drunk's rosy face the whole time who pleaded for his wife not to go.

Joseph drove a sobbing Margie back to his mom's house to grab a few things and rest a little. Then they drove back up to Albuquerque for over 4 hours hardly saying one word until they reached his driveway. He let her inside and got her settled as the sun rose up. Before he left to get Robert, he offered her to stay at his place as long as she needed and she could help watch baby Robert while they found her a job and she figured out her life. She nodded yes.

The arrangement with his cousin was perfect, she was great with his baby and cooked Joseph a meal every day and packed him a lunch, saving him grocery money by not eating out. He helped Margie find a 30-hour a week evening job at Dunkin Donuts opposite of his schedule and they took turns working and watching Robert. She demanded to help pay a little rent and took care of his cluttered house, even organizing his Police paperwork by date. Robert loved how she was always singing or playing music everywhere she went. Joseph also noticed a lot of his cop buddies wanted to drop in for visits more often too.

On April 1st 1984, one day before his 45th birthday, the great singer and songwriter Marvin Gay(e) was staying at his parent's house in an upscale neighborhood near Crenshaw in Los Angeles, CA. Police reports indicate Marvin had been getting clean off cocaine and had spent days locked in a bedroom, allegedly spending his hours in a maroon bathrobe with a pistol in the pocket. Around noon his mom had come into his room to check on him and his dad began shouting across the house to her about an insurance letter. Marvin yelled back and the dad came in his room, where they began arguing. The dad and Marvin began physically fighting, the Sr. getting kicked and aggravated. Marvin got off his dad and went back to his room and sat with his mother to get ready to leave.

Then the dad entered Marvin's room and raised a .38 snub-nosed revolver at his son. The mom screamed, but the dad fired into Marvin's right chest and Marvin screamed from the impact of his lung being exploded. He slumped as his dad fired again. He fell to the floor and died. His dad walked downstairs and went outside to his front porch, where he threw his gun onto his front lawn, lit a cigarette and sat down waiting for Police. Just like that the world lost one of the greatest voices ever known, to domestic violence. Joseph read the newspaper article the next day and shook his head at the realization of family crime extending all the way up to the rich and famous.

1984 was a very busy year in the world and as the Spring season transitioned to Summer in 1984 the city of Albuquerque's crime heated up with the weather. The summer started with a 13-year-old kid obsessed with horror movies murdering his parents in bed while standing on stilts and wearing a Jason mask he had made himself. Police had previously suspected him of wearing a mask and throwing a severed pitbull head into a gas station on Gibson Blvd that had kicked him out earlier. Doctors had to wait for hours for the mom to pass out to operate after she refused a blood transfusion because of her religion. A younger sister escaped with her baby brother, now orphaned.

In the summer of '84 the Cubans and Juaritos gangs had started killing each other over the newest drug craze-Crack cocaine. Undercover Detective Jimmy Zamora was the first Officer to learn of the drug when his CI or confidential informant came to him one day with a rock in his hand, the little skinny 5.7 Chicano said "Hey check what these negritos sold me down the street." As Jimmy studied the small rock, smelling it and slightly wiggling his nose, his face was confused. Jimmy had no idea what it was, but soon the entire city found out.

Pretty soon cartels, gangs, and mobs from Juárez, El Paso, Los Angeles, Phoenix, Chicago and even Memphis came into town to battle the other 130+ local gangs over the rock cocaine market. Smoking a single hit offering users a body euphoria of 10 minutes, Crack was going for $3 a rock in some cities, but lucrative Albuquerque was hooked at $15, $20, even $25 to the fiends. Users acted hyper bizarre and their appearance often turned disgusting rapidly before they even knew they were hooked. Loss of teeth, scabs, uncontrollable mouth spasms and body tweaks.

The Crack War had spread from the major cities into the streets of Burque and its 325,000+ residents. Crime rose, violent crime rose, the amount of daily drug transactions skyrocketed. As more and more rip-offs occurred or battles for turf initiated it led to lots of shootings. Mainly concentrated in the "Warzone" along Central Ave from San Pedro Drive to Gibson/Louisiana Blvd's SE, as well as in South Broadway, Downtown Barelas and in parts of the South Valley SW. The bad areas in the Westside and North Valley still had more of a heroin problem, but Crack Wars were prevalent there too. It was sad for Joseph to see these nice communities with small problems begin to develop into nasty areas with big issues. Many normal everyday people were ruining their lives on a glass pipe, crack had exploded in use across the city. By the mid 80's crack overdoses became commonplace in the 3 emergency rooms in town.

Even though Joseph was broke living month to month and fighting dangerous crimes while being a single widow father, he refused to take part in a department incentive to curb crime amongst immigrants. Citing the growing Crack Wars, Albuquerque Police offered $15 per head to its Officers for any illegal immigrant round up and successfully turned over to federal authorities for deportation. Dedicated to community policing, Joseph cringed at the bonuses a few fellow officers bragged about, over $100 on a paycheck in some cases, which was a pretty penny in those days on their salaries.

After a long conversation with Al Byrnes one night about the implications beyond the bonuses, Al and Joseph knew that this measure was instilling fear in the many Spanish-speaking communities around Albuquerque and Bernalillo County. Most of Joseph's informants spoke Spanish, witnesses he relied on to solve crimes spoke Spanish, shop owners, merchants and hard workers spoke Spanish. Illegal or not, Alvarez needed these people to come forward to testify against dangerous criminals, without fear of deportation. Cases were going unsolved because witnesses were afraid to come forward to tell the truth in fear of consequences.

In a perfect world any and all immigrants would take the appropriate avenues to legally visit or work in the U.S., but who was anybody kidding, undocumented illegals are a common fixture and they are willing to work hard for a lot less money. On the other hand, Joseph firmly believed that Americans deserved the jobs first and any one entering this country should be documented. Joseph had no problem calling on Federal Agents to deport lawbreakers he deemed unsuitable for society. Using his discretion case-by-case, Joseph turned over many illegals to Border Patrol, but never accepted a bonus for doing his job. A bonus for doing your duty crossed ethical guidelines and he felt it was against S.O.P and HR regulations on a number of levels. Joseph earned a lot of overtime hours because the department lacked translators, which was odd because Albuquerque had such strong ties to Mexico and Latin America.

On July 18th, 1984 tragedy shocked the nation. A married father of two walked alone into a McDonalds in San Diego, California near the border of Mexico. Children were on the playground having fun while the parents ate food and watched. Workers took orders and prepared food. Then the 41-year-old married father entered carrying a shotgun, 9mm pistol and Uzi gun. He unleashed terror as he proceeded to shoot up everyone he could in the restaurant. For several minutes he fired over 250 bullets, systematically murdering 21 people including babies, small children, elderly and additionally severely injuring 19 people.

The majority of the victims were of Mexican descent being near the border. Finally, a SWAT team sniper was able to end the terror with a precision shot, but the city and nation were left with the largest mass murder it had ever scene. In Albuquerque the Police Departments top brass gathered together to devise a protocol for a similar incident if it were ever to take place within the city. Many ideas were bounced around including talk of expanding the SWAT team, purchasing better weapons and training Officers how to make entry in pairs. Similar meetings took place across the country after the shooting that shocked the nation. This was very uncommon in that point of time.

BACK IN ALBUQUERQUE two Police Officers received a tip telling them that a lady wanted for fraud would be out at one of the Corners bars, Gary's Game Room, a pool hall. On August 18th, 1984 Officers Vic Webb and Rick Foley went into the bar shortly after 10:30pm to see if they could spot the fraudster. As they walked in to make rounds, a young Black guy on parole pulled out a pistol and pointed it at their faces, ordering the Officers to drop their weapons. The gunfight was on, but the random guy had the drop on them and the Police instinctively dodged bullets while unholstering.

Webb was shot twice in his shooting arm, dropping his gun and pinning him defenseless in a dangerous spot with more bullets flying. Foley had made it out the door and was radioing for assistance as shots just missed him. He took cover behind a rolling dumpster in the parking lot and aimed his gun at the door. When additional units arrived, they immediately made entry and found Webb with blood pumping out of a severed artery in his arm, his service weapon stolen. The shooter wasn't found for

17 years when he was picked up on 429 Lenox Avenue in Harlem for vagrancy, giving NYPD a fake name, but a fingerprint database matched him to face the consequences for the Police shooting in New Mexico.

Shortly after the Webb shooting, at the end of August his cousin Margie was planning a move to Los Angeles to stay with aunties then work and audition for commercials. She had been such a great help, it was nice to have a feminine touch around, Robert adored her. The cousins had helped each other out to save money and organize their personal lives. With Margie moving soon Joseph was thinking of ways he could somehow make more dough. He never once considered the deportation incentive measure and it soon faded out after a year, the Department would no longer reward vigilante immigration patrols. Meanwhile, Joseph signed up for the next Detective exam, one day after his 26th birthday on September 12, 1984.

The stars aligned for Geraldine Tanner when Joseph came into her office early one October morning, after checking the scores for the Detective exam. He smiled and asked her, "How's Johnny Lee doing?" Sgt. Tanner grinned and replied, "He's somebody's girlfriend for the next 55 years." They both laughed slyly before jinxing the same comment by simultaneously muttering, "Not long enough!" Joseph chatted with Gerry for a few minutes about their kids and her pregnancy, then he let her know that he passed the Detective exam.

Gerry had a court appearance to make and had Joseph accompany her through the building down the service elevator to the lobby. In the lobby Geraldine took out her business card and wrote directions on the back then looked at Joseph and said, "Tomorrow I want yous to come over to my house around four AM and meet the Sex Crimes unit. We are all crewing for the Balloon Fiesta and we have a little daycare set up for the kiddos so no worries bring your boy." Joseph was excited and accepted the invite. He had seen the hot air balloons every year he lived in Albuquerque, but this was his first visit to the largest balloonist gathering in the world.

The next morning at 4am Joseph met the Sex Crimes squad at Tom and Gerry's house off of Paradise Blvd NW. Joseph made instant friends when he showed up with a bottle of Kahlua for their coffees and hot chocolates. He was at least 5 years younger than everybody and had to ride in the back of the chase vehicle with a couple old salts who didn't talk much. It was freezing in the bed of the Ford truck on the way to the Coronado mall parking lot. They took a special entrance for pilots and crew, then they parked at a designated spot in the large lot, cleared of cars for acres.

Joseph had fun removing the red nylon fabric balloon from its giant sack with 6 other Officers and laying the long layers across the lot some 30 feet long. As dawn approached, Joseph drank hot Kahlua coffee with a couple of the guys as hundreds of other balloons were all being set up the same way. It was cold. Joseph marveled at the hundreds of different colored balloons and looked forward to taking Robert the next year. The crew used a giant ground fan to inflate the vessel for 20 minutes before its shape was ready for tilting it upright along with the gondola basket. Joseph could feel the warmth of the helium burner as it shot test flames up into the neck of the red balloon to maintain its inflated shape.

As the sun began to peak over the mountains, the Police turned Chase Crew waited for the Head Zebra or flight official in striped referee shirt, to okay the weather for ascension, thumbs up for take-off. Then an Officer/ Pilot named Mark Bralley asked Joseph to help hold down the basket shaped gondola until one of the Zebras gave them the ok to fly. Joseph and Gerry put their weight on the tan gondola, feeling the balloons desire to take off. "Alright Joe, are you Red-Eye?" asked the Pilot Mark. Joseph could hardly hear a word as Mark pulled a cord shooting a giant flame up the balloon, but he shook his head yes. Then suddenly Tom Tanner and 3 other Officers picked Joseph up from behind and shoved him into the gondola or basket. "Welcome Aboard!" they shouted and waived from the ground to a smiling Joseph as the balloon rose to join the dozens of other balloons in the first wave.

Too shocked to think of anything to yell, Joseph was quickly overtaken by the beauty of the ascent. Joseph got nervous as their "Red-Eye" Balloon lightly pressed into the yellow Zia balloon in midair. Mark cordially parade waved to the Zia pilot and riders before the balloons calmly separated.

Rising to 8,500ft. Joseph never saw the mountains or city look so beautiful as he spotted his house from miles away.

The hot air balloon casually drifted West towards the river cruising about 5mph for 10 minutes before coming over the water. The pilot allowed gravity and the burner to ease down to splash and dash in the Rio Grande, inches away from a giant turtle that was disturbed by the intrusion to their habitat. Flames shot up and they climbed back up and drifted over the thousands of cottonwood trees in the Bosque along the river.

Tall flames from burners of balloons sounded off in all directions in bursts, lighting up each balloon's unique colors in the early dawn. Joseph listened curiously as the Balloonists shouted out warnings to each other of approaching power lines and Mark elevated to avoid a few by more than a couple football fields. They spotted a small pack of coyotes off in the desert just minutes before their slightly rough landing in a huge dirt lot in the village of Corrales where the crew had chased them to.

What a ride, he had never seen Albuquerque so majestical with its mountains, river forest and never-ending desert. Folding the balloon back up took teamwork and it was an intimate way to bond with new friends. This had been a very special day. The Police crew all celebrated with a champagne ceremony commemorating a centuries long tradition since the first ballons launched in Annonay, France in 1783.

After that day, Gerry put in the request and snagged Joseph up, welcoming him aboard officially on November 1st, 1984. He truly needed the position and was ready for the challenge of being promoted to Detective, more than doubling his pay to $11.31 an hour.

In early 1985 his second cousin's husband Sam Baca was appointed Chief, he was 37 years old and had been with the department for 15 years. He had married one of Dino's nieces and Joseph met him the day he graduated and they were friendly after that.

Chapter 22

Sex Crimes

WITH THE ADDED COMFORT of his new promotion to Detective, Joseph took off running in Sex Crimes. He was assigned a top-of-the-line tape recorder and a pager to be reachable and on call 24-7 at times. Working diligently to help clear the board of unsolved crimes as new ones rolled in almost every day. Geraldine maintained over an 88% clearance rate and in 1984, 207 of 232 rapes brought charges to a suspect by year-end while Detectives worked tirelessly to solve the other cases. She was a master of logic and could literally write the book on interview and interrogation techniques. Geraldine could pick a part anybody's story and when she confronted suspects with the facts, the guilty ones no matter how hardened, would feel the hair on the back of their neck stand up. Her demeanor was always on point and she could adapt to each situation and interview according to the person's behavior.

Interrogations were a game of cat and mouse with the morally depraved. She was especially polished after May of 1982 when a Child rapist was released from prison on a technicality and called Gerry at work to ask how her own 2yr old son was doing. How stupid can I be, she thought, removing all pictures of her own family from her office and the desk that she had twice interviewed the cuffed rapist from. From then on, she only put up NY Rangers hockey stuff in her Office to protect her families' identities from criminals who would have plenty of time to plot revenge while incarcerated.

Everything indescribable happened in Sex Crimes, men attacking women, women attacking men, men attacking men, women attacking women and the worst of all crimes, "kiddy Chester's or Chester the molesters" as they were known amongst other criminals in prison where they were despised. Joseph worked directly beside Gerry Tanner for one week to study the clockwork of the unit. Every day that first week he encountered something atrocious and he realized that he would have to sacrifice a lot of mental health to fight and solve these repulsive crimes.

Shadowing other Detectives the next week, Joseph learned some pretty clever interview techniques. One thing was certain, Joseph was going to start carrying cigarettes, he saw multiple people relax and talk after a few drags. He saw one Detective give a guy half his sandwich, cutting it into two halves while the suspect watched. Then he poured half a coke in a cup and offered the guy either the can or the cup. These little tricks might develop a certain likeness that even some of the darkest criminals could appreciate. He quickly realized the game, that even though you wanted to strangle some of these degenerate pigs, you had to show them common courtesy.

Joseph grew up in the church and had only been with one woman. Yet within days he was meeting the worst people while getting a crash course on all kinds of stuff he didn't want to know about, but that came with this particular promotion. Joseph could never get used to the variety of sins involved, but after the first victim he interviewed as a Detective, he finally felt his professional purpose in life, to save lives and prevent future victims by ensuring prosecution.

Detective Alvarez responded to his first Rape as lead Detective near the University of N.M. "student ghetto" on Stanford Drive SE. As he pulled up in his brown Crown Vic, a beautiful young college student in a green lycra dress stood in front of a small adobe guesthouse. The blond haired green-eyed 19year old was obviously the victim by the fret in her demeanor. She walked out to the car and seemed hesitant towards

Joseph as he exited his vehicle and he had a feeling she was expecting a female Officer. “Hi I’m Detective Alvarez, Joseph, is there somewhere we can talk,” he asked soothingly. The traumatized young woman was upset and studied the Officer up and down in a slight trance. He saw her look right at his wedding ring and then she looked up at his eyes and when he smiled back with his lips, she shook her head yes then led him onto her small private front porch.

She had a few chairs outside and he pushed the red record button on his tape recorder as they sat and she recounted the assault. Krystal Harris had been walking home from a Cultural Geography course and noticed a suspicious man walking behind her. After a block or two she tried changing up her path and he remained behind getting closer. The man picked up his pace and when he was within twenty feet she tried to run and yell, but he produced a large knife and threatened to kill her if she screamed again, then grabbed her by the back of the neck and led her into a nearby alley. It was broad daylight in the middle of a densely populated neighborhood, but nobody was outside at that time to hear her initial yell for help.

Joseph looked at this beautiful young woman resembling his deceased wife and said to her, “If I have to chase him for 20 years I will find this dirtbag, but I bet you I can get him tonight if you help me…before he has a chance to hurt anyone else.” He saw the words register with the victim and she came out of her trauma state then gave him the detail he needed to catch the animal. “He had one testicle Sir.” Joseph didn’t blink, “Okay that’s great, that’s exactly what I need to catch him, you’re doing great so please what else can you tell me about him? Take your time and remember everything you can.” The young woman rattled off every last detail she could. Joseph then drove her to the Rape Crisis Unit and some nice S.A.N.E. nurses took care of her and collected her clothes for evidence. With the help of the victim’s testimony Joseph captured the deformed animal within 10 hours and Krystal’s account helped send away the 42-year-old husband and father of two, for 15 years.

Capturing that first suspect felt good and the other Detectives were proud, they knew Joseph had it in him. It would never be easy, but Joseph vowed to help hunt down every last one of these animals he could. His tenacity and empathy for victims would be his greatest motivators to help him stay sharp in the field and follow the law to prosecute these horrible offenders for as long as possible.

His first victim Krystal went on to become a Police Officer in Tucson, Arizona after graduating with a degree in Criminology from U.N.M and she sent Joseph a Christmas card addressed to Sex Crimes every year.

Being a Detective helped Joseph's finances, but working in Sex Crimes can warp your psyche. Perverts and pedophiles preyed on the innocent and can get the calmest of human's blood boiling. Archaic laws made things difficult to convict in some areas like the raping of prostitutes or husbands forcing themselves on wives. Over 230 rapes occurred in 1984 and another 238 were reported in 1985. In NM husbands could still rape their wives until the law changed in 1997. There were some real sexual psychopaths in the world and delving into that underworld uncovers a variety of freaks. The sexual predators appeared in a variety of forms, the trespasser, the voyeur, the prowler, the jealous spouse or lover. He learned of their subterfuges or deceitful tactics to lure victims, the jogger, the drunk, the dog walker, the meter checker, lost with a map and dozens of other ploys.

One case nobody in the department could clear was an ether rapist, who passed out victims with a cloth over their mouth dipped in the chemical. He struck twice around the University area in '85 and '86 and then seemed to vanish. Joseph had also heard of an ATM thief who used chloroform to knock out money guards, but when he tried to chase that lead, he found the chloroform guy was a former employee who had been convicted and in jail on the dates Joseph was looking for.

COOKING FOR KIDS can be fun if they are not picky. Joseph was happy that Robert ate just about everything. With Detective pay Joseph could finally afford some regular groceries to invent some bachelor recipes, but one drawback was he was always on the phone talking to other Detectives. Little Robert was a quiet kid, he read a lot and when he saw Joseph was on the phone he would watch TV and twist the volume to a low level. One night Joseph was sitting with Robert eating macaroni and cheese with hot dog bits watching their new favorite show MacGyver when Robert was disappointed that the phone rang. He knew what that meant, he would watch this episode alone. Joseph excused himself.

When he picked up the phone all he heard on the other end was, "Motherfucker." Joseph smiled, he recognized the Detectives voice as Tom Tanner. Sex Crimes had taken a partially burned computer to him hoping he could recover information about one of their own. A civilian chaplain that volunteered for the Police had been using an online chat forum, completely new to Detectives. On this forum he liked to befriend teenage boys and coaxed a couple to perform tasks for him in Albuquerque.

They set up a stakeout and saw the dirty chaplain empty a large bag into a trash alley behind his house. After waiting, a Detective took it. That's where they found the burnt computer inside with stacks of broken floppy disks. After dozens of hours and curse words, Tom finally was able to uncover the deleted chats.

Joseph brought Robert over to the Tanner's house and Tom watched the boys while Joseph and Gerry went to the chaplain's house with a SWAT team and a court order.

AROUND THE TIME Route 66 was officially decommissioned, Joseph began to sprout his first noticeable white hairs. "My tresses," his eyes were in shock as he probed the intruders. One day in the office Gerry Tanner came by and took claim for his new Zeus patch, "Oh no what have we done to you!" She said in a motherly tone. "Ooh I don't want to hear it. I'm dying it back and then moving to Mexico to be a male prostitute so that I can hopefully gain at least ONE OUNCE of my dignity back from working with you people," Joseph said jokingly stroking the patch with his fingertips. Bursting into laughter, she gathered herself and smacked him with a file, "Buddy they will use you like a Piñata DON'T!" Detectives spent a lot of intense time together, sharing unhealthy snacks and jokes are the best way to survive sometimes.

Back at Sandia National Laboratories, robotics engineers and chemists developed the *Remotec Andros 5A* bomb detection robot, the first of its kind in the world, now Department standard. One of the benefits of having some of the top scientists in the world located in your State with a multi-billion-dollar annual budget from D.C. It looked part tank, part car and part human. One early feature was a loaded shotgun that could be aimed and a round discharged to set off an explosion if their acquired target couldn't be remotely diffused or secured by the robots' arm clamps. It was gifted to the department's Bomb Squad in 1985. There were some car bombing incidents in the late 60's and 1970's. Including outside Chicano advocates La Alianza's headquarters at 1010 Third Street NW. Milwaukee, Wisconsin lost 9 officers to a bomb once, inside their Central Police Station.

IT HAD BEEN POURING RAIN across the Duke City for two days straight after previously going 107 days without any measurable rain. Officer Alvarez had just got off-duty one evening and trying to hurry home to relieve the sitter and catch Miami Vice on TV with Robert. He was driving on 4th Street NW to head East on Montaño when he realized traffic was jammed because the busy intersection's lights had gone out. Joseph hit his top lights and drove up onto a median, passing vehicles on his right. After calling it in, he parked his car at the edge of the median facing the middle of the intersection so that people would slow down to the emergency vehicle as its lights reflected all around.

Still in uniform, he had a traffic kit in his trunk and opened his glove compartment to put on an orange safety vest over his jacket. Getting wet, he went to his trunk and pieced together his traffic gear, a 5C cell Mag-lite with Cel-lite aluminum baton that had a red traffic cone attachment. Rain poured down as he jogged to the intersection of 4th and Montaño where the lights were completely out, not even blinking. Traffic started to flow slowly as people paid attention to Alvarez with their windshield wipers going.

As Alvarez conducted traffic, he was facing West down Montaño when Joseph heard tires screeching. The screeching tires got louder towards his position and he turned around to see a station wagon sliding his way. He jumped up at the last second and smashed his side onto the front windshield of the speeding car causing him to flip over the roof and trunk. The car skidded to a halt facing East on Montaño the wrong way and Joseph laid on the ground motionless about 20 feet away.

Civilians stopped their cars and exited in the rain to check on the Officer, fearing the worst. Joseph was dazed and first thing he did was check to see if his gun was still holstered, it was. Drowning out the good Samaritans, Joseph rose up like a corpse from Thriller and charged over to the car, opening the driver's door. He was going to yank out the driver and hook'm up, when he realized it was just some scared teenagers out on a double date. There was one young couple in back and one couple in front, all four crying. Joseph wrote the driver a citation for reckless driving, but didn't cuff anybody or even call the kids folks. To add irony to injury, the stoplights came on as he finished the citation.

A week later after hitting Officer Alvarez with his car, the Judge was ripping the teenager driver in court, rearing him as brutal of a tongue-lashing as anyone has ever endured. When the Judge asked the plaintiff Joseph if he had any physical or monetary damages incurred, Joseph said, "Yes sir your honor" and handed the bailiff a sheet of paper. The bill read for an $11.95 Casio watch from Target and a $3.50 dry cleaning bill for his dirtied uniform. Joseph didn't get hurt, he never even went to the hospital like he should of or called a backup unit for that matter. The defendant offered to buy the Officer any watch he wanted and the Judge would have ordered it. Joseph replied, "Thank you sir, but I don't want a Rolex. I just want my $11.95 Casio from Target replaced! Its waterproof, tells the direction, has an alarm and its digital, even at night." The stalwart bailiff smirked in approval of the Officer's wish.

A few days later Joseph checked his cubby and found a small box containing two $11.95 Casio's from Target with a handwritten apology note. After that night's briefing Joseph traded the extra watch to Lt. Ali Surod Jawan in exchange for half his burrito and some Rolo's, then he tossed the note in the trash after reading it once. As Joseph set his replacement watch, he remembered learning in the Academy about Patrolman Donald Redfern who died conducting traffic during a flash flood in 1951. It was rainy outside and a car driven by a drunk driver slid out of control through an intersection into Redfern. Realizing how close he had come to the end, Joseph used his next day off to draw up a Will to Robert and have it notarized.

Chapter 23

Executive Decision

AUGUST 2ND, 1986. ALBUQUERQUE INTERNATIONAL SUNPORT. CONTINENTAL AIRLINES.

A week after being ran over, Joseph was sent with another Detective to Albany, NY for a 5-day seminar on Stalking. Sgt. Tanner made Joseph and Detective Pete Lesinski promise to eat a street dog for her before they left. The other Detective brought his young wife Caroline and Joseph took Robert along, courtesy of the department, just a month before he started kindergarten. As law enforcement they were allowed to carry their weapons on flights in those days. It was a 6-hour flight and both Officers snored the entire trip while Caroline taught Robert card games.

They all shared a rental car and checked into the hotel where the conference was being hosted. When checking in for the conference itself, Joseph noticed how very few Sex Crime Detectives wore wedding rings. Detective Lesinski happily took his gorgeous wife to the hotel restaurant for dinner, while Joseph and Robert hit the streets looking for the perfect hot dogs. When they found a little Italian man vending by the Capital building, it was so amazing they ordered another round.

The next morning instead of leaving 5yr old Robert with the other Officer's Wife and attend the seminar, Joseph told Robert in their hotel room, "Executive Decision, we're going to Cooperstown!" Robert had no idea what it meant other then he got to spend the day with his dad so he was excited and pumped his fists. Joseph had looked into his sweet child's blue eyes and realized that he didn't want to be in Sex Crimes anymore. His entire personality and sense of humor was becoming morbid after all the terrible things he witnessed as a Detective of such carnal abuse.

His most primal fears and rage existed in this field of degenerates. Joseph despised pedophiles and predators and there was no reward greater to him than bringing a filthy animal to justice, but at what cost to himself. Sex Crimes Detectives have a tough, tough job that requires dedication beyond their salary and eats away personal lives. Joseph was a handsome bachelor in his physical prime, but had only been on a couple dates since his wife passed in 1981 and none since joining Sex Crimes in '84. Joseph was married to his job and was so busy in 1986 that he had forgotten to sign Robert up for t-ball in time with PAL, the Police Athletic League. Baseball had meant everything to him growing up.

After some thought, Joseph told the other Detective that he was taking the rental out and had decided to spend the day with his son. It ended up being such a great spontaneous decision. Joseph hadn't even planned it, but one of his favorite childhood ballplayers was being inducted that day. Now father could teach son about the greats and they watched the induction speech from Willie McCovey of the San Francisco Giants as well as Bobby Doerr of the Boston Red Sox and the family of the late Ernie Lombardi who was National League MVP in 1938 with the Cincinnati Reds. The ceremony was such a breath of fresh air for Joseph and he suddenly just felt relaxed for the first time in years. He forgot how much he loved baseball. Robert wasn't bored, going through some new packs of baseball cards and eating the sticks of gum that came in them.

Main Street in small town America is the ideal setting to experience charm and Cooperstown is one of the top examples Joseph thought. He continued to enjoy the day with his son, spending a few hours visiting the impressive museum itself. Afterwards they had a delicious dinner at the Doubleday Café on Main Street around 6pm Eastern. Joseph had spent the entire day dressed for the Stalking Seminar, wearing black slacks and shoes with a long sleeve white collared shirt tucked in and accessorized by an auburn necktie. Presenting himself as law enforcement, attached to his black belt he wore his Police badge on his left hip and on his right side, he had his black leather gun holster exposing his wood revolver handle for everyone to see.

ROBERT WAS FALLING ASLEEP during dinner and when Joseph asked for his check at the café the short haired waitress in glasses Zoey told him, "Oh no Officer a gentleman over there bought you and your sons' meal," pointing to a table across the room. Joseph left a nice tip and then walked over to the crowded table with Robert to pay respect. Suddenly as he approached, he recognized the tall generous man as the greatest Hitter to ever play the game.

"Mr. Williams thank you very much for our meals Sir, my Dad is never going to believe this. He fought in Germany and Belgium with the Army Air Corps and we are huge fans," Joseph said respectfully. The distinguished gentlemen replied "no Thank You Officer and call me Ted," and reached out his hand to shake Joseph's, then the man asked Joseph what his dad's name is and he greeted young Robert as Joseph replied "Dino Alvarez." "Too bad Greenberg is sick," Williams said to his friends as he produced a ball from a bag to autograph. "To Dino for VE Day! Ted Williams," the legend passed the ball around his table to fellow famous World II Vets and Hall of Famers, Bob Feller, Stan Musial and their guest of honor Bobby Doerr. Joseph had been so distracted by Williams aura, he was late to process the table of legends. While the other 3 men signed the ball, "Teddy Ballgame" made a silver dollar coin magically appear from behind Robert's ear that he gave to the amused boy before the father and son left the diner with giant smiles.

Back at the hotel in Albany that night, Joseph called his dad to tell him the incredible story. The next morning Dino woke up and called one of his war buddies in Des Moines, Iowa to share the story and catch up for the first time in over a decade. They remembered their pilot, co-pilot, navigator, bombardier, radio operator, nose turret, top turret, ball turret and tail gunners on the Silver Streak. Back-to-back for many harrowing missions, they talked for nearly three hours.

Joseph apologized to Pete the next day at breakfast as Caroline took Robert to get some fruit. Pete said, "Hey it's okay with me, but you've got to explain that one to Caroline why she didn't get invited. She loves baseball, we're both big Pittsburgh Pirates fans." Joseph covered his mouth and took a long shameful blink, that was one of his favorite teams growing up. Caroline had a beautiful face, hair, body, eyes and even gorgeous white teeth. When she found out, she joked with a smile and a glare, "No it's okay I just love watching boring TV all day in hotel rooms."

August 11, 1986. Albuquerque Police Headquarters, Downtown 4th and Roma

Upon returning from the Stalking Seminar in Albany, Joseph was called into one of his Sergeants office's about not attending. The other Detective on the trip hadn't said anything, but the Seminar had called to make sure everything was okay. After a long discussion, both parties decided best for Joseph Alvarez to finish his case load then take a personal vacation while they reassigned him. There were no hard feelings and Joseph always assisted the Sex Crimes Unit. After he left, Joseph still contributed 4% of his paychecks automatically deducted into the fun for the advancement of the Rape Crisis Center. 4% Sí o Sí.

⚖ ⚖ ⚖

As both a kid and an adult Joseph loved fireworks, growing up near Juárez he had access to some incredible pyrotechnics. One night after filling up his personal Datsun with gas, he was in uniform and stopped on a street where he saw a man was selling fireworks out of his garage. Just there to buy, the man had all kinds of illegal boom sticks, hundreds of items banned in the U.S.A. He made Joseph a very nice care package for $20 and told the Officer he should bring his car back the next day.

Joseph wasn't sure why, but he returned the next day off-duty, with Juan following. On the large property on Mescalero Road NW near the railroad tracks, the man had a huge mechanics garage in his backyard and he kept the Datsun for 2 days. When Joseph got it back it had a fresh paint job on it, a very stylish copper with gold flake and black racing lines. The car looked pretty cool and the man refused any payment, he said he had wanted to practice a new airbrush. "How about a pizza?" Joseph asked. The man smiled with a hand motion and said "Sold!"

EVERY SUMMER Joseph requested about 6-14 days off and he would take Robert on an annual vacation. He never missed a work day technically, having always carefully swapped shifts with others. When Robert was a baby Joseph would only take him to Alamogordo and El Paso to visit his family. Now that his young son had flown across country to New York for his first flight and with his boy entering Kindergarten soon on August 27th, Joseph wanted a car that he could take back and forth to school and take on road trips.

Luck met him at the gas pump one day with the Datsun freshly painted, he was offered $1,200 by a man at a gas station who raced cars on tracks. With a heavy heart he sold it, thinking of Eileen the whole time, but one good thing about cruising the whole city for your job is he had been eyeballing a red beat-up 1966 mustang for $600 parked on the side of an old lady's house. The body was fine, it was ugly from years of sun, but it ran well after a tune up and some new tires. This had been his dream car as a kid, he was going to love to work on it now that he could afford it.

Starting in '86, every summer he had planned father and son road trips where they would travel cross-country in that Mustang. Joseph hated the hair bands and soft rock of the 1980's and always played Classic Rock on his 8-track in "The Stang." Joseph and Robert cruised to Hendrix, Black Sabbath, Pink Floyd, Zeplin, SRV, Jethro Tull, the Eagles, Skynard, Cream, the Stones, C.C.R., Allman Brothers, Santana and all the other great guitar bands of his era. Metallica and Prince were his exceptions. And he always made time for Roswell, New Mexico's own, John Denver. Jim Morrison was good too, who grew up in Albuquerque school's once upon a time.

Robert's favorite two 8-tracks had belonged to his mother, *Stuck in the middle* by Stealers Wheel and the *Rumours* album from Fleetwood Mac.

With his new ride, Joseph took 12 days off on August 14th while the department changed his assignment. He decided to drive his son to Austin, TX to see his beloved Cowboys scrimmage vs. the Houston Oilers at Texas Memorial Stadium. They drove through El Paso and stayed a night with his folks. Then they left for San Antonio to stay a night and go see the Alamo. The tour guide didn't find Joseph very humorous when he asked her where Ozzy Osbourne had peed, she didn't field the question. They ate at a delicious restaurant in the heart of Downtown San Antonio called Mi Tierra before leaving to go catch the game in Austin at 7pm. It took them about 55 minutes to drive Downtown San Antonio to Downtown Austin.

That night the Cowboys won the scrimmage and afterwards the two spent the night in Downtown Austin. Several young gals complimented Joseph with son and he couldn't believe how many pretty girls were downtown in Austin. The place was a gold mine, everywhere he went some gorgeous vixen called him handsome, told him what a cute kid he had or smiled at him. He couldn't believe his luck when he put Robert up for a nap and went to get some ice in a bucket.

A beautiful young brunette gal in a summer dress and cowboy boots at the front desk was flirting with him, Kay Day from Texarkana reading a criminal justice textbook. He thought she was joking when she asked Joseph out that night when she got off. He desperately wished he had a babysitter so he could head to the famed 6th Street to hang out with her. Young, handsome and lonely he contemplated the move for about 2 seconds, but there was no way he would ever leave his son alone in a hotel room for any longer than he just had. No matter how secure it seemed.

That next morning, dad and son ate pancakes at Kerbey Lane Cafe on Guadalupe Street, it had replaced a restaurant Joseph had visited as a senior in high school when UT was recruiting him for the 1500m and 4x400m relay race. His tall beautiful waitress Sandra recommended a store, Terra Toys, to pick up something fun. After breakfast and the toy store, with a new Teddy Ruxpin they headed up Interstate 35 to Dallas to attend a Texas

Rangers vs. Chicago White Sox game the next night in Arlington, checking into a Travelodge motel. They went to the famous book depositary, the grassy knoll and walked about enjoying the downtown's history.

After the Rangers won 3-2, Joseph was cruising near Downtown Dallas with their windows down in their red Mustang and looking for a McDonalds to buy Robert a Happy Meal for the motel room. After locating the giant yellow arches sign, he pulled up to the drive thru to order. They were waiting in line behind two vehicles when Joseph and Robert heard a woman scream and tires screech in the McDonalds parking lot. "GET DOWN on the floor and don't move," Joseph ordered Robert, unbuckling his son's seatbelt and pointing to the floorboard below the glove compartment. Joseph always carried his maroon fanny pack off-duty, that was really a quick draw gun holster with a zip pouch for badge and handcuffs. He threw his car into park in the middle of the drive thru, took the keys and exited the Mustang while strapping on his fanny pack and pulling out his .38 revolver. Robert did as he was told, sitting in fear on the floorboard, never seeing what transpired.

Right in front of Joseph, a screaming woman in a long blue dress was running to save her life from a lifted blue 1970's Bronco that was revving its engine and aiming at her. The hardtop Bronco had its two windows rolled down and the blond-haired male driver was alone. The jealous ex-husband had been stalking his former wife who had been eating at a Luby's Restaurant next door and when he saw her exit into the parking lot with coworkers, he tried to run her over, but he was careful not to smash his precious truck into parked cars. As the pretty brunette hid between two vehicles and took her heels off, the ex-husband continued to rev his engine and scream obscenities at her and that he was going to kill her. His engine and voice continuing to rev up until Joseph emerged on foot to the side of the mad driver, with his badge and gun pointing five feet from the angry man's face. "SHOW ME YOUR HANDS OR DIE!" Joseph roared an ultimatum.

The surprised man looked down the barrel of the gun with wide eyes and raised his hands in compliance. Joseph shouted, "PARK YOUR

CAR WITH YOUR RIGHT HAND SLOWLY…DO IT SLOWLY… YOU REACH FOR ANYTHING AND I WILL KILL YOU." The man was still raging, but snapped back into some form of consciousness while staring down the revolvers barrel. After parking the car, the man seemed to know the routine and he kept his hands up while Joseph barked more commands. Joseph took a half step left for a better view as the noise from the truck engine stopped before he continued his commands. "Now stick your left hand out the window and open the door slowly from the outside, keep your right hand up." As soon as the door was open Joseph didn't see any weapons and grabbed the man's left arm to judo slam the raging lunatic down onto the parking lot, cuffing him tight as the man growled for the Officer to, "Take it easy man, I didn't do anything!"

When Dallas P.D arrived and secured the bruised faced criminal, Joseph was giving an initial statement when he remembered to check on Robert. Poor kid was still on the floorboard with his new teddy after several minutes and Joseph hugged him tightly realizing how scared he was. The McDonalds crew had witnessed everything and made Joseph two cheeseburgers, fries and a drink then gave Robert a fresh Happy Meal, boxed with two different toys, free of charge.

Two weeks later Dallas Police sent a thank you certificate for the off-duty heroics, but Joseph didn't care he just wanted his black handcuffs back, they were his original pair from his Academy days. Gone forever despite weeks of requests.

Chapter 24

Field Investigator

AFTER 18 MONTHS IN SEX CRIMES Joseph was assigned to be a Field Investigator and work across the city. Field Investigators had a very interesting job, they still patrolled around like any Officer, but also responded to crime scenes to photograph, investigate and collect biometrics. They might take the average 6 calls a night or just 1 depending on the intricacies of the investigation and crime scene. When computers were first installed in patrol cars, Joseph remembered that every night that first week a Field Investigator had to photograph a fender bender involving a distracted cop. Three guys in his own squad and dozens of Officers did the same those first few months with computers.

Field Investigators drove a patrol cruiser, but also carried a Detective kit in a fishing toolbox with black TurtleSkin gloves, Latent Index provisions for fingerprinting, a splatter test kit/trajectory rods, barium antimony gunshot residue tests and other miscellaneous tools. Referred to as F.I.'s, they were also issued a 35mm Canon high-powered lens camera with unlimited access to rolls of film. Other departments might get a set number of pictures they could take. To this day, even with the advent of digital cameras, some Police around the world are lucky to have any way to visually document a homicide, let alone other crimes.

Joseph's first night as a Field Investigator was a tough night to stomach. He arrived to a mobile home park off 98th St. and I-40 SW in reference to a suicide. Joseph's job was to talk to Detectives and photograph the scene. It was disgusting, the man had sat on a chair and put a shotgun under his chin in front of his wife. He found out from a Detective that the man had previously shot himself in front of his wife with a pistol and wore a glass eye. The old salt Detective said this very nonchalant matter of factly, while Joseph was always flabbergasted by these crazy details.

This was a messy scene and they were hoarders, Joseph didn't know where to even begin, but the first thing to do was focus his camera. He aimed at a nearby table and started to fidget with his zoom when he just freaked out and quickly exited the mobile home. Joseph had found the man's glass eyeball and focused in on it unknowingly. It was staring right at him all creepy on the table amongst dozens of items. He had to gather himself for a moment outside. Looking up in the sky, he took some deep breaths and a couple shakes with shivers. The Detective didn't say anything when he returned after a couple minutes.

The scene was the gift that kept giving as Joseph got home after that shift and found brain particles in his own hair and clothes. When he saw it looking in his mirror he again was disgusted and hurried outside. He hosed himself off outside in the cold, both freezing and disgusted. After drying off and warming up, instead of relax he had to go pick up his son and of course already in a hurry, he came out to find there was more yuck in the car.

That morning, he got Robert ready for his first day of school on a step stool in front of the mirror. As they combed his hair Robert looked up and asked "Why are you crying daddy?" Joseph smiled at the kid's purity. "Everything buddy, you are getting so big!" Joseph said after a hard night, after a hard five years.

Dropping him off was beautiful, walking him in to see all the adorable kids with backpacks bigger than they were and a classroom decorated with motivational posters. His dual kindergarten teachers seemed wonderful and it was only a half day afternoon schedule. They had a couple neighbors on the cul-de-sac that picked up their own kids and Robert was always included if Joseph couldn't make it. Having his son in school actually helped Joseph as a Cop by allowing the single father some extra sleep or giving him time to put out some crime photographs on his table at home while Robert was gone. He turned his garage into a darkroom so he could develop photographs while being at home more hours.

As a Field Investigator you became an expert in data collection and in determining cause of crimes and pattern injury identification. Additionally, Joseph studied photography and Law in his spare time to improve his documenting techniques. Being a Detective before he was a Field Investigator helped him know what types of clues or documentation to look for in a crime scene that would be important for prosecution or clarity. When Joseph rolled up with his camera to a scene, most of the time Detectives just let him do his thing.

Every Officer contributes a unique skill set. Alvarez was invaluable to his department because of his ability to speak Spanish and the department rewarded him and a few others with a $1 per hour foreign language pay increase in the recent contract negotiation. Detectives were happy to see him as their F.I. in Spanish speaking neighborhoods, he had an intimate grasp of the culture. He once impressed his Sargeant by recommending to a homeowner to paint the Virgin Mary on his casita wall facing a garbage alley that kept getting graffiti. Months and years later the Virgin was left untouched all around.

Investigative prowess is crafted and Joseph furthered his techniques as an F.I. Working across the city now, he was learning how certain neighborhoods were trending to specific types of crime and if different Police Commands could connect the dots, they could be proactive about issues. Joseph became an unofficial liaison to different squads as an F.I., the department constantly adapting to changing trends in crime. His sons favorite baby sitter Sharon was married to Detective Robert Valtierra who did his own form of crime mapping before everything went digital. Valtierra and Alvarez both led briefings often and were able to get squads looking for specific things in certain areas, that would end up occurring.

Domestic disputes were the most common call. Drugs and alcohol fueled the majority of violent crime, all crime really. Property crime would commonly rise by population increases like a new apartment complex, combined with value of drugs and items desired by criminals. If the price of drugs went up in a neighborhood Valtierra might predict shootings go up and then sure enough more rip-offs happened. The Detective knew what times businesses did their nightly drops and had lists of owner's home numbers.

As businesses evolved with security measures, criminal's habits changed and new ways to commit old crimes were always invented for Police to figure out. Joseph got called to photograph the scene of an ATM machine stolen by a tractor. He arrived to nothing more than some holes in the ground. A security camera caught a grainy image of the heist, then the inventive brute vanished. The camera didn't show that they most likely used a drag behind them to cover their tracks as the ground was graded so.

In the late summer of 1986 Joseph was up in Santa Fe for work with one of their Detectives. It was only the second time Joseph had been there, the first was with Eileen. What a charming beautiful downtown. Everything looked half luxurious half suspended in time from 300 years ago. At a teahouse on Canyon Road, he met a lovely Detective wearing a wedding ring. They struck up a good conversation. She had been in a long marriage and found Joseph very charming and handsome. Enchanted, she did something she had never done before and invited him to dinner the next weekend. She winked at him and said in her seductive voice, "We'll just leave this ring at home.

⚖ ⚖ ⚖

HE WAS NERVOUS ALL WEEK, but that next weekend he left Robert at a sleepover with the Tanner boys and hesitantly came out to Maria Isabel's restaurant in Downtown Santa Fe. The sisters were beautiful ladies, Native American with gorgeous dark hair from the Pueblo of Ohkay Owingeh and the husband of the Santa Fe Officer worked at Los Alamos Labs. The Detective had hooked Joseph up, her sister looked like the singer Sade, with the same caramel complexion and elegance. Her long black hair pulled back and braided down her back. The sister enjoyed when Joseph spoke in Spanish to the pretty waitress, making the lady laugh and then bring another menu. At one point they looked over and saw the Governor sitting across the room and everybody was having a great time. Joseph hadn't taken off his wedding ring in years.

The sister had traveled all the way from Boston where she was a teacher and hadn't been home in a year. Missing home and longing for the nightlife, she wanted to go out imbibing after dinner. Making the best decision he had made in years, they said goodnight to her sister and brother-in-law and went bar hopping at different nice hotels and then dancing at Evangelos nightclub near the Plaza. Joseph was in a dream sequence all night, separated from his profession and all obligations. He hadn't relaxed in years and that night he forgot every care in the world for hours.

After last call, they went outside with all the remaining patrons and she walked over to use a payphone. Chilly for a summer night, Joseph watched in awe at her body in a long black dress under a street light, while others moseyed about in front of closed shops and art galleries in all directions. She smiled and gave him a cabeceo as she hung up. They slowly walked together enraptured in each other's affection, taking their sweet time up West San Francisco St. Her lips like velvet. Thousands of stars lit up the night sky with a mountain silhouette in the distance.

They passed the Five and Dime store and shopping center along the main Plaza and continued up to the beautiful Hotel La Fonda, a giant adobe structure just before the town's Basilica. They walked into the extravagant lobby up to the carved wood reception and her friend slipped them a key. A rush of excitement hit him. Joseph hadn't even touched a woman since his wife passed, but these opportunities happen once or twice in a lifetime if you're lucky and they went up the elevator together. The next morning, he woke up a new man as she slipped off into the day, leaving her contact info in Lynn. He wore a smile for the next 72 hours straight at least. Smooth operator.

STAYING ON TOP of union matters, Joseph was a regular at the Fraternal Order of Police Lodge and he tried to understand the State Legislature. New Mexico has a pretty fair balance politically, with the Republican Party dominating the majority of the land and rural areas. The Democratic Party has the big cities vote and the political pendulum swings for Governor every other generation historically. In November of 1986 New Mexicans elected Republican Garrey Carruthers to lead the State, an agricultural guru. He would replace outgoing Governor Toney Anaya who shocked everyone by commuting the sentence of Gerald Clines killer, from the death penalty to life in prison. Now the family would have to deal with parole board hearings for years to come. The Governor had previously commuted sentences of Santa Fe prison rioters who helped "negotiate" the end and release of prison guards taken hostage.

Politics were always complicated. When Joseph attended college, as a freshman he witnessed a mini-riot on campus in El Paso. There were some Palestinian radicals chanting and Joseph watched them clash with other students and then Police came in and mostly separated the groups. The scene left an impact on Joseph and he didn't like to be near large groups or gatherings of people after that. He kept the images of that day in the back of his mind, randomly thinking about how irrational individuals in a group could be when they start intensifying emotions. As a Field Investigator, sometimes the radio would make a specific dispatch requesting the services. One night Joseph took a call to a curious address.

1600 Pennsylvania Street, NE 87110.

Joseph showed up expecting the White House, but instead found a drab two story apartment complex. Avenue must be French for fancy, he thought as he parked. Victims are often waiting outside once they've called Police and Joseph arrived to three men waiting to his dispatch of "homeowner arrived to a break-in." The three men waiting at the foot of the stairway were foreigners who spoke English and at first, he thought they were Mexican, but realized quickly their accent was not Spanish. The men were nervous as they led him to an upstairs unit. Joseph saw the door showed no signs of forced entry and he drew his weapon and flashlight. Upon entering, he saw the place had been tossed. As he took a minute to clear the rooms, he noticed that every single room was rummaged through, almost like the way he and other Detectives did on Police raids.

Noticing a few curiosities, Joseph put on his gloves and asked the men to wait in the living room while he got out his fingerprint collecting kit. The TV hadn't been stolen and in one bedroom he had seen an empty box of .22 ammunition. Only these were glazer rounds or snake shot, typically used by farmers or desert dwellers. These rounds also can potentially serve terrorists for airplane use as they won't puncture a cabin window to cause loss of pressure, but could put a person down. Joseph had learned about these in a briefing when the FBI raided the home of an Albuquerque man in 1981, former green beret Eugene Aloys Tafoya, who had all kinds of Libyan terrorist materials about a network both in the U.S and abroad. Out of sight, Joseph took off his glove and placed a thumb print on a table lamp.

Returning to the living room, Joseph carried the lamp carefully with his gloves on. He asked the men if any of them had touched the lamp and showed them his own fingerprint that he had planted, much larger than their hands. The middle-aged men shook their heads no. Joseph faked a radio transmission about the fingerprint and then waited for the radio to announce anything, pretending it was a response for him. That's when Joseph asked them to take their fingerprints to compare them to the large print to determine if this was from someone that broke in to the apartment. The men spoke for a moment, a long minute. One of them convinced the other two. They each gave their prints on a card Field Investigators carry stacks of and the last of the three was sweating at the hands so profusely that Joseph had to wipe his hand twice before inking them. Joseph showed the men how the large thumbprint was different and he collected it, lifting it onto a card and tagging it for "evidence" in front of them.

Ready to leave the curious apartment, Joseph was walking out when he mentioned something else that wasn't stolen. He made a comment about a beautiful gold plaque they had hanging by their front door written in a foreign language. "It's a good thing they didn't steal this plaque of Israel." One of the men's faces changed and he rushed over to Joseph by the door, getting right in his face and almost bumping him. The man pointed to the plaque and then Joseph and said "That is the great nation of Palestine and don't you forget it." Joseph tilted his head back a little and snapped back, "My apologies. Palestine, is that where the bible was written?" The two men looked at each other intensely and then wished each other a good night. Joseph left and called in a long lunch break and went straight to the FBI office in town.

That particular incident always bothered Joseph, he never heard anything of it and always wondered. The U.S. Marines and French soldiers lost in the Beirut barracks bombing in '83 and the USS Stark attack fresh in his mind. Being a Field Investigator was full of memorable incidents. He found the work intriguing, often gruesome, but he was a bit desensitized from working the rotten animal kingdom of sex crimes. Still several scenes were shocking to him, every week something appalling happened in a major city.

One day Joseph was called to photograph the first person he had ever arrested, an old man wife beater who now years later had been killed by his wife. The same lady Joseph and Ted Keoppinger had driven to a hospital and taken to a domestic violence shelter a week later as a Rookie. Once this same woman had tried to poison the abusive husband with tea. It was still legal to rape your wife in New Mexico throughout the 1980's. The elder lady finally had enough of his abuse and walked over to him as he was on the toilet and shot him in the chest with a shotgun. With ligature scars on her neck from previous incidents, she called the Police on herself and smoked her only cigarette of freedom while she waited.

The worst things Joseph ever photographed involved Cops or kids. One warm summer night tragedy struck both. A Police Officer arrived home and had placed his gun high up and out of reach of his toddler, up on top of a stand as tall as Joseph. In the time it took for him to use the bathroom, the toddler climbed up and took the gun out of its holster. The little boy pointed it towards his baby brother in a chair.

It was very hard for Joseph and anyone else to document that crime scene. The lives of the brother, dad and mom would be altered forever after the loss and all had long term issues. At home Joseph would always do the same exact thing with his gun, with an almost identical piece of furniture. Robert was a very well behaved mature young boy, but Joseph never left his gun unattended again.

Chapter 25

Partners in Crime

JOSEPH DIDN'T HAVE MUCH OF A SOCIAL LIFE, but when word got around that he played college baseball, he was recruited in the Summer and Fall of '86 to playing in a men's softball league on a team with 11 other Cops. He couldn't refuse as games were scheduled on his nights off and with 15 other teams in the league all sponsored by businesses, it sounded fun. The team's name read across the left chest of their blue shirts, proudly displaying in white lettering F.O.G., for flatulent old guys. Beards weren't allowed on the department, but their variety of mustaches and sideburns gave each of them a certain masculine flair. They didn't wear hats or helmets, most of them had some nice 1980's wavy hair, or the short and shag haircut, two guys were rocking the baby mullet. Whoever scouted did their job. The guys won most games big and looked good doing it.

One of his teammates, he had previously met the night Eileen passed away in the hospital, when Joseph met several Police Officers. There was a handsome Rookie that night from the Academy class after Joseph's, named John Carrillo. Athletic with Hollywood good looks, Carrillo had played baseball locally for St Pius X. He had a pregnant girlfriend Daphne who had worked with Eileen at Carrows and she would sit with Robert at the games or he would play with other Cops kids and sometimes go off on sleep overs with them.

ONE NIGHT after beating a team pretty good, the dozen lawmen on the team all went and celebrated with a couple beers in the parking lot. Most of them had come in their Police cruisers, but they drank out of the back of a truck for over a half hour. Rich in jubilation and exercising decorum, the team was hanging out in the lot of Los Altos Park a little after it had closed. It was nighttime and the fields had turned off their lights. The evening quiet, one of the guys had his radio on low and monitored the city after hours.

Coming from the street, they watched as a Police cruiser showed up to the parking lot sporting their new top lightbar with built in PA. Before anybody could see who was coming, the car hit the group with their spotlight. A few of the guys worked that beat and held up their badge or flipped off the silhouette of the vehicle as they covered their eyes at the bright light shining. Meanwhile Ofc Brichetto said, "It's just Allen" and he flashed a full moon, prompting the car to honk its air horn and making everybody start laughing until John Carrillo said, "Oh no Dude stop it's the Chief." Joseph and everybody's eyes got huge and they just kept laughing pointing at Ofc. Brichetto as he desperately raced his britches back on. They were still laughing, but trying to gather themselves.

The Chief was not amused, he turned off his spotlight and stuck his arm out of his window, calling Joseph over with a wave and shout "ALVAREZ." Joseph wasn't expecting his name and got serious real fast, as did the others at the call out. Everyone listened in as Joseph approached to the baritone voice of, "You know anything about some reports from neighbors of loud drinking at the park?" Now Joseph was very serious and before he could respond, the Chief continued, "Anyone not drinking?" With lowered smiles, Brichetto and Carrillo raised their hands as the air stood still. The Chief stroked his chin and contemplated the situation in a long pause. "Time to wrap it up," he told the group. "Yes sir," Joseph said sheepishly. Now feeling about two inches tall as the Chief long paused again…then asked him, "Did you guys win?" Joseph nodded and smirked as the Chief remained stoic in another long pause. "Alright Joseph, you all be careful tonight. Keep it down. I'll see you around."

Even though they were related by marriage, Joseph was surprised to hear his first name come out of the Chief's mouth. Then the Chief took out his flashlight and shined it over to the group and said, "No more drinking in public and no DWI's tonight, sleep there if you need to…I mean it!" It was silent. Then the Chief shined his light on one particular culprit hiding in the back with a cap on, pulled low. "And you, I don't know who you are, but I can guarantee you…you need to get some sun on those cheeks." The guys were trying to hold their laughter until the hard-nosed Chief shook his head and said "Have mercy on me eyes," then drove off with no expression.

⚖ ⚖ ⚖

Saturday night February 21, 1987.

Joseph got called out with another F.I. to a wealthy neighborhood at the base of the mountains, he had never once even been near that pocket before. Each of them had to park some ways away from the address as a sea of lights lit up the dark neighborhood, revealing multiple agencies, neighbors and news crews gathered along the street. Even the new RV mobile command center was there, a tan Southland motorhome with the department's logo on the passenger side. Joseph collected his camera and he and the other F.I. met the Chief for a quick briefing outside the beautiful two-story home, before he entered the scene with his partner.

At 11:32pm a tall slender Rookie, Officer John Messimer, 23, was dispatched as the secondary unit in reference to a domestic dispute at 4613 Hilltop Place NE. The youngest guy in his squad, he was recently cut loose two months ago to ride alone. The call was originally dispatched that a female called on the phone hysterical, saying that she was being beaten and then the phone line hung up. Officer John Carrillo, 27, had been dispatched as the primary unit. While enroute to the call, Ofc. Carrillo asked the 911 Dispatcher to call the number back. The Officer was informed the phone was answered, but then hung up immediately.

Officer Messimer turned on Larchmont St. in the affluent neighborhood near the mountains and saw Ofc. Carrillo awaiting his arrival inside his vehicle. When he spotted Messimer they proceeded forward together up the street. They parked their vehicles a couple houses down at the bottom of Hilltop Place and they approached on foot. As they came up on the address, 4613, Carrillo used his radio to confirm the numerical location through the dispatcher. It was confirmed and as they approached the house on a sidewalk, Messimer saw lights on upstairs get turned off.

It was a big house, meticulously landscaped. You could easily fit 6 cars in the driveway and 10 along the yard. They passed the long driveway and walked up a brick path from the sidewalk to the front door. Ofc. Carrillo knocked on the nice custom wood door that was facing South with a double-paned thin rectangle window that was vertical in the middle from their waist up to the eyes view. Messimer peaked into a separate window on the side and didn't see anyone as Carrillo knocked again.

The partners switched and Messimer knocked while Carrillo looked around for any signs of a victim, then a light came on that Messimer could see through the front door window and as it illuminated it exposed a staircase. "See anything?" Officer Carrillo asked. That's when Messimer began to see the silhouette of someone coming down the staircase. Messimer nodded yes as he fixated on the figure and Carrillo announced "ALBUQUERQUE POLICE." After a few seconds more lights came on and the door opened.

An older White male, balding, wearing glasses appeared. He was about 5.5 and 170lbs, dressed in black slacks, dark socks and a white t-shirt. The man just stared with intense eyes and raised his eyebrows to field an inquiry. Ofc. Carrillo asked, "Is your wife here?" The male stated, "I'm not married!" Ofc. Carrillo then asked the male, "Do you have a girlfriend?" "NO" the male said annoyed. Messimer asked "Do you have a daughter?"

Further annoyed, the man said "I'm the only one here, you can look around if you want." The Officers accepted and stepped in.

Officer Carrillo asked dispatch to again call the phone line where the 911 call originated from. All three men heard the kitchen phone start ringing. Carrillo then told the man that a female called from this residence saying that she was beaten. The male then stated, "The master bedroom is upstairs…I'll show you." Officer Carrillo gladfully accepted, "Go ahead," advising the male to go first with his arm. The male then proceeded to walk upstairs with Carrillo behind and Messimer third.

At the top of the stairs was the bathroom door to the right. The large room became a big square with 3/4 of the space a bedroom and 1/4 a bathroom/closet combo. You could walk around the bed to enter and exit the closet from the top of the bedroom or enter the bathroom at the door near the stairs and connect to the closet. Inside the bathroom there was a sink vanity then a quick turn right to a set of sliding doors separating the sink area from the toilet space and the toilet from the closet. Well-furnished, the bedroom itself was bigger than most people's apartments. On the unmade king size bed, Officer Messimer noticed a woman's brush. The Officers watched the man keenly and looked all around, but didn't see anyone.

Next the men walked downstairs with the male leading. They started to clear the house and in the dining room Messimer saw a door open leading outside. The tall Rookie walked closer to reveal a sliding screen door that he then unlocked and stepped out onto a patio leading to a beautiful backyard where he shined his light around and saw nothing but a nice lawn. Back in the kitchen when Messimer entered and closed the screen, Carrillo asked the man, "Who's comb was that on the bed? The male replied, "What comb?" Ofc Carrillo then said, "The comb on the bed." The male defended, "It's my comb!"

Gesturing like he wasn't trying to hide anything, the male then proceeded to take the Officers through the rest of the lower part of the house. For a few minutes they proceeded quickly through two downstairs bedrooms, a den and a bathroom to look for any female, but again turning up nothing. Having exhausted the house, Carrillo persisted about the bed upstairs, "The comb looks like a female comb, who's is it?" The agitated male then replied, "My attorney will answer that!" His bad energy protruding, the balding man walked back towards the kitchen and the Officers followed. That's when the ornery male picked up a grey cordless phone off its base, extended the antenna out and began dialing. Cordless phones were expensive and rare to see in those days. An assertive Messimer spoke to the pacing man, "Look we're not here to give you a hard time, a female called us and said she was being battered at this address."

Paying attention to the phone, the male ignored the Officers and started walking upstairs with his phone and the Officers followed behind. When they arrived upstairs the man went left and began speaking to someone on the phone and went and sat on a chair. "*The Police are here, at least that's who they claim to be. They broke in....No they're just holding me now.*" Messimer gave a glance to Carrillo who tapped his tape recorder to remind the Rookie this is all being recorded. The male then hung up the phone, got up from the chair and walked over to a dresser and picked up a briefcase. He then proceeded to walk away from the Officers into the restroom with the case.

The Police followed passed the stairs to the sink as the man entered the restroom and turned right into the toilet area and told them, "I'm going to go to the bathroom" then tried to slide the door shut behind him, but Messimer stuck his foot in the way to prevent it from closing. "This is my house, Cop," barked the man in protest. Ofc Carrillo then said "That's ok" and nudged the Rookie Officer who then took his foot from out of the door which quickly closed and locked.

"Where does the bathroom go?" Carrillo asked his partner. "Theres another door on the other side" said Messimer and both Officers went to go walk out the bathroom to go around the bed. Officer Messimer was exiting the doorway into the bedroom at the stair top with Carrillo behind him next to the sink when the male shouted to them, "Close the door" Officer Messimer fired back, "It's not my house." Then he saw Carrillo reach for his gun and a gunshot went off. Ofc Carrillo fell inside the bathroom as Messimer spun around and unholstered.

Messimer yelled "John…John" and then instinctively reached down and drug his partner back towards him just as the male cleared a jam and fired another shot at both Officers from back inside the closet. Covering his partner Messimer returned two shots back and pulled out his radio announcing "442 PD-83" as the scurrying male shot a few rounds again at them. Drywall pieces and cabinet shards were spattering onto the Officers as gunfire erupted and bullets whizzed close. Zeroed in, Messimer shot two more and radioed, "442-PD-83 Officer Down!"

The male continued his onslaught firing back towards them in double bursts, using a mirror to aim his trajectory closer with each round. As Messimer protected his partner he and the crazed homeowner made eye contact through the mirror and the man fired another round towards the Officers, using walls to conceal his body. The man fired just above Carrillo and next to Messimer, missing both by inches. Now the man could come forward and shoot the downed Officer again or run out of the closet and flank them from behind in the bedroom.

Messimer fired two more rounds and the man fired one back. When Messimer went to fire again, his gun clicked and he realized he was out and then he jumped behind a chair with an ottoman to get cover. The Officer was separated from his partner now by ten feet and he flicked out the cylinder of his revolver and before he could load one bullet the man opened the sliding door from the closet to the bathroom and started to charge near his downed partner. The Rookie instinctively closed his cylinder and pointed it at the sliding door and stood up, the man saw in the mirrors reflection and stopped his charge then winged a shot at Messimer and took cover back in the closet.

"Freeze, drop the gun," Officer Messimer commanded as he tried another quick reload. He put all 6 bullets in mere seconds and ran to cover his partner, then heard a sliding door open and the male appeared in the bedroom from the closet door across from them and started firing at him from another angle then dashed back in the closet. Messimer fired one shot back at the door then mirrored his dash and fired one into the closet after passing over his downed partner. He almost got him and had the man pinned in a corner of the closet from his angle as he covered his downed partner. He yelled to the man, "Drop the gun and come out with your hands up!" Just then he heard a door crash open downstairs and he could just catch a glimpse down the stairwell opening of one of their squad members. "Stay there Richard," Officer Messimer yelled, informing the arriving Officer not to walk up into the line of fire. 3 long minutes had passed.

Time stood still as Messimer focused all of his training on ending this so that he could get his partner to the hospital. Carrillo was on the floor struggling to breathe, shot in the chest, he was writhing in pain. Messimer engaged the man intensely, "Drop the gun, and come out with your hands up!!" The man replied, "I don't even know who you are." Messimer yelled a plea, "I won't shoot you, come out with your hands up!" A thin plume of smoke had filled the bathroom and Messimer took sharp breaths to control his adrenalin. The male then stuck his hands out from the closet door exiting to the bedroom and threw the gun on the floor. Messimer sidestepped over and took command, "Put your hands on top of your head and come out!!

Showing his hands the man then came out from behind the closet door across the room into view and walked out into the bedroom, placing his hands on top of the dresser he had originally grabbed the briefcase from. The back of the man's white shirt sweaty and his balding comb over hair was wild from the gunfight. Messimer had carefully tracked his movements and while moving he was able to look down the stairs to glance at Ofc. Dannenbaum and said "Help John." Dannenbaum hurried up the stairs with his gun drawn. Messimer rushed over to the male and pulled him by the back of his shirt and pushed him onto the bed. Rookie John Messimer handcuffed the male and searched him. When the man was secured, Messimer looked up and could see another Officer in the room above Carrillo, who Messimer asked, "Is he alright?" Ofc Buck replied, "No he's 10-7!"

They rushed Officer Carrillo to the hospital, but he was already dead before he would ever get to see his newborn boy grow up and go on to play college baseball. That night as his squad members arrived to the scene, some of them had to be controlled from hurting the 47-year-old physicist from Sandia National Laboratories. His 9mm had outgunned the Officers and with plenty more ammunition it was actually a second jam that likely caused him to surrender. He had indeed picked up a prostitute that night on Route 66 Central Avenue and violently attacked her in the bedroom upstairs. She was able to escape to a neighbors and call Police. This psycho had somehow obtained a top-secret security clearance to work at a nuclear facility, despite the investigation revealing a sordid past.

After not losing any Officer in the 60's or 70's, Albuquerque Police lost another great one in the 1980's. A brutal decade for the department. As a result, the Chief made an executive order to purchase 9 millimeter semi-automatic handguns to the current Academy and additionally all current Officers could come trade in their old six-shot .38 revolver for a 9mm with 15+1 round in the chamber. If they wanted to, they just had to qualify at the shooting range with the new weapon.

This would be the last time the department sent police out with six shooters. Most made the transition, while a few old timers stuck to the model they had used their entire career. The old Wild West revolver would be phased out with each passing year as the old school retired off into the sunset. Each Officer with the new weapon could have two extra magazines on their belt, putting them at 46 rounds on duty.

SHOTS ALLEGEDLY FIRED BY CHAMBERLAIN

HOMICIDE
4613 HILLTOP N.E.
JOHN CARRILLO
87-14840

approximate scale: inch equals 1 foot
drawn by:
Guy A. Pierce 3-10-87

UCR

OFFICER JOHN ARTHUR CARRILLO, EOW FEB. 22, 1987. AGE 27.

Officer Carrillo's brother George was a member of the Department and his son became a lawyer, just to show you how deep an influence can go beyond the grave.

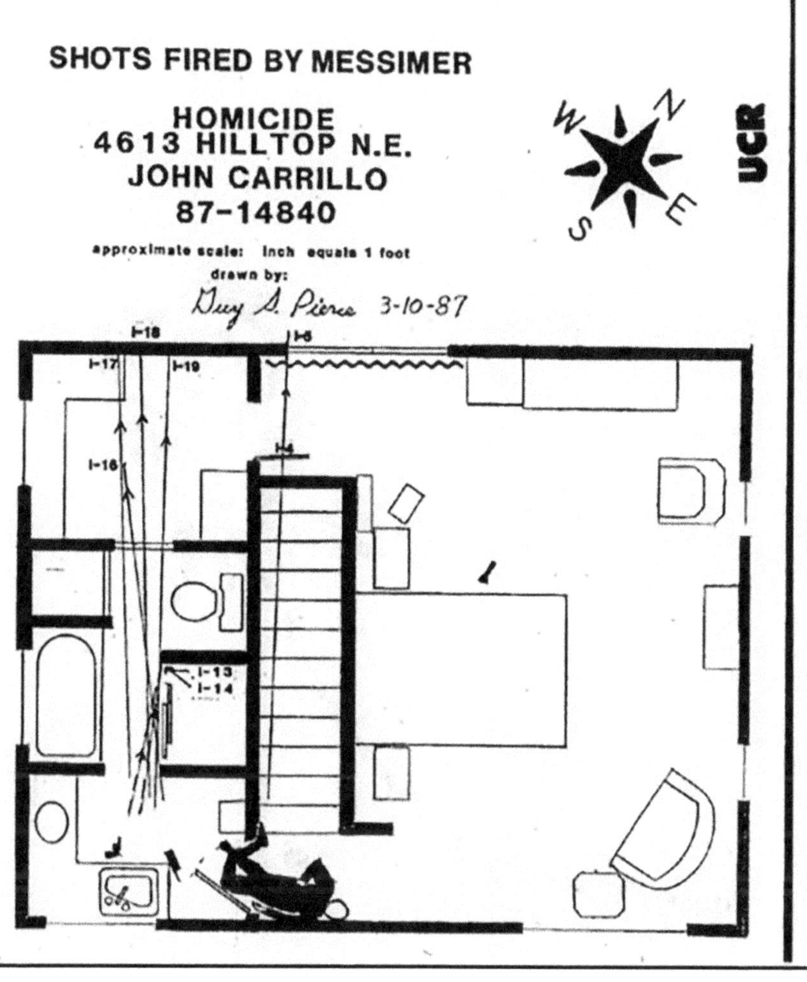

John Messimer was awarded the Medal of Valor for his actions, the highest award in the department, seldomly presented. He would go on to marry an Officer with the department and serve a distinguished career as a SWAT operator. Spending his career encountering many dark situations, none would hurt him more than that night.

Chapter 26

Code of Silence

REELING FROM THE LOSS of another great Officer, the department's union started to get organized. Officer Carrillo was not wearing a vest the night he was killed, Messimer and others who wore them had to pay out of pocket. Many different working conditions needed change and after losing an Officer every other year that decade, tensions ran deep.

There had been several times where politicians failed Officers with policies or lack of funding that put them in danger. After Carrillo died without proper equipment, no vest, some Officers may or may not have left a black rose and a note with a drawing of a certain State Representative with a knife in the back, who had history of bad policies and slights. The message was that they had been stabbed in the back, but it was perceived as a death threat by the Representative when he came to his desk and found it. The ensuing Black Rose Scandal led to 3 Officers being suspended and Gabby's Family Restaurant holding a fundraiser for their legal defense, selling a white shirt with a long single black rose on the front. The shirts sold out immediately and they had to order hundreds more after the first printing to support Officers Greg Williams, Dave Heshley and Sgt. Henry Nuñez.

⚖ ⚖ ⚖

It wasn't the first time the department was marred in controversy. It's hard to find any Police Records pre-1981when a mysterious fire occurred, that damaged files, but not any structure. Lost forever were dozens of heroic Police reports for historians to understand the city a little bit more in-depth. Coincidentally the department had recently come under fire for running surveillance on dozens of politicians, lawyers, judges and other prominent figures. The City Council requesting Civilian Oversight to look into the matter, curiously just before the fire consumed much of the department's files. Police make better friends then foes.

JOSEPH HAD ONCE MADE SOME ENEMIES and/or gained the respect from of his departments higher brass one day at court when he worked Sex Crimes. Two young police officers had taken turns having some consensual fun with some girls on back-to-back nights, in their squad car. Only on the second night one of them became very aggressive when his radio tone came on and he was violent with one of the girls to finish after he received a dispatch. The young girls went to the Police and turned out to be 16-year-olds. Earlier that summer Joseph had been in El Paso for a week with Robert and had two twin cousins aged 16, Yvonne and Carmen, that were so sweet to Robert.

When Joseph was ready to testify in court for the prosecution, the two officers entire unit hierarchy showed up to testify to one of the officer's character. As they sat in the hallway outside the courtroom, a lieutenant made a comment along the line of, "He was just a young 22-year-old tricked into dating a lying little girl." Joseph's cackles raised, he was a young Detective, but he stood up and set their entire squad straight right there. "All of you get the fuck out of here!! Respect this badge. I'm going to reveal details about your boy that will prove how fucking ignorant you are to show up here right now like this. He and that other pig are both going to jail!" Towering above the strangers he looked at all of them, up and down the row they sat, connecting eyes with each as he pointed to the stairwell down the hall. His gun and clean badge attached to his hips. They all thought about it as they stared back intensely and then they collected their things, got up and walked out, never making it in the courtroom.

Years later one of those two officers convicted by Joseph's team would go on to escape prison with a separate group that included one of the most notorious cops kicked off the department in its history. Robert Earl Davis and six others escaped the Santa Fe Prison on July 4th, 1987. Independence Day for 7 really bad guys, who had smuggled a gun into the State Penitentiary and kidnapped one Guard to enter a control room where they shot another Guard Todd Wilson, who luckily recovered. Kidnapping a third Guard to get past doors to climb up onto the roof, they then used a pole to vault over the barbed wire fence in a planned escape. By the time authorities were alerted, the men were gone for nearly a half hour and hundreds of Police around the State began a search.

Robert Davis had already escaped a Los Lunas prison in similar fashion with 4 other inmates in 1985, producing a gun inside the jail and fleeing. He was caught with some of the escapees after he was wounded twice in a shootout at a house with a group of Albuquerque Patrolmen, Bernalillo Sheriff's Deputies and New Mexico State Police on Drake Avenue in the Paradise Hills Subdivision. Davis also had charges for having a gun in a Torrance County Jail in 1983. He had always been a mastermind, even in defeat.

Graduating the Academy in 1969, Davis worked his way up to Burglary Detective by the mid-1970's. A tall strong man with trimmed dark wavy hair, short sideburns and a firm jawline, he was intimidating physically. He even played on the departments best softball team that sometimes traveled. Some of his own squad began to suspect him of criminality when burglary suspects kept reporting someone stealing from their house while it was being searched. Eventually time caught up with Davis in 1977 when he was pulled over by a motorcycle cop for speeding in a sedan. Only the car was stolen, belonging to a man he had jailed the day before who posted bond and came home to find his car missing. The crooked cop's partner was also fired as a result of not cooperating with the investigation and Davis did a small amount of jail time as the State suspended his sentence for probation. Officers in the Penitentiary can have an extra level of liability.

Time caught up with Davis again in March of 1981 in Farmington, NM when he tried to rob a Furr's Cafeteria late at night. This was no ordinary arrest, upon gathering intel and evidence, Davis was linked to a string of robberies with 3 other policemen or former policemen with the Albuquerque Police Department, including a cadet at the Academy. Each sang like birds on the others and revealed their accomplice in more than 40 burglaries of businesses across the State and into at least Colorado and Texas. A sophisticated operation, they had radio crystals for different cities to plug in and pick up on different Police frequencies stretching from Oklahoma to California. This led to a sentence of almost 70 years for Davis and one of the departments biggest black eyes.

Now escaped, Davis was free again with 6 other fugitives, each with lengthy criminal pasts. While State Police conducted a search with Federal Agencies and multiple helicopters, city Cops were on high alert with 7 escapees possibly headed there way. Joseph and all his squad members did everything in twos until further notice. He stayed on and rode an extra shift with Kenny Williams as a passenger that first night in the succeeding squad, tensions were that high.

Luckily for public safety, Davis was captured after 2 days, in the back of a semi-truck trailer 40 miles South of Albuquerque headed towards Mexico. The rest of the prisoners were found one by one, but one of the other prisoners carjacked a family in Flagstaff, Arizona and had them drive all the way to Barstow, California. This same guy had once escaped a Wyoming prison and had no intention of going back. He left the family in a hotel tied up then took their young daughter to Garden Grove, California. Later on, she was spotted by Police walking and helped lead them to the man. With no honor amongst thieves, the perverted escapee led authorities to the remaining two fugitive's motel after 3 weeks on the lam.

There is absolutely nobody more dangerous to society than a badge that has gone rogue, but unfortunately bad cops are born out of human nature. In the late Summer of '87 Joseph was called into the Chief's office. The Chief said he needed someone he could trust for a position, but that he was concerned with Joseph's dealings with certain members of the union. Having recently been voted as the vice president his mood grew concerned, he liked being an F.I. Unfortunately for him, the Chief told Joseph he would finish out the year in Internal Affairs, investigating his own department.

Joseph spent the next 7 months in misery. None of his buddies would talk to him anymore while he was in I.A. Investigating your own Police Department is one way not to make friends. The Department had over 800 sworn Officers by then, so things did happen. Internal Affairs is a necessary function for the checks and balance of a department, but not fun to work. It also disorganized Joseph personally, the new hours were hard to be there at home for Robert after school. He was embarrassed every time he picked up his son late from Rose and Juan's or Robert and Sharon's, Tom and Gerry's or any of the others who helped him survive fatherhood.

CHIEF BACA was the first leader in the departments history to hold a Master's Degree and he had encouraged Joseph to finish his degree after reviewing his file. Joseph talked to the admissions department at UNM and his previous credits from El Paso would expire after 10 years. He was surprised to find he was only about 2 semesters away from a Bachelor's degree in Sociology. He would need a little bit longer, but he did start to chop away with a class per semester at 8am every morning before work.

Finally in early 1988 Joseph was reassigned to be a Claims Validation Officer. The schedule was nice, he was able to take his son to school, get to class, go to work and arrive home about an hour after his son everyday if he didn't run into something. He also had weekends off for the first time in some years and now he could spend whole days with his son. There was even enough time to visit El Paso if they wanted to for the weekend. Robert always made Joseph watch DuckTales episodes after school and on Sundays it was pizza night and Joseph put on 21 Jump Street.

In Claims Validation, different Officers would come to Joseph, usually with some type of injury documented by a medical professional. Joseph would approve their paperwork and then try to find them a temporary desk job. With over 800 action figures working on the department, nicks and sprains can accumulate. Sports hernia, umbilical hernia, dog bite, nose bitten by a prostitute, infection from a needle poke, walking pneumonia infection and all kinds of other things happened every month.

A strong burly Officer came to Joseph's cubicle one day, verbally upset that he was being put on light duty. Roger Hoisington had a fierce persona and a fierce mustache. He was one of the premier SWAT operators with the department, often training the others. Roger had a heart incident on duty and wound up at Joseph's desk. When Joseph asked him where he was coming from and found out it was SWAT, he immediately knew where to place him and offered him a spot in Civil Litigations. "Hell no, I'm not wearing a suit all day." Then Joseph shook his head and said, "I know man, but SWAT keeps getting sued left and right and maybe you can offer some insight into why you guys are always destroying houses, save the department some coin!" Joseph smirked and his eyebrows raised. Hoisington smiled and accepted. He would be instrumental in improving the departments legal defenses against barricaded suspects and in rewriting Standard Order of Procedure to protect everyone.

⚖ ⚖ ⚖

One Saturday morning Joseph picked up the newspaper and was very sad to see one of his Academy classmates on the front page. Four days earlier on February 15, 1989, defensive expert, Officer Stephen House of the Titusville, Florida Police Department was shot and killed while serving a narcotics search warrant in the residence of a suspected dealer. Stephen was a member of the Emergency Response SWAT Team.

SWAT Operators wore armor with ballistic helmets and dressed in Nomex balaclavas to offer protection from the searing effects of gas or chemical flash fires, stun munitions and flying debris. Steve and his team quickly took the suspect in custody, but his dad ran into a bedroom and barricaded himself. House negotiated with the man to no avail. Steve and his team prepared to make entry after no success communicating with the man. Officer House began to lead the entry team into the bedroom by using a noise/flash diversion device, when the occupant began firing through the doorway. As he released the diversion, Officer House was struck in the left shoulder, which was not protected by his protective vest, and the bullet entered his chest cavity. He was survived by his wife and four children.

Joseph called Drew Banks and left him a message on his answering machine and when he called back later, they reminisced about the toughest guy they ever dealt with.

Officer Stephen Franklin House, Titusville Police Department, FL. EOW Feb. 15, 1989. Age 36.

Chapter 27

The Good the Bad and the Ugly

THE WILD WEST of New Mexico has produced some of the finest nature artists like Georgia O'Keefe and Edward Gonzales, sculptors like Maria Martinez and Glenna Goodacre, architects such as Mary Colter and John Gaw Meem, authors Mabel Dodge Lujan, Ernie Pyle, Tony Hillerman and Rudolfo Anaya and fine Native American artists like R.C. Gorman and Pablita Velarde. Art, jewelry and pottery have a long tradition in New Mexican culture. Collectors from around the world shop Santa Fe, Taos and Albuquerque or visit the Pueblos for fine art every day of the year.

One evening at the Crown Plaza Hotel, one of the city's finest hotels, a Police involved shooting took place that destroyed thousands of dollars of art. Police had been in vehicle pursuit and chased a subject to the 12-story luxury hotel. The man exited the stolen vehicle and ran inside the elegant hotel lobby. Several Police Officers pursued and could see he was armed or heard it called out on the radio as they rushed behind to protect any citizens in the large open lobby.

When they entered, the man had run a circle to nowhere and began pointing the gun at his own head while workers and people in the lobby scattered about as Officers fanned out. Officer Steve Nakamura had entered first with a shotgun and tried to calm the man, but he didn't comply and as he was starting to point his weapon at Officers, 6 Officers fired multiple rounds. The suspect was described by all Officers as looking like a movie scene, taking dozens of rounds without falling. His arms wildly flailing up, but he didn't drop the weapon and the onslaught continued before the suspect finally dropped backwards after a near 10 second barrage. Blood splattered all over the front counter and behind the front desk was a beautiful Navajo rug suspended to the ceiling that was covered in blood, the $10,000 price tag even had a spatter.

While the Lieutenant spoke to the very upset hotel management, a Sergeant had made sense of the entire scene except for 1 bullet that lodged in a giant planter nowhere near the downed suspect. The planter was 40 feet away and down a hallway that was out of view of the 6 shooting Officers. Nobody had noticed it, a housekeeper pointed it out to an Officer. "Hey who has a big caliber gun, a .44 or a 45?" the Sgt. called out to a group of 3 Officers involved. One of them shouted over to another Officer, Jeff Russell, "Hey man check your cannon, you missing something?" Officer Russell was surprised to find he had shot one round. He was the only Officer behind the suspect, entering the situation from a different door when the shooting started. With his gun in his right hand, he just started running for dear life and with a loud barrage of bullets flying he didn't realize he had fired a shot behind him. He had run South and his bullet flew North down a hallway into the planter.

His bullet had struck a tall plant vase, blowing a golf ball size hole into it, but surprisingly having kept 99% of the soil in, it almost went unnoticed at the scene. His Sergeant interviewed him and he did his spot on Clint Eastwood, "Well I asked the planter one question, do you feel lucky, well do ya punk?" The Sergeant gave an expression of "*Seriously*," but the joke wasn't wasted as two other Officers turned bright red with smiles as they struggled to keep their laughter in, around the serious Sarge. Jeffrey Cole Russell owned a ranch in Moriarty which was on the other side of the Sandia Mountains, the area referred to as the East Mountains. Looking like a cowboy movie star himself, Jeff was a huge western movie buff and loved the windmill from *The Outlaw Josey Wales* so much that he had an exact replica built on his own property.

IN THE SPRING OF 1989 Joseph was at his desk Downtown working Claims Validation when a big strong Officer showed up in his enclosed cubicle one day in an arm sling. Wearing a short-faded haircut, the physically fit man outweighed Joseph by 25 pounds of muscle. He explained to Joseph how he had hurt his arm racing motorcycles down in Ruidoso, NM. Joseph validated his medical paperwork with a stamp and a signature and he asked, "Ouch man, shit what kind of motorcycles do you race?" The clean-cut Officer Matt Griffin and Joseph then talked about motorcycles and engines for a few minutes before Joseph made some calls to find Griffin a temporary desk job.

Joseph was really surprised when he called a few departments with a warm body to assist and 3 departments asked who the Officer was and call after call each refused, basically citing Griffin as an asshole. One Sargeant said, "Black Matt Griffin or White Matt Griffin?" Joseph had to be coy not to let Griffin in on the insults as he was sitting in the room while Joseph was on the calls, but Griffin had no idea who Joseph was calling exactly. When Joseph replied "White" he heard "Hell NO" and the phone hung up.

Finally on his fourth try and running out of options a Lieutenant from evidence asked no questions immediately agreeing with, "Hell yeah send them down." Joseph turned and gave Ofc. Griffin a thumb up before hanging up and writing out a slip to validate the assignment. Griffin read the newspaper and gave a look of approval, there were definitely worse jobs to have, evidence would be a nice break.

Right after Matt Griffin's claim was validated, Officer Robert Valtierra came to visit Joseph. Standing about 5.8, strong and stout with wavy black hair and thick sideburns, he was one of Joseph's best friends and his wife was little Robert's favorite person that watched him. Joseph greeted him with a nickname and a question by asking, "Hey Valdirty, you know Matt Griffin?" In his distinctly pitched voice, Robert replied, "Which one White or Black?" Joseph said, "The White one." It was obvious Robert knew both as he nodded yes and perked open his eyes to receive a question.

Joseph asked, "Why doesn't anybody want to work with him, I just had three Sergeants turn him down before evidence took him, everybody needs a warm body so I was a little surprised." Valtierra replied, "Well you know he got fired by the Chief for not returning a $75 witness fee from a case he didn't testify in and then the Union got him hired back after he made a big stink, maybe that has something to do with it. He's been involved in some other controversies, he was fired by State Police I believe before he came on here." Joseph answered surprised, "Really? What's your take on him?" Robert said, "Well whatever I think about him, all I know is he possibly saved my life once." Joseph then remembered the shooting that Robert Valtierra was just involved in had included a number of other Officers.

A SNOWSTORM WAS BREWING one cold winter night in Albuquerque in January of 1989. In his Dodge Diplomat patrol car, Officer Valtierra witnessed a speeding car and attempted to initiate a stop, but the car led him on a pursuit towards the mountains. The speed of the chase increased as two additional units joined, one driven by Matt Griffin and the other by Sergeant Paul Heatley. After nearly six miles of giving chase the driver came onto Tramway Boulevard, the last major street before arriving to the neighborhoods of fancy houses that adorn the mountain side. As the driver came onto Tramway his car couldn't make the turn and he skid into a median and onto a rock, his tires were lifted in the air spinning, rendering the vehicle useless as it crashed into a halt. The driver began to exit his vehicle and so did each Officer.

Being the lead vehicle, the first Officer out of his car into the cold air was Valtierra, but as he tensely exited and began to draw his weapon, the situation took on a new danger. With Griffin and Heatley exiting their vehicles Valtierra had a gun pointed at him as the man looked for an escape. Valtierra's whole body instinctively stopped in reaction and he fired one shot at the man as a 4th Officer Steve Nakamura arrived in the backdrop drawing his gun. The bullet just missed its target and the middle-aged White male turned to flee, but kept pointing his gun over his shoulder as he ran across lanes towards a waist high barricade that lines Tramway then leads to houses. That's when a double volley of bullets from Griffin's 9mm rang out just as the man aimed back and was ready to jump the divider. As the man fell, he motioned and Heatley shot his .40 caliber one more time. The fleeing man had been hit in the back repeatedly in front of Nakamura exiting his vehicle, causing an ugly mess of flesh to blast out various body contents across the pavement.

All four of the Officers started screaming at the man to show his hands from four different vantage points. Further complicating matters a heavy snow began to fall onto the scene as they radioed in "Shots fired." The four took no risk and approached the still man with caution and guns drawn, the thick snowflakes liquified on hot barrels. The suspect was already dead as they placed his limp body into handcuffs. Valtierra looked around for the gun the man had pointed at him and nobody could find it, the snow growing heavier. He looked for over a half hour with other Officers before being removed for questioning.

Back at the Police Station, Internal Affairs separated the four Officers. Matt Griffin pissed them off when he refused to speak without a lawyer. Valtierra, Heatley and Nakamura gave statements. After hearing the various accounts, they focused on why Nakamura didn't fire, which he was adamant that because of his angle he didn't have a clean shot. He wasn't convincing investigators that he definitely saw a weapon in the suspects hand and there was no weapon found or recovered now hours later with dozens of Officers having scoured the area. Investigators began to suspect foul play and a cover up.

Then the media announced that there was no gun found on the suspect on a television in the station. Once one of the three Officers giving statements heard that, they got so pissed the other two could hear their tirade off in their separate rooms. The Officers were furious at the premature announcement and Valtierra insisted that they continue the search for the weapon. Back at the scene, the media stayed all night into the morning. After 12 hours it was finally discovered deep in snowy mulch, down an embankment the suspect was about to jump down into, the .22 pistol loaded with one in the chamber ready to fire at triggers pull.

WORKING DOWN in the Main Station, Joseph was able to see a lot of old friends in his day to day. Once he saw Ted Keoppinger and Al Byrnes in the same day, separately. It was nice to catch up, he was able to find out how their families were doing and tell them all about Robert. An aging Keoppinger was training Rookies at the Academy now and Byrnes was actually with a young ride-along Carol Oleksak that seemed squared away already. Always about business, both of his former Field Training Officers had asked about or mentioned the Ninja Bandit after exchanging pleasantries. He told them both that all he heard from one of his former F.I. buddies was that the guy liked to steal Camaros.

The Ninja Bandit was a serial bank robber in 1988 and 1989. The media had dubbed his nickname due to the stealth like manner he robbed banks, face covered dressed in all black from head to toe. Athletically jumping bank counters and controlling people. The guy was good, in and out, automatic weapon and a radio, assertive and gone in a flash. Robert Valtierra, Paul Heatley, Steve Nakamura and Matt Griffin had all sat in on briefings regarding the highly sought after suspect who had hit their district a few times using a modus operandi that nobody had seen the likes of, yet.

One morning a National Guardsmen came out to find their grey Camaro stolen in Jan of '88. The next day the soldiers Camaro was reported used in a robbery of the New Mexico Federal Savings and Loan bank. Next, the Bandit was seen in June at the Sun County Savings Bank, same thing and gone in a flash, fleeing in a stolen grey Camaro with a Colorado license plate. In September a Western Bank, using a grey colored Camaro with a separate Colorado plate than the one identified before. Detectives and FBI Agents were informed by a bank security guard that the Ninja Bandit had an Uzi automatic pistol with a brass catcher to collect any fired casings so as not to leave evidence in a shooting situation. High level planning for an individual.

Bank tellers were terrified around the city. Police recovered the Camaro, but it had been wiped clean. Another rusty brown Camaro was reported stolen by auto Detectives around New Years. Then the First Interstate

Bank was hit in mid-January of 1989 in a rusty brown Camaro. On April 3rd a Trans-Am that resembled the Camaros, was being stolen from its parking space. The owner came out to confront the bandit and was shot four times and murdered. Now the Ninja had entered new territory, but that didn't stop him when on April 17, 1989 the Bandit returned to the Sun County Savings Bank he had robbed the previous summer and struck again in the Trans-Am. This guy was a terrorist and athletic.

Robert Valtierra took a very special interest in the Ninja Bandit case. He had been doing his own crime mapping for years, banished to the garage by his wife to set up his mad lab. Blending his old school Detective skills with his advancement in modern technology, Valtierra had a suspect after months of plotting and connecting the dots. He had first found the timing of the robberies very peculiar to his own schedule.

Then Valtierra remember talking to a couple buddies, including conversations with Joseph and he put in some legwork over the next two weeks. He made a file and went straight to the Chief's office. On his way up he stopped to request a specific Deputy Chief of Detectives to be in the room. This was very uncharacteristic. Up top he showed them the file. They took it.

SITTING BEHIND a desk in an 8x8 open top enclosed cubicle wasn't ideal, but it offered some perks. Joseph learned a lot just by leaving his door open and mingling with Officers. Working Claims Validation was great in the comradery of meeting new faces and usually getting to see them a second time around when they were ready to go back to their old assignment. Roger Hoisington brought him a burrito in appreciation of his "help to the SWAT legal defense fund." Joseph wasn't there when it was Matt Griffins turn to be validated for a new assignment on July 10, 1989.

Out of his sling and ready to get back to patrolling, Griffin sat in the desk across from the female Claims Officer Clingenpeel. She was cordial, stamping his paperwork and then excusing herself out the door to make copies. Griffin sat inside the cubicle. When the door opened again 2 SWAT operators entered behind him and immediately placed their Swedish K submachine guns onto his head and back, the Lieutenant ordered. "Place your hands on the table." The Ninja Bandit listened and was disarmed then taken into custody.

"WHAT THE HELL?" Joseph said in astounded wonder that night when he arrived to see Robert Valtierra at his house to pick up his own son. The whole department was shocked by the news, it would be on all the stations for weeks to come. Valtierra gave a little insight, "He could have got away with it, but I started thinking…all these robberies occurred on our days off. Then there was a wild car chase with one of the Camaros and he winds up in a sling working evidence. Then BINGO, the shooting and I think, who has access to guns they can manipulate? So we just checked all the guns in evidence matching the Trans Am shooting."

Griffin had been stealing parts off a 9mm gun already in evidence. He changed out the barrel and bullet ejector with his own gun. After he used his weapon in the Trans-Am murder, he went and swapped out the parts back into evidence. Only he forgot to swap out the firing pin extractor that leaves unique little microscopic striation marks on bullets casing when it pulls them out upon firing. They were able to match him to the murder and then link up the rest of the crimes. The Ninja Bandit Griffin was sentenced to life for murder, plus 50 years in prison for his crimes.

Chapter 28

Land of Enchantment

BEING ONE OF THE LARGEST AMERICAN STATES in size, but one of the least populated, there was something majestic about the State of New Mexico that attracted Joseph to it. Although he happened to work in a job that allowed him to see the worst aspects of society, Joseph lived in a neighborhood where he didn't have to lock his door at night. He was really safe compared to most big cities in the U.S. and many parts of the world. Albuquerque was a big city surrounded by rural towns and Joseph's wild job wasn't really a reflection of how safe it was. Albuquerque had 190^2 miles of land plus 30^2 miles of South Valley, so even bad parts of town had their nice pockets full of vibrant culture and honest hard-working people.

To Joseph, New Mexico was always a place where anyone could relax in its enchantment. The State had less then 1.5 million people, but it was huge, the 5th largest in the U.S.A. behind Alaska, Texas, California and Montana. It was about the exact same size as Poland, just a little bit bigger than the country land wise. Joseph always found it funny when people would ask him if he had a green card or say that he spoke good English when he traveled and said he was from New Mexico. It happened all the time. *Seriously?* he thought, *Hadn't they heard of Billy the Kid or Georgia O'Keefe, the Atomic Bomb, Bugs Bunny...something?*

Joseph was a true Texan though, registering his Mustang with a Texas plate and a bumper sticker colored like the State Flag that read the State's newest anti littering slogan, "Don't Mess with Texas." Joseph loved the Cowboys in football, Rangers in baseball and Spurs in basketball having grown up watching the likes of Tom Landry, Roger Staubach, Tony Dorsett, Jim Sundberg and the Iceman George Gervin. He liked to attend UTEP vs UNM basketball games or work them if he could.

New Mexico was huge into sports, but only had one AAA minor league baseball team for the entire State. The Albuquerque Dukes had been the Los Angeles Dodgers affiliate since 1969 and played in the Pacific Coast League. Other than that, the University of New Mexico in Albuquerque and New Mexico State in Las Cruces provided the only other mid-major team sports. The Connie Mack World Series was held in Farmington every summer, bringing in baseball prospects from teams around the country. Boxing was extremely popular in the State and New Mexico had produced many champions including Bernalillo County Sheriff Deputy Bobby Foster of Albuquerque who went from boxing in the Air Force to World Champion fighting Muhammad Ali in 1972, a bout refereed by the future Judge, Mills Lane.

What really drew Joseph to New Mexico and prevented him from leaving were the landscapes and the wonderful weather. Albuquerque experienced all 4 seasons for about 3 months each and saw over 300 days of sunshine per year. Even on a snowy day, the sun would usually emerge for a few hours. The city and most parts of the State almost always had a bright blue sky above. New Mexico had kind of always been home, as a child his father Dino would take him every summer to Alamogordo and Joseph would play with his cousins in every landscape known. Across the State, mountains had emerged millions of years ago from volcanoes and earthquakes to form the southern Rockies. Bosque's or forests sprang along scarce Rivers and small lakes dotted the State, mostly in the North.

Joseph preferred Northern New Mexico because it was green and had more population than the southern half of the State. His father and mother loved the southern part of the State for day trips from El Paso. The Zia

State is mainly a dry desert where hummingbirds quench their thirst on cactus flowers as wily coyotes chase bunnies and roadrunners every day, but Northern New Mexico is very lush with trees, although fire danger is always high. Many parts of the State have amazing lighting storms and in some cases a single strike has caused thousands of acres to burn.

Southern New Mexico was hot and arid with cool nights. The North had all 4 seasons of weather for about 3 months each, with the summer or winter being the longest depending on the year. Anywhere in New Mexico it could be windy one day, snowing for a week after that and then clear skies for a month in the blink of an eye. The clouds in Albuquerque were brilliant and across the city there could be dozens of different colors to the clouds at any given time, oranges, yellows and pinks in the West and lots of wispy purple and blue hues in the East. For the most part though, it never got too hot or too cold for longer than a week or two at a time in the Duke City. Everyone had a list of complaints a mile long living in Albuquerque, but good food and weather weren't on anybody's list.

The Spaniards had once conquered New Mexico from the Southwest Pueblo Indians and called the land New Spain from 1535-1821. After Esteban the Moor scouted for riches, the Coronado expedition came in 1540 looking for the legendary Cibola 7 cities of gold and then Oñate's in 1598 setting up El Camino Real or the Royal Road, from Mexico City up to Taos, New Mexico. The Spaniards introduced horses and guns to the Pueblos and learned their techniques about farming. When they couldn't master the climate and their crops failed, some Spaniards began to steal from the Pueblos. After being exploited long enough, the great Pueblo Revolt took place when the Natives of Tewa, Taos and surrounding Pueblos that once warred, banded together to kill over 400 Spaniards to retake Santa Fe and claim the territory back from 1680-1692 after forcing the Spaniards to retreat from Santa Fe down past El Paso, TX. Natives burned dozens of large Mission Churches across the State in subsequent coordination.

Having lost so much by surprise, the Spaniards wrote their Monarchy and the Catholic Church for help. After regrouping and rearming over a dozen years, the Spaniards returned, surrounding Santa Fe with artillery cannons and negotiating a peaceful surrender. Back in control, the Spaniards searched for the Seven Cities of Gold and again forcibly converted the already monotheistic Pueblos to Catholicism by rebuilding Churches and Plazas in every town they likened to.

While tensions existed, so did many stories of love. With over 500 years of coexistence, many Native American's today have Spanish Surnames and all 19 Pueblos of New Mexico have a dedicated Santo or patron saint and celebrate special Feast days every year in their honor.

New Mexico had many strategic positions and trading posts, enticing Mexico to fight the Spaniards and take over the territory from 1821-1846. Then for two years the land was heavily fought for during the Mexican-American War, especially after Mexico had already lost Texas. In 1848, Mexico entered the Treaty of Guadalupe Hidalgo ceding the New Mexico Territory to the United States and ending the War. The southwestern border of New Mexico was formed during the Gadsden Purchase in 1853 and the Eastern border with Texas was drawn up by a judge to show where slavery ended, with New Mexico being free land.

A famous Civil War battle was fought in Northern New Mexico, for two days at Glorieta Pass in March of 1862 between about 1300 Union volunteer Soldiers and 1100 Confederate rebels. The North vs. the South for control of the West. The Union victory forced the rebels out of the territory and changed the overall strategies of the entire War and thus the outcome of the territory. There would be no sea to shining sea to connect the Southern slaveholding confederates to the West Coast, thanks to New Mexico volunteers' resistance. The next 100 years saw New Mexico turn into the Wild West, with adventurers like Civil War General Kit Carson surviving every element imaginable, great Warriors like Geronimo leading his people against all odds and outlaws like Billy the Kid wreaking havoc.

In 1912 both New Mexico and then Arizona, officially became the 47th and 48th United States. NM was known as the Sunshine State in those days. Until the Zia symbol that dawns the State Flag was put on license plates in 1934. The Zia symbol of perfect friendship among united cultures is a symmetrical design from Zia pueblo. The Flag is yellow with the red Zia, a circle with 16 points, 4 points in each direction. The two inner points are long and the outer points are about 3/4 the length of the long points. They symbolize the 4 stages of life, baby, adolescent, adult and elder. The 4 seasons, Spring, Summer, Fall, Winter. The 4 directions, North, East, South, West. The 4 sacred parts of ourselves, the heart, mind, body and spirit.

Officer Alvarez really enjoyed re-learning the history of New Mexico and the Southwest with Robert. The States most significant contribution to the world was during World War II when the Atomic Bomb was developed in Los Alamos. The project was led by scientist Robert Oppenheimer and General Leslie Groves, who had previously developed the Pentagon.

The Manhattan Project in Los Alamos was also where the Rosenberg's spied for the Russians to obtain specific research that helped Russia and eventually the world to advance their own nuclear ambitions. The Rosenberg's penalty for their treason was electrocution, but they had undoubtedly achieved the most successful piece of espionage in modern history. The first atomic bomb the world ever saw was test dropped on July 16, 1945 at the Trinity Site in Alamogordo in southern New Mexico. Having exceeded expectations, it led the U.S government to strike two Japanese cities just three weeks later. Hiroshima on August 6 and Nagasaki on August 9th 1945, marking the beginning of the end of World War II in the Pacific.

History tends to forget the downwinders, regular U.S. citizens exposed to radiation from the nuclear testing. In the following years, Abo Elementary in Artesia, New Mexico was the first public school in the country to be designed underground, to serve as an advanced nuclear fallout shelter. Not a far-fetched precaution, opening in 1962 just before the Cuban Missile Crisis.

Joseph appreciated the Land of Enchantment's pink and orange sunsets, the wild desert, the migrating birds and he loved the Indian Reservations with their beautiful landscapes preserved in time forever. The State was mainly rural and also had 19 Indian Pueblos with small populations rich in culture spread across the land. Whenever Joseph got a free day and the weather was right, he would take Robert fishing at the Zia pueblo or to the mountains of the Jemez Reservation an hour Northwest of their home.

Just like his *Tartarabuelo* guided his *Bisabuelo* who instructed his *Grandfather* who showed *Dino* a family tradition to pass along to *Joseph* so that one day he could teach *Robert,* how to respect the spirit of the fish. Like generations before, Joseph showed his son how to always place the fish carcass facing North so that it could forever swim upstream for its sacrifice. Joseph never hunted, but he could fish all day and be happy catching nothing as long as Robert was there.

Sometimes they would fish and camp out in Jemez with Rose and Juan or other Officers and their families. The father and son duo never lacked friends or options on the weekends. Nonetheless, it was hard for the two to see all the complete families enter their tents at night. It was just Joseph and Robert together alone in the starry wilderness, just them and a few bears, snakes, and mountain lions nearby.

Every time Joseph got home from work, young Robert would tell him to, "Put your hands against the wall and spread your feet." Joseph would assume the position as his son frisked his uniform and all its different pockets for a hidden candy. Like father like son, they both loved Rolos and Reese's Pieces. Robert always laughed after he found the candy because his dad would always sigh in relief and say, "Ahhh now I can get out of this monkey suit," before Joseph shed his uniform to take a shower and change into civilian clothes. He always called his uniform his monkey suit and young Robert always laughed at the expression.

Joseph taught his son to "never watch too much dummy box," and made his son earn television privileges by reading first. Joseph was thrilled when Robert's preference in kindergarten was the front page of a newspaper, just like his dad and grandfather. For every 10 books Robert finished in elementary school, Joseph rewarded him with a trip to the movie theatres, for 20 books they would go to the drive-inn for double matinees. They watched a lot of great movies at the drive-inn, Harry and the Hendersons, the Outsiders, Gremlins, Ghostbusters, Back to the Future, the Goonies, The Karate Kid, Rocky IV, Terminator, Indiana Jones, Red Dawn, Top

Gun, Better off Dead, Breakfast Club, E.T., BIG, Batteries not Included, Beetlejuice, Major League and a lot of other great 80's flicks. Special effects were still in their primitive, but developing stages during the 80's and most of the good movies of the decade relied on exaggerated plots with comedic dialogue or just 1 guy blowing up 100 guys would draw you to the box office.

The 1980's were filled with a lot of great buddy Cop movies loaded with action and Joseph would laugh at how dramatized Hollywood made the heroes. The Untouchables was realistic, but Lethal Weapon, Beverly Hills Cop, 48hrs, Dragnet, Die Hard, The Naked Gun and all 6 Police Academy movies had such wild action and great comedy. Joseph did really good impersonations of Schwarzenegger and Segal, but his best was Dirty Harry and he particularly enjoyed talking to Jeff Russell in their Harry Callahan voices. The two saw The Dead Pool together when it came out. Joseph's favorite movies of the 1980's were Return of the Jedi, Platoon and Stand By Me, his favorite actor Richard Pryor and actress Sally Fields. Robert's favorite movies in the theatre during the 80's were Return to Oz in '85, Ferris Bueller's Day Off in '86, La Bamba in '87, Who Framed Roger Rabbit in '88 and Batman starring Michael Keaton and Jack Nicholson in '89.

By decades end, Joseph had visited 19 States, Mexico and Canada with his son. They went to the Grand Canyon, Las Vegas, Disneyland, Dallas, Wrigley Field, Cleveland and Sandusky, New England and Washington State to visit Drew Banks when he was in Tacoma and he took them up for lunch in Vancouver one afternoon. The father and son also loved traveling New Mexico, fishing for trout in Jemez, Zia, Red River, Chama, Chimayó, Taos, Truth or Consequences and enjoyed camping in Angel Fire or Pecos with Juan and Rose and Tom and Gerry.

Down South they always stopped in Socorro or San Antonio, NM for a burger when they drove to and from El Paso.

Up North, one of their favorite memories together was getting chased by chickens along the river in Las Vegas, New Mexico, one of the hidden jewels of the Southwest. Joseph had to pick up Robert and run for almost a quarter mile to escape the angry flock. Dad and son laughed every time they remembered that chaotic sprint. They of course ordered chicken sandwiches afterwards along the plaza to settle the score. Another time on their way back from visiting Colorado, his dad had actually encouraged law breaking by peeing off the Rio Grande Gorge Bridge with his son in broad daylight.

The land of New Mexico was pure and resilient. Somehow species, flora and fauna all survive without any water for months on end and with constant wild temperature swings. Specifically beautiful to Joseph were the Reservations vast open space, their Pueblo's free from big box stores, franchise food chains and drive thru's. Preserved in time, Joseph was fascinated to visit Isleta Pueblo South of the city. He had once toured Sandia, San Felipe and Santo Domingo on a motorcycle ride with friends one morning and ate a beautiful lunch at Cochiti's Tent Rocks. Every year Father and Son spent a night at El Rincón bed and breakfast in Taos and would tour over a thousand years of tradition at Taos Pueblo. Joseph became friends with the Police Chief and would always bring him some good green chile from down South in exchange for the red chile from up North.

In the Fall of '89 he was invited by an Officer to Acoma Pueblo with Robert for San Estévan day. Over an hour West of Albuquerque, they climbed the hill on foot leading up to the Sky City and were treated to a world of wonder. From below, it just looked like a large hilltop, but once up top there were thousands of people in a thousand-year-old city. Family reunions, multiple groups of colorful dancers in elaborate garments, art displays, songs and games paid tribute to their ancestors, set to the backdrop of a maze of ancient structures leading to ceremonial ladders. Robert made friends with some kids and they were invited into a home for some mutton stew. It was the best of days, absolutely beautiful to experience. No water, no electricity, just Mother Earth and Father Time.

Chapter 29

"Officer Down"

Dec 1, 1989. Pacific Avenue SE. 4:03-4:07pm.

Several Officers heard the radio transmissions of Officer Alvarez spotting a suspect. His whole squad stopped what they were doing and zoomed around their areas to check for him when they heard him call out that he was shot. He was last seen on Edith Blvd passing an Officer, to start their point of reference. His dear friends desperately tried to get radio to confirm his location, but it was unknown. It was a busy afternoon and everyone knew Alvarez as an incredibly smart and capable Officer who was very safety conscious. Shortly after Alvarez's transmissions went silent, dispatch announced an armed robbery at Antonio's Tire Shop, 803 Broadway at Santa Fe Avenue.

That's when every Officer got a lump in their throat and raised their red flag. Everyone within a few miles rushed over to the area of the tire shop, realizing Alvarez found the Armed Robbery suspect(s). Dispatch sent out another call of possible shots fired near Pacific and John St, which was a street up from Broadway and right near the alley where Alvarez pulled behind the blue car, but nobody knew his location. Officer's hearts sank as they tried to radio Joseph and rushed code-3 to the area. Some of the guys had just been talking to him.

About a minute after he was shot, help started coming in. Officer Atencio was the first to locate his friend at the alley, he had a Rookie riding with him Ofc. Mitchell. Atencio was able to call out the location and start to help Joseph. As he pulled him out of his car to begin first aid, Officer Salas arrived to help with a partner Ofc. Gonzales. By his second minute wounded, Officers Wilson, Flannigan, Torrango, Flores, Parker, Vince, Hoyle, Keylon, Stan and Martinez had arrived to start doing their parts to secure the scene and find the people responsible.

An ambulance driver paying attention to the radio responded quickly with his crew to Atencio's dispatch of "Officer Down" and they identified his chest wound to be very serious as they rushed to load him onto a stretcher. Conscious and breathing, he was quickly whisked away by the ambulance to a nearby hospital with a Police escort in front. Other Officers shut down intersections ahead of the ambulance on Broadway at Lomas Blvd NW and Lomas at University Blvd NE then up to the E.R. entrance where a team of surgeon's were waiting and aware of the situation.

911 calls began pouring in from witnesses' moments after the shooting. This brazen act happened in broad daylight in front of men, women and children. Back at the scene Officers found two .22 caliber bullet fragments inside Joseph's car. He had protected his head until they ran out of bullets. From the alley at Pacific there were a variety of routes the shooter(s) could have fled, but it was broad daylight and many neighbors saw the car, saw the suspect(s) and saw the escape route.

Lt. Casey orchestrated every available resource dedicated to helping while his beloved squad member was headed to surgery. Hopefully the small caliber gun didn't damage any organs.

Part III

Chapter 30

High and Low

THE FIRST OFFICERS to arrive on scene were a pair, riding together. Turning on Pacific Ave from Broadway they saw multiple civilians on both sides of the street pointing. Officer Atencio was driving and raced past Joseph's car at the alley, and neither he or his partner were able to see Alvarez slumped over. Thinking the vehicle was empty because maybe Joseph was on a foot chase when he got shot, they scanned West to look for him towards the Railyard.

The Officers gave a short zoom around, but raced over to a yard flagged down by a civilian pointing back to Joseph's car. The 23-year-old Cuban man stood over his fence and told them the cop was shot in the car behind his house and pointed which way the suspects blue car went. Officer Atencio raced back up to the alley, slammed his car in park and ran out to Joseph with his helpful Rookie, Ofc. Mitchell, as more Police cars started to appear.

Multiple people were around outside when the shooting occurred. Joseph had driven by off duty Officer Steve Nix house along his path on Broadway and Nix wife was a witness to the first part of the chase and heard the shots. His house was just around the corner from the shooting and his yard backed into the alley. He had been a member of the 1980 Academy. Nix was working with his brother-in-law on a car out back when he heard the shots from the alley. He came running out to his front yard and up the sidewalk towards Pacific to start stopping kids for statements.

There were three small kids playing and four youth that witnessed the shooting and saw the car. Several different people were in their yards and there was a busy barbershop that heard the shots and saw the getaway. Also, the man whose yard the Police cruiser crashed into and flagged down the first responding Officers got a glimpse of both men. Lots of 911 calls were recorded with descriptions immediately after the gunfire ended.

The little kids and teens all spoke English and Spanish. They were cousins born in Mexico or Fresno, CA and were now enrolled in local schools. There were two 12-year-old boys from Washington Middle school. One said he saw a four-door car cut in front of the Officer with two men and both were shooting. A 9-year-old girl from Eugene Field Elementary said she saw white wall tires on the car waiting and the running man hide, then shooting before he got into a 4-door car. An 8-year-old girl heard the running man say "hurry up" and one man shooting then get into a 2-door car driven by a man in a blue bandana. A 15-year-old girl from Albuquerque High saw the driver wearing a black bandana. One kid saw four shooters, two others saw two. A 13-year-old girl said they drove off in a Ford just like her dad's and the alley man was about 23 years old, others said around age 30. Heavy, slim. Rifle, pistol. The accounts varied juristically. Most saw the fleeing man cross the alley, come back to shoot the Officer with a pistol, then get into a blue Ford with a white top driven by another man.

With the 7 adults near the gunfire it was the same, there were various accounts of the vehicle and two or more suspects. The driver had pulled into off-duty Officer Nix driveway near the tire shop shortly before the shooting. His brother-in-law went to check on the speeding intruder, but said the driver was gone before he got a good look, headed up the street and turning to go behind the tire shop in the alley.

Some of the adults saw blond hair, red hair, dark hair on the suspects. Most accounts distinctly saw a blue car with a white top, but either a Mercury Cougar or a Ford LTD and one Spanish male shooter get into the passenger side of a car with a Spanish male driver, both with black hair. Just like a few kids, there were a few adults who described them both as cholo's. The auto parts owner had the best look at one of the men and he said the same and that they spoke slang Spanish.

Immediately after the shooting, the Officers that arrived called out descriptions for the vehicle and suspects. Born in 1937, Antonio the tire shop and auto parts owner appeared coming down the alley in his El Camino and told them exactly what the armed robber looked like as they attended to Joseph. The ambulance arrived to work on Joseph while Antonio was still in the alley talking to Officers. "Shooter had black hair wearing a brown flannel shirt with yellow plaid and blue plants."

They sent out an all-points bulletin, stop every blue Ford LTD or blue Mercury Cougar, especially blue models with white tops. They knew the car was occupied by two Spanish males, but at least two witnesses state there were four men and Police called out four on the radio also, just in case. As the troops assembled, they began to reel in the chaos and organize. Minutes after the shooting, every Department in the State had a BOLO or Be On the Lookout. The radio sounded off with blue cars getting pulled over across the city, Fords, Mercury's, Cadillacs, station wagons.

Police quickly secured Joseph's vehicle and by radio, organized checkpoints leading out of the city. Officers from every Police station in the city arrived to the surrounding area, hundreds of them and Sergeants began to organize search teams. Teams of 4 Officers were given streets to start a search grid that would knock on every door, from the scene of the crime to the directional path of the fleeing vehicle down William Street. Groups of Officers vectored off and began knocking on hundreds of doors, asking to see inside people's garages. The largely Cuban and Mexican neighborhoods that fanned out from the scene were overwhelmingly helpful, people were quick to show they weren't hiding anything.

In the preliminary stages of investigating the scene, Police had narrowed down the vehicle to two types. Separately, the department of motor vehicles printed out master lists of all Ford LTD's in the State, by zip code and then a list of Mercury Cougars. State Police helped with that action and assisted searching addresses of hundreds of vehicles. Helicopters took to the sky. Minutes after the shooting, Police started pulling over all cars matching the description for the next couple of hours.

Back at Antonio's Tire shop, while a Field Investigator dusted for prints and photographed, a composite sketch artist Detective Bachica interviewed the tire shop owner Antonio. Just by listening and giving the owner little previews, she drew up the armed robber in less than 15 minutes. After getting it right, Police took it to show one of the key witnesses from the alley shooting a series of drawings and without hesitation they chose the tire shop drawing suspect. The other witnesses helped Police Artist Det. Siegel draw up the driver and possible second shooter.

The armed robber was described as a Spanish male age 30, 6.0 190bs wearing a brown flannel with yellow plaid lines and white shirt underneath. Black hair feathered back halfway above his ears and down to the back of his neck. Trimmed sideburns to the bottom of his ears. He had a thick mustache that ran down both sides of his mouth below the lips. Dark eyes and possible chest tattoos.

The driver a Spanish male mid 20's. Wearing a dark colored headband with a blue flannel shirt. Dark wavy hair, dark eyes, no facial hair. A distinct nose and a tattoo of a woman on the inside of his left arm.

Less than an hour after the shooting the sketches of both suspects were released into the media and the Crimestoppers tips started coming in. Police received a few dozen leads, but one particular name came in three times and motor vehicle turned up a blue Ford LTD in the stepdaughter's name and a blue Mercury Cougar in his name. Two callers gave information about him committing other armed robberies and having guns, they also gave the man's prison nickname, "The Ostrich." As they rushed for a search warrant, a peculiar 911 call came in, the transcript immediately typed up for Detectives.

The caller was a man rambling about a Police shooting and the call had a lot of inaudible noise in the background. Detectives later traced the call to a payphone in the South of the city and he was standing by the I-25 freeway probably trying to head towards Mexico. As the man bumbled, the Dispatcher tried to get a grasp of why he was calling. "I won't tell you my name. I'm kind of involved in it. I didn't do the actual shooting." The 911 Dispatcher calmly pressed for more details. The man was not very helpful, but gave some names and an area to look, before they hung up.

One of the longest nights in department history turned into the early morning by the time they had collected what they needed to find one of the suspects. Identified by multiple witnesses as having fired a large gun from his right hand standing outside the Officer's car door. Detectives gathered mugshots of the man whose name kept coming up and showed a photo array of 7 mugshots to Antonio the tire shop owner. Without hesitation he pointed to the ostrich, only he covered the beard in the photograph and said that the thief had no beard. Officers were sent to stakeout a few addresses associated with the birdman in the meantime, while they wrote up everything the way it needed to be for a search warrant.

At 05:00am the next morning an Officer located the suspects Mercury, blue with four doors, parked at 2319 Felicitas SW. They sat on the house and other addresses for nearly two days while Detectives gathered all the information from affidavits and crossed every t and dotted every i for the prosecution. Watching and recording every in and out movement, trailing every vehicle that left in the meantime. On the second day of surveillance a heavy snow fell on the city and prevented Detectives from studying the tire shop alley further until a later time.

Finally with a search warrant signed by a judge, two SWAT teams were sent to the last known address 5808 Gonzales Road SW in armored personnel vehicles, one team for the perimeter, one for entry. Dozens of Officers followed and were staged all around to form a secondary perimeter, with three ambulances in waiting beyond. Simultaneously Bernalillo County SWAT teams and State Police SWAT prepared to raid the apartment of the driver at 1750 Indian School Rd and hit a second known address belonging to family of the robbery suspect at 419 Atrisco SW, Apartment #B around the corner from Felicitas where they found his car. Also, an Impact Team headed to 308 Manzano Drive NE where he had ties. The little ostrich was sticking his head in the sand somewhere.

The shooter should have never been out of jail to begin with, he had been previously sentenced to 230 years for multiple armed robberies. However, an outgoing Governor granted clemency to all death row inmates and to the key hostage negotiators from the prison riot of 1980. Despite participating in the deadliest riot in U.S. History that killed 33, the ostrich was one of the shot callers who negotiated exchanging prison guards for food. And a reduced sentence to end the ordeal 48 hours after it began. With a criminal history dating back to age 13 for heroin possession, the revolving door for a teenage junky extended into adulthood for a now 36-year-old. By the time he shot Joseph, the lowly convict had spent more than half his life incarcerated from multiple arrests for heroin and armed robbery. All that time to read books, riot and not raise his own children.

Chapter 31

Hearts and Spades

CARMEN ALWAYS MANAGED her household with care and constant upkeep. Dino had always maintained a good paying job, but for 30 years drove an hour to and from work. His 9-5 government workday usually kept him out from 8am until 6pm on weekdays. To keep busy she always helped both of their families by watching different nephews and nieces year around even after Joseph moved out. Having grown up ranching and then experiencing extreme poverty in her youth, she always appreciated her modest affluence. She was cooking spaghetti and meatballs one evening for seven kids expecting Dino home soon when she got the call from Chief Baca.

This was a day she had imagined and the thing she prayed against the most, her worst premonitions had come true. She remembered back to when Joseph told her on the phone that he was in the Academy. For almost a month she had cried day and night thinking of how dangerous Police work was. Her baby boy. Carmen fainted and fell pretty hard as all the kids watched TV in the other room. After a dizzy spell she sat up and looked as an older child tried to talk to her. Stunned, she couldn't make out what the girl was saying and realized her hearing aid had fallen out. The phone was stretched down on the ground by the cord. Placing her hearing aid back in, she started crying as the reality set in again and she sat her back up against her fridge and picked up the phone.

ROBERT had just finished a long day of third grade. At school everyone was getting ready for the big Christmas play and Robert had the lead as Santa. He was well read and easily got the part a month before when he auditioned in an authentic stuffed belly, mini-Santa suit that Rose had sewn for him with a beard on a string and everything. Every day he was excused at the last hour to go and rehearse. His dad thought the outfit was hilarious and had a date lined up for the play.

After school at Rose and Juan's, he was in their den watching his new favorite comedy with Juan Jr. about a Chicago Cop and his neighbors *Family Matters.* The house smelt like a simmering stew as the phone rang on the wall by a crock pot in the kitchen. Juan Jr. got up and ran across the room and up two steps to answer. He called for his mom then put the phone down on the counter and ran back, "What did I miss?" the kid asked Robert. "Nothing just commercials," Robert replied then asked, "Was that my dad?" Juan Jr. shrugged, "No but it was the Police." Robert thought that was funny, but as the show came on, he kept watching, only glancing over at the phone across the room as Rose picked it up. His eyes grew when he heard Rose, "Oh my God no, please No, NO, NO, NO." Then when Rose looked over at him across the room and turned away real fast, Robert got butterflies in his stomach.

57-YEAR-OLD HARVEY STALLA had recently been diagnosed with lung cancer and was spending his morning walking the beach with his wife, apologizing for all the things they never got to do. Elsie had gone out to choir practice with her church group in Kailua Kona to practice their rendition of Mele Kalikimaka and Harvey had just got dressed to go out bowling with his friends. Alone in their 2-bedroom condominium he was walking out the door with his bowling bag when he heard the phone ring. By the time Elsie got back he didn't have any tears left in his eyes as he sat at their table and looked up at her. Elsie had only seen him like this once before, "Harv what's the matter darling?" All he could say was,

"Pack your bag.... Joseph!!" as he sobbed into both of his hands and she came to hug him.

WHEN DINO arrived home from work, he saw all the kids were missing and the house smelt like spaghetti, but all the food was put away. He felt a weird aura as he placed his top hat on a rack and hung up his coat, announcing his presence and looking for his wife, "Carmelita?" As he walked into the kitchen he loosened his tie and saw her through a back window in their yard seated with Father Henry. When he walked outside, they both looked at him and he knew something was wrong. The three of them drove up to Albuquerque without stopping, Father Henry and Carmen were saying prayers the whole way as Dino gripped the wheel in stunned silence.

"Pack your bags, Joseph!" as he [illegible] into both of his hands and she came to hug him.

WHEN DINO arrived home from work, he saw all the kids were missing and the house smelt like [illegible] until the food was put away. He felt a great aura [illegible] his [illegible] coat [illegible] his [illegible] and [illegible]. He walked into the [illegible] window [illegible] [illegible] [illegible] [illegible] [illegible] [illegible] them [illegible] [illegible] [illegible] [illegible].

Chapter 32

Final Justice

ANTONIO NÚŃEZ was going about his day-to-day activities at the front desk of his tire shop. Raised in the Great Depression in La Barca, Mexico he had built this business from the ground up and hoped to pass it on to Antonio Jr. one day when he retires. His fingers thick and hands strong from years of honest work. He had bells installed at the top of the door leading into his lobby to attend to his customers, his shop behind him with a couple employees changing tires. When the dark-haired man walked in to his store with a brown flannel buttoned only at the top to fan out downward and expose his white undershirt, Antonio thought he was a cholo looking for tires. Then when the man asked Antonio to use the bathroom, Antonio said he didn't have one, but that the man could head to the Corners bars up the street.

That's when the strung-out man with his thick fu-man chu mustache displayed his true character. "Dame la feria" he demanded money in slang Spanish. Antonio stared down the barrel of the pistol. The armed man repeated in English, "Give me the money." The wise old man opened up his cash box and emptied out the tray and everything underneath onto his counter. The glassy eyed gunman shoved about $100 in various small bills into a small cloth bag he had pulled out.

After stuffing the bag, he told the owner to turn around and saw that he had a wallet and demanded it. Antonio slowly pulled out his wallet and showed a Mexican bill, "only Mexican." The cholo ordered the business owner to the back and Antonio took three steps down a hallway and then paused, but heard, "Get back or I'll shoot you." The hard-working old man continued into his shop and never looked back until he heard the bells ring again when the door slammed open from the robber fleeing. That's when he called his son to dial 911 and hopped in his truck to go down the alley.

ONCE A MIGRANT WORKER, Santiago came to this country with a dream from Chihuahua, Mexico. He had been living happily in Albuquerque for years, owning his own small business that provided for his family. The back of his upholstery shop and ironworks store faced the alley across the street from where Officer Alvarez's cruiser was when the shooting occurred. Leading up to the shooting he was having a typical long day. Santiago peaked out a small dusty window of his shop when he heard a rustle in the bushes outside and saw a man in a brown flannel with yellow plaid, looking like they were hiding in the alley by getting behind a tall cottonwood sapling's brush. Curious, he paused his work and observed.

A few people passed by the window every day, but this guy was in an unusual hurry. That's when Santiago looked over across the man and saw the approaching Police car in the street. He saw a blue Mercury in front of the Police car, driven by a man in a blue shirt with black hair. That's when he saw the man in the alley right in front of him angle to walk sideways onto the street and behind the Officer before sprinting forward and raising a gun, firing multiple shots into the window of the Police car. It happened in an instant. He saw the driver of the Mercury get out for a second and say something to the shooter as the Police car rolled into a brick wall across the alley. The shooter started to hopping around and went to the driver side, then ran back around to the get in the passenger side.

The hard-working man Santiago was shocked at the scene and quickly ran to a payphone to call 911 to give the description and a partial license plate. After the call, Santiago went outside as many Police arrived and he quickly spoke to one driving by. That Officer listened to him, but drove off to chase the people he described. He had given the most detailed description to 911 Dispatchers and to Officers but didn't leave his contact information.

After three nights of not sleeping and terrible flashbacks, his wife helped give him the courage to come forward. The father and husband had been around Albuquerque early in the decade when Police were paid to collect immigrants to deport them. He was afraid of deportation for his family of four if he testified on record. The whole family was offered complete immunity from deportation in exchange for his testimony. The humble hard workingman was just sewing along when he became a key eyewitness to a crime that shocked the whole State.

Everything he told Detectives matched other witnesses accounts, but he gave the clearest picture of the sequence of events and actions of the suspects. He was the best witness, very detailed. Antonio the tire shop owner and Santiago the upholsterer's versions were used as the framework to draw up the search warrant. That's about when the Ostrich called and said he saw himself on the news and wanted to turn himself in.

Both of the criminals identified had long rap sheets that dated back to their youths and had been released several times for major crimes. Maybe time had finally caught up to them as Detectives scoured their history, while SWAT raided their addresses. The prosecution looked solid with multiple witnesses identifying the shooter as the same man Antonio the tire shop owner was able to pinpoint to the armed robbery of his store just before Joseph was shot. Santiago the upholsterer and Antonio the tire shop owner selected the same guy in separate photo arrays. Sure, the kids gave conflicting statements and some of the witnesses around the shooting had bad angles, but they knew they had their man with the two business owners accounts.

Every night the news updated the public on the investigation and Police released their mugshots to the news. Criminalistics Detectives started receiving quite a few calls from business owners who saw the Police sketch or photographs of the armed robber and wanted to update their own Police reports. The suspects in Antonio's Tire Shop robbery and his driver were identified in the robbery of Garfield Laundry at 2624 Garfield SE on Nov 30, they stole guns from Mesa Pawn shop at 200 Coors NW, including a 10 shot .22 caliber revolver on Nov 27. A Church's Chicken was robbed on Nov 14, a Payless Shoe Store at 5555 Zuni SE on Nov 4 and on Oct 30 they had robbed the Whiting Brother Service Station on 5922 Central Avenue SW. All the victims had pointed to the Ostrich in photo arrays and a few witnesses stated they saw the robber run out to a blue vehicle with a getaway driver.

University of New Mexico Hospital Emergency Room 5:19pm, Dec 1.

The night of the shooting when Dispatch announced that Alvarez was dead on arrival at University Hospital, Officers across the city had to pull over and gather themselves. Some Officers went into a rage state and looked hard to find the blue car before anyone else, some drove to the scene or hospital, others found solace in each other's arms. Four bullets had penetrated his vest. The news was shocking to the entire department and a few close friends of Joseph decided they would partner up to go visit 8-year-old Robert before the News broke. They found out where he was staying and called to confirm before driving over.

Looking just like the composite sketch drawing, the armed robber was taken into custody and some of his family processed for harboring a fugitive. The driver was never to be found, Police played the suspicious 911 call after the shooting, to his family and they confirmed that the voice was him. Hotels didn't require a credit card back then, cash was accepted everywhere and you'd be foolish to flee the law without money or an ID. When Detectives found the 19-year-olds ID left behind, they deduced that due to him being the only accessory and a direct witness to the shooter, its most likely he wound up buried in the desert to ensure that he never revealed the truth. *The Prisoner's Dilemma* is taken care of and you can easily blame the other guy if he's dead. The timing of turning himself in, perhaps after tying up a loose string.

Joseph had been pronounced deceased at 5:15 pm an hour after the shooting. The medical examiner performed his autopsy and removed the bullets for evidence. With his alleged killer captured, his funeral was held a couple days after.

People from all over the United States and Mexico came. His best friend Alfredo from high school came from Ft. Hood, Krystal Harris showed up, the first victim he helped as a Detective, now a Cop with Tucson PD. Eileen's parents from Hawaii, Uncle Dave still in the Navy came from Camp Humphreys. Cousins from California to Pennsylvania, Idaho to Mexico. His professors and classmates from UNM. Police Officers from nearly 30 agencies adorned the Church. Robert sat in between his grandparents and watched as they honored a career and life well spent in the short time he was here.

The Priest at Joseph's funeral ended his touching last rites by asking if anyone cared to share words or a story about Joseph. A lot of Officers got emotional, they had so much to say and share about their friend and brother in arms, but everyone struggled to compose. After the Priest left the podium empty for 30 seconds, he began to return when a 8-year-old Robert walked towards the Mic from the front pew. What made every Officer, friend, and family member of Joseph the saddest was seeing the orphaned Robert make the walk up the stairs alone. A chain reaction of people lost it.

Upon approach to the alter, the Priest placed down a booster stool for Robert to step up on and he lowered the mic into the boy's voice range. Dressed in a fine suit his father had bought him for Easter that year, Robert faced the Church audience and panned his eyes left to right, allowing a moment before saying, "My dad always taught me that sad can be healed with laughter, but there is no cure for anger. And don't worry everyone he only had to go to Purgatory for a few hours for all the cursing before he went to Heaven." The crowd managed a small laugh and Robert paused before continuing, "I miss him so much, but don't be mad everyone, remember the funny times because God will give the Final Justice to the people in this world who hurt others. My dad always told me that and I know it has to be true."

The boy looked around and finished with a simple, "Thank you everyone for coming." When Robert stepped down the crowd applauded the brave and eloquent young kid as he left the mic open. He was applauded all the way back to his seat, next to his grandparents. Then Drew Banks of the Washington State Patrol took the attention in his blue uniform as he walked up to the podium, looking as tall as ever.

"Hello to everyone and the Alvarez family. My deepest condolences and words can never express how amazing your son was." Banks said looking down at Joseph's family. "Thanks for what you said kid, your dad was a great man and an excellent cop, I remember how proud he was of you always showing off your pictures. He sends me your school picture every year." Banks said looking directly at Robert, who had no idea his dad had done that. Then with a chuckle of remembrance he continued speaking to the whole church, "I just wanted to share with yall my favorite story with Joe. We were roommates in the Academy so there are plenty, but this one takes the cake. Forgive me father." The crowd perked up. "So this one night Joseph pulled up in front of the Metro Jail booking. I was outside the entrance smoking a cigarette with three other Officers and Joseph talked with us while we smoked. Five minutes later when I finished my smoke Joseph said, *Shoot man, I almost forgot* and Joe walked down to the trunk of his unit."

As Banks told the story he was starting to laugh and before continuing to everyone he said, "Sorry about this next part Chief, but this was way back in eighty two so statute of limitations!" The other Officers in the Church smiled in anticipation. "Next thing I know Joseph opens his trunk and calls me over to help him. I walk down and see this poor son of a gun Joe had hogtied and had put a filthy pantyhose over his head." Banks laughed with the audience and continued, "I asked "*Geez Joe what did he do?*" And Joe looked at me and said, "*He Spit on my face and that was okay, but then he made of fun of my mom and that wasn't okay.*"

The whole Church laughed even the Chief as Drew Banks added, "We always pranked Joseph's cubby after that and bought him different pantyhose's. He must of accumulated twenty pairs, but he refused to wash the one he had and kept it in his trunk for the next spitter, all covered in spit and nasties from the previous users." Banks looked up to see one of the few moments that week that the department was smiling. "The class of nineteen eighty will never forget you Joseph, never! Love you brother!! God bless your family" Banks finished wiping away a tear of pain mixing with his tears of laughter as he blew a kiss to heaven before returning to his seat. Poor Carmen had no idea what the commotion was when everyone laughed about Joseph defending her, she just sat with a broken heart and looked around at all the Officers that resembled her son.

Al Byrnes took the podium next and it was the first time anybody had ever seen him obviously upset. He was pale and anybody who knew Al saw that his bright smile was missing. Byrnes tried to speak, but had to get help from another Officer, who explained to everyone the events leading up the cassette tape recording they were about to hear. Al took a deep breath and long exhale before he pushed play, adjusting the microphone into the small speaker as the recording began. The tape was of Al playing guitar and Joseph singing *Imagine* by John Lennon to all the U.N.M. protesters on the night Lennon was assassinated in New York. Hearing his father's beautiful voice is what finally made Robert cry into his grandma's arms. Sitting in the row behind the Alvarez family, Tom Tanner gave the kid a rub on his shoulders as he fought back his own pain and Gerry wiped away tears with a Kleenex.

The whole experience was overwhelming for the Alvarez family. So many strangers, the giant motorcade, the 21-gun salute, bag pipes, presenting Robert with a folded flag, news vans, everything in English, a cemetery 5 hours from home. His mother and father could barely be consoled throughout the experience. Father Henry too had lost the words for the first time in his life, he couldn't take his eyes off the collage of photos depicting the life of the cherished Officer, his dominos partner. Robert's heart sank forever when they lowered his father in the ground. He sat motionless as a line of hundreds of people placed roses one by one onto the casket, the Officers stopping to Salute.

Chapter 33

Chico's Tacos

PACKING UP HIS HOUSE and saying goodbye to all his classmates the same week you buried your dad was a lot for a little kid. An overwhelming week to say the least, there were so many different people in and out of his house those days, everybody feeling sorry for him. A moving company came and everything they moved and touched was his dad's or his dad bought for him or his dad's friends gave to him. Reminders were all around of a life that will never be the same. He wore his dad's Jim Rice baseball glove for a half hour, holding a baseball while watching movers reshape his entire life. All four of his grandparents tried to cheer him up, but he didn't eat or drink much those days.

Robert had spent a couple months with his Alvarez grandparents by himself in the summers after 1st grade and 2nd grade. Moving down to El Paso wasn't his first choice, he wished he could go with Robert and Sharon or Tom and Gerry, maybe Rose and Juan. He would have no friends now. Then he started to worry about Spanish. How would he ever understand his grandparents. His grandfather spoke perfect English, but preferred Spanish. His grandmother was still learning English and had a heavy accent that she still mixed words in both languages.

With the heartbreaking loss of his father and the move down to El Paso, Robert could feel his whole personality change with the scenery. The back yard grass was dry and the town smelt earthy from the greasewood plant that lined its mountains and desert. His room was much smaller at his grandparents and he would never be able to fit all his posters. Trying not to mope, he took a Ken Griffey Jr. poster out of a tube and his grandma was loud and upset in Spanish as he tried to understand if he could hang it up or not. They were lost in translation.

Dino came home and kissed his wife, who told him the kid was upset and crying in the room all day. He had just put in his retirement paperwork and wanted to tell her, but first he had to help his grandson get settled. Walking to the bedroom this seemed familiar, but it was a totally different situation now for the grandpa and instead of walk in, he gently knocked. "Hello Robert, it's your Abuelito, your grandpa." Robert placed his Walkman headphones on a dresser and opened the door. Dino went in. It was the first time they had ever talked alone really.

Robert was upset about the baseball posters and school, friends, Spanish, everything, his Dad. "And grandma won't stop chasing me around to eat, I'm not hungry grandpa." Dino hadn't eaten much all week and smiled, "She's been chasing me around too!" Robert laughed as he wiped away his eyes and sat in the strange room with boxes of his things packed away. The gentle grandpa told Robert some stories of his dad and the room to put him at ease. Then Dino's stomach gave him an idea, "I haven't eaten all week, you like Tacos?" Robert shook his head yes.

Although Carmen was already prepping to make chicken that night, Dino walked out and told her to grab her coat to join the guys for some Chico's Tacos. He hadn't been in years, but Dino drove down to 4230 Alameda Street and Robert's eyes grew wide at the site of the neon sign and busy restaurant with tall glass windows. Inside the mid-century box shaped restaurant there were tables and benches full of families, multiple arcade games and a counter full of choices served on red trays. Offering hot dogs, hamburgers and their signature tacos, it was a place Joseph loved growing up, but had only taken Robert a couple of times when he was too little to remember. Robert ate 3 taco boats or 9 skinny rolled tacos in cheese and salsa and Dino doubled him up while Carmen ate a hamburger and fries. Dino gave Robert a quarter to play the Cruisin car racing arcade game and gave Carmen a big hug as they watched the little light skinned blond haired boy enjoy wheeling a race.

Robert was very excited to meet Mr. Muirhead his 4th grade teacher, it was the first time he had a male teacher. Thin, but barrel chested he doubled as a part time soldier in the National Guard and had all the kids start their day doing 10 pushups and learning a fun fact of the day. 25 years old, he did great impersonations when he read aloud. All his classmates were upset when Mr. Muirhead was gone one day, deployed to the Gulf War and they never saw him again at the school. After a series of substitutes, a few weeks later they found a nice lady Mrs. Margolias from New Jersey. She was a lot of fun and planned a trip to Carlsbad Caverns in New Mexico and Dino was excited to chaperone. He also had another tripped planned to celebrate his retirement.

⚖⚖⚖

Just after the 1-year anniversary of Joseph's death, Dino took his bride and grandson Robert on Aloha Airlines to go and visit Harvey and Elsie. An added bonus, Robert would meet Eileen's younger sister, his Aunt Laurie. She was home for Christmas from UT-Austin where she studied and worked as a graphic designer. Tall and skinny with blond hair, she wore big sunglasses and a sun hat almost everywhere they went that week.

The Stalla's rented two small condos along Waikiki beach for the occasion. Robert wanted to be next to his aunt the whole time when she took everyone to go see Santa Claus surfing, a cultural phenomenon. Later that day Laurie told him stories of his mom when everyone took a ride on Ed Isaacs Glass Bottom Boat Tour. For four nights in a row, he ate Pecan pie with his grandpa Harvey and twice when Elsie caught them, she gently poked the elder's stomach and reminded him of his doctor's orders. Robert smiled as his grandpa placed the blame on him both times. Hawaii was beautiful, from sunrise to sunset they experienced gorgeous scenery and perfect weather. It was the last time Joseph, Dino and Carmen saw Harvey alive.

CARMEN WOULD GO into Juárez almost every single day to go see her brother or buy her daily groceries. For years she would never let Robert go into Mexico with her. After retirement, Dino didn't enjoy his two pensions as the terrors of Nazi Europe and his owns son's death haunted him. He retired to his room. His grandpa didn't speak much other than to his wife by the mid 90's and most days he sat quietly in his room alone, drinking whiskey while watching sports and news. Robert still hung out with his grandpa for a few minutes every day. The Spanish channels showed a lot of pretty girls, boxing and soccer for Dino, and Carmen had mastered the art of watching her specific Telenovela at 6pm while cooking dinner.

His grandma was a great cook and Robert enjoyed taste testing with her while she explored culinary. Robert's favorites were her amazing green chile chicken enchiladas, roasted tomato bruschetta with capers, migas with nopales and burritos with refried beans mixed with a little peanut butter. Despite her ability to whip up miracles in the kitchen Dino ate the same two meals every day. He had a sausage biscuit and coffee from McDonalds every morning and every night two over easy eggs with green chile, refried beans and a flour tortilla.

Dino wouldn't leave the house for weeks sometimes and one day Carmen refused to go pick up his daily sausage biscuit and coffee from McDonalds. Dino was trying to sweet talk and Carmen blocked it by saying in Spanish, "The doctor said you need fresh air, when you mow the lawn, I'll get your McDonalds." Dino smacked his lips at the thought of mowing their large back yard. She gave him a look and he tisked at the task before walking to the shed to get his gas mower. He tried one last move, "It's out of gas, can you pick some up on your way to McDonalds?" Showing her a red gas can. Carmen walked over and started the mower in one try as Dino clenched his fist and tilted his head back in defeat.

Robert watched from his room window and laughed as his grandma winked to him.

Dino mowed at a leisurely pace while Joseph played Police Quest on his computer. Carmen left to run errands as Dino started the lawn and the second she was out of sight Dino came in and gave Robert a $5 bill to finish the job. "Corre mijito, y cuiadalo." He said for Robert to hurry before the grandma came back and to hide the money. Dino wanted to watch the Dream Team in Barcelona.

Carmen busted them both when she was putting away some laundry and followed a simple grass trail to a sock drawer with a $5 bill. Dino had to walk around the 4-acre park across the street at least one time every morning, followed by a kiss to get his breakfast after that. She also decided to take Robert to Mexico for the first time the next Saturday when the trees needed trimming. They headed to Tío Jesús hacienda.

Police Survivor benefits, for family of the fallen, work in different ways depending on the State. New Mexico gave the Alvarez family a check for $187,428.82 Carmen didn't ask any questions, Dino handled all the big finances. The Will stated Robert would move in to live with Dino and Carmen in El Paso if Joseph were to die or became incapacitated. Joseph had taken out an additional $100,000 life insurance policy that would go to Robert after his 18th birthday, Dino was the custodian. His parents would take custody of the estate in Albuquerque and rent it out to an Officer for no more than $100 more than the mortgage and any extra money would go to Robert's care or the upkeep of the house. Dino didn't need money, but this was a lot, although he would just as soon trade it all back.

A notorious gangster and drug lord made international headlines in December of 1993, when Pablo Escobar's reign as the world's Cocaine Kingpin was ended by Police gunfire in Colombia. A year later on December 19, 1994 Mexico devalued their Peso currency and the banking system in Juárez virtually collapsed overnight. Greedy bankers and corrupt officials made out like bandits, while citizens lost everything, land, homes, cars, small businesses. Crime and desperation increased.

Robert and Carmen climbed Sugar Loaf Mountain every Sunday after Church and in 1995 they would start to bring food, for all the families hiding in the mountain's caves.

ON HIS FIRST VISIT into Mexico, Robert was pleasantly surprised to find out his Tío Jesús owned a candy shop and gave all the kids in the neighborhood one free candy a day. It was a small space attached to the end of the side of his house, it fit one person behind the counter and offered about 50 different options. Some of the kids would grow up and become doctors, architects and skilled workers, others became hardcore criminals, but nobody ever disrespected or forgot the courteous Jesús. His uncle had also been the first person in the 1960's to get that neighborhood hooked up to the municipal water supply after years of carrying buckets. In the house Robert took notice to the boxing regalia and nostalgic photos of his time in the ring that dotted his great uncle's family home. The walls were plastered and the light hues relaxed Robert so much that he took a nap on the sofa watching TV after lunch that first visit.

Robert didn't verbally speak Spanish for over three years until he started high school and met a young girl named Maria Luisa. Short and pretty with long black hair and a light complexion. She was incredibly shy, but nice to him in a Spanish class they took. At one point they were seated next to each other as speaking partners for weeks and as he often troubled, she giggled and would help. He saw that she took the class to learn English and he enjoyed correcting her little mistakes. Becoming friends, he learned *Luisa* crossed over from Mexico every day and took a city bus, then walked to school over a mile.

Like a gentleman, he eventually stopped riding his own school bus and would walk her and a couple of her friends to their bus stop a mile in the opposite direction every day. Then he would start jogging or walking home, a few miles, all just to say goodbye to the pretty girls. Before the Summer started, fearing he might not see her again he decided to get on the bus with them one of the last days of school. The girls didn't believe him when he said he had an uncle in Juárez. Starting in Downtown El Paso, he had been to Tío Jesús house enough times by then that he walked them over in a maze of streets with ease and got them all a free piece of candy from the store when they arrived. Luisa and a couple of the girls were impressed, they only lived about 10 minutes from his uncle.

When they got near Luisa's house, she said something to her friend Yanice. Luisa tried to leave and Robert insisted on seeing her up to her door. Yanice shook her head no, Luisa told Robert in English "Now you go, ehhm with Yanice okay," and tried to say goodbye to him awkwardly. As they debated the importance of walking her home, they all heard a man yell Maria. Joseph knew her as Luisa and didn't realize the approaching man down the street was calling her. She was so tense and her friend told Robert to run. Robert figured it to be the dad and he was raised to introduce himself to parents out of respect. He walked up to greet her tall slender dad dressed nicely in a white and brown shirt tucked in to his brown pants with a nice belt buckle. The middle-aged man threw a single straight right into his face, sending him to the floor. His eye blackened from the instant swelling and as he felt a rush at his nose, Robert quickly got up and ran away as he heard the man laughing and yelling in Spanish in the distance.

He had never been punched except by accident playing Ninja Turtles with a friend once. His head was spinning on the way home and he jogged when he could, arriving much later than normal. Dino was recovering from a mini stroke and was confined to movement in a walker, but usually stayed in his room all day. When Robert came home with the black eye, his grandpa happened to be coming from the kitchen, the first time he left his room all day and had caught a glimpse of his battered grandson.

New motions, dismissals, postponements, reasonable doubt and eventually a hung jury verdict of his son's murderer had really put Dino through the ringer. It wasn't a total acquittal, they had been able to convict the ostrich to jail for the armed robbery of the tire shop and being a habitual offender. He would spend his life in prison, but he walked on the murder and there would be no double jeopardy. Dino had driven up to the trials and explaining that to his wife was as hard as anything. They never told Robert. All he knew was the bad man was going away forever.

Now seeing his injured grandson, but not able to talk well with one side of his mouth, Dino gingered over to his own room and retrieved a box from under his bed. It was a struggle. He returned a few minutes later and knocked on Robert's door. The kid tried to ignore it, but came out when he heard something placed on the ground outside his door and his grandfather scuttle away back to his room.

Chapter 34

A Tale of Two Cities

ROBERT STARTED TO VISIT Juárez on his own after he opened up the package his grandpa gave him. It revealed a set of yellow Everlast boxing gloves and his dad's three city championship medals along with a picture of him in California on a podium in 1st place. Dino also gave Robert home videos from 1963-1980. There was a video of every boxing match his dad had fought in middle school on Kodak Super 8 tapes and his Police Graduation.

That first night he figured out how to work his grandparent's old projector and watched hours of tape, with a pack of frozen peas in a paper towel pressed against his eye that his grandma gave him. Watching the videos was therapeutic and inspring as he sat with his swollen face. Robert had the courage now to fight back, thanks to his grandpa and he had the spirit to fight from his dad. After Luisa's dad punched him into oblivion, he never wanted to experience that helplessness again. He had walked right into the punch the more he thought about the man's demeanor.

At school he found he looked for her for days. He asked all her friends and even a couple teachers about her. Robert wasn't mad at all, he was worried that his friend was embarrassed because of him. Or maybe she had got into trouble from his appearance at her house. He had heard the story of his grandpa having to ask permission and be chaperoned by his great uncles. Maybe he crossed a cultural line. Luisa came to school for one Final exam after that, but Robert didn't see her again for a year. He worried about his friend and wanted to pass by her house, but was afraid.

Luisa's parents met in Monterrey at the University. They met buying popcorn in the lobby of a Cantinflas movie *El Patrullero 777*. Her dad had to join her mom's congregation and attend mass regularly before winning her family's approval. The courtship lasted a few years and they were married at age 21. Shortly after, they moved up to Juárez where he found jobs at two maquiladoras before starting his own business.

Maria Luisa had a wonderful childhood with her mother Maria Teresa. Her mom was the most beautiful soul, always busy, always keeping her daughter close by and teaching her things. Working long hours as a seamstress in a shoe factory, she made sure their daughter went to an all-girls private school for many years. The girls all wore red plaid skirts and nearby Catholic school boys would tease their strawberry skirts by calling them "Fresitas." In high school, the girls she hung out with still called her *Luisa Fresita* sometimes.

Luisa's dad Angelo had been a hard-working, loving husband. He built his own house with his brothers help, two story with four bedrooms near coveted Downtown Juárez. His brother Frederick was a good man and they ran a successful auto body shop together for many years. Things began to go south for Angelo when his brother had a heart attack at work and died. Then a year later, the death of his wife.

At age 11 Luisa's mom died from some type of bladder infection, in seemingly normal health. The widowed Angelo first turned to alcohol then to a life of cocaine. Before long he would often leave his daughter with neighbors, then alone for days on end sometimes. He sold his mechanic shop for pennies on the dollar. After being busted by some crooked police once, they turned him into their worker mule.

When Robert first walked into the Bellavista Boxing Gym with his black eye, the owner knew who the kid was because he knew Tío Jesús and he had trained teenage Joseph a few times. Grown men and young boys worked out at various stations all around and two rings displayed sparring wars. The man went to his office and called Tío Jesús who came down to beg Joseph not to set foot in the ring and to stay out of Mexico. But when his great Uncle got there and saw the kid's shiner, he instead started his training. "If you tell Carmen, she will kill me," he said in Spanish and Robert smirked. His Uncle gave him a stare he had never seen before from him as his uncle warned, "NO! She will kill me!" Robert looked in his uncles diced green eyes and understood that this was all a very serious lifestyle.

At the U.S./Mexico bridge, the Border Agents would marvel at this tall light skinned kid running into Mexico every day with a backpack on. After some months of boxing, he revealed a new athleticism he didn't know that he had. With a lot of unvented rage, Robert was a natural at the sweet science. A southpaw, he was athletic, strong and fast. Then after a growth spurt, he could dunk a basketball by 14 and by 15 excelled at the high jump and basketball team.

His grandmas cooking helped as he grew to 6 feet 170lbs by his junior year. Training boxing once a week for years, he sparred with men often. On the track team for high jump, he had aspirations of taking out his dad's school record of 1.68 meters and he was the co-star of the schools losing basketball team.

Chapter 35

Narcotráfico

STEVE McQUEEN had passed away in Juárez when Joseph was a Rookie, the action star seeking cancer treatment. In the 1980's, the border city became a go to place for alternative medicines during the AIDS pandemic and it was a highly sought after destination for medical tourism. With 6 ports of entry back into Texas, 4 car and 2 train, Americans flocked to the city where you could find anything at a bargain.

Juárez is a beautiful city, rich in culture and history with more than 1 million residents. Busy plazas and finely constructed buildings and monuments adorn the border town, famous for its nightlife and shopping. Everywhere you look people can be seen walking and talking amongst each other in a town where days are long and sunny. Green taxis dash tourists around town to buy clothes and home furnishings for a fraction of the price in the U.S. Entering the United States the limit is 1.5 liters of alcohol before incurring a tax and/or 1 carton of cigarettes amongst other import rules.

Unfortunately, with the lucrative American market up North, the cocaine trade and crack manufacturing began to take its foothold in the once bustling border town of over 1,250,000 people. Divided into 32 States, Mexican Police didn't even carry guns in the 1990's in the largest State of Chihuahua. Slightly larger in land then all of the U.K., Chihuahua State shared 500 miles of U.S. border from the Big Bend of Texas over to Western New Mexico. Home to 4 million and front line to the U.S. supply chain, powerful drug lords used different routes in the Chihuahuan Desert to smuggle North.

In the summer of 1998, the Albuquerque Police Department and Fire Department donated supplies to Chihuahua, Mexico including bullet proof vests, asps, and handcuffs, along with fire suits, helmets and hoses. On the route, a contingent of Officers were kind enough to stop by and visit the Alvarez family, although Dino stayed in his room. Carmen allowed them to take Robert down for the weekend to Chihuahua city in a convoy that included the Mayor of Albuquerque Jim Baca.

It was a four-hour drive in a dump truck, but his grandma handed him a book on Chihuahua. Robert learned that his hometown and Chihuahua had a lot in common. In 1709, three years after funding Albuquerque, New Spain, the Italian born Duke Francisco V Fernández de la Cueva funded the creation of San Francisco de Cuéllar, New Spain which would later become Chihuahua, Mexico. Belonging to the Bourbon Monarchy, the Duke had visited Mexico on military affairs and after his visit was adamant about funding law and order in the New World. One of the first from Europe in setting up courts, tribunals and Policing in the Western Hemisphere.

Robert learned a lot more on an official State visit to the Governor's Palace after they checked into the Plaza Hotel in the Historic Center next to the Metropolitan Cathedral. A lively city of nearly 700,000 people, that night they attended rooster fights in an indoor stadium at a Palenque festival featuring singer Pedro Fernandez. He was fascinated watching as young girls on the stadium floor threw tennis balls with little slits in them to gamblers in the audience. They tossed the wager balls better than the grown men threw them back. Teams of men prepared their fighters, they had their own cases with sheaths of various styles of metal claws to attach to the roosters.

Feathers flying, each battle was one on one, a fight to the death almost every time. Robert stared intensely as one man cried when his prized rooster keeled over and died just after it had finished its opponent and "won" the battle. The man carried away the skilled Gallo, weeping the whole way off. After 50 fights, they cleared the floor and dimmed the lights. A famous Mexican singer dressed in a fine mariachi suit came out with his band and serenaded the crowd. Robert was in awe as roses, panties and bras flew down stage from multiple women of different ages at the handsome singer.

The next day there was a huge ceremony for the gifting of the supplies, the Mexican government brought in multiple media outlets, groups of dancers in colorful dresses and a whole mariachi ensemble, not just a band. Albuquerque and Chihuahua officially became *Sister Cities*.

At an Official dinner that last night, seated amongst a long table for 30, the Cops ordered something for Robert that he had never heard of before. A soup came out and when he took his first spoonful, he looked up to see the whole table of Diplomats and dignitaries watching him.

Robert thought it was delicious, but he dared to ask what he had just consumed. "It's seso soup…cow brains," said a Cop. The words provoking an unmistakable image, Robert paused for a second and then looking around he just dug in for another big spoonful. The whole table cheered and he saw a man in a cowboy hat across the table hand another guy some money while smiling. Robert was having a great time the whole trip.

Back in Juárez, Luisa hadn't attended school in six months. She was working to maintain her father Angelo's desired amenities in their house. Despite being a degenerate gambler living month to month, he liked nice things. Nice tequilas, cable television and new clothes were his forte, but gold was his most desired item. He hovered over his daughter when she cashed her checks from her jobs at Delicias diner and the Hotel Paso del Norte in Downtown El Paso.

Gold watches, gold bracelets, gold necklaces, gold rings and several gold teeth. He was always laced up and wore a white cowboy hat courtesy of his daughter. Born the same year as Joseph, Angelo was the exact opposite type of person and father. Yet Luisa's mother had raised her right and she loved her dad even though he was constantly a menace to her spirit and her finances.

Most of the money Angelo took from his daughter was to finance his drug operation out of their nice gated house. As a result, the kind, but precocious Luisa tried not to be home when her dad was. He drove a 1974 Mercury Cougar and she would look through the white metal gate to see if the long car was parked. The day he punched Robert, Luisa cried the whole night. With each passing day her life seemed more stuck, her childhood dreams long gone with every long hour worked or hidden in a cafeteria.

She couldn't always avoid him and he came home for dinner most nights before leaving. As her dad took on more customers in the lucrative drug trade, Luisa started to notice some seedy characters coming around. Her dad was starting to allow grown men to flirt with her, they were his "business associates." Some of the more dangerous types she saw were two brothers that owned gambling halls or guys that came over to load up car trunks full of boxes. She had somehow maintained her innocence and never really knew what cocaine was, she suspected maybe the boxes were stolen goods.

Moving drugs across the border was a game of luck, but Angelo had a few tricks. He used multiple cars at once, with usually only one filled with a stash of cocaine. Back in 1962, John F. Kennedy had visited Juárez once to settle the El Chamizal land dispute. Now Angelo used El Chamizal Park as a gathering point before his team crossed coke into Texas. At the park a lead car always had a passenger smoke a joint in the car then exit. With the car stinking it was almost always stopped crossing, then searched for a long time and eventually let go. Everyone else just moved along right behind the distraction.

He was connected to a Mexican police officer on the take that had a wife working in the U.S. Consulate in Juárez. Once a month Angelo recruited women with babies, offering them a temporary medical visa and a decent buck to cross over with a baby wrapped up with half a kilo. $100 up front, $100 on completion. Depending on the month he was moving about 10 kilos and in doing so, meeting lots of shady characters. Angelo wasn't the owner of the cocaine, he just pushed it out. As quick as he got paid, he either snorted or gambled away his profits. His addiction fueled his decisions. After he was robbed once, he started to pack a pistol in his car. He would only leave his gun at home if he crossed into Texas leading a drug run.

EVERLAST

Chapter 36

Boxing and Hate

ANTHONY "TONY" BECERRA had boxed in the days of Tío Jesús and was the gyms oldest living former champion. He had been crowned champion of Mexico at 147lbs from 1961-63. Tony had helped a young Joseph develop a wicked fast jab and when Robert walked into the sweatbox for his second day, Tony greeted him in Spanish, "I've been waiting for the day you came in here with the same fire in your eyes as your dad. Let's get started, but look, don't tell your grandma or you can't come back." His uncle had said the same thing the week before, maybe they knew something Robert didn't.

The Bellavista Boxing Gym was the definition of blood, sweat and tears. It had a reputation as gritty and every boxer had to pay their dues. For the parentless Joseph that meant 1 hour of mopping and emptying spit buckets for every 1 hour he trained. He mostly hit bags, most of the guys in there were grown men and despite weighing the same or more than many, he was normally outclassed at every station with whoever he trained with. Anybody could challenge anyone, but Robert was off limits via Tony's orders.

By high school his hair had darkened brown and he was 5.10 already. In 9th grade Joseph's old baseball coach selected gangly Robert on the freshmen team, but he never really played. He was a pinch runner and occasional center fielder for defense, but he could never hit the ball. In the 10th grade the new coaches cut him after the first day of tryouts. However, in the Spring, he maintained the illusion that he was going to baseball after school, but would often go train at the gym. Boxing became a lifestyle and he started to watch some of the great matches of the 1990's and his idols became British Heavyweights and Puerto Rican speedsters amongst others, his favorite big championship fights to watch were Johnny Tapia's from Albuquerque. He started to put on muscle and could run for miles.

When Robert sparred for the first time at 16, he was at super middleweight or 168lbs. His Tío had been a champion at that weight 40 years ago. It was more than 10lbs his dad's weight when he graduated the Police Academy in 1980 at age 21. Tony knew what was going to happen as the southpaw Robert went against a short stocky 19-year-old of the same weight. The two went at it for 2 minutes, twice. All the guys that watched congratulated the young first timer on his effort in the loss.

He lost many rounds at first, but soon honed his skills in the gym. With headgear on he was able to keep most scuffs off his face or blame any on baseball and track to avoid his grandma's detection. The gym was his outlet and he was in really good shape. On the weekend he could run the 40 minutes to the border and 10 more to the gym. The gym and his uncle's house were just across the border.

One day he was enjoying another sparring victory and as he got close to home, he splurged on a coca cola at the gas station down the street to celebrate. When he arrived home, he walked into his living room and his grandma took the coke bottle out of his hand and started yelling at him to sit down. Confused he sat. She went back into the room and came out to show him her hands full of stuffing. She had cut up the gloves his grandpa gave him, his father's gloves. Robert was devastated. He ran out the door all the way to Mexico.

Robert spent a few nights at the boxing gym in Juárez. His trainer gave him some bananas and a cantaloupe to eat and the teen rationed it out over two days while training hard. He was furious about his new life as a huérfano, an orphan.

On the third morning Tony was going to kick him out, but called his grandma instead. She came down to the boxing gym and picked him up, no words spoken. He thought she was going to scold him the whole way back, but even worse she remained silent. It was a hot day and her Skylark didn't have a working air conditioner. The line of cars was in the hundreds to cross the four lanes of entry at the international bridge into El Paso. His grandma rolled down her window to get some air flowing. As they slowly advanced, she bought two bottles of Orangina from a young boy with a cooler in between the rows of cars and she handed one to Robert.

With still 20 cars to go in front of them, she finally spoke, asking Robert to open the glove compartment. She asked him for her cars paperwork and he grabbed it. As Robert went to close the glovebox, she told him to grab a small plastic pack of developed photos that he had hardly noticed. "Ábrela" she told him to open it. He looked at the curious envelope, developed at a Walgreens in Los Angeles and written with *Thanksgiving Juárez 1980*. Robert opened it to reveal a whole roll taken of his mother and father at his Tío Jesús's house while she was pregnant, unbeknownst to the family members in the photos. Carmen had made a call to L.A. to get them for her grandson.

Chapter 37

Innocent Victims

A LOT HAD HAPPENED in Luisa's life since she last saw Robert nearly three years before. She had dropped out of school and been working two jobs full time in Downtown El Paso on a highly coveted work visa. Luisa dreamed of running away, but was pulled by a magnet to the thoughts of the beautiful life she once had. Attending Mass was her favorite hour of the week on Sunday's, her refuge from a life stuck. After service, her hopes were constantly ruined when she would arrive home to find her dad and his girlfriends, they seemed to get sleezier with each turn of the page. She had been able to hide some money from hotel tips and one day planned on just staying in El Paso and taking a bus to California to start a new life with her own place.

By the time she was 16 her father was getting really bad and verbally abusive, something he had never done before. Her once beautiful home became tense and started to accumulate shady visitors. Peeking out of her room she noticed on two occasions, men come over and pay her dad money and then go into his bedroom with one of his girlfriends. Luisa needed out.

One day Robert happened to stop at her restaurant in Downtown El Paso after a morning run with all the Mexican boxers. They had both matured physically. His hair had darkened and she had a beautiful body to accompany her innocent face. Her English had improved and his Spanish was much better.

Robert scrapped up the change to get a burrito every morning he could after that.

He would visit Luisa a few times a week for several months and talk her up when she wasn't busy. If he went to his uncle's first, he always brought her a piece of candy. They were always happy to see each other. One day Robert's demeanor was different when he came into her work. She took her break early and sat with him as the other employees smiled at her from the distance and made kissy faces. Only she wasn't flirting, Robert looked sad. "Are you okay?" she asked Robert.

Luisa showed up at his grandpa's funeral that Sunday. Her long skirt and elegant sweater were some of the only good things about that day to her friend. That and the four Albuquerque Officers that were kind enough to show up to support their fallen comrade's father when they heard. The Army and Air Force also sent Honor Guard to the Church and did escort for the retired Master Sergeant.

Robert and Carmen had heard Dino fall at home one day and by the time he was loaded into an ambulance, he had already succumbed to a brain aneurysm.

When Luisa got home the afternoon of Dino's funeral, she walked into a nightmare beyond her front gate. Her dad was nowhere to be found and these nasty people were in her living room, nine of them. Surrounded by pictures of her mother and her grandparents in Monterrey, the strangers were smoking cigarettes and drinking. Luisa asked them politely to smoke outside and kindly brought out a tray to extinguish. One of the men grabbed her wrist, dropping the tray and when she tried to reject, he grabbed tighter and pulled her over and sat her on his lap. Telling her what a beautiful young lady she was as his friends laughed. Luisa froze and cringed. One of the women came over and saved the girl by seducing the man to relax his grip.

Luisa ran out as the men laughed. She spent the whole night crying at Yanice's, but there were already 6 kids in that small house. The next day she looked into getting a fake ID or a passport to get to the United States from some friends, but nobody really knew how to. For weeks she tried to avoid home. Then one day she stopped showing up to work. After ten no shows, even her bosses were asking Robert where she was. Robert remembered where she lived.

Chapter 38

Fight or Die

ROBERT CAME TO HER white metal gate and it looked like nobody was home, peeking through small billet holes. He asked a kid passing behind on a bike if he knew if anyone was home and the kid looked scared and rode off faster down the street. There was a doorbell button outside the gate and Robert pressed it, then he looked up and saw her. She appeared upstairs behind a gated window. Robert saw the curtain close and she disappeared.

Luisa had run down stairs and came outside to look at him through a skinny opening in the gate. She was all bruised up, begging Robert to leave. Of course he refused, and after some back and forth, he sat down in front of the gate as she begged and pleaded. Her dad would be back any moment. "What happened to you?" He asked concerned. She wouldn't say and defended, "Nothing Robert, please just go." Glancing up he announced over his shoulder "You can come and live with me and my grandma in El Paso, your own room." Luisa's heart dropped. Carmen would never allow it, but Robert knew something was wrong. "Your grandma doesn't even let you buy censored music," she checked his proposal. Robert wasn't budging.

When her dad showed up Luisa was back inside and he parked his car on the street. The first thing Robert saw were his pointy boots exit the car and then his whole body lurched out. He was wearing a lot more gold than the image Robert had of him from their previous meeting. Robert stood up. Exiting his long car, Angelo paused and told the lady in his passenger seat to give him his Cowboy hat and he put it on. Then approaching Robert he smiled and said in Spanish, "I remember you."

Angelo's girlfriend was yelling as he woke up on the ground from a three-piece meal. He spit out some blood and scooched up to his car, gathering his hat. It had been four years since he last saw Robert. This time Robert walked away.

That night Luisa thought about what Robert had said and only 17, she dreamed of running away with him. She didn't love her dad anymore after what he let happen. Now she was locked in for over two weeks. Her dad kept the gate opener and always took it with him. She could escape, but his sleezy prostitute girlfriends were always around and had been instructed to keep an eye on her. The weeks passed and she was a prisoner in her own home, cooking and cleaning for strangers.

HIGH SCHOOL GRADUATION was beautiful for Robert. He took pictures with all his friends and posed one last time with the basketball team. Yanice and Robert shared a special hug, missing their bright hard-working friend. His grandma was so proud. Officers Golson and Hetes from the Albuquerque Police Department showed up and Robert's friends all thought he was a sheik or a king posing with two strong Cops on his side. Now his biggest dilemma was that he had been accepted to the University of New Mexico, Texas-El Paso and Texas-San Antonio. He had been rejected by his top choice UT-Austin.

That summer he spent a lot of time helping out at his uncle's candy store now that the Patriarch was in a wheel chair. Yanice brought four of her siblings by every day. Robert brought his aunt the money around 2pm in exchange for a torta to eat. He decided to stop boxing for college although he heard that Harvard had a boxing team, he couldn't verify if collegiate boxing even existed anymore. July of 99' was the last month he paid dues at Bellavista and he took advantage. He would even show up twice a day sometimes to get in some bag work or help out young ferocious kids.

Leaving the gym one day he was walking back to his aunt and uncle's house to check on them and have a bite before heading back to the gym for a sparring match. Walking the streets, he bought a De la Rosa marzipan circle from a little kid even though he could get them for free in a few minutes. It was a nice day and he was going to miss all this. Unwrapping the plastic, he heard a tire screech and turned around to see Angelo exiting a car and pointing a gun in his face over a half year since they had last seen each other. He ordered Robert into his car and Robert knew this was a death trap, never get in the vehicle to go to a second location. There was just nothing he could do, he got in the backseat. Angelo told a female companion to drive the car and he got in the backseat after Robert, pressing the gun into his side the whole trip.

Back at his compound, the white gate locked behind him and Luisa was nowhere to be seen. He asked Robert "You going to beat me up today boxer man?" Then he pistol whipped Robert behind his ear and ordered him out, behind the girlfriend with a big perm. Robert had never been punched that hard, his whole head was ringing. He reached back to check for blood a few times, but was just sweating.

Inside Angelo went off about how Luisa ran away from her job and family obligation, to Monterrey and owed him money. He and his girlfriend sniffed a quick line each. Then the bandit smiled his mouth full of gold and told Robert to sit down in front of the television. Robert was praying and sat down in compliance as he rubbed behind his right ear. Angelo tucked the gun into his waistband, went to a VCR and pushed in a tape. In Spanish he told Robert, "Mr. Alvarez I have something special for you to watch." Robert didn't expect his name out of the man's mouth and realized he had made a terrible mistake ever getting involved with this guy.

The video showed a clip from an HBO documentary about prisoners of the war on drugs. It showed his dad's killer bragging about surviving prison and the streets by being tough, while incarcerated in Granite, Oklahoma. Robert turned pale like he witnessed a ghost. Robert had never heard the killers voice before. He had always thought that he was rotting away in a California prison somewhere. Angelo laughed at Robert's face, "You like? Keep watching white boy."

After the clip the video went black for a second. The gravity of the situation had fully registered to the young teen by now. Then on the TV Luisa appeared alone on the edge of a bed. The mood further darkened. Robert felt a deep anger stirring as he continued to watch as a grey-haired man in slacks and tie appeared and sat next to her. Robert knew the man from somewhere. The slick dressed man put his left hand on her right leg as she scooted to the edge of the bed and told him in Spanish that she has a boyfriend. The tape continued and showed the sexual assault on Luisa who was overpowered.

Angelo bragged about the money her virginity earned him and laughed when Robert's face turned red. As Angelo laughed like a Hyena, Robert just felt this voice inside him to "*Fight or Die*," so he stood up and yelled out to Angelo, "And where's the money now? Up your nose!" Robert had grabbed an empty glass pint of tequila and threw it like a fastball smack into the bridge of Angelo's nose. Robert dashed across the room as Angelo cupped his nose with both hands to adjust it back into place while blood poured all over his chin, throat and shirt. The old bastard reached down for his gun when he saw Robert coming and tucked his chin to get tackled into his kitchen cabinets. The girlfriend was screaming and throwing stuff across the room as Robert started punching him in the struggle for the gun. Robert was able to somehow get the gun free and he ran out of the house and threw it over a fence before he tried to jump the gate to escape the walled off compound. It was still daylight.

The gate and fence had rows of points along the top and his shirt ripped and he cut himself good across his arm vaulting over. Nobody was out on the street except parked cars and some people way up the road. As quickly as he gathered himself the gate opened behind him and like a nightmare, he just couldn't get away fast enough. Angelo appeared through the gates gap and rushed to hit him with a crowbar in the street and Robert fell forward onto his hands. He tried to get to his feet. Realizing the kid hit harder than he had expected Angelo took no chances and he used a two-handed shove-punch to toss the younger Robert back towards the gate as he tried to get up. In two quick throws Robert was right back on the ground where he had jumped over.

That's when Angelo stabbed Robert on the ground with the long edge of the crowbar, first in the shoulder and digging down to pull it out. As Robert yelled "STOP STOP" in terror, Angelo sunk into him again, this time in the stomach. Seated, Robert reached down and desperately struggled over the bar as it tore into him. When it pulled out his stomach was on fire, then the crow bar smacked on the side of his head and he was done. He glanced up and tried to cover his head and kick his attacker.

This is it Robert thought, this is how I'm going to die, fighting. "Grandma!" he whimpered. BOOM a single gunshot rang out and Angelo fell just inside his own property at the gate, the back of his head caved in and his face blown everywhere including onto Robert's already bloody clothes. Robert laid in shock as blood from his wounds poured and the gate kept trying to close but would open from the sensor being blocked by Angelos body. He was helped up and into the kitchen where he was placed on a kitchen island. It was Tony the boxing trainer. The blood from Robert's shoulder dripped fast on the kitchen tiles and Tony instinctively grabbed a kitchen towel and applied pressure to the wound. Robert's stomach was grinded up, but not bleeding like his shoulder. The girlfriend was screaming outside, making everything feel rushed and Tony started to keep Robert from going into shock, like he was working his corner.

Tony scooped Robert into his arms and began to rush him out the door. With all his might Robert applied pressure to his shoulder with his left arm and used all his remaining might to tug onto a door frame with his injured right arm, preventing Tony from exiting and slinging him back a little. Robert could barely speak, but said "VCR" and Tony realized the kid wasn't budging. Tony hurried Robert to the television stand and Robert removed the black VHS tape with his right hand. Angelo's girlfriend had run back in and was stealing all his things.

When they came outside, Tony spotted a young teen from the neighborhood who came outside on the street when he heard the gunshot and all the screaming. Tony called to the boy "Chuy" to come and help as he loaded Joseph into the cabin of his truck as the evening began to set. When the 5.3 curly black-haired Chuy came, Tony told him to drive Robert to the border and he stuffed a wad of peso bills into the loose pocket of Chuy's black basketball shorts. In Spanish Tony told Chuy, "Get him to the American side and run back to Mexico before anybody can catch you. If you make it back to me, I'll give you more money."

Chuy was only 15 and had barely driven before, but he played enough Arcade games that he got Robert to the border quickly by blowing through all stop signs and redlights on the way. His braking was horrible, but it got the job done. As they pulled up to the American line and authorities, Robert used the last of his energy to beg Chuy to guard the black tape and not let a soul watch it and then Robert began to blank out. Chuy promised to guard the tape, despite knowing Robert would never survive. As they crossed into the United States, Chuy honked the horn to get the attention of Border Patrol Agents before he bailed out of the truck and it rolled into a barrier. Two Agents chased Chuy as far as they could and another came up to the truck with his gun drawn and he recognized the bloody passenger who had crossed over many times before.

Chapter 39

Call of Duty

July 8, 1999. University Medical Center, Downtown El Paso, Texas.

Robert could see a bright white light as he opened his eyes slightly. "Dad?" Robert said as the blurry image of a tall dark haired Albuquerque Police Officer appeared. "Robert, hey buddy?" spoke the familiar voice. Robert began to cry, "Dad I'm sorry you died." The figure spoke, "Let me get a nurse," then left the room. When the Albuquerque Police Officer returned with a nurse, Robert realized he wasn't dead. It was Matt Morales, the Officer that had his pinky broken by Joseph in the Academy who Robert met at his dad's funeral. Officer Morales had been sent down to El Paso by Albuquerque Police to speak to U.S. Marshalls and Juárez authorities regarding a trio of Wanted murder suspects. Morales had rushed down to the hospital from his hotel room when he saw the El Paso News and heard about what happened to Joseph's son. As Robert was trying to make sense and muster up a sentence, he heard Morales plead, "Save your energy kid, let them work on you. You're quite the survivor."

18-year-old Robert had been in a medically induced coma for 48 hours after two surgeries to repair nerves in his right arm and two surgeries to remove 3 feet of his small intestine and repair a puncture to his spleen. The nurse rushed into the room when Morales alerted them that he woke up and two doctors followed shortly after. It was a miracle the young man was conscious and he required round the clock care for three weeks.

It took an additional three months of rehabilitation and recovery before Robert could have visitors outside of his family. When he slept, he was tortured by the images of the night he almost lost his life. When he was awake, he was tortured by not having any idea where Luisa was and if she was okay. He just wanted to sleep every day, his body needed to recover. His grandma practically rebuilt the hospital Chapel.

The hospital had to ward off multiple requests to interview Robert by the media and he refused them all on the phone in his room when they somehow patched through. There was one sports reporter who he trusted. Robert had met the man many times when he played basketball and track in high school. One night Robert scored 20 points in a JV game and afterward the reporter saw Carmen picking him up. He told Robert "Your mom must be proud." When he learned that Robert had lost his mother when he was child, the reporter revealed that he personally knew Joseph, only it wasn't for sports.

The reporter told the story of a car accident claiming his own mother's life. Joseph was a passenger in that accident and had exited the wreckage and then picked the boy up with his baby brother and carried them over to the sidewalk until the Police arrived and arrested his dad's whole truck. The story had always shocked Robert to think about his dad like that, in handcuffs. When Chuy was finally able to visit the hospital and give Robert the videotape, he knew who to call.

Robert's black tape led to a multijurisdictional takedown of high-profile citizens who were involved in drug trafficking and a prostitution ring. The man on the video raping Luisa owned a wealthy Construction company and was favored to appear on the ballot of the upcoming election for City Councilman in the district that included the major border crossings. There was a lot to the story and is it sent shockwaves across both sides of the border. Before he left the hospital, Robert had sent Chuy on a desperate mission to locate an address for Luisa.

After the dominoes tumbled in the Drug Operation, Robert learned that Luisa was in Juárez somewhere and had tried several times to cross the border, but was unsuccessful. Security had tightened with the Media exposure from Robert being a stabbed American dropped off at the border and the ensuing government scandal. It was too dangerous for Robert to go into Juárez especially with the walking cane he was confined to for a year, but he had to get his girl out of there before she wound up on the streets or dead from her father's debts. With 500,000 people in El Paso and near 3 million overcrowding Juárez now, there was just no way to find her after authorities seized her house.

Chapter 40

Slice of Heaven

THE DESERT IS AN EXTREME PLACE. Many migrants die crossing them every year, including thousands trying to get into the U.S. In the same day you can experience above 90 degrees in the afternoon and below 40 degrees by midnight. Wild temperature swings, lack of water and punishing winds make survival all the more impressive. It's so dry in places that the ground hardens and cracks from months of no water. Even if you cross into the United States, you still have to elude authorities, find water, get somewhere, look for work and then build up. If you can find water.

While it looks like there is nothing that could survive for miles upon miles in the desert, all you have to do is relax your eyes and you'll see an entire ecosystem of animals on land and in the air. Surviving on cactus and anything they can find, lizards, bats, roadrunners, rabbits, snakes and wrens are the most common to see. Coyotes can be found alone or in groups. Bears and wildcats are harder to spot, keeping towards the mountains of the Southwestern U.S. deserts. Hummingbirds in dozens of colors are seasonal and along the Rio Grande migratory Sandhill Cranes and Canadian Geese follow the path to warm weather every year.

Around the turn of the millennium, Luisa found a "coyote" couple who could sneak her across into Texas for $1,000. She had been volunteering at different Catholic charities and sleeping wherever she could find. Luisa had lost her work visa, her home, her innocence, but she hadn't lost hope. They told her they would smuggle her over and then she had to cross the desert just a few miles to where somebody would be waiting for her.

AFTER TÍO JESÚS PASSED, Carmen's sisters came from Los Angeles and they drove over 10 hours down to their childhood village Pedriceña for the first time in 50 years. She visited the well where her cousin died as kids and she wept. Remembering Father José Antonio or Joseph Anthony, the Priest they adored from Elche, Spain who ran to retrieve her cousin that fateful day. They visited the Church she grew up in and prayed for her brother and all her family. On the way home she stopped in Lerdo and visited the Church she was married to Dino in. A young widow, she had a hard time living in the house she had shared with her husband and raised both her son and now grandson. She followed Dino's will and sold when she was ready.

When Carmen went to the bank in El Paso, the tellers were very nice to her. They brought her to an office and had a Spanish speaking manager who advised her. Joseph and Dino had invested some coin for Robert, but Carmen received the handsome check. Having never handled finances before, she was so nervous when the manager told her she didn't have to share the money with anybody.

Robert came up often to visit his grandma Carmen in her dream farm that she purchased in Delta, Colorado. With the $100,000 he had "traded" his grandma in exchange for most of the home videos of his father and with the money from the sale of her house, she was mortgage free. She had a nice pension that included a $200 kicker for life from the Italian American Veterans of World War II fund. Dino always took care of her even from the grave.

Carmen had a one-acre lot that backed up to a neighbor's 60-acre hay farm grazed by horses with a small mountain or large hill in the backdrop. A stream of water ran year around on the edge of her property for her garden. After enough visits and with his wife Luisa gaining dual citizenship, he decided to move up to Delta, Colorado with their baby daughter Maite in 2003 after finishing his Geography degree from the University of New Mexico. Selling his childhood home in Albuquerque was very emotional, but his place in Delta was just breathtaking. He had two acres of fertile land with water rights and panoramic views.

Time had passed since he spent over a year going through extensive physical therapy for nerve damage in his shoulder. Recovered, although he could no longer eat grapes or tomato peels, they hurt his stomach. He was back to playing basketball for leisure by the time he got settled in Colorado and he was medically cleared to join the upcoming one semester, 18-week, 746-hour Police Academy to work for the County.

Other than special invitees Drew Banks and the Tanner family, few people in the audience at the Graduation ceremony knew what it meant for Carmen to pin the Badge on Robert. It was as emotional of a day as the following year when he welcomed his own son to the farm, Dino Joseph. The following Spring he planted an apple orchard that his family learned to protect in the snowy winters and they raised a dozen sheep together with their border collie Duke and chihuahua Wolfman.

One day they took The Stang out to go fishing near their house. After a nice catch Robert went to teach his son what to do with a trout carcass, but saw his daughter was already showing her little brother his cardinal directions.

Every summer Elsie flew into Grand Junction and stayed with Carmen to double down some great grandma love. Uncle Dave with his boys Jeremy and Scott and Aunt Laurie with her son Ian visited Robert's family from time to time, usually when Elsie was in town. Life wasn't always easy, there was plenty of occasional action in small town Colorado, but in general, his life was simple and beautiful. He had to shoot a mad cow once, but other than that he just tucked away into his own little slice of heaven.

DEDICATED TO ALL THOSE WHO HAVE SERVED IN THE LINE OF DUTY

&

IN HONOR OF THE POLICE OFFICERS KILLED IN MY HOMETOWN DURING THE 1980'S.

Philip H. Chacón 36 years old, killed by gunfire in 1980

Gerald Eugene Cline 35 years old, killed by gunfire 1983

John Arthur Carrillo 26 years old, killed by gunfire 1987

Kenneth "Shawn" McWethy 23 years old, killed by gunfire in 1986 on Pacific Ave after witnessing a man run out of a tire shop at 8301 Broadway Blvd SE.

FOR MORE ON REAL FALLEN HERO'S GO TO THE OFFICER DOWN MEMORIAL PAGE:

www.odmp.org

Authors Note:

Special thanks to the Albuquerque Police Records Department and the Chief Paul A. Shaver Albuquerque Police Department Museum. The first person to ever read my book in its infancy back in 2010 was Detective Paul Judd. He was the Curator of the new Museum and we both appreciated each other's interest in the history of APD. Paul Judd learned more of E.D. Henry and Robert McGuire's murders from reading my book, I had just looked up the details at the public library on a microfiche. Judd goes on to research and finds out Marshal E.D. Henry never received a proper burial in 1886. Det. Judd located his remains with help from old cemetery records. Then on the 125th Anniversary of their death in 2011, E.D. Henry had a proper burial. Detective Judd had organized a funeral attended by the Governor and with a 21-gun salute and bagpipes, with a donated headstone. Outstanding.

The characters and stories in The Fraternal Order are based off of true people, but some names and events have been changed solely through my perspective and with no affiliation to the Albuquerque Police Department. Some Officers names were changed so I could play with their actions and chronology, while other names weren't changed for admiration or effect. No former Officers or their families ever gave me permission to use their name(s) or stories, but I hope that I've honored the department and all the great Officers who did and do their job the right way, especially those who made the ultimate sacrifice and gave their life.

The creation of Joseph Alvarez was inspired by my dad, retired A.P.D. Captain Francisco "Rocky" Nogales and A.P.D. Officer Kenneth "Shawn" McWethy who was killed in the line of duty at just 23 years old, before he had a chance to start a family of his own and a few months before earning his Bachelor's Degree from U.N.M. while working full-time. One of his brothers was in the Academy at the time and went on to become a distinguished Officer, like their father, the director or Agent in Charge of the Albuquerque Secret Service office and later the Undersheriff.

In 1986 my dad was a Field Investigator who spoke Spanish and right after the Shawn McWethy shooting, he dusted for fingerprints at Antonio's tire shop and photographed the scene, including dusty footprints from the fleeing robber.

Shawn has no relation or connection to the fictional Joseph Alvarez, but I feel his tragic killing on Pacific Avenue portrayed by the death of Ofc Alvarez can be used as a training tool to all Officers to get into the good habit of taking off their seat belt immediately upon arrival to any scene. From stories I've heard Shawn was a really good Officer and super safety-conscious. He always wore his vest and carried an ankle piece. I've heard the Police car referred to as the death box. Ever since 1986, the Academy trains the seatbelt removal upon safe arrival. Makes sense with 90% of Officers being right-handed and the ever-present threat of ambush.

My point of changing his cold-blooded murder is to show that it could have happened to any Officer in the United States. He was just doing his job protecting his community and has undoubtedly saved Officers lives to those who have had the extra seconds in critical situations to remove their belt thanks to the training learned from this incident. His killer died of poor health in prison in Soledad, CA but lived to see old age and was featured on a prison documentary on the War on Drugs visited by his family. Shawn didn't get to experience old age or children of his own. However, Shawn is up there protecting his loved ones in the Kingdom of Heaven for an eternity. I'm not so sure Cop killers get to say that. Like the ones who killed Robert Rosenbloom, Phil Chacón, John Carrillo, Gerald Cline and Mike King/Richard Smith, Frank Sjolander, Max Oldham, Steve House, James McGrane, Daniel Webster and anyone else who has killed an innocent Officer performing their duty. A special tribute to John Messimer! + Jeffrey Cole Russell, didn't forget you Cowboy, EOW Jan. 8, 2002. Also, Joe Harris Jr., your dad SuperJoe EOW July 16, 2009 would be proud to see you follow in his footsteps. -God bless and God Speed to our Officers!

Why I'm a fanboy of LE. In 2010 I was accepted to be a Federal Agent with the U.S. State Department's Diplomatic Security Service. I drove down to Austin for the panel interview. A dream job to protect dignitaries and embassies around the world, joining my cousins Jeremy and Scott. I obtained my top-secret clearance and awaited the call to F.L.E.T.C. with a conditional offer of employment. Then the craziest Albuquerque night, I get rear ended stopped at a light on Coors and Iliff by a stoned driver. I've carried a herniated disc in my back ever since and shrunk from 6.1 to just under 6 foot from age 25 to 40, plus whiplash that comes and goes. I was stopped and the guy was going 50+ and didn't break. The plot thickens. As we awaited Police a homeless guy was crossing West on Coors where I had been turning East. I thought it was a lady because of his long black hair and smash they got hit by a car right in front of us and killed. The car drove right by me and the guy who hit me, and we were the best witnesses. All kinds of Police, Fire and Ambulances swarmed in, the ghetto bird flew around. I'm all jacked up. My Impala is trashed in the rear. This poor person was dead and the responsible party fleeing. I didn't want to use up an ambulance and called my dad who was an Investigator still and he slipped into the area off duty as they shut down multiple roads. The E.R. on a Friday night is like a horror movie mixed with a comedy show, just nuts, total circus. Side note: The doctors saw me for 2 minutes and prescribed me 10 painkillers, I took one of those bad boys and thought I was going to die. Flushed the rest down the toilet and then years later found out what that was all about. Scary. Sorry fishies. Yeah, that was the end of my intent to ever become Law Enforcement. At 25, I could dunk a basketball one day, then haven't been able to touch the net since the accident.

I started this book visiting my grandma's farm in Delta, Colorado on summer vacation as a teacher awaiting my call to the Police Academy. Then after my accident and Police dreams were smashed in my back, I stopped writing this book and incurred severe writers block and many doubts about whether anyone would read it and whether the story would ever materialize into something worthy of the fallen Officers sacrifice. I wrote the entire framework and ending with about 80% of the story on a farm in Delta in one week in 2010 then just stopped. Then I was teaching back in Santa Fe and on Oct 26, 2014 tragedy struck when my friend and fantasy football buddy Anthony Philip Haase of Rio Rancho Police, NM died in an automobile accident, his End of Watch was far too soon. His brother-in-law Michael Hetes working with him that night, his wife Nichole a young widow.

It was an experience that will forever haunt my hometown, they changed the entire dangerous curve on the road his car flew off. He was heading to protect a family in a domestic hostage situation. I remember thinking wow here is this young man 7 years younger than myself and I felt like he had already accomplished so much that I could only strive to be half of what he was. State Champion pitcher, professional athlete, married, career, respected. He lived such a good lifestyle, morally sound, highly intelligent and completely humble to all his accomplishments. When I started writing again, I thought of him often and I will never forget that morning when I awoke to the bad news and all the events from the aftermath. Although I was happy to hear his younger brother followed in his footsteps and joined the Rio Rancho Department of Public Safety to continue a family legacy.

While I continued to not write for years, I couldn't believe how many Police Officers die in the United States every year on the Officer Down Memorial Page www.odmp.org. Month after month the tally is surreal including during the course of me writing this book in New Mexico with 2.2 million residents, Bernalillo County Sheriff Deputy Dean Miera, NM Transportation Officer Robert Porter, Sandoval County Sgt. Robert Baron, Rio Rancho Officer Nigel Benner, Santa Fe Deputy Jeremy Martin, small town Alamogordo lost three Clint E. Corvinus, Anthony Ferguson and James Sides. Hatch, NM lost Jose Ismael Chavez, Las Cruces Jonah Hernandez. NMSP Darian Jarrott and later Justin Hare. There was a helicopter crash claiming the lives of Bernalillo County Undersheriff Lawrence George Koren, Deputy Michael Adam Levinson, Lieutenant Fred Douglas Beers III and rescue specialist with the Fire Department Matthew King. EOW's 07/16/2022.

I'm not sure the General Public can ever give enough appreciation for the dangers faced in upholding Public Safety. When I hear people trash the Police, I can't help but think of Tribal Police Officer Kevin William Schultz, off duty on a Church retreat, setting up camp wearing his badge, gun and handcuffs, when he saw a young boy drowning in a river go by and his only instinct was to jump in and save the boy. The kid made it, Schultz unfortunately did not. Who is willing to do that? The people criticizing the Police always, care to jump in? EOW 8/17/2002

As I taught History in public schools, I couldn't believe how many Officers are attacked in just my city alone. I sat and watched dashcam of the shootings of 4 Albuquerque area Officers on October 26th 2013, the tragic footage of Officer Daniel Webster's murder by a revolving door felon EOW Oct 29, 2015. His widow a Deputy. 30-year veteran Lou Golson shot four times on bodycam in Jan 2016. (Ofc Adam Golson and sister cop, brother deputy, your awesome to follow career). Sgt Brandon Watts shot on 2/19/2025. The danger never stops.

Then I watched as every city that "Defunded the Police" after 2020 saw their crime skyrocket, including Albuquerque. Direct correlation. Lazy Juvenile code, horrible competency laws and removal of qualified immunity is the lack of respect given to Officers by bad policymakers and the nasty sentiment from members of the public. DOJ Decree, Cops getting tried for bullstuff and walking on eggshells. The Department dwindled to less than 400 patrol Officers as the city grew to over 550,000 residents by 2021. Homicide records shattered every year in 2020, 2021, 2022 as a result. My brave cousin Joseph left APD for Irving, TX, he's homegrown. As the world fought over masks, one early morning, only 5 A.P.D. Officers were working an area for 60,000 residents when outside a coffee shop 4 of the Officers were shot on Aug 19, 2021 on bodycam, by a revolving door felon from California with a full auto sear pistol. That technically left 1 Officer for 60,000 people to locate the other suspect. Never caught. Obviously there was a big response, but I could see in studying the Jim Samora, Phil Chacón, Gerald Cline, John Carrillo and Shawn McWethy shootings that the response in the 1980's was really good. Triple the number of Officers were available and the city had about 150,000 less citizens. You can see it in the Cops episodes filmed in Albuquerque in the 1990's. A cooky place, but the Duke City was under control then. The Police working now are absolutely doing an amazing job, but need support from City leaders and the Public. To:Chris Patterson, from a quiet kid in middle school to APD Commander. Hats off.

By December of 2023 I was in the paper for being fired as a teacher for criticizing the removal of Police in schools after 2020, the lack of supervision leading to the shooting deaths of teens Bennie Hargrove then Andrew Burson then Elijah Pohl Morfin. When Pohl Morfin was killed, shot in the head on campus at a basketball game and the school district publicly held a press conference and called it "kids playing with guns" "an accidental shooting." Well, I was fired after the email I wrote the night of the shooting. My heart goes out to all my students. That week I was cast as a guard on the movie Opus, appearing briefly to escort the lead actress, my scene filmed at the devil's butcher shop. Thank you to Albuquerque Aviation Academy Charter School for your Security and taking this stray dog in a week later to teach NM history + Film and Rio Rancho High School for keeping my wife safe before we left for Spain. I love Albuquerque, but it's been very unsafe 2020-2025...

Finally, I turned 40 in Dec of 2024 and had one of them what the hell am I doing with my life moments and remembered that I had wrote a book once. If you read every chapter and thought it sounded real, it's because just about some variation of everything really happened. Even the crowbar stabbing and shooting in Juárez, not to me thankfully, but that happened too. I grew up babysat in the Police station and heard some very interesting stories. With Shawn McWethy compelling me for life.

The term "police officer" is a common noun and should be lowercase unless it's part of a proper noun or used to refer to a specific person. **Or I could just capitalize it out of respect every time for my book to draw your eye to it, Police, Cops, Cadets, Instructors, Detectives. Sorry grammar police. Lesson learned, respect The Fuzz!**

To my friends and family who served and those still serving.
To the men and women in blue, we can't thank you enough.

New Mexico, USA Law Enforcement Deaths (Known as of April 2025) **Justin Hare** Jonah Hernández **James Sides** Anthony Ferguson **Darian Rey Jarrott** Lawrence George Koren **Fred Douglas Beers III** Michael Adam Levison **Jeffrey Allen Pierce** Bryan Vannatta **Sam J. Trujillo** Jeffrey Mark Montoya **Johan Mordan** Houston James Largo **Clint E. Corvinus** Jose Ismael Chávez **Jeremy Martin** Daniel Scott Webster **Robert W Baron** Greg 'Nigel' Benner **James Francis McGrane Jr** Joseph Anthony Harris Sr **Michael R. King** Richard W. Smith Jr. **Jeffrey Cole Russell** Robert Walter Hedman **Damacio S. Montaño** Larry Brian Mitchell **Damon Talbott** Samuel Anthony Redhouse **Kelly Fay Clark** William Harold Sibrava Jr **Horst Harold Woods** Isaac Benjamín Martínez **Victoria Louise Chávez** Jerry Arnold Martínez. **Glen Michael Huber** Nathaniel A. Afolayan **Stephen A. Sandin** John Arthur Carrillo **Sherman L. Toler Jr** Thomas Arlen Richmond Kenneth Shawn McWethy **Travis Haynes** Gerald Eugene Cline. **Robert P. Larson** Benjamin L. Green **Philip H. Chacón** Leopaldo Cesilo Gurule **Richard Gomez** Thomas Chesley Bedford Jr. **David L. Coker** Royce Leroy Bennett **Juan Leo Ortiz** John M. Bloxom **Charles Elwood Wasmer** Edward L. Moreno **James Monroe Vigil** Emilio Mestas **Victor C. Breen** Robert Rosenbloom **Julián Narváez** Gilbert Montoya **Jay Elmo "Jerry" Wignall** John B. Arvizo **Benjamin Herrera** Ishkoten Koteen **Frank A. Sjolander Jr.** Ralph R. Higginbotham **Nash Phillip Garcia** Robert Bush Butler **Clemente Salazar** Lee Pena **Caleb Thomas Hopkins** Juan Ruiz **Ananias "Norris" Green** Truett Eugene Rowe **Mack R. Carmichael** Andres Chavez **Billy Meador** Bernard F. Leonard **Thomas `W. Jones** Apolonio Pino **Manuel Quintana** Harvey S. "Harve" Bolin **John Henry Heard** J.M. Clifton **Henry Clyde Hatcher** Rufus Dunnahoo **Louis Silva** Zaccheus Raymond Sutton **Charles N. Cunningham** Emilio Candelaria **Thaddeus "Thad" Pippin** Lewis H. Mickey **Oscar Davis** William Rutherford **John Watson** George Washington Batton **Luis Abeita** Dwight B. Stephens **Henry M. Love** Alexander Knapp **Thomas H. Hall** A.L. Smithers **Roy Woofter** J.A. McClure **James I. Kent** Charles B. Smith **William E. Tipton** William Joyce Rainbolt **W.D. "Kechi" Johnson**

Edward J. Farr **Kent Kearney** Bud Johnson **Daniel Bustamente** Frank Vigil **James Leslie Dow** John McLeod **Frank B. Robson** William H. Guyse **C.B. Shutz** Robert McGuire **E.D. Henry** Tom C. Hall **John Hurley** Jasper N. Corn **William L. Jerrell** William A. Bergin **Robert Olinger** Jose Antonio Griego **James W. Bell** Antonio Lino Valdez **Joe Carson** Robert W. Beckwith **George Hindman** Manuel Garcia y Griego **William Brady** Owen A. Landdeck **Isaias Alarid** Louis Edward Stiger **Tranquilino Lopez** Luciana B. Gallegos **James Carlysle** Robert Alan Potter **Rene B. Garza** Rodolfo "Rudy" Ledezma **Roger Hoisington** William F. White **James Bundy** James Martin Kirchner **Leonard E. Daniel** William T. Speight **Germaine Ferris Casey** Christopher Mirabal **Ronald T. Baca** Melvin Lee Hodges **Richard Armijo** Leslie Delbert Bugg **Walter G. Taber** Ralph Lee Garcia **Gerald Peter Magee** Louis F. Jewett Jr. **Filimon J. Ortiz** Jose Maria Gonzales **Carl Emanuel Vocale** James Edward Clark **Ralph W. Ramsey** Dominique Joseph Smith **Gregory A. Geoffrion** Philip Olivas **Bruce A. Richard** Antonio Jaramillo **Robert Eric Duran** Daniel C. Rivera Jr **Manuel Olivas** Ronald Edwin Shores **Max R. Oldham** Donald W. Redfern **Andrew Francis Tingwall** Julio Enrique Baray **Ramon Robert Solis** Dietrich Stahl **Wayne G. Allison** Lowel D. Howard **David M. Smith** Ocie C. Gray **Austin A. Roberts** Michael T. "Tommy" Box **Robert Francis Purcell** Warren G. Fleshman **Joseph Ralph Silva** J.V. Cogdill **James F. Haynes** Louis McCamant **Bentura Bencomo** Aniceto Montoya **Thomas Wade Frazier** Stephen Lawrence Ackerman **Ryan Sean Thomas** Andrew John Dominguez **Dean Francis Miera** Michael C. Avilucea **David Tourscher** Ramon Nevarez Jr. **James Andres Archuleta** Luis M. Castillo **Angelic Suzette Garcia** Thomas J. Williams **Jesus A. de la Ossa** Ruben Valles Carbajal Jr. **Charles Lee "Matt" Dillon** Leo Chavez **Lee L. Bound** Dave Serna **Barney Dean Montoya** Bruce Shepherd Bardliving **Wayne M. Stedman Jr**. Alfred Ray Davis **Robert Romero** Bennie D. Williams **Claude Bishop Evans** Robert E. Lee **Joe Taylor Aven Jr**. John Carl "Jake" Ramsey **Colby S. Farrar** Albert Paul **Fred Kenney** Kevin William Schultz **Todd Parkins** Isaac Benjamin Martinez **Anthony Phillip Haase** Lloyd R. Aragon Sr. **Bianca Quintana** K9 Rebel **Timothy Ontiveros** John Kelly **Antonio Aleman** List updated by: Officer Down Memorial Page

www.ingramcontent.com/pod-product-compliance
Lightning Source LLC
LaVergne TN
LVHW050527160826
845677LV00011B/1966